High Praise for Privateer

"Scandalios' debut novel is a high-seas adventure set during the American Revolution.

"In many ways, Scandalios' novel reads like the diet version of *The Count of Monte Cristo* — a tale of revenge and treasure hunting played out against a backdrop of rolling seas and clanging swords... Scandalios fills the novel to the brim with action scenes, plot twists and high tension. He often writes in the vernacular of a modern action film, which gives his battle scenes a high-speed, cinematic urgency. Readers can expect vivid images of cannonballs flying through the air and acrobatic pirates fighting with two swords at once. The book accomplishes the rare feat of seamlessly blending several fiction genres: action, mystery, suspense, romance and even comedy. Carrigan makes for a charming protagonist and readers will feel invested in his quest for revenge...

"A thrilling read that will appeal to young and old readers."

- Kirkus Reviews

"This 18th-century mashup of *Hamlet*, *The Count of Monte Cristo*, and *The Sea Hawk* keeps the pages turning...the action is often intense and engaging...promising high seas adventure."

- Publishers Weekly

PRIVATEER

MICHAEL SCANDALIOS

Acknowledgements

I wish to convey my deepest gratitude for those individuals that were instrumental in guiding this project along its winding journey.

First, thank you to my daughters Jenna, Amanda, and Sarah who encouraged my converting what began as a bedtime story in the Hawaiian islands to the adventure novel it has become.

To the "extended" crew of the *Aegean Clipper* – this book was written with you in mind: John and Jackie (Captain and First Mate), Sally, Brian, Lori, J.P., Kelly, Max, Jack, Nico, Hannah, Zack, Will, Chase, Elle, and Anna. Sailing through the Greek islands with you confirmed that life is about the journey, not the destination.

Additional gratitude and a smart salute to Jack Stephenson and John Rossi for their willingness to jump headlong into the voyage and return with words of encouragement and support.

To my good friend and super-talented author Tracy Grant – thank you for all your ideas, suggestions and editing. Your expertise in writing, as well as your knowledge of late-eighteenth century England, was indispensable. The book is far better for your skillful touch.

Finally, to my best friend and wife, Kathy – I could not have pursued this journey without your patience and loving support. Your suggestion of adding a romantic side to the story is yet another example of how anything I think I can do, I do much better with you!

- Michael Scandalios

"Be not afraid of greatness.
Some are born great, some achieve greatness,
and some have greatness thrust upon them.
Thy fates open their hands."

- SHAKESPEARE, *Twelfth Night*
Act II, Scene V

Table of Contents

✝

Chapter 1: The Match

West England, 1765 - The sunlight glistened off the dew on the roadside grass like a thousand diamonds as the coach rumbled along the narrow country road from Bridgwater to Bristol. The two horses shot warm air from their noses in perfect cadence, as coordinated bursts of steam-like vapor.

Though tired, the coachman smiled at his good fortune in landing the huge round-trip fare. It would be a beautiful day, both in terms of the spring weather and his expanded billfold.

Inside the coach, a well-dressed gentleman sat quietly, regarding the sleeping boy lying on the bench across from him. Miguel Santos Velazquez Allegria de Torrente glanced out the window of the coach and noticed the beauty of the spring morning as they sped through a lush meadow. He instinctively checked his pocket watch, satisfied that they were ahead of schedule.

Mathew slowly sat up on the bench, and stared out of the coach, noticing the sunny morning in store. He stretched his arms out wide and yawned as he turned to Santos.

The rigorous fencing lessons of the summer had seen Mathew's grasp of tactics and speed progress at an accelerated rate, even by Santos' lofty standards. It had been increasingly difficult when sparring for the master swordsman to dominate

1

his young protégé. Every so often, one of Mathew's clever attack sequences would put Santos in a rare position of uncomfortable imbalance.

It had been years since Santos had sparred or fought with anyone near to his own skill with the sword. While he could still best Mathew, he knew the boy's rate of progress and natural ability would likely result in a defeat of the master by the time the pupil was fifteen.

Santos reflected on the irony that the protégé for whom he had searched all over Spain, was the son of a captain in the British Royal Navy. It had been such an intriguing request from the Englishman he had known predominantly through written correspondence over the years. The request was flattering in its admission of Santos' fencing prowess as well as the tacit trust of leaving his son's development to a Spaniard.

However, Santos privately had worried that Mathew was learning only how to fight Santos, rather than how to fence in general. No matter how differently Santos fought – right handed or left handed, slowly or rapidly, in balance or out of balance, patiently or recklessly, he could not possibly simulate every fighting convention.

Today, with a high level of confidence in his pupil, Santos had arranged for a light sparring match with a young lieutenant in the Royal Navy known to be adept with the sword.

As they were within minutes of reaching the wharf area at Bristol, Santos reminded Mathew that the arrangement was nothing but a fun test of the boy's progress. He implored him not to be nervous and that, win or lose, he would be better for fencing against someone other than Santos to see how others fight in a competitive environment.

Santos didn't dare inform the boy that it wasn't a friendly scrimmage, but rather a challenge match for money. Unfortunately, that was the only way he could negotiate the confident officer into a match with his young pupil. To inform Mathew of the stakes, however, would likely make the boy nervous, and Santos knew his protégé would compete most effectively if relaxed.

When they reached the grassy park across from the wharfs,

Santos told Mathew to wait near the carriage while he confirmed the rules and precise venue of the competition.

After a few minutes, Santos returned to the carriage and escorted Mathew to the agreed upon match area. There were a few large, sporadic elm trees providing ample shade to those seeking respite from the mid-morning sun, but the open lawn area was ideal for a friendly outdoor match as it was generally flat and firm ground.

Mathew Hatley was confident that, whatever the outcome, expectations were suitably low for him and that he likely wouldn't embarrass Santos. Though he did not expect to win the match, he felt he could prolong it effectively with his speed and unusual tactics. All he thought about was doing well enough to make Santos proud.

Mathew wore a traditional fencing suit to the event, including a wire mesh helmet. Before donning the protective headgear, he turned to regard his opponent. The young officer seemed athletic and powerful, though Mathew was careful not to make any assumptions before the sparring began. To do so could be a competitive advantage for his opponent. Although he found it somewhat odd that the man kept sipping on a flask of liquor in the morning.

While stretching approximately twenty feet away, Mathew could clearly hear the shipmates of his sparring opponent goading the sailor into the match as though it were a real duel or battle.

"Slice 'im to pieces, Jackie-boy!" said one colleague.

"No quarter, Jackie-boy!" added the other.

"Don't worry, lads. Hold my coat and flask. I won't be a moment!"

Santos walked halfway between the two opponents and called each to join him before starting the match. He provided the young naval officer with a fencing sword matching the one in the hands of his young pupil.

He implored the opponents to fight fairly by the rules of fencing convention. He then informed them that he would be the official scorer and there would be three rounds. The first to win two rounds would be declared the victor. Each round would last either three minutes or when a fencer scored five points, whichever occurred first.

The young officer called Jackie-boy didn't seem to be paying attention, preferring to wave the fencing foil off to the side, testing its weight and balance. It wasn't until he heard the word "victor" that he turned and stuck the rounded tip of the foil into the chest of Santos so hard that the length of the foil began to bend.

"And that's when you pay me my gold, Spaniard."

"Certainly, Lieutenant. As long as you win two rounds."

Mathew's mesh helmet concealed his expression of nervous confusion given the discussion of a contest for money.

Santos looked down at Mathew as though he could sense the boy's veiled countenance. "Mateo, just spar as we do and you will be fine."

His words of confidence immediately perked up the body language of the young boy who backed up a few paces and began stretching and squatting in a few additional rapid pre-match exercises.

"C'mon, lad," implored the one called Jackie-boy. "Do you mind? We set sail this evening and I'd like to be on my ship when she weighs anchor!"

Mathew did not like the sarcastic tone of the naval officer, nor the unbelievable disrespect he showed Santos by sticking him in the chest with the foil. Now armed with all the motivation he needed to wash away any nervousness, he approached the overconfident opponent.

Santos called for the match to begin and, in a lightning-fast series of attacking maneuvers, Mathew scored points seemingly at will. But instead of finishing off the startled sailor for an early round one victory, he intentionally broke off his attack and willed his opponent to go on the offensive so he could quickly and embarrassingly counter the other fencer.

Jackie-boy tried to gain ground, but his short counter attack was easily thrust aside by the young faceless boy. The naval officer fought sloppily, with his arms swinging too much and his wrists too tight. The skinny child then pursued with such vengeance that the sailor never had a chance. Within seven rapid strokes the young boy reached for and tagged the middle chest area of his out-of-balance adversary.

"That is point five. Round one to Mateo!" announced Santos loudly.

"Jackie-boy, what the hell just happened?" yelled his friends in near unison.

"Lucky move," responded the now angry officer. "Won't happen again!"

Then he turned to his smaller opponent and pointed his foil at the faceless mask. "I hope you enjoyed that little bit of dancing, 'cause I'm gonna teach you something now, little brat!"

Behind the wire mesh, Mathew invisibly smiled. He had clearly gotten under the skin of the overconfident sailor. His opponent's crazed anger was just the sort of advantage that Mathew knew well how to exploit.

Round two began with Jackie-boy's friends urging him to beat the kid with such hysteria that Jackie's initial attack was almost entirely emotional. He over-committed himself in several positions whereby it was easy for Mathew to score points while successfully defending his own body. Each clean tap of his foil to the naval officer's body brought an announcement of a point by Santos. With Mathew brimming with confidence, Jackie backed off and screamed in frustration.

"C'mon, Jackie, don't let him beat you!" implored one of the sailors.

"He's just a boy," the other sailor added, "and a Spaniard, at that."

Instead of waiting for the coordinated attack of the boy, the angry Jackie came at Mathew once again, but instead of fencing in conventional method, he fought as though his foil was a saber. He swung the foil over his head to frighten his young opponent and charged hard at the boy.

Mathew recognized the sailor's emotional desperation and knew the fight was over before the officer moved forward.

The large adversary was ten feet away and closing fast, his foil held over his head, ready to come down like a hammer on a nail. Rather than hold his ground and raise his own foil to deflect a thundering blow from Jackie, Mathew threw himself on the ground and rolled in a forward somersault toward the charging fencer.

With the space between them cut instantly, the crazed sailor could not bring his foil down fast enough to touch the boy, yet his forward momentum took him past the gifted fencing pupil and left him out of balance. Instantly coming out of his tucked roll to one knee, Mathew raised his foil and touched the chest area of the officer who had turned to swing wildly and harmlessly above the crouching boy's head.

"That is the fifth point. Round two is over. Mateo wins the round and the match!" Santos proclaimed.

The dumbstruck Jackie turned to his friends who looked on aghast as their provincial champ screamed towards the heavens in defeat.

Santos, too, looked toward the friends of Jackie who dug into their uniform pockets to extract some coins to cover their share of the lost wager. Santos approached them with a smile and an open hand. They handed their coins to him reluctantly, but couldn't help praising the fighting skill of his young pupil.

"Never would have believed it if I didn't see it with my own eyes!" said one of the sailors.

"The kid moves like lightning. I'm glad I didn't agree to fight him," said the other.

The sailor named Jackie walked over, threw his foil down at the feet of Santos, and begrudgingly pulled two coins from his own pocket, all the while eyeing the young fencing protégé over his left shoulder with anger in his eyes.

"Yes, Spaniard. You taught this one well. He's gifted, no doubt," Jackie said as he nodded to his friends to detain the Spanish tutor, "but how well does he fight with a real weapon?"

Jackie bent over and withdrew two razor-sharp swords from their sheaths and walked purposely toward Mathew.

"Don't do it, Jackie-boy," yelled one of his friends.

"It's not worth it, let 'im be," implored the other.

Within a few strides, Jackie approached the boy and unleashed a backhand slap to his head that sent the boy's protective mesh fencing mask six feet into the air.

The startled boy never felt so scared or rattled. He looked up in panic at the officer's menacing stare. |

"No more dancing! Let's see how well you fight someone with a real sword, boy!" The belligerent officer raised his right arm with sword in hand. Mathew was so petrified that rather than run, he threw his arms up instinctively to block the cutlass that was about to slash downward on him.

"No!" yelled Santos, struggling through the grip of Jackie's mates though helpless from a distance of less than thirty feet.

Jackie's right arm came down quickly, but rather than strike the boy, the sword pierced the ground one foot to Mathew's left.

"Relax. I'm not going to kill you, boy," said Jackie. "I'm going to teach you a little humility. The real world isn't about foils and chalk. In the end, you'll thank me. I only intend to cut you a little! Show you how we do things in the Royal Navy!"

"Please, sir. I don't want to fight you!" pleaded Mathew who believed the man would be only too happy to wound him.

"Sensible lad! I wouldn't want to fight me either, but you brought this on yourself by showing me up. Now pick up the bloody sword!"

"Please, sir...I...I don't..."

"PICK UP THE DAMN CUTLASS, BOY!" bellowed Jackie.

Rather than yelling at the lad again, Jackie raised his cutlass as if to attack in the next instant. Mathew instinctively pulled the sword from the lawn and got in a defensive squatting position. His blade met that of the naval officer's only inches from his own head.

"Mateo, move around!" called Santos, still struggling to free himself from the clutches of the two sailors.

Mathew turned and bought a moment of time by sprinting to one of the thick elm trees. His aggressor was only a few feet behind him though, and when he reached the tree, unleashed a frantic barrage that sent wood chips flying in all directions. The probability of hitting the boy was low, but the biting sound of the steel sword hitting the trunk and pieces of flying bark were intended to frighten the boy.

Immediately, Mathew moved to run to the other tree some thirty feet away, again with Jackie in close pursuit.

"That's it, boy! No more games, I'm going to make you fight

now!" growled Jackie in disgust.

The few defensive maneuvers Mathew had made had successfully thwarted the attack and put the bully officer out of position. With every second, Mathew's confidence grew. He had decided on a move that he'd toyed with while sparring with Santos. It was certainly an unorthodox move from the standpoint of fencing. It was an acrobatic move his mother had taught him when he was a few years younger. He had performed it successfully in sport with Santos, momentarily leaving his tutor in a defenseless position. If it worked now, it could possibly save his life. Santos read Mathew's mind and watched intently, knowing the surprise that was to come.

Mathew was ten feet from the tree running full speed directly at its wide trunk, with Jackie now less than ten feet behind him and gaining.

Instead of stopping at the tree or running to one side or the other, Mathew, using his own momentum, ran three strides up the trunk, pushed off and completed a perfect back flip in mid-air, landing on the other side of the disbelieving Jackie.

As the officer turned, his astonishment had cost him, for he had not kept his guard up. Mathew made six strategic thrusts with the sword which Jackie had great difficulty defending. So mercurial was the boy's offensive barrage that Jackie soon found his own sword thrust from his own hand and lofted into the air.

Jackie picked his sword up off the lawn, raised it and charged the boy. He counted on the boy not daring to strike him in his advance. He was wrong.

Mathew made a quick defensive half slash so rapidly the young officer never saw it coming nor had time to get out of the way. Mathew had not tried to hit the charging man, but rather wave the sword so as to discourage his advance. However, the enraged officer moved in stupidly and too fast. The very tip of Mathew's sword caught the skin just in front of his attacker's right ear and tore as through air, leaving Jackie's skin near the nose.

Jackie let out a piercing scream, covered his bloody face with his hands and dropped to his knees in agony.

The sailors detaining Santos immediately let him go to rush to their fallen colleague. Santos pursued close behind, grabbed his protégé by the arm and pulled him away from the commotion. Mathew and Santos ran to their carriage without ever looking back.

What happened:

Fencing match—
Mathew beats
Jackie (Naval Sailor)

†

Chapter 2: The Venture

In the late summer of 1774, a frail, learned-looking gentleman entered a three-story building on the southern side of a long thoroughfare known as Pall Mall in the St. James's area of London.

As he slowly ascended the stairway within the building to a suite of offices on the third floor, the man tried to appear confident, though he realized the extremely low likelihood of achieving his objective. He was fifteen minutes early for his appointment with a representative of the Royal Court.

The gentleman knew the vast majority of visitors were turned away with a small, near valueless token of His Majesty's appreciation of their interest in his well-being or regaled with exaggerated exploits that left visitors feeling ashamed to have asked for even a moment of the king's precious time.

A few moments later, the man sat upright on an intricately decorated chair outside the office of one of the Counselors to His Majesty. He focused on the hunting scene depicted in the tapestry on the wall across the large waiting room, wondering in his mind how best to present his idea to the King of England at the palace in the unlikely event he would be granted the opportunity.

The first course of business would be to convince the counselor that a private audience with George III was warranted. It would be a monumental task, for the visitor was determined not to reveal any details of his proposed discussion to the royal counselor. If he had but a few moments with the king, the aged gentleman was certain that his Sovereign would find the discussion irresistibly intriguing.

A well-dressed young man opened the double doors across the room and approached the gentleman on the ornate, cushioned chair.

"His Lordship will see you now," said the young assistant in a rather condescending tone.

"Thank you," said the older gentleman, rising up and following the rude assistant who had already turned around and was heading for the office doorway, leaving the guest to trail behind.

As the visitor reached the doors and entered the larger and more handsomely decorated room, James, Lord Roberts looked up from some papers on his desk and regarded the approaching guest.

"Good Lord, Professor Hutchins!" said Lord Roberts, as he bolted from his high-backed chair. "This is indeed unexpected. To what do I owe the pleasure of your company this morning?"

The visitor smiled warmly, touched by the instant recognition by one of his former students and the undeniably sincere greeting. As he approached the large desk of the royal counselor, he silently recalculated that his odds of success had just climbed appreciably.

"I am here to arrange a private conference with His Majesty," said the professor in a direct tone.

"I see," remarked Lord Roberts.

Hutchins met his former student's gaze, flicked a glance at the assistant at a desk to the side of the great room, and then looked back at Roberts.

"Jeremy, would you be so kind as to leave us in private for a few moments?" Roberts asked.

"My lord?" the assistant stammered, seemingly pleading to remain and listen to what Hutchins would say.

"Please, Jeremy...a few moments?"

Though it again was framed as a request, it was clear that the young assistant knew better, and shuffled dejectedly toward the doors. He left the office and pulled the doors closed behind him.

"Now, Professor, it is indeed delightful to see you again. May I inquire as to the nature of your requested audience with His Majesty?"

"Well, to begin with, I recently took a one-year leave of absence from my post in Ancient Greek and Roman History at Oxford.

"My favorite of all my tutorials," added Roberts, "and a well-deserved rest, no doubt."

"Thank you, Lord Roberts. Actually, I have been spending most of that time conducting research in the Mediterranean where I came across something I believe, most sincerely, that His Majesty will find intriguing."

"It sounds fascinating, Professor. You certainly have my interest."

"The thing of it is, Lord Roberts...that is..." Hutchins coughed. "I dare not divulge anything more of this unless it is to the king's own ears."

"Professor Hutchins," Lord Roberts protested, "I cannot take you to the king without knowing what this is about. I appreciate the delicacy of your situation, but you must give me some idea of what you mean to say to the king. Think of how it may make me look if I took you to the king and you produced a...a magic lamp, for heaven's sake."

"I am asking you to trust me, James. You've known me for twenty years. I assure you I would not seek an audience with the king to show him an old lamp, ancient manuscript or arcane treasure map."

"You put me in a difficult situation, Professor..." Lord Roberts let the sentence hang for effect. The translation in the professor's mind was instant: *Last chance to tell me something or I must regrettably turn you away.*

"Lord Roberts, I am very sorry to have wasted your time. I simply cannot tell you any more – I am certain the king would prefer it this way. You must trust me on that count. If you cannot grant me the audience I seek, I will not take the rejection personally. Good morning."

"Just a moment, just a moment, Professor." Lord Roberts altered his negotiating tactic, seemingly fearing his fate if the king found out he hadn't allowed access to the professor who indeed had something of supreme interest.

With most individuals, Hutchins suspected, Lord Roberts was a master at delicately extracting information. Hutchins, however, could see he had just gained the upper hand in their polite negotiation. Sweat was beginning to build on Lord Roberts's brow.

"Professor, if I were to grant you the audience you seek, will my king be pleased with me?" Roberts asked.

Professor Hutchins' suppressed a smile. He had won passage to the king without confiding his secret after all.

"Exceedingly so, Lord Roberts!"

Three mornings later, King George III was in a rather fragile mood. For all his trappings, he was prone to occasional bouts of depression and self-pity. The slightest change in his schedule or routine usually took a toll upon his temper. He scowled down at Lord Roberts from his throne in the main receiving hall.

"Explain to me again, Lord Roberts, who I am to receive this morning and why you cannot tell me what the meeting is about?" the king grumbled slowly and loudly.

"Your Majesty, Professor Hutchins is from Oxford University. He is England's leading authority on ancient Greek and Roman history, and has recently returned from a research trip to that part of the world with what he says is intriguing information for you, and you alone. I have known him some twenty years now, first as a student and since as a friend, and he swore he could not divulge the topic of his intended discussion, even to me."

"And yet you admitted him."

"Yes, Your Majesty. I...I trust him."

"In that case, Lord Roberts, I shall be intrigued to hear what the good professor considers so important," remarked the king with enough levity in his response to bring the haughty advisors surrounding him to a round of bellicose, if perhaps sycophantic, laughter.

Lord Roberts visibly brightened with relief as it seemed the king was suddenly interested in his upcoming audience with the professor.

Professor Hutchins made the return coach ride to Pall Mall, however his coach pulled up to the main entrance of St. James's Palace rather than the offices to the side.

He knew the most difficult part of his project was already complete. It was highly probable he could convince the King of England to undertake his venture. The trouble was that if the king declined, the professor had no reasonable alternative. He wondered if the king would deduce his own bargaining strength and negotiate a far less attractive arrangement for the professor.

His carriage had only just come to stop when a powerful looking soldier in full dress uniform quickly pulled the door open. Professor Hutchins' confidence waned as he stepped forth from the coach.

The imposing edifice of the palace had a powerful effect on the psyche of many a visitor, and it was absolutely intentional. Even the most confident man was humbled upon entering through the main gate.

Seven stories tall with battle parapets atop two octagonal towers that flanked the massive twelve-foot high oak doors, the main entrance to St. James's Palace had two armed soldiers posted as sentries. The guards were more than window dressing, and the professor knew well that this was special duty for these men to guard the king at the palace. No doubt they had proved themselves capable and brave on the battlefield to even be considered for this post. They gestured to Professor Hutchins but didn't speak, and he, in turn, did not utter a sound to them.

Once summoned forward into the greeting hall, Professor Hutchins approached the entry doors slowly, worn leather book satchel draped over his slight shoulder.

As he entered the grand hallway, his eyes quickly fixed on the

King of England in the distance, sitting on a receiving throne. This was neither what Hutchins had intended nor expected. Surrounding the monarch on either side was as many as five advisors. No doubt the king intended for them to listen to Hutchins' story and make their recommendations shortly thereafter. This was absolutely unacceptable to Hutchins, but unlike in Lord Roberts' office, he was not in a position to negotiate the terms of the discussion.

He approached the king who sat on his throne three small steps atop a platform, bowed genuinely and, unlike most visitors, remained in a bowed position until told to rise by his Sovereign.

"Welcome, Professor Hutchins, please rise. You do me honor with your visit. What shall we discuss?" began the king.

"Your Majesty, I am a professor at Oxford. I teach ancient Greek and Roman history, and took last year off to conduct research in the Mediterranean. It was there that I made a remarkable discovery - a discovery of something so vitally sensitive that I wonder if I may humbly request to relay it to your ears only."

Hutchins could see in the body language of the king's reaction that his Sovereign's mood was starting to shift against him.

"Afterwards, Your Majesty," he quickly added, "if you decide to inform your royal advisors, of course I will accept your decision unconditionally."

King George sat pensively as the eyes of the room returned to him and, with each second of silence, the king looked increasingly uncomfortable. He shot an admonishing glance down to Lord Roberts before speaking. Lord Roberts visibly winced.

"Professor Hutchins, what you request is rarely ever granted. Dignitaries and royalty from abroad are generally not afforded private time with me. I would never have considered meeting with you this morning if it were not for Lord Roberts. He is one of my most trusted advisors, and if it were not for his kind and trusting words on your behalf you would not be standing here."

"I understand, Your Majesty," confirmed the penitent man.

"Very well. You shall have the next ten minutes to tell me

your tale in private, and - for your own sake - I hope you have not betrayed Lord Roberts' trust."

"Thank you, Your Majesty. I am confident you will be pleased with what I will tell you," answered Professor Hutchins.

As they left the receiving area and approached a nearby chamber, one guard leapt up quickly to open the large oak door. Once both men were inside, the guard pulled the door shut.

"Your Majesty, how much do you know about ancient Greece and Italy?" asked the professor awkwardly.

"Professor Hutchins, please assure me that you have not gone to such lengths to secure my private time in order to give me a history lesson!" snapped the king.

"No, Your Majesty. I beg your pardon. I'll get right to the point. The study of the golden ages of Greece and Rome is filled with many remarkable accomplishments and traditions that carry on to this day. But because it was so long ago and much of their history was passed on orally, many great exploits, and people, and even cities lie under thousands of years of decayed marble, rocks and dirt and may never be confirmed. For these undiscovered tales we give the title 'legends' suggesting that they may have actually existed or taken place, but they cannot be confirmed by physical evidence as yet."

"And you have discovered physical evidence substantiating one of these…legends? Is that correct, Professor?"

"Yes, Your Majesty. I have," Hutchins declared.

"Oh, don't keep me in suspense, Professor," mocked the king. "You've discovered the tomb of Achilles…or was it Agamemnon…or Alexander the bloody Great!"

"I've discovered the location of the ancient Treasury of…"

The king shot the professor a very serious stare, awaiting the rest of the name.

"Ancient Greeks, Romans, Egyptians, and others used to store their wealth on certain islands in the Mediterranean Sea. These islands would essentially serve as large, heavily guarded depositories. Royalty, wealthy gentry, travelers to the Holy Lands, and even pirates would store their valuable possessions and artifacts on certain small islands designated as treasuries."

"So, you have tracked down the location of an ancient

treasury of sorts?" inquired the king.

"Yes, Sire, though quite by accident…"

"Congratulations, Professor Hutchins," interrupted the king. "If this is true, you have indeed made quite a significant archeological discovery. England is proud of you and your scholarly efforts. You shall be hailed as a hero and given full credit for your educational contribution."

"No!" snapped the professor.

"I beg your pardon, man?" the king exploded.

"Forgive me, Sire. But a discovery like this can never be publicly proclaimed. It would invite all sorts of looters and freeloaders to the site and corrupt the sanctity of the ruins of the ancient city, not to mention my research. I humbly request that you keep this a secret, Your Majesty."

"I don't understand, Professor. Why would you ask for a private interview to tell me something which I should forever keep confidential?"

"Only you and I know of my discovery, Your Majesty," confirmed Hutchins, "But that is not why I've requested this audience."

The king fixed Hutchins with an intent stare.

Hutchins took the satchel off his shoulder and laid it on the table in front of the king, opening it slowly and carefully. From it he pulled a linen cloth tightly wrapped in a small ball and untied the ribbons methodically.

When the ends of the cloth were pulled back, the king's eyes opened wide in disbelief. He could mutter no audible reaction. There on the linen sat three sparkling ancient gold coins.

"Your Majesty," Hutchins explained, "only a very small percentage of the thousands of islands in the Mediterranean Sea are occupied by people. I had arranged for a local fisherman to take me to a particular uninhabited island so I could conduct research on its ancient ruins. I stumbled upon an undisturbed underground chamber; an ancient depository…intact."

Professor Hutchins let the last word out slowly and watched the king lift his gaze from the coins.

"Did you say 'intact,' Professor?" questioned King George.

"I did indeed, Your Majesty,"

"Remarkable!" whispered the king. "Can you describe what you found?"

"I discovered what I believe to be perhaps the largest depository of gold and antiquities the world has ever known. Scholars knew of the existence of many of these depository islands, but no one before had proof."

"Tell me, Professor," queried the king, "What is the approximate *value* of this depository?"

"I spent most of my return trip to England trying to estimate its value in my head. Of course, some of the pieces are priceless antiquities – incalculably valuable - but for which there is no real market to trade. The gold however was enough to easily fill perhaps twenty large chests."

The king blinked as if clearing his eyesight would help him register the staggering amount of gold.

As King of England, George III lived a tremendously wealthy lifestyle and had no need to increase his own personal wealth, and yet so much gold would be an important windfall to retire the massive debts of the Seven Years' War, finance the growth of England's robust colonization effort globally, improve its already top flight military, and perhaps even add to the arts, which was of high interest for this particular monarch.

"And you would like to *recover* the artifacts and gold from this cave and transport them safely back to England."

"Precisely, Your Majesty. And now you understand my reasons for requesting a private audience."

"I do indeed, Professor."

"I could go to a shipping company and charter a vessel to transport the depository, but with such a find, I am uncomfortable trusting an *undisciplined* crew."

"You wish me to commission a naval vessel to transport the depository. That way, pirates would not be an issue and you would be dealing with men of unimpeachable discipline and honor."

"Precisely so, Your Majesty. And I would be willing to compensate each of the crew handsomely for their discretion once the depository arrived successfully. Perhaps a fifteen percent collective share would be agreeable?"

"I see," the king said in a thoughtful voice.

"And for my king," added the professor, "I would be willing to share most of the gold, say seventy-five percent, as long as I was entitled to the antiquities for my research and the balance of the gold. After my research, I would donate the antiquities to the Museum of Ancient History at Oxford as well as the Royal Academy, which I understand you have generously supported from your own personal wealth."

King George's face brightened perceptibly. "In that case I accept your offer, Professor Hutchins. I shall have three of my most trusted admirals here tomorrow to plan the venture and nominate the most honorable and seaworthy crew to complete it successfully. Other than the admirals, and the selected captain of the ship, no one else will know of the...err...*cargo*. Is that satisfactory to you?"

"Yes, thank you, Your Majesty," said Hutchins noticing that the king never took his eyes off the golden coins on the linen cloth.

"Sire, you may keep these coins as a gesture of my gratitude for your kindness and discretion."

"Thank you, Professor Hutchins. You have done an incalculable service to your Crown and country. You shall have the gratitude of this king for all your days. In addition, you will soon likely be one of the wealthiest men in England."

- Hutchins meets with king
- Doesn't tell anybody what he told the king
- Island with ancient treasures - lots of gold

✝

Chapter 3: Duplicity

𝒯hree days after Professor Hutchins' visit with the king, the calm quiet of an overcast morning was interrupted by the driving hooves of two fast moving carriages along the Pall Mall.

The horse-drawn coaches bearing Admiral Terrence Reynolds and Admiral Simon Hughes arrived at St. James Palace simultaneously. While the palace guards looked on in impassive silence, the admirals turned and exchanged a glance before proceeding through the main entrance.

Two of the highest ranking and most decorated naval officers in the entire Royal Navy strode down the long entrance hall, three paces behind their silent escort. Their gazes fixed straight ahead, each wondered why King George had called for their attendance on such short notice.

As the two admirals were led to an ornate chamber, the coach of Admiral Josiah Watts reached the main entrance to the palace.

When Admiral Watts was escorted into the chamber, Hughes and Reynolds rose and greeted him. After hand shakes at the head of the rectangular table in the center of the meeting room, the admirals sat down and waited for their monarch to arrive.

The taut silence was interrupted by the sound of Lord Roberts entering the room from behind them, through a second door. When the admirals turned to see who had entered, Lord Roberts lifted his chin and made the appropriate formal announcement preceding the king's entrance:

"George the Third, by the Grace of God, King of Great Britain, France and Ireland, Defender of the Faith."

"God save the king," echoed the admirals in unison as they stood.

King George III entered behind Lord Roberts and passed him swiftly and silently. Lord Roberts exited and closed the thick door. The king gestured to the bowing admirals to be seated. He was carrying a parchment rolled into a cylinder and fastened with a purple silk bow. The admirals noticed the excited gait and glint in the eye of their monarch as he approached.

"I have summoned each of you to assist in planning a very special naval assignment," the king began. "But before I begin, I will warn you that what I will say must be kept in absolute confidence. I would consider any breach of this trust as treason against the Crown, and would quickly and without remorse exact the appropriate punishment for anyone betraying this trust. Do I make myself clear?"

"You do, Your Majesty," confirmed Admiral Hughes as the other admirals nodded their unconditional agreement.

"Very well." The king untied the ribbon on the parchment and laid out on the table in front of the admirals a large map of Europe. The admirals held the corners as the king handed them small weights to keep the map flat.

Then the king pulled from his pocket the three shining ancient gold coins and tossed them onto the middle of the map. The admirals' stares had been fixated on the map, but now focused, wide-eyed, on the coins.

One coin in particular spun around like a top for what seemed an eternity. No one spoke or moved until it finally fell flat.

At once, the men looked up to the king who clearly enjoyed the drama of bearing captivating news.

"What you see before you are three coins from an ancient depository in the Mediterranean," the king declared. "The location is marked on this map and has been undisturbed for what appears to be thousands of years, until it was recently discovered by a British scholar while traveling through the islands. Outside of this scholar and me, and now the three of you, no one knows about its existence, let alone the location of the depository."

The admirals looked at one another before turning back to the king as he continued speaking.

"I need you to work out the logistics of sailing there, accompanied by the scholar of course, secretly collecting the artifacts and gold from the island, and returning to England. You, as well as the select crew of men you recommend, will be rewarded handsomely for your efforts should the contents of the depository be recovered and transferred to England successfully and in secret. Any questions, so far?"

"Yes, Your Majesty," Admiral Reynolds said. "Has this scholar given you any idea of the size of *cargo* we are to recover?"

"An excellent question," the king answered, "According to the scholar, the gold alone would conceivably fill more than twenty large chests."

The mouths of all three admirals dropped open as one.

"You gentlemen will study the map and agree upon the most appropriate ship and crew given the distance and the likely route. Inform me of your selections and I will make certain you have everything and everyone you request. The scholar will join the venture and is to be accorded every possible courtesy and comfort for its duration. Upon his return, the scholar will personally confer with me. Only when the cargo is safely at the palace and the scholar has reviewed all its contents can we release shares of the gold to you and the crew."

"Thank you, Your Majesty, for honoring us with this assignment. It shall be completed successfully," Admiral Hughes confirmed.

"Very well." The king waved a hand. "As a token of my faith in your discretion, each of you may keep a coin. But remember, reveal neither the coins nor the venture to anyone. Only the captain of the ship will know the true mission at its commencement."

The admirals stood as one and bowed in silence as the king

exited the room by the same door through which he had arrived.

♦

Across town, the stale air of a pub was filled with acrid pipe smoke, spilled ale and body odor, as the usual clearing sea breeze was conspicuously absent.

Four naval officers sat near the back of the large open air tavern known as Livingston's, sweating from the heat of the muggy June afternoon air, playing cards and drinking rum as though it were water.

A young boy waiting tables approached cautiously and stopped when his eyes met the glare of all four men.

"Pardon me, sirs, but there is a message for the one called Wilson," the lad announced in a quavering voice.

The roughest looking of the lot answered, "I'm Wilson. Who's looking for me?"

The boy approached slowly and extended a hand with a small note. As soon as he had put the note into the man's open hand the boy quickly withdrew his arm and moved back nervously toward the bar.

Wilson glanced at the scrawl on the note:

Meet me now in the private room behind the bar.
- A friend

Wilson looked up and willed his eyes to focus for a few seconds near the bar area for a sign of whom it was that wrote the brief note. He remained motionless for a moment, considering whether or not he would venture to the private conference requested anonymously.

Curiosity narrowly won out over his state of fatigued inebriation and poor hand of cards. He withdrew his pewter tankard of rum from the table, bid his mates continue without him, and sluggishly retreated to the bar area.

Placing his empty tankard on the bar, he noticed the young boy nodding his head toward a door down the short, dimly lighted passage behind them. Wilson lumbered out of sight down the hallway, knocked twice, and quickly entered the small room.

He was in what appeared to be a storage area, filled with casks of rum, wine and ale stacked floor to ceiling along the walls. No one was in sight, just a lantern hanging in the middle of the small area, casting ghostly shadows over the walls.

"Good day?" offered Wilson cautiously while peering into the room, though not quite committed enough to close the door behind him completely.

"Good afternoon," came a calm voice from the shadows.

"Who's there? Show yourself!" Wilson demanded.

"Calm yourself, my friend. I merely wish to have a brief word with you in private." The voice came from a shadowy figure standing between some large casks across the room.

The older man stepped forward into the flickering light. Wilson gasped, recognizing him at once, and stammered an apology.

"Please don't give it a second thought," said the man as he approached from the shadows. "And I apologize for the need for secrecy, but I believe I have a rather intriguing proposition for you."

◆

Captain Thomas Hatley, senior officer of the HMS *Pinnacle*, bolted upright from a sound sleep. Next to him stood a small man with a candle in one hand. His other hand was clenched on Hatley's shoulder, jostling the captain out of his fitful slumber. He drew back his hand quickly as Hatley sat up.

"Please report, Professor. What is the status of your operation?" Captain Hatley inquired formally. As he rubbed his eyes, he glanced up and noticed that the five carefully selected sailors that knew of - and had assisted in - the operation were standing a few feet behind Hutchins.

"The extraction and loading of the antiquities has been completed without issue, Captain," reported Hutchins in a tired voice.

"Excellent news, Professor," Hatley said as he held a pocket watch close to the professor's candle to deduce the time. "Three forty in the morning. We will set sail at dawn. Did you receive any inquiring looks from any of the crew?"

"No, Captain. The boat is silent," answered one of the sailors from behind the professor. "The only crew we've seen is the night watch on deck, and they were entirely uninterested in our activities."

"Probably think we're daft to have come all this way to collect some ancient broken marble artifacts!" Hutchins added.

"Just so," replied the captain, "Your part in this operation is done, Professor. Go below and get some well-deserved sleep. That goes for the rest of you men, as well."

"Thank you, Captain," Hutchins said. "I shall be very pleased to report directly to His Majesty how clever and resourceful you have been. The explanation of collecting historical antiquities for the Royal Academy in London, and marking the crates as such, was brilliant."

As Hutchins and the men left the cabin, Captain Hatley leaned over and lit his bedside lantern. While the professor's long day had just concluded, Hatley's was just beginning.

He swung his feet to the floor and re-opened the pocket watch hanging from the thin gold chain around his neck, though he was not focused on the time. He stared at the portrait, on the inside panel, of an uncommonly beautiful woman and a young man with the deep blue determined eyes of his father. The watch had been a gift from Hatley's wife Sarah three years prior, when their lone child, Mathew, had left home for college.

As he stared at Sarah's striking features, he recalled how he had immediately fallen in love with her so many years ago in the distant British colony of Virginia. In such a vibrant land and with such a close-knit family, Thomas had been as surprised as he was elated when Sarah accepted his marriage proposal and relocated to England.

Thomas' wealthy parents had died two years before the naval assignment that sent their son to Virginia, leaving Thomas with a considerable fortune and an expansive estate in Bridgwater on the Bristol Channel. After Thomas and Sarah's first few months together in London, the newlyweds happily had relocated to his family's estate, eschewing the social expectations of an aristocratic family and embracing the sanctuary away from the teeming city.

Since Thomas was often away at sea, young Mathew had been raised primarily by Sarah. With no concept of how children were to be brought up in England, she had spent a great deal of time with the boy on outdoor activities that would have made most adults in England wince, and most children fantastically jealous.

Since the estate grounds were vast, there had been abundant tree-climbing, archery, gymnastics, swimming and riding – all kept private from neighbors and friends.

In addition to their diverse athletic activities, Sarah had developed in her son an amazing acumen for chess at an early age. They would play for hours on end. When Thomas had occasionally played, he'd found it embarrassingly inexplicable that such a young boy could occasionally defeat a decorated military tactician.

Mathew also had a passion for reading, which - like his skill in chess - was advanced beyond his years. His appetite for literature had been born from his love of stories.

From early childhood, young Mathew had been riveted to his father's tales of the sea. At first, these were Thomas' best attempts at short bedtime stories, more fantasy than fact, meant to merely entertain and open young Mathew's mind to exotic areas of the world. In time, Mathew developed a heightened interest in everything nautical.

The estate's library was perhaps Mathew's favorite room of all, and he had often curled up in a large leather chair devouring classic literature including Homer, Euripides, Virgil, Cervantes, and Shakespeare.

In later years, he listened intently to every naval discussion with his father, whether about the type of rigging on a particular ship or complex naval tactics.

By the time he was nine, Mathew knew the name and purpose of every part of a large sailing ship, the ranks within the navy, and the tactics used in many of the most famous naval battles in history, from the Greeks unlikely defeat of the Persians in fifth century BC, to the more recent British victory at the Battle of Quiberon Bay during the Seven Years' War, in which his father gained additional notoriety.

Equally as impressive as his knowledge of the sea and naval history was his general nautical skill. Thomas and Mathew would enjoy racing small sailboats across nearby lakes and, on occasion, in the challenging Bristol Channel. Thomas could see his son rapidly develop an extraordinary sense of wind direction and tactical sailing efficiency.

However, the most impressive of all of Mathew's generally hidden talents was his prowess with the sword. His passion for fencing blended his insatiable appetite for classic literature with his enthusiasm for physical training.

How many valiant battles and heroic confrontations had he imagined as a young child immersed in works from Homer to Shakespeare? Thomas would occasionally find young Mathew running about the large home, reenacting the vivid descriptions of legendary duels from Sinbad to Achilles to pirates of the Spanish Main. As Mathew would later recall to his father, these swashbuckling scenes would continuously play in Mathew's head as he lay down to sleep each night.

When Mathew turned eight, Thomas had finally, though reluctantly, agreed to teach his son basic swordsmanship. Each lesson with blunt wooden play swords was cherished by Mathew, and he voluntarily practiced several hours each week. Thomas had been consistently astounded at the pace of the child's progress.

By the time Mathew reached ten, Thomas could see that his son possessed a very rare combination of speed and balance. Regrettably facing the reality that his time at home was too irregular, and his skill too limited, to tutor Mathew anywhere near his full potential, Thomas had resigned to hire a private fencing instructor.

Mathew eventually grew into the most gifted pupil his demanding private fencing tutor had even trained. He recalled marveling at his son's speed and grace during matches with the master swordsman at the estate in Bridgwater. *Lightning* was the term the private tutor used most often to describe Mathew's blinding speed and lethal skill. By the time Mathew was sixteen, the pupil would defeat the master as often as not.

How long ago it all seemed to Thomas who now studied his son's face in the pocket watch portrait. A wave of pride filled the Royal Navy captain as he remembered the more recent past.

Just three years prior, Mathew had postponed his dream of joining the Royal Navy in order to enroll at Oxford's Warwick College. Warwick had been an obvious preference given its unparalleled distinction in the areas of classics and literature.

However, his decision had come with an odd request - he wished to enroll at Oxford not as Mathew Hatley, but under a pseudonym. As he had delicately explained, his desire was to achieve success purely based on merit and not trade on the famous name of his heroic father.

Thomas and Sarah had patiently considered their son's preference for anonymity, and reluctantly agreed for him to use his mother's maiden name, Carrigan, while at Warwick.

While his son's academic advancement had been exemplary, Thomas knew his son would likely seek to join the Royal Navy as an officer candidate upon graduation. It had been the constant topic of conversation when the two would helm a small sailboat together on the Bristol Channel during school holidays.

A creaking in the floorboards of the deck above him stirred Thomas from distant thoughts of his family. He began every morning away from home in thoughtful meditation on his home in Bridgwater and the faces of the two people he loved even more than the sea. He smiled as he realized that on this particular morning, with an earlier start than usual, he would be heading home to England.

"I'll be home soon, my dearest," he said aloud as he closed the watch lid and stood to get dressed for the day.

An hour after the cargo had been quietly stored in the *Pinnacle*'s rear hold, Hutchins and the five sailors who had assisted him were fast asleep. The ship was silent and motionless in a secluded Mediterranean bay, and the narrow sliver of moon provided almost no light.

The ship's first lieutenant slowly walked onto the quarterdeck and gave a nod to burley seaman Ramsey, who turned and gave the same nod to sailors Forsyth and Laughton.

Forsyth and Laughton turned and nodded to Beckett and Putnam who moved quickly across the foredeck and disappeared below. When they returned topside precisely ninety seconds later, they nodded back to Forsyth and Laughton, signaling that their initial task was complete. Forsyth turned and nodded to the lieutenant while Laughton began climbing up the rigging to the crow's nest.

A tired young seaman, Adrian Lyle, was startled to alertness by the creaking of the rope rigging moving under him. Although he was undeniably fatigued, it seemed far too early to be relieved from his shift. He peered over the edge just as Laughton reached the bottom of the nest.

"Bit early tonight, Clyde," said Lyle, "Not that I'm complaining, mind you."

Just as Laughton climbed over the side, Lyle recognized that this man wasn't his scheduled replacement.

"Oh," Lyle recovered quickly, "I thought you was Clyde-boy taking me place."

"Clyde's not feeling right, so I've come to relieve you," responded Laughton.

"Bit early, aren't you? What time is it?" Lyle asked.

"Look, you want to be relieved or not?" Laughton shot back. "Get some rest!"

"Alright, alright" Lyle said, stifling a yawn. "More sleep for me…suits me fine."

As Lyle turned away from the conversation to descend the rope ladder, Laughton instantly pulled his knife from its leg sheath with his right hand, grabbed the tired young sailor with his left arm, and pulled the blade of the knife quickly across Lyle's throat.

Laughton gently lowered Lyle's limp body to the floor of the crow's nest platform and wiped the bloody blade on the dead sailor's coat, replaced it in its sheath, and descended the rope ladder rapidly. When he reached the deck, he turned and nodded to Forsyth.

At that moment, Beckett and Putnam appeared through the main hatchway having silently completed another task below deck. They turned around to face the lieutenant waiting near the aft deck. Putnam made a gesture by crossing his arms on his chest, with each hand on the opposite shoulder.

Ramsey approached and whispered to the lieutenant, "Time to pay a visit to the captain."

While the lieutenant and Ramsey moved slowly to the captain's quarters, the other four sailors scurried below deck.

Ramsey's knuckles tapped on the captain's closed door. The two visitors were somewhat surprised to see the faint but distinct light under the door, from flickering candles across the cabin. The captain was awake.

"Who is it?" the captain called.

The lieutenant opened the door and stepped in, followed by Ramsey, who quietly closed the cabin door behind him. Captain Thomas Hatley held a hand up just below his eyes, to shield his vision from the glow of the candles on his desk, and squinted into the darkness of his cabin.

"Begging your pardon, Captain," Lieutenant Wilson said. "I would have waited until daybreak, but I saw your light was on, and thought I might discuss something with you briefly."

"Come in, First Lieutenant," Captain Hatley responded, sounding exasperated at the intrusion, but thinking of no legitimate excuse to turn his lieutenant away. "What is it?"

"Thank you, Captain," stalled the officer as he approached the wide oak desk. "You see, Captain, it's come to my attention that we may have an outbreak of some sort of rash among the men. I've never seen anything like it. Seaman Ramsey, show the captain your arm."

While Ramsey approached the captain around the left side of the desk, the lieutenant slipped around the right side of the desk. Ramsey bunched up the sleeve of his left arm which was dangling straight down as Captain Hatley adjusted his wooden chair to face the sailor and leaned forward from his sitting position to get a better look.

In a flash, Ramsey raised his left fist connecting a powerful uppercut to his captain's chin. The force of the punch knocked Hatley backward in his chair. From behind, Wilson wrapped a twisted cloth around his captain's throat. Stunned from the blow to his chin, a confused Hatley felt himself spinning off into unconsciousness.

Hatley awakened slowly as his lieutenant patted his cheek. His mouth was gagged with a cloth tied tightly behind his head, and his jaw felt like it was broken. His wrists had been tied securely with thick leather straps to each armrest of the chair, as had his ankles to the chair legs.

As Hatley blinked in an attempt to focus, Wilson leaned in, speaking softly and disturbingly.

"Well, well, Captain. It looks as though I'm in control now, doesn't it?"

Bound, silent and helpless, Hatley still managed to shoot his lieutenant a piercing stare.

"Yes, I'm sure you're thinking: 'why didn't he just kill me?' I could have, you know. I let you live so that you may suffer slowly and painfully. Had I liked you or even respected you, I would have done you the courtesy of killing you instantly, but as it is, I think it is appropriate that you experience a nice slow death."

Hatley stared defiantly at the lieutenant, as his senior officer explained himself.

"You never should have recommended against my promotion to the rank of captain last year," Wilson admonished. "Oh yes, I know it was you and Captain Poole that voted against my candidacy."

Hatley continued his intense gaze, wondering how many men were part of the apparent mutiny. He had personally requested the majority of the officers, specifically for their trustworthiness, though one of the few exceptions had been Wilson himself, placed on the HMS *Pinnacle* by the Admiralty.

"I know what's in the crates, Captain! My men are taking it off the ship as we...I mean...as I speak. Why split all that gold with several hundred, when it can be split into a handful of shares?" he added rhetorically.

Hatley struggled against his bonds while he wondered how the lieutenant could possibly have discovered the true nature of the cargo.

"I'm not one for surprises, Captain. You should know that we've set enough charges to blow the *Pinnacle* and its crew to Kingdom Come. The crew will almost certainly be killed by the blast, but if any should miraculously survive and swim to shore, they'll be shot on sight by my men."

An anger he'd never known before surged through Hatley. He tried with all of his might to jerk out of the chair, but could barely move.

"Yes, the blast will kill the men," repeated the lieutenant looking up at the ceiling, "but, it probably won't kill you."

Hatley was suddenly still. He realized the blast would likely knock him over, but he'd be sparred the instant death of the crew only to suffer the prolonged agony of drowning helplessly.

A tear welled in his eye, not at his imminent disturbing death, but at the realization that he would never see his beloved wife and son again.

"Do have a nice swim, Captain," Wilson said as he leaned over the table to blow out the candles. The light below his chin gave his face a ghostly, demonic look as he pushed out a quick breath and turned the cabin into sudden blackness.

The thud of boots followed by the creak of the door indicated that Wilson and Ramsey had left the cabin.

Not knowing how many minutes he had left to live, Hatley continued in vain to break free from his bound position. His wife and son's faces swam before his gaze and tears fell freely from his eyes. Had he let his wife know how very much he loved her? Had he communicated adequately to Mathew how proud he was of him?

Nearly fourteen minutes after Wilson and Ramsey had left, an eternity to Hatley in helpless captivity, the deafening blast from inside the ship threw him backward in the air several feet, landing hard on his back on the cabin floor.

Hatley felt the deck of the cabin suddenly changing planes, and slowly felt the gravitational pull of his weight toward the cabin door. His bound body and chair began to slide across the floor to the low point in the room. He heard the sound of water rushing into the room from under the door. It would be just a minute or two more.

One hundred yards away, two jolly boats glided onto the soft sand of the shore. The sailors stopped rowing, pulled their oars up and watched as the HMS *Pinnacle* slowly sank.

The middle half of the vessel had disappeared in a fireball with millions of wooden shards launched in all directions instantaneously. The remaining foredeck and aft deck were pinching towards one another, sinking slowly.

As the last of the remaining portions of the ship dropped below the surface of the water, the lieutenant turned to the four sailors still facing the water.

"Lads, please tell me someone remembered to pack the bloody rum!"

- crew gets together
- Mathew's page
- Wilson takes over ship and blows it up

†

Chapter 4: Reactions

The merchant ship *Avalon* sailed unscheduled into the port of London with a handful of survivors from the HMS *Pinnacle*'s dramatic destruction. News of the tragic loss of nearly her entire crew spread rapidly throughout the dock area.

Within an hour, King George had been informed of the disaster and demanded a debriefing from Admiral Hughes.

Due to the highly secretive nature of the unorthodox mission, Admiral Hughes personally addressed the handful of survivors. One by one, he questioned the injured and still shaken crewmen privately. As delicately as he could, he tried to extract precisely what had happened to the ship and its secretive cargo.

After two hours of collective questioning, the admiral was sufficiently convinced that none of the survivors had any idea of the true nature of the cargo. Each had separately but consistently recounted that, a day or so prior to the accident, some crew had apparently gone ashore on a small deserted island and collected remains of some dilapidated marble statues and ancient artifacts.

Unfortunately, only one officer survived the harrowing tragedy. Though he honorably tried to deflect blame from his captain, his testimony was indirectly a scathing indictment of Captain Thomas Hatley.

It was far too incredible for Admiral Hughes to believe.

Hatley was known to be a fastidious naval tactician, placing his crew and ship's safety above all else. In a battle, there was no doubt that Thomas Hatley was one of the most lethal and cunning captains in the Royal Navy, but in peace time, no captain was more cautious and genuinely concerned with the welfare and state of his crew and ship.

After multiple questions, the version of the events as recalled by Lieutenant John Wilson pointed to Captain Hatley making a series of rash and reckless miscalculations that ultimately cost England one of her finest ships of the line and most experienced crews, not to mention her irreplaceable cargo.

Apparently, Hatley had gone against the admonitions and recommendations of his own corps of officers, and pushed on through a dark-as-pitch night at full sail in a rugged summer sea storm that the accompanying civilian scholar had referred to as a *meltemi*.

The storm had knocked the *Pinnacle* off her intended course and resulted in the ship smashing violently into the tall, jagged cliffs of the small Maltese island, Filfla.

The gunpowder had ignited and the entire ship exploded. Only a few of the crew, who happened to be on deck at the time of the collision, were thrown clear from the ship into the darkness before the explosion seconds later.

Each of the crew had recalled, through voices choked with emotion, a similar version of their last moments before impact. There was darkness all around, and all of a sudden...whoosh...they were thrust off the ship, flying over the bulwark toward the darkness of the sea or rocks. Some of the men hit rocks and had died instantly. The few survivors knew that they were indeed fortunate that they were neither crushed on the rocks nor burned nor drowned.

The sheer cliffs of Filfla dropped down below the surface to an immeasurable depth. Even in the clear Mediterranean water the next day, the remains of the ship were clearly lost to the dark abyss far below. With no beach access, the heroism of Lieutenant Wilson was all the more impressive.

The account of the horrific events visibly devastated Admiral Hughes, who had the unfortunate assignment of debriefing the king directly.

He communicated that, based on the consistency of the individual accounts from the few survivors, Captain Hatley had apparently acted carelessly and recklessly, directly leading to the death of over four hundred crewmen and the loss of one of the finest ships of the line, as well as her secretive cargo and lone civilian. Admiral Hughes added that, due to his careful line of questioning, he could confidently conclude that the survivors knew nothing of the gold.

Once the debriefing concluded, Admiral Hughes left the palace and traveled by coach all the way to Bridgwater to personally deliver the tragic news of the HMS *Pinnacle* disaster to the unsuspecting wife of its deceased captain.

Hughes had the decency to spare Sarah the unflattering details he'd learned from the *Pinnacle* survivors the prior day. While her initial reaction to Thomas' death was abject shock and disbelief, within seconds she broke down in the admiral's empathetic arms in a torrent of tears.

The shock of losing her beloved husband to a sailing accident in the Mediterranean was incomprehensible. He had fought valiantly through several battles over the years, and suffered only minor injuries.

While Sarah was unaware of the specific details of the mission, Thomas had assured her before his departure that he was traveling to a relatively nearby region and that it would not be a military assignment. There would be no battles at sea with foreign navies on this particular duty. He had even mused that it would be one of the easiest and safest missions he'd ever led.

And now he was dead. Within moments of Admiral Hughes' sorrowful news, Sarah's mind shifted to Mathew, who likely had not learned of his father's tragic passing.

♦

Mathew Carrigan walked through the driving wind with a purposeful gait, leaving the rigors of a profoundly challenging, yet successful academic week behind him. The late afternoon wind seemed to cleanse any lingering anxiety away with each step closer to his residence. Within sight of his building, he began to focus on the card games scheduled with his college mates that evening and, eventually, retiring to his warm bed for much deserved sleep.

Mathew climbed the six marble steps of his college and reached for the sturdy doors, taking one last breath of the cold, biting air before entering.

"Good afternoon, Carrigan," a fellow student offered as Mathew strode through the foyer.

"Greetings, Daniel," Mathew responded with uncharacteristic elation, as he stopped in his tracks and pivoted to face his friend reclined on the common room sofa. "Make sure you bring plenty of money this evening as I'm feeling rather lucky!"

"Once again, your confidence will be your undoing, old fellow. I shall be the one retiring a few pounds heavier tonight."

"Daniel, we both know I've taken far more off you than you off me. If you were truly interested in increasing your wealth, you shouldn't invite me to play in your card games."

"A mere canard, Mathew. I let you win occasionally to keep you coming to the games."

"Interesting. However, with that kind of immutable logic I believe a career as a barrister is improbable," Mathew jeered.

"How else can I insure the attendance of so many attractive young ladies?" Daniel finally confided.

"We both know they come to see you, Daniel," Mathew said, though he knew Daniel was correct.

"That reminds me. There's a rather attractive lady in your room right now," Daniel remembered. "She's been here for a couple hours. Said she'd wait until you arrived."

"Relentless. Who is she?" Mathew inquired, more irritated than interested.

"I don't know. I've never seen her before. She's certainly not one of the town girls come early to spend extra time with you. She's a lady, that one."

"Fine," Mathew said as he pivoted back toward the wide stairway across the foyer.

By the time he reached the door to his room, Mathew's mood had swung back like a pendulum to more curious than irritated.

He opened the door and walked in.

Across the modest room at the set of windows opposite the door, a woman immediately rose from the leather armchair.

"Mother!" a surprised Mathew announced. "This is indeed a pleasant..."

His greeting was interrupted by the realization that something was wrong. The look on Sarah Hatley's face was unmistakable. She stared silently at her son with a sorrowful expression for seconds that seemed like an eternity. Her lips began to quiver as she attempted to speak, but the rush of emotions overwhelmed her. She burst into tears as she crossed the room to Mathew's embrace.

"Mathew," she started as she held her son tightly, "I have terrible news. Your father is dead."

As news of the *Pinnacle* disaster quickly spread from London to the outlying areas of England, Captain Thomas Hatley's image was severely tarnished, while the reputation of Lieutenant Wilson was dramatically enhanced.

Within a week, the name of Thomas Hatley evoked resentment and hostility from people who had never met the man. Scorn and derision followed his name, and unfortunately found its way to his devastated and unprepared wife.

As if she had commanded her husband to purposely destroy himself and the crew, the town of Bridgwater turned hard on her.

What began as rude treatment quickly escalated to taunting and open hostility. Her colonial background, initially viewed as quaint, set further flame to the town's scorn. The American colonies were increasingly unappreciative, and in some cases, openly hostile toward England's governance and supervision.

Sarah began to receive direct threats. Initially, hostile notes were posted at the gates of the Hatley estate. Gunshots were fired at the house, breaking some windows. In one particularly frightening incident, someone had breached the gates in the middle of the night and attached a rather graphic warning note to the front door with a large hunting knife.

Sarah fled to the safety of her husband's closest friend and former naval colleague. A prominent shipping magnate, it was he who looked after her for the following week at his estate just outside of London. And when she had elected to return as soon as possible to Virginia, he agreed to monetize the Hatley estate and provide her safe passage to the American colonies. Longtime friends, the man reluctantly agreed that she should leave England, at least for the foreseeable future.

Though grateful for the man's generous assistance and resolute to return to Virginia before putting her host in danger by any association with her, Sarah was torn at the prospect of leaving England without saying good-bye to her son in person.

Before leaving, she penned a detailed letter to Mathew at Oxford, describing the unfortunate threats she'd been receiving and requesting him to join her in Virginia after his graduation in a few months. Unlike her, he did not share his father's last name and so was in no immediate danger. She mentioned her husband's former naval colleague as a point of contact in England and apologized that she was unable to deliver the message herself.

Begging his forgiveness, she closed the letter with: *Your loving mother, Sarah.* The ink of her signature was smudged from the tears she shed in writing her goodbye.

Back at Oxford, news disseminated through the general student population of the destruction of the *Pinnacle.* Weeks after he had first learned of his father's death, the topic was still a major point of discussion among Mathew's friends and colleagues. Even with the constant reminders, it was still unbelievable to him that his father could be dead.

His father was a long time captain in the Royal Navy and he had felt there was a dash of immortality in the man. He had survived countless sea battles in recent wars and had sustained no injury more than minor cuts and bruises.

And now he was dead. How? There was no explanation or detail other than his ship had been dashed into jagged rocks on an island in the Mediterranean during a storm and exploded killing nearly every sailor. There was no mention of a battle, no pirates, no danger other than the storm itself.

As a young boy, Mathew had often sailed with his father in the Bristol Channel and, on a number of occasions, in suddenly inclement weather.

Thomas Hatley was an expert in guiding ships, no matter the size, to safety in high seas and treacherous winds. With his own eyes several years prior, Mathew watched his father calmly negotiate a fierce storm that had suddenly turned on their small sailing vessel. He had also been decorated by the navy two separate times for saving so many sailors due to his resolve and tactical decision making during ferocious storms.

This made the account of the *Pinnacle* explosion all the more specious to Mathew. Something felt out of place.

The shock of losing his father was replaced within a few days with confusion and anger. There was no discussion of an accident or a stray lightning bolt or something beyond Captain Thomas Hatley's control. No, it was deemed that recklessness destroyed the *Pinnacle* and the blame lay squarely at the boots of her captain. To make matters far worse, England had turned against his mother, too.

England was much more than a country to Mathew. It had been a supreme ideal created like a fortress in Mathew's mind, brick by brick, layer upon layer and stone by stone forged over the years from his father's loyalty and service, by the history books he cherished, and legends passed down through generations.

How mighty the fortress had been. And now – in one broad sweep of events - how tarnished and beaten down it had become. The ideal that had taken most of Mathew's life to create in his mind, came crashing down in the few silent, emotional moments the young scholar spent staring teary-eyed at the distant hills beyond the Warwick College grounds.

Mathew was immediately torn by the complexities of his situation. He still had one term to go to complete his Oxford degree. His father would want him to finish as scheduled, on this point he had no doubt. It also made no sense to give up, so close to that particular journey's end. But what next?

He had always assumed he would attend the Britannia Royal Navy College and become an officer in the navy. And now the very name that would have surely granted him admission to officer candidate school was bound to prevent him from joining the navy at all.

Much as he tried, he could not force himself to seriously consider alternatives outside the British navy. He made up his mind to look up his father's friend, Andrew Dunn, following graduation and openly discuss his predicament.

Upon commencement from Oxford, Mathew traveled straight to London rather than Bridgwater. His cherished possessions amounted to several books and maps, three swords, and a series of letters from his father to him over the years since childhood that he kept in chronological order in a leather folio entitled *Tesoro de Familia*, Spanish for "Family Treasure".

Two other trunks were predominantly filled with clothes. Once the carriage he'd hired was loaded, Mathew turned and glanced back towards St. John's clock tower, across the immaculate greens and gardens connecting the four stone clad school buildings and two residence halls.

He slowly drank in the last view of Warwick College and its adjacent town. The memory would have to last quite a long time, Mathew assumed, for he knew he would likely not be back for several years.

What had once seemed a cold and daunting institution, evoked the warm feeling of home as he prepared to leave.

As the carriage pulled away, Mathew was already facing the opposite interior wall of the carriage, eyes closed in silent contemplation.

Mathew recalled meeting Andrew Dunn a few times as a young boy. He remembered how his father downplayed Dunn's praise and loyalty. The two old friends had been very close and Mathew actually looked forward to seeing Dunn again.

Then Mathew thought of his mother. His father had loved her so much and treasured every moment with her, and Mathew often considered her the backbone of their family in many ways.

Undaunted, courageous and lovely – she embodied so much of what Mathew admired. She had left a comfortable lifestyle and close-knit family in her native Virginia as a young lady to start over in a new land. That could not have been easy, and yet she made the tremendous sacrifice without a second thought because of her love for his father.

Mathew also thought about his childhood fencing mentor, Santos. He recalled his father originally describing the Spanish swordsman as the ideal candidate to tutor young Mathew. Miguel Santos Velazquez Allegria de Torrente was the most skilled swordsman Thomas had ever witnessed. He had marveled at Santos' unparalleled speed and acrobatic footwork while attending a local festival during a layover in Santa Cruz de Tenerife of the Canary islands nearly two decades prior.

Santos' fencing expertise was unmatched. He had been a decorated naval hero in the Spanish navy but had fallen out of good graces with King Ferdinand VI. Apparently discharged from the navy dishonorably, the true account had never been made clear to Mathew's father.

Thomas and Santos remained close friends through years of periodic correspondence, though their contact abated during the latter portion of the Seven Years' War. In 1761, Spain had declared war on England who was already fighting France. At the conclusion of the war two years later, England had gained key Spanish colonies including Havana in Cuba, and Manila in the Philippines, as well as Florida.

Mathew recalled how his father had been tentative about writing to Santos immediately following the hostilities, but eventually Santos reached out to him, indicating that their friendship was far more valuable to him than any political, military or geographic constraints.

Thomas had been overjoyed to receive a reply directly from Santos suggesting that he would be delighted to visit England and train young Mathew in the ways of the sword. His lone condition was that their arrangement be kept private - a condition valued equally by Thomas.

Mathew smiled, with eyes still closed, remembering his first fencing lesson with Santos, as though it were the day before.

For an initial assessment of Mathew's skill, they had sparred privately on the terrace that overlooked the expansive ground of the Bridgwater estate. They had donned the appropriate white protective jacket, in addition to the gleaming knickers and gloves, and prepared their foils by running colored chalk up the blade and around the point in order to leave a mark on one's opponent, whether by a point or a slash, thus proving a score.

Santos had turned toward Mathew and stood very straight. He held his foil in his right hand, though Mathew knew from his father's stories that the Spaniard was equally adept with either hand. The young boy had wondered if he, too, would ever posses such a rare and impressive advantage.

From a distance of fifteen feet, both fencers stood at their respective *en guard* lines. Santos brought the hilt of his foil up to his head as Mathew did the same, respecting custom and signifying to one another their mutual readiness to commence.

"En guard. Pret. Allez!" Santos barked, and Mathew quickly assumed the initial en guard position.

The cultured sport of fencing was governed by priority rules aimed to encourage sensible fencing and reward initiative and circumspection at the same time, and to penalize fencers for attacking in a manner that could be lethal with sharp blades. The first fencer to initiate an attack or the last to make a successful parry or defense receives priority, which favors this fencer in terms of points on simultaneous hits.

The master approached the student slowly yet steadily. He would be the aggressor first. Mathew noticed how gracefully Santos slid. His body moved quickly in a line and yet his head never changed its vertical plane. The movement in his legs did not lead to any discernable movement above his waist. It seemed a remarkable illusion.

Mathew successfully parried Santos' initial and direct attack. The two sparred for over ten minutes before Santos halted the skirmish by standing erect and raising his left hand. As he removed his mask and starred intently at Mathew, the young boy lowered his foil and raised his own protective mask, returning Santos' glance, silently searching for some expression in the Spaniard's weathered face.

"Muy bueno," remarked Santos, nearly whispering while slightly nodding his head.

Mathew's face burst into a wide grin. He liked the Spaniard very much and was pleased to have seemingly surpassed his tutor's initial expectations.

Over the course of the following six years, Santos worked tirelessly with Mathew. Mathew knew his speed, fluidity, footwork, balance and stamina were exceptional. However, it had been his intellect that had intrigued the master swordsman the most. Though a powerful fighter, Mathew relied on a fast and analytical intelligence, processing strengths and weaknesses of different opponents as simulated by Santos. He fenced as he played chess – in control and detached from emotion.

When they weren't fencing or training in obscure exercises or playing chess, Mathew would often ask Santos about Spain, the Mediterranean, the Caribbean and other parts of the world with which the Spaniard was familiar. After several summers together, Mathew even began to pick up the Spanish language quite well.

He had learned much more than swordsmanship and a new language from the kind Spaniard, and Mathew considered Santos a close uncle in many respects.

While neither he nor his father had heard from Santos during his university years, Mathew recalled with great fondness the mix of rigorous discipline and ever-present optimism instilled in him by his private tutor. He credited much of his adolescent growth to the wisdom imparted by Santos' lessons and direction.

It was still a mystery as to why Santos had not responded to Mathew's letters.

He knew that in 1759, Charles III succeeded his half-brother Ferdinand VI on the Spanish throne. Ferdinand had carefully forged a delicate balance of neutrality over the decades in the conflict between England and France – refusing to be tempted by the offers of either into declaring war on the other.

Charles, however, openly detested England and broke Spain's neutrality to fight with France against the English at the close of the Seven Years War. Spain took on England again in a clash over the distant Falkland Islands in 1770.

But Mathew refused to believe that Charles' open animosity

toward England permeated through the entire Spanish population. There had to be another reason why Santos had not replied to Mathew's correspondence.

A large bump in an otherwise relatively smooth ride jostled Mathew back to his original thoughts. As the coach rolled south-eastward towards London, the great city just visible in the distance, Mathew felt optimistic that Andrew Dunn, a relative stranger, would be able to shed some light on what would be the right course of action.

~Mathew goes to live
with Andrew Dunn
- Last name is descriminated
~ Changes name

†

Chapter 5: A New Old Friend

*M*athew arrived at Ardsley Manor at Clivedon, the home of Andrew Dunn, and took a moment to regard the splendid estate of his father's longtime best friend.

The magnificent mansion was set atop a hill surrounded by 35 acres of lawns and gardens overlooking the River Thames, just to the west of London. Mathew's eyes drew across the expansive side-gabled roof, noticing chimneys on both sides of the home.

He detected slight movement in an upstairs rectangular six-paned sash window, suggesting his arrival had been noticed and he would soon be greeted by his host in the warm, spring evening.

A moment later, Dunn came out the panel front door at the center of the home and headed down the wide, marble steps of his estate.

"Greetings, Mathew," he spoke and grasped Mathew's right hand in his own, as the coachmen carried Mathew's trunks up the small flight of outer stairs and into the foyer of the large house. "I confess I didn't expect to find you'd grown so tall."

When the coachman was out of listening distance, Dunn continued, "I want you to know how very sorry I am for your loss. Your father was an extraordinary man."

"Thank you, sir" replied Mathew, "and I appreciate your kind hospitality," he offered as he motioned with his eyes to Dunn's beautiful home.

"Think nothing of it!" countered Dunn, "Even though we haven't seen each other for over ten years, I feel I know nearly everything about you from your father's proud descriptions. You are welcome to stay as long as you wish!"

"You're very kind, sir," Mathew said.

"...as long as you make an honest effort to dispense with the formality," Dunn admonished, winking. "The last time we saw each other you called me 'Uncle Andy.' But then again, you were only a small boy. Perhaps just 'Andy' will suffice from now on."

"Very well," Mathew replied through a broadening grin. It was the first time he had smiled in quite some time.

"I mean it, lad," added Dunn. "I want you to be very comfortable here. If there's anything I can do for you, do not hesitate to ask. I'm sorry we've come together again under such sad circumstances, but I must admit I look forward to the company."

Mathew then remembered that Dunn's wife had died about eight years prior. "And I'm sorry for your loss, as well," he mentioned. "Mrs. Dunn was a delightful lady - my parents always spoke so fondly of you both."

"I appreciate that. Now, let's get inside and get you situated," Dunn gestured toward the stairs. "I expect you're famished and rather tired from the trip. You're in for quite a treat. My housekeeper, Mrs. Whalen, is preparing a hearty supper in your honor."

Mathew pulled his leather satchel over his right shoulder and slung the duffle over his left. "That's sounds wonderful, Uncle Andy," he answered.

A few minutes later, Mathew was settling into the guest bedroom. It was a spacious chamber, complete with a sofa next to a large set of windows overlooking the expansive front gardens.

While unpacking his belongings, Mathew was optimistic about his decision to visit Dunn. Perhaps a short stay here would provide that confidence in direction he so desperately desired.

Nonetheless, just to be able to finally end his prolonged silence and speak with a friend of the family about his father's death would be welcomed at this point.

As he dressed for dinner, Mathew recalled how Dunn and his father had originally met. Both were young sailors in the Royal Navy showing great promise. Thomas Hatley, however, was dedicated to a career in His Majesty's service on the sea, while Andrew Dunn was ultimately focused on starting his own shipping business.

Ever the idealist, Dunn often talked to Hatley about open trade with exotic ports around the world and making a difference in the lives of those he served in business as well as those he managed within his firm. Dunn's fate was a marriage of commerce and the sea, and no man, according to Mathew's father, was as intelligent and enterprising as young Andrew Dunn. Every bit as good a seaman as was in the Royal Navy, his father would boast, but with the entrepreneurial spirit to start his own enterprise and see it prosper exceptionally.

After Dunn eventually left the navy and started his shipping company, Hatley was not surprised to hear of his immediate, burgeoning success. He was a natural financier - a master of accurately assessing the risk to voyages and underwriting his business properly. He was a firm believer in limiting his risk, for some agreeable portion of his profits, by insuring cargo shipments through various other parties.

Dunn's reputation for underwriting risk was legendary. Interestingly, the nautical risk management cooperative known as Lloyd's (named for the dockside coffee house in which these business ventures were transacted) would often come to Dunn to help underwrite particularly large or complex shipping ventures. Sometimes, he was offered and would take a stake in a venture. Other times he would merely inform Lloyd's of his assessment of the risks and what he felt was the appropriate level of compensation to accept the risks. In no time at all, Andrew Dunn became an extremely wealthy and respected man.

Mathew recalled how his father would go on about how idealistic Dunn remained through his meteoric success. Dunn remained focused on providing the best service possible for his clients and creating a large number of good jobs for many men at all levels within his organization. Dunn was genuinely as concerned for the welfare of his sailors as he was with that of his captains. His thoughtfulness and compensation schedules, including payment to injured crew, were legendary. There was no finer commercial shipping operation where a knowledgeable sailor would desire a place.

Dunn had tried many times in vain to lure Mathew's father to his company, even offering him a partnership position, but to no avail. Dunn knew the Royal Navy ran thick through Thomas Hatley's veins and that Hatley was only content in leading men in a different, albeit more dangerous, business, and Dunn respected this. While the proposals continued through the years, they became more a familiar salutation to both men rather than an offer anticipating genuine consideration.

Both men remained as close as brothers through the years, though very few people knew that they were even acquainted. The typical form of correspondence was a letter. Occasionally, they would privately get together at Dunn's home when Hatley was either going to, or returning from, a naval mission.

At dinner that evening, Mathew sat at the splendid teak dining table and watched his host pensively select a bottle of wine from an immense oak cabinet across the room. Though Dunn was strong and confident, Mathew clearly sensed the kindness and empathy at which his father never stopped marveling.

The young gentleman prided himself at being keenly perceptive in judging a man's character. Back at Oxford, he had a reputation during late night card games of "looking into the very soul" of his opponents and knowing the strength of their cards from the mere expression on their faces or the most innocuous facial tick, gesture or body movement.

Mathew saw Dunn as a highly intelligent and driven man, with a curious dose of abundant compassion. Every gesture and word spoken outside when he first arrived had been sincere and heartfelt. A man of great style and taste - a true gentleman, thought Mathew.

Mrs. Jessica Whalen, widow of twenty years and Dunn's housekeeper for the last thirteen, entered the dining room, and Mathew instinctively stood. She immediately shot Dunn an approving glance.

"Oh, this one *is* a proper gentleman, Mr. Dunn, and handsome, too. You'll not likely see much of him when the young ladies discover his presence in London."

"Now, Mrs. Whalen," warned Dunn in a serious tone, "his presence here is not to be announced. This is vitally important. Mathew is here for well-deserved rest, relaxation and, above all, sanctuary."

Then he softened his admonishment and winked at Mathew before asking Mrs. Whalen, "I don't believe it would be very relaxing with teams of young ladies parading about the grounds for his attention at all hours, do you?"

"No, sir" replied Mrs. Whalen, "I understand." Then turning to Mathew, she added, "It is indeed a pleasure to meet you, dear. You just let me know if you need anything."

"Thank you very much, ma'am," said Mathew, feeling a rare grin once again break across his face.

Mrs. Whalen ladled some aromatic vegetable stew while Dunn poured Mathew a glass of Bordeaux. The smell of fresh bread and roast lamb wafted from the kitchen to the dining room, and Mathew instantly realized how very hungry he was.

Mathew recalled his father describing his visits to Ardsley Manor in glowing terms. Dunn was, above all, an excellent judge of character, his father had said. It was a faculty that had served Dunn well over the years in underwriting the risk of countless commercial shipping ventures, for weather and pirates were not the only risks on the seas.

Dunn's secret for accurately assessing and valuing risks at sea placed a great weight on the *people* that would be in charge of the journey. He could apparently spot courage and leadership right away and would look for both in a captain and officers when underwriting a particularly long, complex, or dangerous venture.

"You've been through quite a lot, Mathew," he said as they began the first course. "I suspect you'd like to talk about your father's passing with someone who knew him well."

"Oh, yes, I certainly would." Mathew straightened up quickly in his chair, relieved that it was Dunn who had brought the subject up first.

"Your father was like a brother to me. You are like...," Dunn stopped mid-sentence and corrected himself, "You *are* family. I want you to know that I am willing to help you in any way that I am able. But you should not be in any hurry to decide anything. You are at an important crossroads of life, and your decisions should be well thought out and considered."

"I appreciate your offer, Uncle Andy," Mathew again purposely used the familial title because he felt a deep sense of connection to this man he hardly knew. And he realized that one of the only regrets in Dunn's life was not being able to have children and that the uncle reference would be both respectful and favorably received.

As they began to eat, Mathew opened up the conversation on his father. "I don't believe the accounts of what happened the night of the accident."

"I know you don't, Mathew, and for what it's worth, neither do I," Dunn said. "The facts, as they have been reported, are not at all consistent with the man I knew."

"That's true," Mathew added, excited and relieved that he could at last speak with someone openly about the incident; someone who understood the sea, someone who understood his father.

"My father would never have put the ship and crew in harm's way. He was a fanatic about safety."

"Yes, that's what puzzles me, too," Dunn agreed. "I've had many discussions over the years with him about cargo shipments making up time by sailing through the night. It is one thing to do so in the open sea, but in the Mediterranean, with thousands of small islands? I can't imagine the circumstances or cargo that would drive Thomas to do so."

"And apparently during a severe storm, besides," Mathew added. "The risk would be increased dramatically, not to mention the fact that they wouldn't be able to navigate by the stars."

"Valid points, both," Dunn concluded.

Mathew and Dunn picked at their meal distractedly, absorbed

by the complexity of their discussion.

"Mathew, you should know that I've used my influence to look into this matter directly. After I heard the news, I discreetly contacted Admiral Simon Hughes with whom I had served in several campaigns during my Royal Navy years. It turns out that of the Admiralty here in London, it was he who interviewed the survivors and debriefed the king himself.

Mathew's face brightened and posture improved instantly. "Really?"

"Hughes didn't know that Thomas and I were close friends, you see. So I appealed to him simply as an interested merchant attempting to learn as much as possible about the accident in order to better assess the risks for my own ships in the Mediterranean."

"And he was cooperative?"

"Fully, though he was unable to provide much insight. Hughes said that the accident occurred in the middle of the night, hence the scattered few sailors on deck at the time of impact with the island. The explosion was so horrific as to consume nearly all the men below deck instantly, and the men that were on deck at that hour were thrown far from the ship into the sea or onto jagged rocks."

"Dreadful! But what were they doing near Malta?" Mathew inquired.

"Come, Mathew. You know very well Hughes would never confide the nature of a naval mission to a civilian, even a former naval colleague."

"Of course. That was a rhetorical question, I suppose," Mathew offered while shaking his head. "But does it make sense to you that the *Pinnacle* was alone on that voyage?"

"It does not," agreed Dunn. "She was a grand ship of the line; one of the best in the Royal Navy. What she was doing alone near Malta will likely remain a mystery, I'm afraid. I can only presume she was not expected to engage in battle or she would have been sent with other ships."

"There's another oddity, Uncle Andy. How did the survivors get back home?"

"A British merchant ship, the *Avalon*, had the good fortune to pass by Malta early the next morning. She claimed the few survivors and came straight back to England."

"Curious," Mathew remarked.

"Indeed. The probability of the *Avalon* passing on the very next day was extraordinarily low. The survivors were most fortunate"

"Yes, the timing was certainly remarkable, but also that the *Avalon* could see a few injured men from out at sea."

"What are you saying, Mathew?"

"I'm not quite sure. It's just that there are too many fantastic coincidences for my taste," Mathew answered as he lowered his head before speaking again. "I realize my father is dead and nothing can bring him back, but I do not accept the navy's account as truth. There is a missing element somewhere that we may never learn, but it is something that ties these odd events together better than the story you've been told."

The conversation paused for a few moments while the two men continued their meal.

"Then let us back up and examine this from a different perspective," Dunn directed. "We agree Thomas would never push the ship under normal circumstances. So what would motivate him to drive at full sail in a stormy night through a labyrinth of jagged islands?"

"Running from something, you mean?"

"Perhaps."

"Another navy?"

"Highly unlikely. We're not at war with Spain, France, or Italy."

"Corsairs?" Mathew mused, as he lifted a glass to his lips.

"Even less probable," Dunn calculated. "While North Africa is littered with pirates, particularly along the Barbary Coast, they would not aggressively pursue a Royal Navy warship."

Mathew nodded agreement while stirring the last remnants of his stew, staring in deep thought at the center of the teak table.

After the meal, both men stood and retreated to the terrace. The night air was warm and the view of moonlight dancing on the Thames River below them was spectacular.

Dunn filled his pipe with tobacco and motioned for Mathew

to take one of the leather chairs facing the water in the distance. Mathew declined to smoke, but readily accepted a glass of port.

"How's your mother?" his host inquired.

Mathew shrugged his broad shoulders and looked outward across the river and up into the night stars. "I don't really know right now, but I expect she is in a far better place than here."

"I don't mean to bring up another sensitive subject, Mathew. It's just that I think of Virginia every time I light this pipe. The most magnificent blends of tobacco come from there."

"That's alright, Uncle Andy. Thanks to you, she's gained safe passage home. I expect we'll hear from her soon and I imagine she is happier to be in the American colonies again after the tragedy. I'm just upset that in her time of need, the people of England turned on her. I'm angry and embarrassed. Everyone loved my mother, until the accident."

"Mathew," Dunn began, changing the subject, "while you're here at Ardsley, I want you to carefully consider your future. You have several choices. I know your mother wishes you to follow her to Virginia, I suspect you may wish to enlist in the Royal Navy, and I'd like to add another option for you to consider: come work for me. You would sail the world over, see exotic lands, one day lead a crew of men. Not to mention the fact that you would be more financially secure. I understand you don't want any favors, and I won't give you any. If you prefer, you can start as a mate on a ship and earn your way up over time by merit."

"Your generosity is overwhelming, Uncle Andy, and I would be a fool to refuse without giving it a great deal of thought. But I must tell you that I still have a desire to join the Royal Navy as an officer's candidate. I have focused on that objective for most of my life thus far, and it is so close. I'm afraid that I may regret not pursuing my goal several years from now when it would be too late. Can you understand?"

"I think I can, Mathew. I see the same boundless determination in you that I saw in your father long ago," Dunn observed. "And I'm aware that you know more about naval operations and tactics than most officers in the navy today - your passion and your tutelage have seen to that. There's not a question in my mind that you would come through Britannia Royal Navy College with honors and ultimately captain a ship."

"I need to do this, Uncle Andy."

"I know," Dunn calmly responded as he turned to look out at the river. "I assumed you'd feel that way. There's only one problem: you cannot get into officer's school as the son of Thomas Hatley."

Mathew winced at this stark reality. "Yes, I know."

"It's odd really. You would have been welcomed with open arms before the accident, but now that your father's been publicly scorned, you really have no chance."

"Actually, I wasn't thinking about joining as my father's son," Mathew said.

Dunn turned to look at him. "I see. So as at Oxford, you would take on another iden..." Dunn's voice trailed off as he realized what Mathew meant. "Of course!" Dunn smiled wryly, turning from the view of the Thames back to his guest. "You apply as Mathew Carrigan!"

"Precisely. Only one barrier would remain," cautioned Mathew.

"You need a sponsor," surmised Dunn. "Well, that is a predicament, I must say."

Mathew couldn't tell if Dunn was sincere or having a little fun at his expense. In any case, it was too awkward to directly ask his host to sponsor his candidacy, especially so soon after arriving at Ardsley. Mathew was hoping that Dunn would offer once they got on the subject.

"I suppose I could sponsor you, Mathew."

"Thank you, sir!" Mathew burst out overjoyed. "Are you sure you don't mind?"

"Nonsense," Dunn countered. "You are the best candidate the navy could hope for. There is no logical reason why you shouldn't be given the chance. All we have to do is come up with a solid story of how we know each other, and I'll arrange a candidate's interview for you."

"Absolutely," Mathew agreed.

"Oh, but let's be clear about the consequences. Once you go in as Mathew Carrigan, you can never go back to your former name. Do you understand that? Not only would your career be put in serious jeopardy, but I would be in big trouble, as well."

"I understand; I'll tell no one."

"Come on in now, Mathew" said Dunn. "You've had a long day. Please go up and get some rest. Tomorrow is Saturday, and I've got a lot planned for us."

Mathew gave an inquisitive look to Dunn as he was not expecting such a busy and important man to have set aside so much time in advance for him.

"We'll be out in my sailboat all day. We'll work on our story on the water where there's plenty of privacy! How does that sound?"

Mathew paused. There was so much he wanted to say, but he was overwhelmed. "I don't know what to say, Uncle Andy. Thank you."

"You're entirely welcome. Good night, my boy, and God bless you."

Mathew turned and headed inside. In his dreams he could not have hoped to have such a generous advocate with whom he could speak freely and who had the ability and desire to help him greatly.

As he climbed the stairs to his room, Mathew realized just how tired he was. The excitement had masked his fatigue temporarily, though his eyes were growing heavier with each step upward towards the second floor landing.

By the time his head finally hit the pillow, Mathew was resigned that sleep would win out quickly. His last thought that night was how miraculously and quickly his path had been clarified.

- Mathew moves in with "Uncle Andy"
- Close relationship

†

Chapter 6: The Royal Navy

A month after arriving at Ardsley Manor, Mathew met at the Britannia Royal Navy College with the officer in charge of interviewing applicants.

The waiting room was filled with twenty young men. Though the two windows of the room were already opened, the absence of a sea breeze in the morning provided no relief from the stale air of the crowded room.

Many of the applicants gave off a haughty air as though they had already commanded hundreds of men on countless military skirmishes and numerous acts of valor. Rather than being concerned about his chances in the presence of such unbridled self-confidence, Mathew could not help but find these men amusing.

In the corner, three would-be officers were in heated debate regarding the proper method of tying a square knot. None were correct. In the middle of the waiting area, two young men who apparently knew each other were amusing themselves by studying each candidate officer in the room, commenting out loud regarding each candidate's chances for making officer.

"Not a bloody chance!" said one.

"Well I sure as hell hope not," added the other with a laugh.

Mathew was unaware what they had concluded about his own

prospects, as he was deep in thought by the time they turned and studied him.

Individually, each candidate met with the interview officer, providing responses to his inquiries and letters of reference. When summoned into his interview, Mathew stood and approached the door with purpose and eagerness. He was keenly aware not to speak before being spoken to by an officer. He imagined that this would be something of an initial test.

The interviewing officer sat at an oak desk at the back of the room, reading over some paperwork. "Come in," beckoned the man without looking up.

"Yes, sir," Mathew replied as he strode to the center of the room and stood at attention beside a conspicuously placed lone chair facing the interviewer. Mathew knew not to sit down until invited to do so. This was not so much a rule of the navy as a rule of common courtesy. Nevertheless, Mathew was sure someone had, or would, make the mistake today of approaching the chair and sitting down uninvited. He felt sorry for the poor candidates that did.

The interviewer glanced up and was noticeably surprised that Mathew had not already sat down. He grinned slightly, apparently pleased that this particular interview had already started out much better than most others. He motioned to the chair with his hand holding a quill pen.

"You may be seated. Now then, you are Mathew Carrigan. Is that correct?"

"Yes, sir."

"Good. I am Lieutenant Simon Atkinson. I am to interview the candidates and review their letters of reference. You may have noticed twenty men in the waiting room, and they'll be another twenty this afternoon. There were forty yesterday and forty more scheduled for tomorrow. From this lot, no more than twelve candidates will be selected to begin training as a candidate officer in His Majesty's navy," continued Lieutenant Atkinson. "What percentage of candidates will be permitted to train, Mathew?"

"Ten percent, sir," Mathew responded instantly.

"At most, Mathew, at most!" added Atkinson emphatically.

"Last year was a decidedly thin class of worthy candidates. Only eight were selected from over 135 applicants. However, if His Majesty's navy is to continue as the greatest naval force the world has ever known, we must be highly selective. Would you not agree, Mathew?"

"I would indeed, sir."

"How old are you, lad?" queried the lieutenant.

"Twenty, sir."

"Tell me about the last five years of your life," asked Atkinson.

Mathew was careful not to ramble – a sure sign of nervousness and disorganization. He discussed his schooling at Oxford and his long summer days spent sailing in the Bristol Channel, as well as his swordsmanship training under the tutelage of a Spanish master.

While the Royal Navy extended candidate officer training to some university graduates, Mathew knew it was often seen as more of an impediment than useful preparation. Conventional thinking was that intellectuals would not have had the time at sea to truly become knowledgeable of the most important lessons to a naval officer – leadership, seamanship, and military conflict. University-educated young men were often regarded as soft and unable to endure the rigorous physical and mental training eventually awaiting candidate officers.

However, Mathew clearly appeared sturdy and fit, and his experience in relatively challenging areas of the open sea would be regarded as an asset.

The swordsmanship, however, would certainly warrant further inquiry.

"How did you come to train with a Spanish master?" Atkinson asked.

Mathew's response was truthful in every detail, except that he replaced his father's contributions and instead credited his introduction to Santos to his candidacy sponsor, Andrew Dunn.

"Whom?!?" demanded the recruiting officer, shocked at the mere mention of the name.

"Andrew Dunn, sir," confirmed Mathew, noticing that the name struck a chord with the lieutenant.

"Please bring your reference to me, Mathew."

Mathew knew that recruiting officers ordinarily wouldn't review references before interviewing the applicants, preferring to remain objective during the discussion. Undoubtedly, many applicants brought in letters of reference from wealthy and influential people, only to end up as otherwise poor applicants.

This particular reference, however, clearly carried real weight and was as rare as it was impressive. A letter from Andrew Dunn was as good a reference as one could have. He was legendary for his military as well as commercial nautical exploits, though he had rarely given letters of reference before. This made it all the more special.

Lieutenant Atkinson silently read the letter, though his eyes grew wide. Mathew, having reviewed the letter's contents the prior evening, was not entirely surprised by Atkinson's reaction.

Andrew Dunn's reference was well written, sincere, and polite. He did not demand or assume Mathew's candidacy. Instead, he clearly laid out the qualities that he saw in Mathew and modestly suggested them as critical elements to leadership that would keep the Royal Navy the envy of the world. The letter was stirring in both its simplicity and conviction.

Atkinson had apparently seen enough.

"Quite an endorsement, Mathew," offered Atkinson. "Congratulations. I will grant candidacy to you, as I am confident there will be no candidate more qualified in person or by reference in the entire set of applicants."

Then the officer took an admonishing tone.

"Please do everything in your power to confirm Mr. Dunn's confidence and my personal judgment on your behalf."

"Yes, sir," replied Mathew through an uncontrollably widening grin.

Mathew progressed rapidly through the academic portion of the naval college, impressing each of his instructors along the way.

The one critical area of training that was impossible to measure in the classroom, and many argued was impossible to teach, was an ability to lead men at sea. Thus, the bulk of each candidate's training as a potential naval officer was at sea under the watchful eyes of some of the hardest and most critical judges, the captains of various war ships.

Most of the captains in the pool with responsibility for developing young officer talent were invited to participate due to their thorough record of excellence and abrupt communication style. For most candidates that eventually became officers, this period of apprenticeship was looked upon as their worst year in the Royal Navy. Many buckled under the constant and intense emotional, as well as physical, pressure applied to them by their captains, leaving the Royal Navy without ever making the grade.

The average candidate lasted only six months, and many quit sooner. A number of captains were actually proud of the number of candidates they had sent scurrying back to either commercial shipping or a career on land.

By completing the academic portion of his candidacy at the top of his class, Mathew drew the immediate and unenviable assignment of sailing under Captain Randolph Isaacs aboard the HMS *Constellation*, a fate designed to supremely test only the most promising candidates.

A wager surfaced among some of the naval instructors as to which month Isaacs might break the impressive young officer candidate. Fortunately, Mathew never learned of the wager, which essentially predicted him leaving the navy by month nine. In a way, it was a relative vote of confidence in that most otherwise promising candidates sent to Isaacs usually lasted less than three.

Captain Isaacs was a burly curmudgeon; an old sea dog that did not like officer candidates in general. Thirty-years a veteran of the Royal Navy, he felt a strong sense of personal responsibility to weed out those candidates that could not take the heat of battle or the intense sea conditions that they would undoubtedly be faced with down the line.

He had been highly critical of many of his fellow captains for allowing candidates to pass through without really testing their levels of seamanship, leadership, and self-defense. The fact that the last twelve candidates assigned to him all quit within five months of service meant to him that he was conducting a rather important service for the navy.

Over his first few weeks at sea, Mathew's interaction with the crew was watched closely. The sailors respected his rank, but not yet the man. As was customary, they narrowly toed the line between respect and insubordination, in order to see for themselves what kind of man was leading them.

Initially, the crew vetted his every movement intently and listened to any other officers who might mention information about the candidate's past. Yet nothing was known or discovered about Midshipman Mathew Carrigan, though a number of the crew were quite adept at prying. He was thus nicknamed "ghost" as he seemed to have appeared out of thin air.

By the end of his first month at sea, Captain Isaacs had thrown all manner of moderately challenging, though subtle, tasks and tests at the candidate officer, and Mathew had passed each with high marks.

Mathew ultimately learned the crew's moniker for him and smiled wryly. *If they only knew how right they are*, he thought.

While Mathew's commanding presence and manner were just as strict as those of Captain Isaacs himself, there was something else the crew could see in the young man. No one could quite place it, but they agreed that Mathew had certainly gone through some amount of tragedy and suffering already in his young life. There was something about him that did not suggest privileged upbringing, but rather effort to earn his place. Here was a man entirely capable of creating and controlling his own destiny.

There was also something refreshingly genuine about Mathew, for he did not seem to observe – or only casually so – the unseen dividing line between sailors and officers. He often made small, supportive comments throughout their voyage, including some well-timed humorous barbs. He was adept at self-deprecation, too, which the sailors found as delightful and enduring as they found it strange.

When Captain Isaacs gave an unusual command, every crewman obeyed though they may have silently questioned the command in their mind. When Mathew Carrigan gave a command, there was obedience without doubt. Carrigan had quickly gained the trust and loyalty of the sailors, and Isaacs could see this from decades of experience at sea.

During the third month at sea, an unusual event occurred on the deck of the *Constellation* that would seal Mathew's fate in the eyes of Isaacs.

On an otherwise calm sea one morning, a verbal quarrel among two sailors quickly escalated to blows. Rather than rush in to stop it, the crew on deck surrounded the scuffle and goaded the sailors on. Captain Isaacs saw this as an interesting test for Mathew, and ordered him to stop it immediately.

Contrary to Isaacs' expectations, Mathew did not instantly bark out the command to stop the two men from fighting. Instead, Mathew threw himself down to the quarterdeck, quickly moved across the ship to the location of the fight and threw himself into the fracas as he gave the command to stop. But the tempers of both men at that moment were far greater than their obedience to rank or common sense, and they kept fighting.

Mathew got in between the two fighters and pushed them momentarily apart. Turning slightly, he knocked down the first sailor with a direct lightning-like barrage of three combined moves that appeared in a blur to the crew still surrounding the action, dropping the sailor instantly, and harmlessly to his knees. While the first sailor was down, the second crewman tried to approach from behind Mathew and deliver additional blows to the man kneeling on the deck. Anticipating this reaction before the other sailor reached his felled opponent, Mathew turned, reached up, and grabbed the man's neck in a ferocious grip, stopping the man dead in his tracks. The grip was getting impossibly tighter even though the sailor raised both of his hands to pry off the strengthening hands. The man helplessly lowered to his knees and Mathew finally released the hold on the man, assisted him up to his feet again

"Stand down, man! It's not worth it," Mathew admonished, as the man slowly nodded his agreement though his head was still lowered.

Mathew walked over to the other sailor who had propped

himself up on one knee, and assisted the fallen fighter to his feet again.

"What the bloody hell was that?" asked the sailor still disbelieving he had been so effectively immobilized so fast.

"I can show you later when tempers have subsided," responded Mathew, as he pulled both sailors by the hand toward each other. "Now, face the captain, bow, and shake hands with each other," Mathew commanded very quietly, though both adversaries were reluctant.

"Now!" barked the officer's candidate through clenched teeth, at which point both men complied with the command.

Mathew turned himself to face Captain Isaacs on the aft deck and declared loudly, "Just some harmless sport among the men, Captain, nothing more."

Brilliant, thought Isaacs. Carrigan had boldly thrown himself into the fight, which very few officers would have done, thereby gaining the respect of everyone. And he deliberately made up the bit about the fight being for sport in order to save the two men from certain punishment. His quick thinking endeared Mathew to the two fighting men, as well as the crew.

He put himself in harm's way and risked irritating the captain in letting the fight go unpunished. While risky, the act had served a valuable purpose. If any of the men had doubted Mathew's capacity to lead them in battle, there was no remaining doubt.

Captain Isaac's little test ended up a tremendous success for Mathew, and Isaacs had to admit that the young man might actually make the grade.

Three months later, Mathew began his second tour in the Royal Navy, aboard the HMS *Intrepid*. She was a third rater ship-of-the-line, one hundred seventy-five feet in length, double-decked with sixty-four cannon, and a crew of five hundred. Crafted in 1760, she had performed valiantly in the Seven Years War, having bested seven French and two Spanish vessels while suffering only mild battle damage herself.

The *Intrepid* had had only one captain since her inaugural launch, Captain Simon Shaddock, one of the most decorated heroes of the Royal Navy. A serious battle tactician, it was rumored he was soon to be promoted to the rank of commodore and lead his own fleet. He had no family other than the navy, and was utterly disconsolate on land. Shaddock was also one of the strictest by-the-book senior officers in the Royal Navy.

Their mission was to sail to the Mediterranean Sea, meet up with two other Royal Navy warships at various locations on predetermined dates and conduct maneuvers for a period of three weeks. After these maneuvers were fulfilled completely and satisfactorily, the caravan of ships would be escorting a convoy of British merchant ships through waters infested with North African pirates.

As the *Intrepid* sailed away from England toward a far off destination to the south, Shaddock was impressed overall with the way the junior officers led the crew through the launch, but he made mental notes of several minor errors committed by some of the officers. He would admonish each man who had made a mistake in front of his peers at an officers' meeting in the evening. Like Captain Isaacs, Captain Shaddock liked to test the mental fortitude of his officers as well as their physical abilities.

By the time they reached the rendezvous point on the Greek island of Mandrakos, Shaddock was confident that some of the officer candidates might even be molded into adequate and capable seamen.

He was especially curious to watch the development of the young Mathew Carrigan. Not only had Carrigan come highly recommended, but he was told this young man might be one of the finest swordsman in the Royal Navy. That ability would come in handy if they came across any Barbary pirates; an event that Shaddock privately calculated to have a better-than-even probability.

A month later, the *Intrepid* lay anchored in the tranquil bay of Pali on the island of Mandrakos. The intense heat of the day had finally given way to a comforting light breeze and a much cooler temperature.

Most of the crew came up on deck in the evening, taking in

the most pleasant part of the day in the open air. The day had been as productive as it had uncomfortable, and the men knew they were soon to be rewarded with rum rations. There was anxious anticipation among most of the crew for a night of relaxing.

At the light meal in the officer's quarters, Captain Shaddock had been especially complimentary of the young officers in discussing their last several days of leading the ship's activities. His uncharacteristic praise was as welcome to his officers as was the generous portion of wine that was served at the dining table.

Unlike his colleagues that evening, Mathew stopped drinking after his first glass of wine. As pleasing as the taste was to his lips, he was certain that an alcohol-induced headache in the raw heat of the Greek islands would be doubly painful for anyone who imbibed too much. He also had a suspicion that the generous portions may actually be another test of Captain Shaddock's to discern which officers had enough discipline to stop drinking.

Later that night, after most of his colleagues had stumbled to their hammocks and awkwardly crawled in, Mathew sat on deck taking in the brilliant stars above that seemed twice as close to earth from his vantage in the Mediterranean than they did from England.

He picked out a number of famous constellations and recalled some of the stories behind them that the ancient Greeks had established long before.

A moment later, a man approached. By the weight of the feet, Mathew could tell it was the big first mate and he was probably searching for him. Mathew perched himself up on one elbow to get a better look.

"Evening, Lieutenant Carrigan," the mate said as he approached. "The captain thought you might be up here and not passed out below like some of the others."

Mathew began to stand, and the mate helped him to his feet.

"Is something wrong?" asked Mathew.

"No. The captain just wanted a private word with you is all. Believe me, it won't be the tongue lashing some of the other officers are going to get tomorrow morning!" the large man laughed, seemingly pleased that there would be some rather uncomfortable headaches among the foolish young officers then. "What were you doing up here anyway?"

"Just staring at the constellations and recalling the ancient legends that accompany them," Mathew offered as he turned to walk away.

"You're an odd one, Lieutenant" the first mate commented as he craned his neck toward the night sky, seemingly lost on how anyone could see any pictures in the myriad stars or find their ancient stories fascinating.

"You wanted to see me, Captain?" asked Mathew as he stood at the open door of the captain's private quarters.

"Yes, for just a moment. I'm glad to see you haven't overindulged in the wine tonight."

"No, Captain."

"Well, that's part of the reason I called you here. You see, part of our mission was to rendezvous with the *Voyager* here today and sail together for some open sea maneuvers tomorrow."

Mathew acknowledged by nodding his head.

"As you can see, the *Voyager* didn't make it today, so we can't very well set out tomorrow," the captain continued. "I'm afraid we'll have to wait for her. Meanwhile, we sit in this beautiful bay at least another day. Even if she were to arrive in the morning, the mission calls for an early morning tandem departure. Do you know what that means for us?"

"Yes, Captain. I believe I do. A day off."

"Precisely, Carrigan. A day off it is. Only the men don't know that. So keep that to yourself tonight, otherwise the lot of them would drink themselves stupid."

"That's probably true, Captain," agreed Mathew.

"Because I know you'll be right in your head tomorrow morning, please lead the dawn shift. When they come to deck, you can have the honor of announcing the day off. Only announce it softly, I'd like to remain asleep as long as possible tomorrow. Sleep is the only time I'm comfortable in this part of the world, the blasted heat!" the captain confided.

Mathew saluted and turned to leave, but pivoted back to face Shaddock again. "Captain? Since it is a day off, may I take the skiff and sail a bit, perhaps around the island?"

"Can't get enough of the sea, my boy?" Shaddock shook his head from side to side. "They told me about you. 'Never get him off the sea', they said. Very well. You finish the first shift early and take the boat, only get back before sundown in case the *Voyager* arrives."

"Yes, Captain!" Mathew answered with a broad smile. "And thank you, sir. Good night."

As he lay in his hammock staring at the cabin ceiling a few feet above him, Mathew imagined the constellations he had seen earlier in the night. Breathing in long, meditative rhythms, he felt himself falling into sleep.

The wood planks of the ceiling suddenly vanished, and he was staring into the open sky again. There was a noticeable breeze that passed him, and then it was gone. A voice faintly called out to him. It was a familiar voice - the voice of his father.

"Mathew…"

"Father? Where are you?" Mathew felt himself calling out.

"Mathew…I am here."

- Mathew starts to become part of Royal Navy - Favored by Captain - doing a great job - boat with an leutenants and the mother sets sea.

✝

Chapter 7: Xirokos

𝒯he skiff from the *Intrepid* was lowered into the placid water by four seamen, all smiling as this would be their last physical duty during the day.

Mathew sat alone in the small sailboat, looking northward out to sea and studying the shadowy contour of the island called Xirokos, approximately five miles away. He recalled learning at Oxford that there were over two thousand Greek islands, but less than three hundred were inhabited. According to the *Intrepid*'s nautical charts and accompanying information, Xirokos was a small, uninhabited spit of land with no strategic or economic value.

As soon as the skiff reached the water, Mathew was busy casting off the lines that had lowered him into the water, and raising the sail that would harness the wind. He was very much looking forward to the day, knowing he would likely be the only person for miles. The following day, he would be back in cramped quarters except when he was on duty, engaged in a series of naval maneuvers.

The wind and sea that day were fairly calm until Mathew reached the open area between the islands. Seemingly out of nowhere, the winds swept down with enough force to speed his small craft across the water at an accelerated rate. Exhilarated,

Mathew kept a firm grip on the tiller to keep on his course. At one point, the spray of the warm sea on his face caused him to look down and back. In that moment, he could see he was approximately as far from the *Intrepid* as he was close to Xirokos.

The sun was high enough in the sky to light up the intricate coastline of the rather diminutive island. Within a couple hundred yards of the island itself, Mathew veered his small vessel to the west, with the idea of circumnavigating the barren isle that seemed as high as it was wide.

Three-quarters of the way around the island, he came upon something of a hidden cove. He would have sailed right past it had he been in a larger ship and therefore further out at sea on his approach. The opening was not exposed directly to the sea. It had one high wall of rock jutting out to sea and curving so as to give the appearance of just a rugged coastline. In fact, the cove would not have been discovered had Mathew passed its opening in the other direction. What a stroke of luck, he thought, to have arbitrarily sailed around Xirokos in a clockwise direction.

Mathew proceeded into the opening at a slow speed, as the winds of the open sea were blocked by aegis of the high, narrow peninsula to one side and the island to the other. As Mathew came around the bend of the entrance formed by the cliff walls, he took a deep breath. A little more than three hundred yards in each direction there was a long, white sandy beach stretching around nearly three-quarters of the secluded cove.

As the skiff glided slowly across the center of the cove, Mathew glanced down through the shallow, crystal-clear water. Even in the shadows of the mid-morning, he could make out small shells in the sand twenty feet below the skiff, as well as occasional tiny fish darting about.

All of a sudden, he saw under the water just ahead of him a dark mass, less than ten feet below the surface. At first, he presumed it to be an outcropping of submerged rocks.

Once at the dark shape in the water, he lowered the sail, picked up his oar and adjusted his rowing so the boat would slowly come to a stop just above the mysterious mass.

He shuddered. This was no rock formation. This was clearly a large ship that had sunk many years before. He could see that it was the stern of a ship pointing up towards the surface, though because of the shimmer on the sun-drenched water, he could not make out the name just above the window portals. He could see a mass, perhaps seaweed or some other undersea growth that had covered over part of the large ship's name.

Mathew's heart leapt and his youthful imagination got away from him. On this magical day, on this fantastic island, he imagined a sunken pirate ship with a bounty of gold within. He instantly longed for some way to view the shipwreck more clearly.

He replaced the oar and picked up his telescope. He slowly balanced his weight at the stern of the skiff and leaned over the side. Cupping his hands around the opening to block out the sunlight, he lowered his head, closed his right eye and peered through his cupped hands with his left eye. He dipped the other end of the instrument a few inches under the surface of the water. Amazingly, he could suddenly see under water with great clarity.

The large mass was indeed a ship, and a warship by the looks of her lines. Mathew's heart began to pound. She was jutting out of the sandy depth as though the front half were buried under the sand.

How long ago had this ship sunk? And what would have caused her to turn downward and sink perpendicular to the water surface in the cove?

He moved the instrument to look beyond the deck of the sunken vessel. He could now see the remains of the ship's bow jutting from the sandy bottom. It was as though the middle third had been cut away from the ship, and the two remaining pieces sunk next to one another. Now, at least he understood why the ship sections were positioned the way they were. But what would cause such a wreck?

His skiff had drifted along the line of the two submerged ship sections so he was now nearly over the bow. He pulled himself up fully onto the skiff and put down the looking glass. Taking up the oar again, he repositioned the skiff directly over the stern.

Once he'd repositioned the skiff, he quickly reached for the telescope and delicately balanced his weight while leaning over the stern again. Peering through the instrument, he could see that the first several letters were covered by some undersea growth. He read slowly from the left to the right the few visible letters.

"C-L-E," he said aloud as though he were talking to someone on the skiff with him, writing down this information. The three letters meant nothing to him at this point. What was that letter that preceded the C-L-E that was only partially covered by the growth? Mathew studied the exposed right half of the letter that sloped downward from left to right.

"And that looks like a lambda," he again spoke aloud. Then it occurred to him that it couldn't be a Greek ship, for he knew well the Greek alphabet only had a few letters similar to the Latin alphabet of his native English language. There was no "C" or "L" in the Greek alphabet.

"Not lamba," he corrected himself. "Then an 'A' I suppose," he added, pleased with his deductive reasoning.

"A-C-L-E...ACLE...ACLE," he repeated to himself slowly.

Then it hit him. The impact of his discovery of the name shocked him into such a spasm that he accidentally fell over into the water.

"The *Pinnacle*!" he blurted as he popped out of the cool water. *My God!* he thought. *How is this possible? I'm nowhere near Malta where the Pinnacle reportedly crashed on jagged rocks.*

Mathew held onto the side of the skiff as he tried to make sense of what lay less than ten feet below him. There was no immediate explanation.

He collected himself within seconds and glanced down through the water under his chin. He stared at the large bank of windows of the ship's aft. If this was indeed the *Pinnacle*, then he was hovering over the captain's cabin - his father's cabin.

Looking upward toward the sun, which was now near the middle of the expansive blue sky, Mathew reached over the skiff's bulwark to grab the bowline. He took in a deep breath to fill his lungs with air and dived down under the water. Only eight feet below the surface, Mathew tied the bowline to a part of the stern of the sunken ship.

After surfacing for another deep breath of air, Mathew dived again, clearing the growth from the other letters of the ship's name. He could see through the clear water that the ship was indeed the HMS *Pinnacle*.

Surfacing again for another breath, Mathew decided to enter the captain's cabin through a broken window.

Because the sun was almost directly overhead, its light reached through the cabin remarkably well. Hovering weightless in the middle of the cabin space, he could see that the cabin's furniture had sunk down to the front of the cabin, pulled by gravity once the ship itself had settled in the sand. Mathew could make out the captain's desk on its side down ten more feet below. On top of the desk, the captain's chair seemed to be awkwardly positioned on its side.

As his lungs began to hurt and beckon him to the surface for air, his attention focused on a small gleaming object near the captain's table. Mathew went up for air and decided he'd dive again for a closer look deeper into the cabin.

He reached the surface just as his aching lungs gave way and gulped for oxygen, while his eyes stung from the salty water. He reasoned that he would not be able to spend so much time in the cabin. It would have to be a bullet dive - down fast and up fast. The gleaming object was the target. *See it, grab it and get out*, he thought to himself as his breaths slowed to a calm cadence.

He dived under and kicked hard for the bottom of the cabin a full twenty feet below. The mystery object still glistened below with the sunlight directly upon it. Mathew extended his hand and touched the object. It was smooth and thin. It was a sword, exposed only a few inches outside of its sheath, just enough to catch the brilliant sunlight.

He pulled at the sword to bring it to the surface with him, though just as he turned to push off the cabin wall and launch himself up again to the skiff, he looked to his right at the chair resting on its side on top of the table.

Staring back at him was a skeleton, seemingly sitting comfortably in the chair. Mathew was so startled by the sight that his mouth burst open and bubbles of air exploded upward. His legs pushed hard, and he sped to the skiff again.

As he rested for a moment at the skiff, his arms draped over the bulwark supporting his predominantly submerged body, he examined the sword. Slowly pulling the weapon from its once decorative sheath, he looked for the engraving that would identify its owner. His eyes scanned the area of the blade near the hilt. The cursive lettering read quite clearly, *Captain Thomas Hatley.* He dropped it into the skiff and considered what he'd just seen.

That is my father's sword. That was my father's chair. That must have been my father in the chair.

As the initial gruesomeness of the sight waned, Mathew's intellect took over. *Why would my father be sitting in his chair while the ship sank?* And with no jagged rocks in the cove, there had to be another explanation for the ship's destruction.

His mind jumping around in a panic state, he summoned his breath for another bullet dive. Speeding to the collection of furniture lying on the front wall of the captain's cabin, he kept his vision on the high-back chair. He gently pulled the chair away from the skeleton, but the collection of bones, tissue and clothing remained loosely affixed to the chair itself. Puzzled and out of air, he went to the surface once again.

On his next dive, he stopped at the stern of the ship just eight feet below the surface and untied the bowline of the skiff. He came up to expand his lungs and make one last dive.

He took in another large gulp of oxygen and submerged down into the sunken ship with the bowline in his hands. When he reached the captain's chair, he tied the bowline quickly and sprang to the surface.

After collecting himself for a brief moment, he clambered aboard the skiff and began to slowly pull the chair and its long dead occupant up from the depths below.

As the dilapidated chair reached the water's surface, Mathew grabbed it and carefully hoisted it on to the skiff.

He immediately noticed the leather straps that had been used to bind his father's limbs to the chair. Pure rage tore through him. It was obvious that his father had been bound to the chair, intentionally drowned.

Once tight around the man's full wrist, the leather straps had become loose as the skin and muscle had long since decayed in the water leaving only thin bones.

Mathew untied the straps and delicately freed the skeleton

before throwing the chair back into the water.

He stared at the remains, wishing there was some mistake, some clue that would allow him discover that this wasn't the remains of his father in front of him.

As though it had a mind of its own, his arm extended forward and reached under the area of what used to be the figure's collar. His fingers wrapped around a thin chain, on the end of which was a pocket watch. His nervous hands gently negotiated the clasp, releasing the outer cover to reveal the non-functioning chronometer. The time reflected was 4:10 and, on the inner panel, was the portrait for which Mathew and his mother has patiently posed five years prior.

His energy depleted and eyes burning from the salt water, Mathew felt the full impact of his discovery. Though he initially fought the emotion, tears began streaming down his cheeks as he imagined his father's helpless last moments alive and harrowing death.

Mathew lowered his head and tried to make sense of all the thoughts that cascaded through his mind.

The piercing call of a hawk circling high above the hidden cove snapped him back to attention. Forming his thoughts in a more organized fashion, he rowed the skiff to the beach.

Silently, he pulled the skeleton from the small boat and gently laid it on the sand in a shady spot under a fig tree, before beginning to dig a large, deep pit in the sand. When the pit was nearly three feet deep and six feet long, he gathered his father's remains and placed them in the earth. He turned and hurled the leather straps into the thick foliage nearby, all save one.

With his left hand and teeth, he slowly tied the remaining strap to his right wrist. After it was firmly tied, he looked down at his father's bones in the makeshift grave and began to speak.

"I don't understand why you were murdered, Father. But I swear to you here and now that I will wear this band that once bound you to a horrible death, until I avenge your murder."

Mathew began replacing the sand from the pit, covering the remains of the legendary Captain Thomas Hatley. When his chore was complete, he bowed his head in prayer.

Mathew had lost track of time. The sun was now sinking well

past mid-day. Certain that there was nothing left for him to do, he shoved the skiff off the beach and into the small bay. He rowed gently past the sunken *Pinnacle* and out the unusual cove entrance.

Once he was free of the narrow passage, the wind found the skiff and Mathew raised the small sail. As he sped back toward the *Intrepid*, he glanced downward at the objects found earlier – a sword and a pocket watch. Neither would be difficult to sneak back to his gear on the large ship.

As the skiff sped across the open sea, Mathew yelled out loud to clear his mind. On the desolate stretch of the Mediterranean, no one heard him.

Questions sprang up in his mind likes weeds in an untended garden. *What was the Pinnacle doing inside a secluded cove on a Greek island over six hundred nautical miles from Malta? And how did the ship end up in such a strange position under the water?*

As he stared across the sea to the distant island of Mandrakos, clues presented themselves in his mind.

The explosion was no accident. There were no rocks that could have torn the ship apart, so she had to have been blown up by charges around the middle of the ship. The charges would have had to be sufficiently lethal and carefully placed to leave the two remaining sections so well intact.

The story of the wreck that was reported was so far from the truth that Mathew had just discovered that it was clear the survivors must be the perpetrators.

No doubt Captain John Wilson was the leader of the deceitful mission. Instantly, Mathew acknowledged Wilson as the target of his revenge.

But what possible motive would he have to murder the men of the *Pinnacle*? Mathew quickly considered several – power, financial gain, duty.

The first two seemed highly unlikely since Wilson could not have been assured that his account would have been so uniformly believed back in England, and a Royal Navy vessel would not carry any wealth.

That left what Mathew considered the most immediately plausible motive: duty.

Could this have been a plot to destroy the Royal Navy from within? Were the survivors spies sent out to destroy the ship and murder the crew? But which country could possibly place such spies?

Or maybe it wasn't a foreign country after all, but a faction *within* Great Britain.

His reasoned thoughts gave way once again to emotion, and the raw rage for Captain John Wilson burned inside him as he approached to within a half mile of the *Intrepid.*

Bounding through the small waves in the open sea, he felt the salty sea spraying on his face. He imagined himself in front of his father's presently faceless murderer and slowly began to smile.

There was no doubt in his mind that he would take great pleasure in killing the man, but he was resolute to wait until he understood two facts: what was the motive and who else was involved?

Additionally, he would endeavor to restore his father's good name, though he realized it would be a massive undertaking with little chance of success. To build an immutable case against the guilty, Mathew would have to collect abundant and irrefutable evidence, likely over many years. Even then, there could be no certainty of justice prevailing.

Exonerating his father was also in direct conflict with his overwhelming desire for revenge. He would not be able to kill Wilson nor any accomplices, for he would need them alive to stand a trial that could vindicate Thomas Hatley. If a trial did occur and they were ultimately acquitted, Mathew would be the prime suspect if the accused came to an untimely death. Additionally, he himself would likely become a target of the murderous men either before, during, or after a trial.

There must be a way to clear my father's name, Mathew felt, but he shelved this distant concept in favor of the violent retribution upon Captain John Wilson that dominated his thoughts.

As he approached the *Intrepid,* a number of seamen waved to him to come about. He pulled alongside the large war ship and lowered the sail. With the ropes thrown from the deck of his ship, he secured lines to the aft and bow of the small vessel, and in less than two minutes, was hoisted to the deck by the strong crew.

He climbed out and turned at once to go below decks to his quarters.

"Have a nice day on the sea, sir?" asked one of the crew respectfully.

Mathew wasn't sure how to answer the straightforward question at first. "Wonderful," he lied. "How was your free day?"

"Wonderful!" answered the man with unimpeachable sincerity. "But the *Voyager* is here now, so it's back to duty tomorrow."

Mathew glanced across the deck of the HMS *Intrepid* and saw the HMS *Voyager* had indeed arrived, anchored less than a hundred yards away.

That is as it should be, thought Mathew. *The sooner we get back to work, the sooner we get back to London.*

"Oh, yes," the deck hand started again, "Captain Shaddock saw you were coming about twenty minutes ago. He told me to tell you that he'd like to see you in his cabin."

"On my way, Seaman," Mathew nodded as he turned to go below decks. "I'll just drop off my gear and put my uniform back on," he called back.

Mathew's knock at the captain's door was immediately followed by a loud "enter" command by Shaddock.

Mathew strode in, swept off his hat, stood at attention in front of his captain, and snapped a formal salute. The captain, seated at his desk, returned the salute far less formally and gestured Mathew to take a seat in the nearby chair facing the desk. Once Mathew sat, the captain began to speak.

"Lieutenant Carrigan, how was your day?"

"Splendid, Captain," Mathew said. He wanted to inform his captain of what he'd discovered earlier in the day but judged it prudent to keep it to himself for the present. He would tell no one but Andrew Dunn of what he'd found that day. Until he could learn the motive and the extent of mutiny, absolutely no one else could be trusted.

"That's good to hear, Mathew. And where did you go?"

"I ventured toward Xirokos and veered off to the island on her right, Kynthera, I believe," Mathew said, choosing his words with care. The captain's interest disconcerted him. Could Shaddock be involved in the plot? Or was he seeing ghosts everywhere? "After circling a few times, I saw no one, so I put in to a rocky shore and read underneath the shade of a tree. I'm afraid I must have fallen asleep because I didn't plan to stay out so long."

"Quite all right, Mathew, quite all right," Captain Shaddock said. "You're back before sunset as I requested. No harm was done."

"Yes, Captain."

"Mathew, tomorrow is a big day. We begin our naval maneuvers with the HMS *Voyager* which arrived about two hours before you did. Did you happen to see her across the bay?"

"Yes I did. She's beautiful. It's good to see another Royal Navy ship in the area, sir."

"I agree. Strength in numbers, to be sure. By the way, that is why I've summoned you here. I have a surprise for you."

Mathew feigned interest though there was nothing that could possibly surprise him more than what he'd discovered earlier in the day.

"I want you to meet the commanding officer of the HMS *Voyager*, Captain John Wilson," announced Shaddock as though Wilson was already in the room.

"A great pleasure to meet you, Lieutenant Carrigan," offered a smug voice from a few paces behind Mathew. "I've heard so much about you from Captain Shaddock, I had to stay and at least meet the young man that is the talk of the Royal Navy."

Mathew's eyes nearly popped out of his head when Shaddock announced Wilson's name. He stood and turned slowly to greet the approaching man. The man who was responsible for the death of his father; the man that Mathew had sworn a private oath an hour prior to track down and kill.

Certain that this was neither the time nor place for his revenge, Mathew greeted the loathsome murderer as though he'd never heard of the man. His mind was resolute, but his eyes were not prepared for the additional shock when he saw the face of

Wilson.

Mathew recognized him instantly, for there along the right side of the man's face was a long, deep scar. A scar delivered by Mathew's own blade in Bristol some ten years before.

"Are you all right, Carrigan?" Wilson asked. "You look like you've seen a ghost!"

"I'm fine, Captain," Mathew answered directly to Wilson. "I was just startled as I assumed no one else was in the room."

"Never assume anything, young Carrigan. A *good* officer is alert and never caught off guard!"

"Yes, Captain," Mathew accepted the criticism, though he burned internally, anxious to rip the man to ribbons with his blade.

"Please forgive the surprise, Mathew," Shaddock said, "Captain Wilson and I were going over the details of tomorrow's exercises when we saw you approaching in the skiff. He asked me where you'd been, and I said I didn't know. I told him how impressed I am with your skills, sense of seamanship and leadership. He wanted to meet you, that's all."

"Yes, I must say I found it intriguing that you chose to sail on your day off, Carrigan," Wilson said.

"Oh, that's not peculiar," Shaddock offered before Mathew could respond. "The young man cannot be kept off the sea! He's the best sailor on the ship, including me!"

"Is that so? Well, did you see anything interesting today, Carrigan?" asked Wilson. Mathew was sure the other man was seeking confirmation that his secret was still safe.

"No, Captain. The sailing was exhilarating, but as for the sights, there is nothing interesting to report. Just some arid, rocky islands, and a few goats climbing on the hillsides."

Captain Wilson nodded slowly as he walked behind Mathew. "Very well, Carrigan. It was a pleasure to have met you. I wish you all the best in your career in His Majesty's Royal Navy, and if I can ever be of service to you, please don't hesitate to seek me out for advice or counsel."

"The pleasure was mine, Captain," Mathew said, his voice easy though the lie was bitter on his tongue, "and I will be sure to seek you out in the future." There, at last, he spoke the unvarnished truth.

Captain Wilson turned and saluted Captain Shaddock before leaving the captain's quarters to rejoin his own ship across the small bay.

- Mathew finds fathers ship and un remaing of his
- Swears to kill Wilson
- Meets wilson again as a captain of another war ship

†

Chapter 8: Mettle

𝒯he following morning was a sweltering one, even by Greek standards.

Nearly an hour after Mathew went below decks to escape the searing mid-day heat, a loud shout came from the deck. The *Voyager* was running up a new communication with her flags.

Mathew grabbed his telescope and returned to the main deck. The *Voyager* was perhaps five miles ahead to the west and had spotted one of the rendezvous ships further on. Mathew deciphered the message quickly: HMS *Rubicon in sight to the southwest, prepare for battle!*

It was not clear whether the message was meant as part of an elaborate naval exercise or there might actually be danger ahead. All sailors upon the *Intrepid* were told to treat every exercise as though it were the real thing. Walking through the motions without urgency would not, under any circumstances, be tolerated.

The three British war ships regrouped to form a tight battle line in order to fend off a three-ship grouping of Barbary corsairs. Mathew could see they were clearly not British ships and this was certainly not an exercise. His heart raced as he sized up the imminent skirmish.

It was entirely possible that in a fevered battle, there would be close hand-to-hand deck fighting. Mathew's training in fencing had been complete for years, but at last he would be wielding his saber versus pirates with a painful death the likely outcome to the loser. He also reminded himself silently that no enemy, but especially pirates, could be presumed to fight fairly.

If it was to be that he would not see the end of the day, Mathew was strangely calm, perhaps due to his training and confidence in his instincts. And if he were to die, so too would Wilson in all likelihood.

As the short line of Royal Navy ships bore down on the pirate caravan, Mathew double-checked that his three pistols were loaded and ready to fire. He touched the hilts of the swords he wore on each hip several times while staring out at the approaching ships. The battle would soon begin.

Captain Shaddock had never been louder in the preceding months. Not only were his commands short and clear, but they were delivered with such volume and authority they inspired the crew to a high level of conviction and confidence.

The HMS *Rubicon* sliced just to the left of the oncoming pirate ship. The initial confrontation was a mismatch as the eighty-gun *Rubicon* would likely dominate its smaller counterpart. The roar of the *Rubicon*'s cannons brought a loud cheer from the decks of both the *Voyager* and the *Intrepid*. The battle was on.

Within one minute the other two British warships engaged their own targets, sending a barrage of twenty-four and thirty-two-pound cannon balls from the thirty-eight guns on each ship's starboard side. The first pass through the line produced an advantage in firepower to the larger, more lethal British ships. It would only be in close quarters that the pirates would be able to gain any kind of advantage.

Deck fighting was to be avoided by the British at all costs, for it was in extended hand-to-hand combat that the frantic fighting style of the pirates could potentially do the most damage to a ship's crew.

The return volleys at the *Intrepid* and *Voyager* produced only modest damage.

The second act of the battle meant another pass by the quickly aligning Royal Navy ships. When the *Rubicon* reached her prey she actually steered toward a very close passing of the enemy, nearly teasing the pirates into thinking that the English were too close to fire their huge cannons again and intended therefore to board.

Upon their captain's command to adjust the sails and turn hard left, the *Rubicon* seemed to momentarily stop and bank hard to the left, thereby raising the firing line of her cannons to point at the deck and sails of the pirate ship, rather than its hull.

With outstanding precision in timing, the side of the *Rubicon* suddenly belched out a combination of heated grapeshot, chain shot, and multiple bar shot. The intent was to strafe the deck with red-hot iron devices that expanded like a bolo as they approached their target. The shrapnel blasts shredded sails and pirates alike, and took a serious toll on the pirates' masts, rendering a complete scene of chaos on board the pirate ship. Marines from the *Rubicon* fired upon the pirates with their rifles dropping dozens of pirates in their confused tracks.

With her adversary essentially disabled, the *Rubicon* would be able to stalk and blast her enemy at will from angles that would not place their ship at comparable danger.

The *Intrepid*, under Captain Shaddock, had similar success damaging the second pirate ship, for the *Intrepid* had an even greater size and firepower advantage over its prey than that of the *Rubicon*. Mathew watched in awe how the captain and crew geared the ship precisely capturing the wind advantage and revealing an impressive talent for timing the blasts from the cannons.

The *Voyager*, however, was under threat. She had surprisingly broken from the attacking formation line prevalent in the strategy of the Royal Navy for over one hundred years.

Her first pass at their own prey was a firestorm that rendered both ships badly damaged. She took heavy losses on its initial pass and, by the time the crews of the *Rubicon* and *Intrepid* noticed, she was being stalked for boarding.

"Jesus, Wilson, you idiot!" blasted Captain Shaddock as though Wilson were able to hear him across the sea. "Why did you break the damned line?"

"She's taken heavy damage below decks," Mathew answered.

He turned and glanced at the pirate ship that the *Intrepid* had badly damaged. She was immobile, on fire and would probably sink within the half hour.

"Get me to the *Voyager*!" Mathew said to Shaddock.

"What?! You're mad!" was Shaddock's incredulous reply.

"Get me to her now, with a complement of marines and we'll defend the *Voyager*!"

"You're out of your mind, Carrigan! We'll come about and fire on the pirate ship from the other side."

"And we'll risk killing our own men, Captain," Mathew insisted. "Get me close enough to that ship so I can board!"

"Thirsty for some deck fighting, are we, Carrigan?"

"She'll be taken in minutes if we don't even the score!"

"And are you willing to have the lives of the marines you take with you on your conscience should your plan fail?"

"Yes, Captain. Please, we have to act now."

Captain Shaddock turned to face his crew on deck. Within three seconds, the captain had weighed his options.

"Hard to port! Bear down on the *Voyager*, lads. We'll board her opposite side," Shaddock's command boomed like thunder. "Carrigan, have your marines in ready boarding position in two minutes!"

"Aye aye, Captain!" Mathew responded, "Marines! I need twenty volunteers to board and defend the *Voyager*!"

He heard Shaddock start to mutter a protest at his requesting the men to volunteer rather than ordering them to join him. But before Mathew finished his request, thirty-two marines stepped forward.

As the *Intrepid* pulled up to the wounded *Voyager*, the deck fighting was in full swing. Once the pirates had climbed aboard, pistol shots were exchanged, but by the time the *Intrepid* pulled alongside, the fighting was all swords and knives as reloading a pistol on deck was near impossible given the time and focus required and the dangerous slashing of swords around everyone.

The *Intrepid* marines who did not volunteer to board the *Voyager* laid down a fierce barrage from their rifles killing or wounding several pirates that had boarded the *Voyager*, but had not yet jumped into the fighting.

The instant the *Intrepid* was within swinging distance Mathew launched himself with a loud scream which seemed to further invigorate the marines that joined him only a second later. As he flew over the bulwark of the *Voyager*, he let go of the rope and dropped six feet to the deck below with a solid thud, followed by the collective thunder from the boots of the marines joining him.

Each marine had a rifle with bayonet affixed which they each drew off their respective shoulders and pointed into the rush of pirates running at them. In a solitary burst of sound and flame, sixteen pirates were stopped in their tracks. Though eight pirates somehow evaded the sea of bullets, their attack advanced only ten feet further, as they were stabbed by the bayonets of the marines' first firing line.

Three of the advancing pirates got off knives or axes in the air before they reached the soldiers, but only one struck a marine, a glancing wound to the man's shoulder.

Another swarm of pirates pulled off their attack on the *Voyager* crew to deal with the marines from the *Intrepid*. They were met with pistol fire from the soldiers who held their rifles in one hand and pointed pistols from a leather strap on their torso. Other pirates scrambled to reload their pistols and blunderbusses, but they were cut down efficiently by the marines still aboard the *Intrepid*.

Mathew's attack plan was working to perfection. Mathew himself had already separated from his marines and moved purposely from the bow toward the stern of the ship, firing each of his three pistols in successive strides killing three men instantly, dropping the pistols to the deck as the dead pirates likewise collapsed.

Within his next two strides, he had drawn his swords from opposite hips and was slicing away at blades that seemed to suddenly surround him.

Within twenty seconds he had killed a man with each sword.

Another twenty seconds later two more pirates hit the deck with wounds serious enough to take them out of the battle. His rapid engagement caused a brief pause in the battle, for after the first two waves attacked him with no success, others were reticent to suffer the same fate.

Mathew looked up to the quarterdeck and saw Wilson struggling with a fast and aggressive swordsman, just as another pirate was climbing the short set of steps leading to that deck to overwhelm the captain of the ship. Mathew had only a few seconds in which to act.

Suddenly a marauder launched at Mathew from the left, catching him off guard, but only for a split second. By the time the pirate was close enough to do damage, Mathew extended his own sword to easily ward off the man's aggressive charge. The pirate's body weight was over-extended toward Mathew, who quickly pivoted and raised his elbow, connecting squarely with the shocked face of the pirate.

Mathew turned to face the quarterdeck and threw his saber thirty feet through the air, landing it precisely in the back of the second pirate approaching Captain Wilson.

Wilson was barely holding his own versus his pirate adversary, and almost entirely on the defensive. It was clear to Mathew that he would not likely last an additional two minutes, so he ran forward and jumped up to the aft deck to assist, passing the dead pirate laying face down and retrieving his other sword from the marauder's back without breaking stride.

The pirate sensed Mathew's approach. He lunged toward Wilson quickly. His thrust was parried by the worn out British captain, but the two men were within two feet of each other. The pirate lifted his leg, placing a foot in line with Wilson's stomach, and kicked hard, sending Wilson sprawling backwards to the deck.

Mathew took up the fight, but unlike Wilson, was neither tired nor in a frame of mind to be on the defensive.

The pirate, a skilled fighter, swung his sword hard a few times in order to ward off the advancing Mathew and catch his breath. Mathew took a lighting quick step to the man's right side that brought the intended reaction from the pirate. With his footwork awkwardly out of sync with his position, the pirate slashed horizontally at Mathew. With his right hand cutlass, Mathew met and slapped the stroke away, further knocking the tired pirate off balance and exposing his entire right side with no defense.

The speed and precision with which Mathew next struck was

a visual blur. One step toward the exposed pirate, one clean and deep stab through the rib cage, one quick step backward while pulling his cutlass from the pirate, all with his left hand. The pirate dropped to his knees and looked up at Mathew vacantly, which Mathew answered with a roundhouse kick that sent the dying pirate to the deck hard. Only seven seconds were required for Mathew to dispatch Wilson's attacker.

Mathew turned to Wilson who had caught his breath and was slowly lifting himself up. Surprisingly, Wilson neither nodded nor verbalized any gratitude. The thought of killing Wilson right there and then ran across Mathew's mind momentarily, but as he knew Shaddock was watching the whole encounter, he could not touch him.

Your time will come, filthy bastard, thought Mathew. *If I have anything to say about it, no one will harm you until I exact my revenge!*

Upon witnessing the brave assault on the scattered pirates, the men of the *Intrepid* cheered loudly while the remaining pirates ran to jump overboard, preferring their chances in the open sea to hanging from a yard arm or facing this expert swordsman.

The threat neutralized, Mathew turned and walked back toward the marines he had brought on board from the *Intrepid*. Only three of them were wounded and none seriously. He approached them waving his arm to return to their ship.

"Just a moment, you!" bellowed Wilson from behind him.

Mathew stopped in his tracks and turned around. *It's about bloody time*, he thought. *Finally, the wretch will acknowledge my assistance in some form.*

He was wrong.

"Just what the hell do you think you were doing?!" Captain Wilson demanded. "Who gave you permission to leave your ship and board the *Voyager*?"

Mathew knew it was Wilson's shattered pride talking and that there was no risk to him whatsoever if he did not reply. Instead, he turned and gathered his men, moving to the ropes on which they would swing back to the *Intrepid*.

"I'm talking to you, goddammit! Don't you dare turn your back on a captain of the Royal Navy!"

"ENOUGH!" burst out Captain Shaddock, no more than

thirty feet away at the bulwark of the *Intrepid*. "You impudent fool! This man saved your bloody life, your bloody ship and the lives of most of your bloody crew. You would have been routed mercilessly! I witnessed the entire scene. If you wish to lodge a formal complaint, do so with me now in private, but do not think for one moment that you have the right to talk to this officer in that manner!"

— Pirates attack
— Mathew Wilsons Saved life

†

Chapter 9: Illumination

Six weeks after routing the marauders on the *Voyager*, Mathew returned to Ardsley Manor.

He explained the entire episode of discovering the HMS *Pinnacle* and his father's bound corpse, proving Wilson had murdered his father and the crew, and how later that very day he had been introduced to Wilson on board the *Intrepid*. He also described the irony of Wilson being the older version of the young officer Mathew had scarred in a fencing match a decade prior.

Dunn listened intently after pouring Mathew and himself a glass of wine. By the time Mathew finished his part of the story, Dunn could only sit in silence for a few moments and shake his head, stunned by the news.

"Good heavens!" he finally said. "That's almost too incredible to be true, and yet it explains a great deal. I *knew* your father wasn't at fault!"

"Right, though I'm still thoroughly confused as to why the mutiny took place," Mathew added.

"Indeed," Dunn agreed. "The more information is discovered, the more puzzling the heinous crime becomes."

"Why not confront Wilson? I'm confident I can make him talk," Mathew said as he pulled a large shining knife from a boot sheath.

"Too risky," Dunn said. "Besides, Wilson's probably not the architect. Someone placed Wilson on the *Pinnacle* to gain from something, though I don't know what. It could be someone as high as the Admiralty. And what if you can't get Wilson to talk. If he dies first, so too does the trail to the architect."

"Bloody hell!" Mathew pushed back his chair in frustration. "That's unacceptable! That bastard lives until we learn why the mutiny was committed and who planned it?"

"I'm afraid so, Mathew."

Mathew drew a deep breath. "What are our next steps?"

"Let's take one path at a time. Perhaps if we discover *why* they committed the atrocity, we may shed light on *who* was the planner."

"Agreed," Mathew conceded. "Why would six men kill four hundred men?"

"We already know...mutiny."

"No, technically mutiny would be if they took possession of the ship," Mathew pointed out. "But they didn't, the ship was destroyed intentionally."

"Maybe they were part of a larger group than six. Perhaps it was a more even struggle and only six lived to tell the tale."

"It was six from the beginning, Uncle Andy," Mathew said. "The entire middle third of the ship was disintegrated, and the remaining pieces dropped below the surface. The stern was facing up as was the bowsprit. It was as if it were a giant egg that someone cracked and left the two open shell portions facing down next to one another."

"Good Lord, an internal explosion?!"

"I can't think of any other way to tear a ship like the *Pinnacle* in half. Given the location of the ship, the size of the cove and the state of the wreckage, I'd say the explosion occurred at night. That way most of the crew would be asleep down below decks. The six could easily coordinate taking out the few sailors that stood watch, lock in the sailors below, and somehow set coordinated charges to scuttle the ship."

"What a macabre scene! Destroying their own ship and crew!"

"And they knew that the *Avalon* was somewhere nearby to pick them up, so they were never really marooned," Mathew added.

"But what possible motive would those six have to commit such an atrocity?"

"Well, it wasn't for financial gain. It was a Royal Navy warship, there would be no valuable cargo to steal."

"True."

The two sipped their respective wines, thinking silently for several minutes before Mathew spoke up again.

"What did my father say when you met the evening before the *Pinnacle* sailed?"

"Nothing out of the ordinary, I think," responded Dunn. "Let's see. We were here at Ardsley, we ate our meal, and had some wine."

Dunn closed his eyes as though imagining the events of the night several years prior. With his eye lids still shut, he motioned with his hand as though he could turn back in time and see himself with Thomas Hatley.

"We went out to the veranda. I made my usual appeal that he resign from the navy and captain one of my ships or help run our overall operation."

"And what was his response?"

Dunn opened his eyes. "The same as all the other times I tried to recruit him over the years." He waved a hand. "No, Andy. Thank you for the generous offer, but my place is in the Royal Navy."

"Yes, I imagine that would have been his response," Mathew agreed, nodding his head.

Their silence resumed, but lasted only thirty seconds.

"Wait a moment! There was something different! I can't believe I remember this. It seemed like nothing at the time," Dunn said.

"What is it? What did he say?" Mathew leaned forward in his chair.

"He mentioned that he might retire from the navy soon anyway, and rather than take another job, he would spend more time with his family," Dunn said.

Mathew released his breath with a scrape of frustration. "Well, that's nice, but I don't see how that helps us?"

"Thomas and I were very close. He had never intimated before then that he might leave the Royal Navy. I remember that I was surprised. It was a rather sudden decision he said; something to do with that probably being his last mission. I congratulated him and got up to get a much better bottle of wine to celebrate, but he stopped me. He intended to retire *after* the mission that started the next day."

"Go on." Mathew's senses quickened again.

"Well, I implored him to leave the navy right away, but he was most insistent to complete the one final mission. Something about a momentous impact it would have."

"And he didn't give more detail about the mission?" Mathew asked.

"He couldn't and he wouldn't. Your father was the most honorable man I ever knew. He would never tell me details of missions, nor would I pry," Dunn explained. "But he did say that as important as the mission was, he'd be back in a few months and that it wasn't going to be dangerous at all. In fact, he said it was more of a *scholarly* endeavor."

"A scholarly endeavor?" Mathew repeated, to which Dunn simply nodded.

"Does that mean anything to you?" Dunn asked hopefully.

"Not offhand, but given that the true scene of the crime was the Greek islands, I wish we could ask Professor Hutchins. If there was any tie between my father's scholarly endeavor and the brutal murder of four hundred sailors, he might have a guess."

"Hutchins?!" Dunn bolted upright on the couch.

"Yes. Professor Elwin Hutchins from Warwick College, Oxford. He was considered the foremost authority on ancient Greece and Rome in all of England. But calm your enthusiasm, Uncle Andy, he died just before my third year at Oxford. I was even scheduled to study with him that autumn."

"That's it! Don't you see?" Dunn burst out.

"I see a dead end, Uncle Andy."

"And I see an open door, my boy!"

"What are you talking about? Hutchins is dead."

"Yes. Hutchins is dead, but the trail isn't! You said it yourself, you were going to study with him at Oxford. You didn't because he died. Where did he die?"

"Somewhere in the Greek islands, conducting research."

"The same time your father died, Mathew!"

"A coincidence, Uncle Andy, Hutchins was old and he made many trips over the years to that part of the world. Anyway, he was a civilian, and would not have been on board a Royal Navy ship."

"I'm not so sure, Mathew. I actually met the man on a number of occasions. He often boarded one of my ships bound for the Mediterranean for his research trips."

"All right, you knew the man. What are you getting at?"

"I was invited to attend the service for his passing held at Oxford. A rather splendid little affair, if you ask me. The man was very well-liked among both the academic and aristocratic crowd."

"And your point is…?"

"My point is that it was a *service*, my boy, not a funeral."

"What?" Mathew perked up, suddenly understanding Dunn's meaning.

"That's right, a memorial service…there was no body!"

"No body…" Mathew whispered his understanding in a mesmerizing state of disbelief.

"Consider that Hutchins died in the same general area, at the same general time of the *Pinnacle* disaster, and add to that the fact your father called this a *scholarly* endeavor…," Dunn laid out the facts as they understood them.

"My God," Mathew concluded. "Hutchins was on the *Pinnacle*!"

"I believe he was, Mathew. Otherwise why would they have canceled his lectures at Oxford and held a service without a body. Someone in England had to know that he was positively dead and not just sick or lost, or otherwise extending his excursion."

"It certainly seems too coincidental, but I'm not sure how this will help us. You referred to this as an open door."

"Yes, indeed! We need to investigate this further right away.

This could be the biggest clue in the whole puzzle."

"But how? Hutchins is dead."

"Yes, but his daughter is quite alive. I've met her a few times and saw her again at the service. She might be able to answer some of our questions."

"And where is she?" asked Mathew.

"Warwick." Dunn sprang to his feet. "We'll take the coach right away!"

Diana Hutchins opened the door of her cottage and invited Andrew Dunn and Mathew Carrigan into the home. There was something interesting about the men who wished to discuss her father, especially the tall one with sharp blue eyes who claimed to be a former student of his.

Diana welcomed the discussion with two distinguished gentlemen. She taught at a local school for children, had never married, and spent her time away from teaching by reading, sewing, cooking or gardening in the quiet of the country home shared, at one time, with her loving widowed father. Now alone, her father left her a generous inheritance on which to live, including the home itself.

"Miss Hutchins, we hate to impose, but we'd be ever so grateful to learn more about your father," asked Dunn as he removed his hat upon entering the home.

"That's quite alright, gentlemen," she responded. "I am over the shock of his passing. Please do sit down. What would you like to know about my father?"

Both men sat after Diana seated herself. Lieutenant Carrigan began the first of many questions.

"When was the last time you saw your father, Miss Hutchins?"

Diana didn't even have to think back, for the answer was at the forefront of her mind. She closed her eyes as if to replay the scene in her mind.

"It was the morning he last left this house, the morning before he sailed back to Greece."

"Did he say specifically or even generally where in Greece he would be going?" Dunn asked.

"No."

"Do you recall his mood or temperament that morning?" Dunn said.

"It is peculiar you should ask that, because I remember him being strangely happy, almost giddy."

"Why would that be strange?" Carrigan asked.

"Normally, when he traveled long distances he rued the journey as a necessary annoyance to reach one's destination. He loved both Greece and Italy very much, but he hated the voyage."

"I see," Dunn said sounding interested, "and did he perchance discuss the purpose of his ill-fated trip?"

"No. Nothing more than continuing his research, for which you know he had an insatiable appetite."

"Miss Hutchins, I own a shipping company and your father had traveled on my ships on a number of his trips to the Mediterranean. Did he happen to inform you of the name of the ship on which he traveled that last time?"

"No," Diana said, surprised herself at this realization. "On most other occasions, he would leave me a rough itinerary and the name of the outgoing vessel."

"Are you sure he did not this time?" Carrigan asked.

"Positive. In fact, I asked him the name on the morning of his departure, and he said he forgot, which is also strange in that he had an unparalleled memory. I didn't think much of it at the time."

"How is it, Miss Hutchins, that you were made aware of your father's demise?" asked Dunn, choosing his words with obvious care.

"A representative from the Royal Navy came to our home and informed me that the navy had knowledge that my father had perished in Greece and that his body was regrettably not recoverable."

"And that was all they told you? Did you ask any questions?"

"Believe me, gentlemen. I loved my father dearly and I must have asked fifteen follow up questions: Where? How? How did they know? But they sent me someone who didn't know any specifics. I sought more information through other channels, but never got any more explanation. I forced myself to try to believe that there was some mistake, but since he never returned...I lost hope at some point along the way."

"What about his colleagues at Warwick? Were they able to shed any light on your father's disappearance?" Carrigan asked.

"No, unfortunately they were no help at all. Like you, I was searching for answers in every place I could fathom. After my father was officially declared dead by the Crown, I received a written proclamation from the Royal Court for services to England and a touching service at Oxford. Following the service, several of his colleagues stopped by our home and delivered their condolences along with his belongings from his room at Oxford."

"What kind of belongings?" Dunn inquired.

"Books, research, papers, notes, small artifacts - I kept his notes and research, but I gave the artifacts back to the college for its museum. I presume he would have wanted that. Anyway, ancient artifacts were really not my idea of a decorative touch for the home."

Both men laughed understandingly.

"Other than that, I kept the famous leather satchel and diary with which he always traveled."

"I recall the satchel and the man were rarely separated," Carrigan said.

"And you kept those for sentimental reasons, no doubt," Dunn said.

"No, actually he instructed me to hold on to them in case anything ever happened to him."

"Really?" Dunn and Carrigan said in unison, exchanging a glance.

"May we view them?" Carrigan asked.

"Certainly. Only I hope your Greek is good because he didn't make entries in English!"

As Diana Hutchins stood and left the room to retrieve the professor's satchel and book, Mathew audibly confirmed what Dunn was thinking.

"Perhaps there will be a clue in the book that somehow ties

Hutchins to the *Pinnacle*."

When Diana returned, she paused before handing over the well-worn leather satchel.

"Gentlemen, before I agree to show you his book, would you kindly tell me why you're so interested?"

"Of course, my dear, you're entitled to that," Dunn said.

"Miss Hutchins, allow me to express my sincere sympathy for the passing of your father," Mathew added. "I, too, lost my father while he was on a journey far from home, and I understand how difficult the loss can be."

Diana met his gaze for a moment. "Then I am sorry for your loss, as well."

"You see, Miss Hutchins, we have a theory about your father's disappearance. It is only a whimsical notion at this point and requires much more evidence before we feel we can communicate it to you. We wouldn't want to get something so important wrong."

"I see. In that case, I will allow you to review his book, but under two conditions. One, it doesn't leave this house, and two, you must promise to inform me of this theory if it becomes more substantiated."

"Madam, you have our word on both counts," Dunn said.

"Agreed," Mathew confirmed.

Diana Hutchins nodded her trust and extended the satchel draped over her hand to Mathew, who accepted it without taking his eyes off hers. He smiled softly, communicating his appreciation.

When he opened the tanned leather satchel, he found one item inside: the worn leather bound notebook in which her father had inscribed countless notes over that past twenty years. The binding on the spine had long ago become so flimsy that two intersecting leather straps served to hold the book together.

Mathew laid the notebook on the table in front of them and slowly untied the straps. As he turned the pages with care, he noticed they were filled predominantly with neat hand-written text, but every few pages contained an illustration or a map. As Diana had warned, the bulk of the text was in Greek, although Mathew noticed several pages in Latin, as well.

Since he had been proficient in Greek and Latin long before he went to Oxford, Mathew had no trouble reading through the professor's various notes.

He instinctively turned to the end of the book, where he found there were only about fifteen pages yet to be used. He flipped back page by page until he found the last few with writing on them.

He turned to a page that was filled with text, though it made little-to-no sense. The references were obviously coded in case someone else read the book.

The facing page was nearly half-filled with a continuation of the incomprehensible description, but there was also an interesting enlarged illustration of what appeared to be an ancient coin.

At the top of the page there was an inscription in Greek, which Mathew silently translated. He schooled his features not to betray the shock that ran through him.

"Miss Hutchins, have you ever heard your father discuss something called *Trapeza apo Midas*?"

"I'm afraid I don't speak Greek or Latin, Mr. Carrigan, but I don't believe I ever heard him utter that particular phrase before," she admitted, while smiling apologetically to Dunn.

Dunn returned her smile while Mathew turned the book around to show something to Diana Hutchins.

"Have you ever seen a coin that looks like this, Miss Hutchins?"

Diana leaned toward Mathew and peered at the expanded size drawing. Suddenly, her eyebrows rose and she let out an audible gasp of recognition. She stood back and looked at Mathew, then Dunn, then Mathew again.

She excused herself and left the room. Within thirty seconds, she reappeared with a silk handkerchief.

"Something tells me I can trust you two gentlemen." She placed the cloth on the table and unfolded it to reveal a shining gold coin.

Mathew reached out for the coin, slowly picked it up and held it higher to catch more light. His eyes went back and forth from the coin to the book, coin, book, coin again, book again. He placed the coin back within the silk on the table and looked up at Dunn, nodding that they were identical.

"He brought it back the last time he returned from Greece," Diana explained. "He said he purchased it from an antiquities dealer he'd known in Athens for quite a bargain."

"Were there any others like this or just the one?" Dunn inquired.

"There were three others. He took them to London one morning to donate, I think. I'm sorry I don't know to whom. I assumed it must be the Royal Academy."

"London? Are you sure?" Mathew asked.

"I am positive, Mr. Carrigan. I remember presuming he was going to give them to colleagues at the university, but he said he was headed for London for an important meeting."

Mathew and Dunn exchanged looks. Then Mathew turned to Diana and thanked her for her time and cooperation.

"Was I of any help?" she asked hopefully.

"Tremendously so," Mathew said. "You've provided an intriguing clue for us to pursue."

"Really? And do you think this clue could lead to some kind of treasure?"

"In a manner of speaking, Miss Hutchins."

"More coins like this one?"

"Something far more valuable, my dear," Dunn interjected, "...the truth!"

Diana smiled. "I wish you kind gentlemen luck and ask that you remember me if you find either,"

Dunn also stood. "Miss Hutchins, you have our solemn word that any good that comes of this matter will be shared equally with you. We can't thank you enough for illuminating our path." Then his tone became serious. "Have you talked to anyone else about this book or the coins?"

"No. No one has asked and I hadn't put things together as you did."

"That's good. I don't mean to alarm you, Miss Hutchins, but for your own sake, please don't mention the book or the coin to anyone else. Find a safe place to keep them."

She agreed and bid farewell to the two men who were pulling

together pieces of the puzzle that was her father's death.

The cautious optimism inside the coach en route to the Hutchins home was replaced by confident elation on the return trip home.

"All right, Mathew. Let's have it. What's the importance of the coin?" asked Dunn.

"The Greek phrase I asked her about. She had no idea what it meant," Mathew reminded Dunn. "It was written at the top of the page of the enlarged coin drawing. *Trapeza apo Midas* is Greek for *Treasury of Midas*."

"Good Lord! More coins like the one she showed us?"

"Probably many more - too many to carry himself," mused Mathew. "But the important point is not the amount, but the location!"

"What do you mean?"

"On the opposite page from the coin drawing, there was a crude map with a small inscription – just one letter in length…but a letter that likely ties Hutchins to the *Pinnacle* after all! The letter 'X'."

"X?" Dunn asked. "What does that tell us?"

"X marks the spot," replied Mathew. "There are over two thousand islands in Greece, but very few that begin with an 'X'. I believe the 'X' means Xirokos, which just happens to be the island where the *Pinnacle* was destroyed."

"By Jove, you're right!" Dunn said. "Good thinking, Mathew! Only it's unfortunate that we don't know the names of the people to whom Hutchins presented the three coins in London."

As Dunn regarded Mathew, he noticed the young naval officer break into a confident grin that couldn't be contained.

"What is amusing?" Dunn asked.

"Actually, we do know who the recipient of the coins is - and it was one person, not three. I just didn't want to reveal it in front of Miss Hutchins."

"We do? How? Who is it?"

"In his book, under the illustration of the coin, there was an additional, cryptic inscription in Greek," Mathew said.

Dunn gasped as he shifted forward in his seat across from Mathew, his eyes nearly popping out of his head with anticipation.

"And?"

"The translation of the inscription means *Charon's Toll - G3*," Mathew said.

"Well, who the bloody hell is Karen Stoll? I don't know any Karen Stoll!" Dunn threw himself back in his seat.

"No, not *Karen Stoll*," Mathew said with a laugh. "*Charon's Toll*...a *toll* paid to *Charon*. In ancient Greece, people believed that when they died, their soul would be transported across the river Acheron...their version of the path to heaven, by Charon the ferryman, as long as they provided an obolus."

"Obolus?" inquired Dunn.

"A coin...as remuneration for transport. Literally, a toll. Corpses were buried in ancient Greece with a coin under the tongue in order to compensate Charon in the afterlife."

"Oh, right. I think I remember," Dunn said, "but wasn't it the river Styx?"

"That's a common misconception, originally suggested by Virgil in his *Aeneid*. However, most historic references, including Pausanias, as well as Dante's *Inferno*, cite the river as Acheron."

"Oh, very well. I'm not going to tangle with a classics scholar on this subject," Dunn conceded. "Anyway, I still don't see what the reference to a mythical figure tells us."

"I believe it is an allegorical symbol for someone else. Who in London could provide safe passage, to presumably gather and transport the entire Treasury of Midas?"

"But we've already established that, dear boy - the Royal Navy!"

"Yes, but who commands the Royal Navy?" Mathew let the rhetorical question hang in the air. Dunn's face lit up again and his eyes met Mathew's.

"Good Lord, G-3...George III...King George!" Dunn exclaimed. "Of course, if the take was so vast and so heavy, Hutchins would barter with the king to transport it home. For a fractional share, he could *borrow* a naval warship and trusted crew by the command of the king."

"The king would be his partner, too. There's a bit of safety in that, or so one would have thought," Mathew added.

"Then he gave the three ancient coins to the king as proof of his discovery and a pledge of good faith in their partnership," Dunn said.

"Someone in the Royal Court or the Admiralty sold my father and his crew out to take the gold for himself," Mathew added. "Until we find out whom, we can't speak of this to anyone. Whoever was behind this has already killed and would clearly do so again to protect himself."

- Mathew gets back from ship trip
- Starts talking with Dunn about mystery
- Meeting with Hutchins daughter

†

Chapter 10: Mixed Emotions

*M*athew returned to the Royal Navy offices as requested, and was ushered into an unoccupied private office by one of the naval administrators. Within two minutes, the doors burst open.

"Mathew Carrigan!" Captain Isaacs shouted. "Welcome back, lad! It is a delight to see you again."

Mathew was taken aback by Isaacs' unusually ebullient expression.

"You have no idea what I'm about to tell you, do you?" Isaacs asked, somewhat surprised.

"No, Captain."

Isaacs shook his head in disbelief. "How is that possible, boy? The whole wharf area is raving about your heroics off the Barbary Coast. Selfless bravery and skilled fighting that will soon become legend!"

"I just returned from a few days away. I'm afraid I wasn't present to correct any exaggerations, Captain."

"Exaggerations?!?" Isaacs boomed. "Those were the precise words of one Captain Simon Shaddock! Mathew, there are not many men in the Royal Navy as hard a soul as Shaddock, except for maybe me. He took you on that mission because I had recommended you highly. You impressed the hell out of me on your first mission at sea, and word had since spread about your seamanship and leadership. I dare say, you've won over yet another hard heart."

"That's kind of you to say, Captain," Mathew murmured, trying sincerely to sound modest, though inwardly relieved that his recent actions at sea were remembered as selfless bravery rather than reckless and irrational.

"Mathew," Isaacs began slowly and with a widening grin, "it is my distinct privilege to inform you that you have been promoted to the rank of captain in His Majesty's Royal Navy."

"Captain?" exclaimed Mathew, more shocked than pleased. "Are...are you sure?"

"Congratulations, Captain Carrigan. You are the youngest I can ever recall making that rank."

"Captain?" repeated Mathew, still not sure he had heard Isaacs correctly.

"Mathew, some men *consider* themselves leaders," Isaacs said, "...but you proved it. Asking for volunteers and having men willingly jump into battle with you? Incredible!"

"Thank you, sir"

"Don't thank me. You earned the rank as much as any of us. Do you know you have to be nominated by at least two other captains to be considered? Only in your case that was no problem. A recommendation for promotion from Shaddock and me is unique enough, but what really won over the Admiralty was the testament of the sailors from your last voyage."

"Really?" Mathew asked.

"Yes," Isaacs assured him. "The Admiralty was taken aback by the references from the crew of the *Intrepid*. Shaddock brought a team of them in – a most unusual occurrence. The men were unanimous in their support for you. One said he was pressed into service over two years ago and he would gladly serve under you even if it meant going into dangerous battle. The Admiralty board was most impressed. They asked the sailor what made you so special and his response got you the promotion on the spot!"

"What did he say?"

"He explained that no one ever dared disappoint you."

"Very kind words." Mathew's voice was somewhat faint to

his own ears. He still could not quite believe the fantastic news.

"Mathew," Isaacs added, "the men are entirely behind you. It would be extremely difficult, not to mention foolhardy, for the Admiralty to disregard that level of obvious leadership."

"Who else knows about this?" Mathew asked, wondering if he'd be able to tell Dunn the news firsthand.

"Who doesn't? The word is out all over town, my boy."

"I'd like to inform Andrew Dunn myself."

"Certainly. Go to Dunn now. Take the rest of the day, but report back tomorrow morning to these offices. There will be a brief, but formal ceremony - full uniform."

"Yes, Captain," Mathew agreed as he snapped a salute to Isaacs. "And thank you, sir."

"Congratulations...*Captain*!"

As Mathew approached the door, he turned back to Isaacs with one more question. "I beg your pardon, sir, but might I inquire as to my first duty as captain?"

"Well, since you'll find out tomorrow morning anyway, I suppose I can tell you one day in advance. But keep it to yourself – and act surprised when they tell you officially."

"Yes, sir," Mathew promised.

"America!" Isaacs announced. "Brutal colonists are proving resilient thus far and the Royal Navy will assist in an all-out assault to quell the rebellion once and for all!"

Mathew felt as though he'd been slugged in the stomach. As pleased as he was at his early attainment of his life's pursuit, he was not prepared to fight in a war directly against his mother's beloved land, to which his mother herself had returned.

He tried not to show any emotion, simply nodding at Isaac's announcement.

Upon leaving the naval offices, he elected to walk to Ardsley Manor rather than ride by coach. With each stride, he thought of his mother back in Virginia, wondering if she was safe from the ravages of the war so far.

He recalled long discussions with his father about how England should avoid war with the American colonies at all costs, and how revolution had been understandable and even predictable given the way the king had treated the colonists in recent years.

Many intelligent men on both sides of the Atlantic had spoken and written at length on the merit of some form of compromise over the colonial grievances, but the king and his counselors were adamant that the only method of dealing with dissent was with political disdain and overpowering military force.

By the time he approached Ardsley, Mathew was so deeply lost in his thoughts and concerns that he nearly passed Dunn's magnificent home.

The celebration at Ardsley Manor was bittersweet. On the one hand, Andrew Dunn had jumped from his chair when Mathew informed him of his promotion. However, before he could scurry off to fetch a bottle of champagne, Mathew waived off any celebration.

"I appreciate your support and kindness, Uncle Andy, but the news isn't all positive."

"Nonsense, my boy! What could possibly be wrong?" inquired the bewildered Dunn.

"My first duty as captain is to lead the HMS *Endeavor* to America for a large scale assault on the colonists," Mathew replied.

Dunn's brows drew together. "Oh, I see," was all he said.

Over the following few days, the more Mathew learned of the mission, the more personal conflict he felt.

He would be part of a convoy transporting a massive influx of soldiers and supplies to meet up with General Howe in the colony of New York. There, the Royal Navy would bombard the Colonial Army from the sea, as Howe would lead as many as 12,000 soldiers against an out-manned and inexperienced colonial militia.

Ironically, as his father had done in the past, the evening before the voyage Mathew dined with Andrew Dunn at his estate. However, they spent far more time looking over nautical charts than dining.

Mathew took control the following afternoon of the HMS *Endeavor*, a one hundred eighty foot, double-decked third rater with seventy cannons and a crew of over four hundred. From the port of Dover, the *Endeavor* and four other ships of the line were to sail the following morning southwest along the English southern coast all the way to Land's End, the southwestern tip of England. There, they would meet up with a large naval convoy sailing south from the Royal Navy port at Bristol.

The crew of the *Endeavor* began the mission with bright spirits and energy. They all realized that their mission, while relatively safe, had important strategic value in breaking the colonial rebellion. With fair weather and no colonial navy to contest their efforts, delivering supplies and bombarding coastal targets from the sea involved a very low level of risk.

Additionally, the crew was aware that their captain was the most heralded young officer in the Royal Navy for years. Several had served with him when he was a junior officer and had communicated earnestly to the rest of crew that there was no finer, braver captain under which to serve. There was a strong sense of pride that they would serve under the famous Mathew Carrigan.

Mathew was aware of his celebrity and took it in stride. Though there was a novelty of being such a young captain, he was careful not to try and prove his rank at every turn. Many of the crew and even some of the junior officers were older than Mathew, yet every one of them admired him for the confidence he exuded with every spoken word and each step across the deck.

On the third day at sea, Mathew appeared to his junior officers as physically ill and weakened. His hunched body, white pallor and slowed speech were evident throughout the morning. Twice while standing near the helmsman on the quarterdeck, he nearly fell over. Though he corrected his balance before falling, his awkward movement caught the attention of both the first lieutenant and the helmsman.

"Captain, you should get some rest in your cabin. You don't look well at all and we're another day and half from Lands End,"

First Lieutenant Sutherland commented. "You'll stand a far better chance of recovery to full strength by the time we reach the Bristol fleet."

"Nonsense," Mathew argued, "I'm certainly able enough to manage. We need to stay focused on the task at hand, and I don't feel as badly as I might look."

"I'm certain you're able, Captain. It's just that we're hugging the English coast at eight knots on a calm sea. There are no issues or decisions for you to make. I am merely suggesting you get some rest now when everything is calm. I, for one, would rather have you on deck when we're in the open sea and the winds are gusting, sir."

"Perhaps you're right, First Lieutenant. I may go below for a brief rest at this time as everything seems in order. Please wake me if that should change for any reason."

"Of course, Captain."

Mathew saluted his first lieutenant and turned to descend the short flight of stairs down to the main deck and the quiet privacy of his cabin underneath the quarterdeck. His pace was slow and measured and his posture was stooped.

Upon entering his cabin, Mathew shuffled to a chest of drawers against the wall. His shaking hands opened the top drawer and he reached in to remove a small bottle. He removed the stopper and took one sip of the dreadful tasting concoction, replacing the cork while grimacing as the foul liquid nearly made him wretch. He pulled off his coat as he stumbled across his cabin and collapsed on his bed without taking the time to remove his boots.

In the late afternoon, the ship's physician attended to Mathew and noted his rapidly climbing fever. By the evening, Mathew had taken another turn for the worse and was now barely able to stand on his own on the deck and bark out orders. At the repeated insistence of his fellow officers and confident the men could handle the easy duty, he resigned early again to his cabin to take more medicine and rest.

In the middle of the night, the HMS *Endeavor* glided slowly through the calm, dark sea approaching the Bill of Portland. With a quarter-moon rising in the sky and stars shining brightly,

Mathew struggled to his feet to leave his cabin and get a breath of fresh sea air.

He waddled up the steps of the aft deck and spoke briefly to the night helmsman. Mathew looked down to the ship compass and ahead off the bow. He informed the helmsman that he would be out for only a moment to plot their location and course and would return to his cabin to sleep. The helmsman nodded and refocused his attention ahead.

Once back down on the main deck, on the port side, Mathew doubled over and vomited violently. From his hunched over position, he turned slowly and noticed the helmsman's sympathetic face in the moonlight. He felt a second wave of nausea, staggered to the bulwark, and vomited again, this time into the sea.

Mathew straightened up long enough to silently chart their location with his sextant. After ten minutes, he looked up and saw that the sailor in the crow's nest was looking out to the distant horizon, forward and to the starboard. Mathew glanced in the same direction and could see the faint outline of a thin stretch of land oddly jutting out from the English mainland, the Bill of Portland, approximately a mile away. He turned back to the helmsman who was staring intently into the darkness in the starboard direction of the island.

After cutting through several small swells, the helmsman refocused on the compass to confirm their intended path. The faintest whiff of vomit reached his nose, reminding him that his captain had been on deck moments before. He had seen Captain Carrigan doubled over, expelling whatever was left in his tender stomach. Given the calm sea and moonlit night, it was certainly some kind of illness that plagued the man, rather than the motion of pitching seas.

The helmsman looked down to the main deck and noticed that the weakened captain had had the good sense to return to his cabin for the remainder of the night.

- Mathew gets Promoted
- Sets off to Sea
to America to fight
- Hesitant because that
Is where his mother lives
- Mathew gets sick

†

Chapter 11: Mariposa

A approximately midnight, in a small cabin beneath the deck of the merchant ship *Falcon*, a quiet man known as Señor Mariposa lay down in a warm bunk to get some much needed rest. By his calculations, the *Falcon* continuing on its present course and speed would be near the French Bretagne peninsula by the time he awoke in the morning.

As the man waited patiently for sleep to overtake his waning energy, he contemplated his recent release from incarceration and imminent arrival in Santander, Spain. Though he was a prisoner no more, his freedom had come at a notably large expense.

◆

By the time dawn lit up the eastern horizon the following morning, the winds had picked up and the seas had grown in terms of swell size and ferocity. The morning crew of the northward charging HMS *Endeavor* came out to deck to begin their shift.

One of the sailors approached the rigging in order to climb up and spell the sailor in the crow's nest. He sprinted up three lengths of the rigging before stopping as something strange caught his eye. Looking down, he spied some sort of blue garment hanging over the side of the ship, wedged against the outer bulwark and the ropes. He dropped down to the deck loudly and reached over the side to grab the garment. To his horror, it was an officer's coat, and the epaulettes on the shoulder reflected the rank of captain.

He looked down on the deck and noticed a sextant that had been dropped on deck in a small pile of vomit. He turned and held the jacket up to the watching lieutenant who was making his way to the sailor from the raised aft deck. The lieutenant grabbed the coat as panic swelled in his face. He turned and ran into the captain's quarters, hoping to find the senior officer asleep in his bed, but fearing he would find the quarters vacant.

In a moment, the lieutenant returned to the deck in full sprint and yelled for everyone to look for the captain. Within fifteen anxious minutes, they had deduced that the sick and weakened captain had fallen into the sea sometime in the middle of the night. The night helmsman had recounted his memory of seeing the feeble captain vomiting near the bulwark around midnight, when they were near the tip of the Bill of Portland, near Weymouth. When he turned to see no captain on deck, he had presumed he had returned to his cabin.

The *Endeavor* was speedily turned around and a course was set for full sail to the approximate point of when the captain had last been seen aboard the ship. Within a few hours, they reached the narrow peninsula called the Bill of Portland, where Captain Carrigan had last been seen on the ship. However, there was little reasonable hope that the captain would be found alive in the chilly water. The most one could have hoped for was that Carrigan had somehow swum to the land, although it had been nearly a mile away when the ship passed in the middle of the night, and Carrigan's weak condition would have impaired his ability to swim any meaningful distance.

As the *Endeavor* reached the tip of the peninsula, long boats were released to fan out and search the surrounding area of the coast while two teams of marines went directly ashore to inspect for signs that their captain made land during the night. The entire crew searched for over two hours before a man in the crow's nest called their attention to a small object off the port bow. The crew stood at the bulwark staring dumfounded at Captain Carrigan's floating hat. Reports from the returning long boats were sorrowful. No body, no footprints. There was nothing. The HMS *Endeavor* would continue its intended mission, joining the other ships bound for the American colonies with the most harrowing news they could imagine. On his inaugural voyage, one of the most celebrated young officers of the British Royal Navy had perished in a tragic accident at sea. Captain Mathew Carrigan was dead.

◆

Señor Mariposa, remained in Santander throughout the mild winter of 1776. He was a well-liked, charming man of presumed considerable wealth, though he was an enigma to many. He customarily wore expensive suits of resplendent colors made from the finest wools and silks, yet also had long curly hair, a thick black beard and bushy moustache, giving him the appearance of a common beggar from the streets of Madrid. An eccentric, thought the people of Santander who knew him.

In the early spring, Mariposa informed his friends he was returning finally to his home in Málaga. His journey to the southern coast of Spain would afford him some time in Madrid, as well as a venture to the east, to the Mediterranean coastal town of Valencia, to see an old friend.

Once in Valencia, he discovered that his longtime friend had been taken away quite mysteriously in the middle of the night some months prior by a detachment of King Charles III's royal battalion. While he initially feared the worst, Mariposa eventually convinced himself that his friend was no direct threat to the Royal Court and that prolonged imprisonment, torture or execution was unlikely.

Rather than dwell on his friends absence, he continued on to Málaga and booked passage on a Spanish merchant ship bound for the Caribbean, just south of the American colonies.

The day of his ship's departure from Málaga, Señor Mariposa arrived at the docks at dawn, intending to embark his transport before the docks teemed with people. As he surveyed the boarding ramp to the merchant ship *Sensato*, he noticed another gentleman approach the ramp with the same idea of an early boarding. Interestingly, as the gentleman reached the summit of the ramp and was about to step down onto the ship, he was hurriedly turned away by two sailors. Strange, thought Mariposa - the *Sensato* was a merchant ship, not a navel vessel. Who cares if one of the passengers boards a few minutes early? As early boarding was obviously out of the question, Mariposa remained in his seat at the window of the dockside tavern, ordered a cup of tea, and continued to watch the ship intently.

Less than an hour later, halfway through a biscuit and marmalade, his thoughts were interrupted by a boarding whistle from the foredeck of the *Sensato*. Mariposa glanced at the watch in his vest pocket - seven-thirty in the morning. Rather than board immediately, he lingered in the shadows of the docks, watching to see who else would be traveling with him to the Caribbean.

The *Sensato* was a cargo ship whose primary purpose was transporting goods, not people. There would not be many passengers on this voyage as the cabin space below was limited. The handful of people he watched board all seemed Spanish, by the sound of their discussions. Most were men, though there were two young boys - probably mid-teens - and one woman - at least forty years of age. Mariposa knew none of the boarders, and since the ship was apparently on a strict boarding schedule, he proceeded up the gangway, leading three porters carrying his luggage.

Confident that he was a stranger among strangers on the *Sensato*, Señor Mariposa felt more comfortable than he had in months. His long, unruly hair and beard insured that the other passengers would likely leave him alone. During the day, he kept to himself near the bow of the ship or to the stern. He could indulge in the fresh sea air and fine weather this way, and avoid the uncomfortable discussions with other passengers near mid-ships, when they did, occasionally, come up on deck.

To the other passengers the thirty-five day journey would seem a painful marathon of seemingly endless days cascading into the next. For Mariposa, however, the trip would be too short and the isolation most welcome. As long as he had a good book, he could never truly feel bored.

On the third day at sea, a normally unremarkable sight severely rocked Mariposa from his serenity. A boy, no more than 10 years old, strode to the deck and walked around for a few minutes of fresh air and sunlight. This was no one Mariposa had seen boarding a few days prior. He had mentally catalogued each of the passengers, by their cabin numbers, from merely observing them come and go from their respective rooms thus far. Every person that had boarded had been accounted for - until now.

Mariposa was careful not to stare. He would glance up occasionally from his book to see the lad walking in roughly a large square shaped pattern on deck, certain that the boy had not noticed his infrequent glance upward from his book. Then the boy stopped in his tracks most peculiarly. He turned slowly and faced Mariposa.

Mariposa's nose was pointed back down at his leather-bound book when his curiosity got the better of him. Hearing the boy beginning to walk again, and in a direction away from him, Mariposa slowly looked up. The boy had indeed walked away a few steps, but backwards, with an eagle eye on the shaggy-haired man. Mariposa gave a slight grin and tilted his head to the young boy, in a familiar manner as to suggest "good morning."

Mariposa had not considered how his rough appearance muted the intended effect of his gesture. The boy was shaking. He seemed quite pale by comparison to the other passengers. He returned no smile, and Mariposa thought he saw concern in the face of the lad.

In a moment, the boy turned and vanished just as quickly as he had come, and Mariposa shook his head before returning to his book. Other than the presence of a very young, pale, and unaccounted-for passenger, the day was peacefully uneventful.

The next morning, Mariposa took up his strategic position at the very bow of the ship fairly early, leaving almost no deck space around him that might allow other passengers to join him or invite conversation. At one point, he had put down his book and fiddled with some stray rope. His hands moved quickly and effortlessly, completing several complex knots.

His thoughts were suddenly interrupted as he saw the pale boy begin to walk the deck again. Mariposa continued to tie and untie knots without looking down. This time, he made no attempt to look away from the boy. He nodded politely never taking his eye off the young stranger. The boy was now close enough for Mariposa to notice two things.

First, he had the hands of a young student, not someone who had spent much if any time on any kind of farm or other physical labor. Second, the child was mesmerized – his eyes focused on Mariposa's rapid tying and untying of complicated knots. The bearded man from Spain saw he had an audience and was prepared to impress.

As the boy inched closer, Mariposa started a variation of two complicated knots. This particular knot had no name that the man had ever learned, and had more appeal as a magician's trick than any practical utility. The overly complex knot had grown in size before the attentive stare.

Silently, he gestured to the boy with one end of the rope extended. As though in a hypnotic trance, the young child calmly reached forward and held the one end of the rope tightly. As he looked up, Mariposa's eyes met those of the boy and he pulled on his end of the rope. The knot disappeared. The boy was confounded, and let out a broad, beaming smile.

"Bravo! Muy bueno, señor!" exclaimed the child.

"Gracias, amigo," Mariposa answered, though he could tell right away by the boy's few words that he was not Spanish, but probably English.

"Por favor...otra vez?" asked the boy, still holding onto his end of the rope.

Mariposa elected to respond this time in what he presumed to be the native language of the boy. "Certainly I can do it again. I can even show you how it's done."

His friendly gesture of speaking in the boy's native tongue had an entirely unintended affect. The child instantly dropped his end of the rope while his face noticeably paled.

"What's wrong?" Mariposa asked.

"You...you're English!" answered the frightened child.

"That's right. And you're from the American colonies," Mariposa said, though he wasn't sure why the boy was so frightened. Then it dawned on him that to this boy, all Englishmen were probably considered the enemy, especially with the war in the colonies escalating.

"I have to go now," replied the boy casting an anxious glance round the deck as he turned to walk away.

"Just a moment, young fellow! You don't have to be afraid. I think it is wrong the way King George has treated the colonies, and I admire the brave men that are fighting for independence."

The boy turned back around. "You do?"

"Absolutely. Why, I've even read the colonial Declaration of Independence and think it's one of the most remarkable documents I've ever seen."

At this statement, the boy smiled proudly.

"In fact," Mariposa leaned in closely to the boy, more for effect than to prevent others from hearing, "I'm part colonial, too! My father was from England, but my mother is from the colony of Virginia. I am traveling to America to visit her."

"Really?" responded the boy enthusiastically, seemingly wanting to trust the stranger.

"So you see, young fellow – we're practically related! Why, I could be your uncle! My name is actually Dunn, Mathew Dunn." Though he had not uttered his new surname out loud before, it had a comfortable ring to Mathew's ear. He extended his hand down to the rather slight child.

"I am very pleased to meet you, Mr. Dunn," responded the boy formally, shaking Mathew's hand. "My name is Smith...John Smith."

After a half-hour of conversing, young John retreated below decks. Mathew was partly upset with himself for opening up so much to the stranger, but he reasoned that he had done no lasting harm as this was merely a child, whom within a few weeks, he would not likely ever see again.

He had told John he was a graduate of Oxford traveling to

visit his mother and her family in Virginia and start anew. After assisting on their farm for a few months, he would look for work as a professor at one of the colleges in the colonies, teaching classics.

While he certainly had the capability to fulfill this noble profession, he was still driven by, and to, the sea. He truly intended to work the farm with his mother's family for a time, but then he planned to head back to sea, perhaps in a commercial capacity, after the revolution's surely imminent conclusion.

The boy had said he was from Maryland, just to the north of Virginia, and was returning after visiting a relative in Spain. He was the son of a clergyman / farmer. His father had taught him Latin and some ancient Greek already. Mathew had not had an occasion to speak Latin since he left Oxford, and he enjoyed their brief discussion as much as he was surprised by the remarkably broad and deep intelligence of the small boy.

As he grew more easy in Mathew's presence, young John finally acknowledged that he was not traveling alone. His father was with him, though badly ill below decks. He had only made it up to deck a few times and only for a few moments at a time. When Mathew inquired as to his malady, John was hesitant to go into detail.

Mathew told John that he hoped his father would recover soon and that he could meet him. While polite and appreciative, John suggested that that was entirely unlikely. Still, they made an agreement to meet again the following day and discuss Latin poetry, magical knots, and Shakespeare.

That evening, Mathew returned to the deck of the ship for a few moments before settling down to sleep. There were six Spanish sailors, but no passengers, atop that evening.

After gazing for a time at the moon's reflection in the relatively calm Atlantic night, he reached under his coat and brought out a strange looking mechanical device. He held it close to his eyes for a moment and pulled it away and down to make some adjustments, then held it up again.

From behind him, near the aft of the ship, a door silently opened a few inches. A young face peered out to see what it was the tall stranger who was his new friend was doing. Was he a magician? Was he conjuring spirits in the sky? While the young boy's mature grounding immediately refuted these flights of fancy, he couldn't tell what the instrument was in Mathew's hands. Perhaps he'd get a better look if Mathew turned? Perhaps he'd ask Mathew in the morning.

Just then, a hand touched the boy's shoulder, sending a shock wave of fright up his spine.

"Go to your room, John. Get in bed and go to sleep."

In the child's place, the man remained, silently watching the large stranger near the front of the ship fiddle with his odd mechanical device. The man wore a tattered wool cloak covering his head and most of his body. His eyes were fixed on the stranger on deck who suddenly turned to retreat to his cabin for the evening. In that brief instant, the man behind the door could see the device clearly in the glow of the moonlight and the recognition caused his heart to skip a beat.

Mathew awoke at six in the morning, stood in the tight cabin and stretched his arms wide, his back and rib cage expanding with his long stretch. He ran his hands through his bushy mane of hair. Though he was badly in need of basic grooming, a haircut and a shave, he had elected to prolong his marooned look and wait until a day or so before reaching America.

Even little John was noticeably less comfortable with Mathew of late, though Mathew knew it wasn't his lack of grooming. Something else had changed in their brief relationship. He hadn't seen young John out on deck the rest of the prior day.

Mathew slowly and silently made his way from his cabin to the deck. The sun was already rising in the morning sky behind them. He could feel the crisp sea air chill him to the core. But he would not be on deck long enough to be uncomfortable. The morning air was more of a method to fully awaken.

Instead of taking his usual position near the bow, Mathew retreated toward the stern of the ship where there was more protection from the following wind. He was about to return below decks when the door that led back to the captain's cabin slowly opened near him. He was standing behind the door slightly, hidden from sight.

A man slowly walked out into the morning air, but Mathew could see it was not the captain. This man was rather short and stout. He had an old wool cloak about him, like a Franciscan monk. This was no monk, however, thought Mathew. The shoes, barely visible under the robe, were of very fine grade leather, in well-kept condition, with shiny silver buckles to the side. The style was more consistent with aristocracy than a monk who would have given away all his worldly possessions before serving God.

Mathew remained silently transfixed on the corpulent stranger, for here was another passenger that was unaccounted for. How many passengers had spent the night on the ship before she sailed from Málaga?

After taking five or six strides out toward the bow, the man looked from side to side and, once satisfied that no other passengers were on deck at the moment, proceeded with a brisk walk the entire length of the ship. When he reached the bow, he faced out to sea and completed a series of odd stretches and deep knee bends. The one thing Mathew couldn't yet see was the man's face.

Realizing that he'd been on deck long enough and was fully awake, Mathew began to feel the cold cut through his clothes and numb his fingers.

At the same moment, the stranger at the front of the ship slowly turned and retraced his steps back to the doorway to the passage leading to the captain's cabin. After three long strides the man's eyes rose up and met Mathew's. Clearly, the man was startled, but he kept moving toward the door, walked past Mathew and shut the door behind him.

Mathew saw surprise in the man's weary eyes, but not fear. Probably just thought he was alone, Mathew reasoned as he strode to his entrance off the deck and made for his cabin, more than slightly chilly.

Later that morning, Mathew approached his familiar spot on the bow of the ship. It was to be another clear and sunny day. Having recently dunked his head in a bucket of water, he welcomed the natural warmth the sunshine and light wind provided. His wet locks hung down quickly drying in the warm sea breeze. There were other passengers on deck this morning, but no sign yet of young John Smith. Two hours later there was still no sign of the young boy. Perhaps he wasn't well. Though mildly concerned, Mathew dared not search out the lad.

After another hour or so, John slowly came out into the midday sun. He awkwardly avoided eye contact with Mathew, so much so that Mathew resisted the temptation to approach the young boy. In fact, Mathew turned sideways looking up to the south when he wasn't engrossed in his book. It took about fifteen minutes, but at last John slowly walked up to Mathew.

"Did you lie to me?" John asked. He seemed careful to ask a question rather than make an accusation.

"What are talking about, John?" responded the equally cautious Mathew.

"Well, you said you were going to your mother's farm in Virginia and then perhaps teach at a university."

"Yes, John. That is my sincere intention. Why do you doubt my veracity?"

John's face screwed up with concentration, as though he was wrestling with himself over whether or not he should explain his doubts. "I saw you last night," he said at last. "You were standing on deck when I peeked out to get some night air. I saw you holding an odd looking device. I didn't want to disturb you, but I was curious. I explained what I saw to my father. He said that it was probably a sextant and said that I should leave you alone and not go near you any more. Is that what it was, Mathew, a sextant?"

"Yes, John. That is precisely what that instrument is called. But I don't understand why that would bother you, or your father."

"It is a device used by sailors to navigate, is that correct?" John asked.

"Yes, that is correct."

John's shoulders dropped at Mathew's response and his head turned down.

"John, why are you supposed to avoid me? I hope you know I mean you no harm."

"Oh, I believe you, Mathew. But my father thinks you are a British sailor, and, as we are at war with England, I would do well to avoid."

"I see," Mathew said, trying to hide the shock of the boy's unseen father knowing so much about him. Was it possible that someone was on board had recognized him from his days in the Royal Navy?

"Are you a British sailor?" asked John, looking straight up into Mathew's eyes.

"No, John. I am not a British sailor. I am English and I have sailed before, but I have left England for good, seeking a new life in the New World. My mother, Sarah, is really a Virginian," Mathew answered.

"Now listen to me," he added, leaning closer to the child. "I mean neither you nor your father any harm. You have been a brave young man to open up and be honest with me. If you choose to avoid me the rest of the trip, I will respect your wishes and leave you alone."

"I don't want to avoid you, Mathew," the boy smiled. "I think you're one of the most interesting people I've ever met!"

Mathew smiled with appreciation at the intended compliment, but wondered how many people, interesting or otherwise, the child had met as the ten-year old son of a colonial farmer-clergyman.

"So, where does that leave us?" Mathew inquired before extending his hand to John. "Friends?"

"Friends!" John agreed, shaking once again the large hand of the man. "Tell me more about your mother and her farm," John said. "How did Sarah end up back in the colonies?"

Mathew explained in vague terms that his father had died many years ago and that his mother took the opportunity to return to her family's farm in Virginia. Mathew was joining her now as he had recently completed his degree at Oxford. The farm, he explained to the inquisitive youth, was in an area near a town called Suffolk, not too far from the sea.

John had told Mathew that he had been to Virginia twice, and that both times he found the colony to be exceptionally beautiful and the people friendly. He assured Mathew that he would unquestionably be happy there.

The more time he spent with the exceptional child, the more questions Mathew wanted to ask. But he sensed John was most comfortable asking the questions, not answering them.

By the twelfth day at sea, Mathew had become a trusted friend to the child. They spent most of the rest of their time together discussing Shakespearian sonnets which with the boy was, remarkably, more than familiar. Mathew wondered if he also had such an intelligent command of the legendary English poet when he was John's age.

After poetry had been thoroughly discussed, they conducted a normal conversation switching from Spanish to Latin to Greek. Once speaking, they began to discuss Greek mythology. The young boy's knowledge of ancient Greek history and mythology was also particularly amazing to Mathew.

It occurred to Mathew that in his own young life he'd only known two American colonists well thus far - his mother and young John. While the vast majority of England's citizenry regarded colonists as little more than brutish and unrefined, Mathew's admittedly limited experience told him otherwise. The schooling in the colonies must be exceptional, for his experience of colonists was completely opposite of the conventional belief back in England.

Over the next week, Mathew and John met many times atop the deck of the ship. In the time since he had first met the child, Mathew had decided that he would like to maintain contact with the impressive young lad. He even harbored thoughts of becoming his guardian if the boy's father's serious illness were to become fatal.

Since his mother had left a sizeable amount of the family wealth for Mathew with Andrew Dunn, money was not an issue for Mathew. He had always known that he might one day be in a position to do something wonderful for a relative stranger, as Andrew Dunn had done for him. In fact, it was Dunn himself who suggested that the best way of repaying his own kindness to Mathew was to pass it on to someone else in need at some point in his life.

The timing and the person or persons, assured Dunn, would one day become clear.

- Matthew go to America cargoboards ship
- Meets John Quincy
- Saves John Quincy by claiming him as his nephew

✝

Chapter 12: Interception

𝒯he next morning, Mathew uncharacteristically slept in. The sea and the sun had drained him of his normal vitality, or so he assumed. It was closer to 7:15 than 6:00 by the time he awoke, hearing a slowly building commotion from scattered conversations passing in the passage outside his cabin. The discussions were in rapid Spanish that was difficult to follow. Mathew cracked open the door to his cabin and heard two men discussing the large ship on the horizon.

Mathew shut the door, relieved that the commotion was not about someone falling off accidentally or any serious problems with the integrity of the ship. He began his morning calisthenics, when a terrible thought crossed his mind.

In this part of the world, a large sailing ship might be a British naval vessel. Then again, it might be another passenger or cargo ship. For a fleeting moment, he allowed his mind to wander to the lowest probability but highest danger scenario: pirates.

His curiosity besting him, he made his way up to the deck with his spyglass under his arm. As he got to the deck, he noticed the passengers facing slightly forward off to the starboard side.

He raised the spyglass to his eyes, although he could already see that it appeared to be a British naval frigate. Upon magnified inspection, he confirmed the large Red Ensign flying from the stern, and, by the line the ship was taking, that she was not just passing by coincidence. She was heading straight for where the *Sensato* was headed – a collision course. There was no question in Mathew's mind that the Royal Navy intended to board the Spanish vessel.

He drew a breath and quickly looked among the passengers on deck for young John, but the boy was nowhere to be seen. Mathew looked again toward the frigate with his spyglass. Estimating the frigate would pull alongside his cargo vessel within fifteen minutes, Mathew went below and hid his spyglass.

Upon returning to the deck, he sought out one of the ship's sailors, and inquired in Spanish as to what was going on. The mate confirmed what Mathew already knew. When he asked why, Mathew was told that it was fairly common for the British to search commercial vessels from time to time in these waters to ensure there were no secret caches of munitions for the colonial war effort. By the lack of anxiety in the mate's voice and response, Mathew could sense there were no munitions aboard.

"No munitions?" he asked in Spanish half-jokingly.

"No munitions, señor," confirmed the sailor.

Mathew returned to his cabin to prepare it for possible inspection. He took a mental inventory of his belongings. His cylindrical case of swords was sure to bring attention, but that was thin enough to be relatively easy to hide. The sextant, compass, and spyglass could raise some interesting questions, too. All were small enough, however, to be easily concealed as well. The only concern left was someone recognizing him, and that risk he dismissed immediately as he sincerely doubted his own mother would recognize him with his long hair and beard.

He lay on his bed, after having pulled from the bottom of his trunk a Spanish version of the bible Santos had given him many years before in efforts to assist the young boy learning the Spanish language. The appearance of reading the book, any book, in Spanish would further substantiate his identity as a Spaniard.

Above him Mathew could now hear the yelling of English naval officers, barking commands at the Spanish captain and in a rather supercilious tone. He could understand the need to check certain ships, but surely it would behoove the navy to do so with the utmost respect and courtesy.

The voices were on top of them now, commanding all the passengers and sailors to the deck. Their orders were drowned out by the *Sensato*'s sailors repeating the orders in Spanish. Mathew reluctantly rose off his bed and moved toward the deck.

It was when he came out onto the sunlit deck that Mathew first heard the plea for help - in English - from a small boy, and looked up to see young John, struggling to break free from the grip of a large British marine. A stocky British lieutenant had just boarded the ship and strode toward the wriggling boy.

"Silence!" yelled the officer as he approached John. He refrained from striking the boy, but barely.

"Search the entire ship!" he turned and barked to his men.

Instantly, fifteen Royal Marines ran the length of the deck and disappeared below.

"Who is the captain of this vessel?" the British officer demanded.

"I am here, sir. Capitan Miguel Torres," offered the captain of the *Sensato*.

"Well, Captain Torres, I am Lieutenant Aaron Hawthorne of His Majesty's Ship *Sentinel*. We wish to search your ship, sir. May I have your permission?"

"We have nothing to hide, Captain," responded the Spanish captain. Mathew noted that his refusal to answer the question directly seemed as obvious as Hawthorne's disdain for having to ask the question in the first place.

"Well, if that is indeed the case, then you have nothing to fear," exclaimed Hawthorne. Something in the arrogance in his voice however seemed to Mathew to suggest that he, Hawthorne, was absolutely certain that some secret cargo was about to be found. It was as though he had been tipped off by spies. Mathew could only hope that there was no secret store of munitions in the ship's hold.

Just then, the Royal Marines reappeared on deck.

"No one below, Captain," yelled the first marine.

"What?" Hawthorne barked, visibly shocked.

No *one* below, repeated Mathew in his mind. They weren't

looking for *something*, they were looking for *someone*.

Hawthorne turned to the boy still held captive at the ship's bow. "And I suppose you are traveling across the Atlantic on your own."

"He's with me!" interrupted Mathew, in a perfect King's English.

The British officer spun around and eyed Mathew from afar quizzically. He looked down at the boy once more and then turned and walked briskly to Mathew, the look in his eye implying that he sincerely doubted the pale young boy was with the tanned, bearded Englishman. He inched closely to Mathew and spoke to him quietly.

"Who is the boy to you?"

"He is my nephew."

"And who are you?" Hawthorne asked coldly.

"Professor Dunn, Classics Studies and Literature, Warwick College, Oxford. I am bringing my nephew back home to my sister, his mother."

"Oh, I see...Professor Dunn, is it? You know you really don't look like an Oxford don to me."

Mathew's retort was both quick and self-assured.

"I don't look like this when I'm teaching, Captain. I've just finished a sabbatical in Spain studying renaissance art and literature."

Hawthorne was entirely unconvinced. "And what was the boy doing with you?"

"My nephew is an exceptional student, Lieutenant. My sister wanted him to spend time with me at Oxford and in Spain. Don't let his youth misguide you. He knows more about Shakespeare than most of my students."

Hawthorne smiled a loathsome grin.

"*Something so sweet can never be fatal. I weep cruel tears,*" Hawthorne spoke. "Now, Professor, is that from *Hamlet* or *MacBeth*?"

"Neither," Mathew countered calmly. "It is from *Othello*, and the correct phrase is *So sweet was never so fatal. I must weep, but they are cruel tears.*"

Hawthorne's brows drew together in frustration. He turned

back to Mathew and asked his sister's name.

"Sarah" replied Mathew with false confidence while feigning a sense of annoyance with the British officer, hoping to add to the fabrication.

It had no affect whatsoever on Hawthorne, who quietly strode back across the deck to where young John Smith was being held. On his way, he stopped and turned his face toward Mathew with a foul smirk, as though he knew he was about to catch the pair in a lie.

He soon reached the young boy, bent over putting his hands on his knees for support. He leaned in close to the boy's face. From across the ship Mathew could see the panic in young John's eyes.

Hawthorne asked a number of short questions, any one of which might land Mathew and young John in a lot of trouble.

"Who is that over there?"

"Mathew Dunn, sir."

"And what does he do?"

"He's a very talented man," John said, forcing his voice to be steady. "He is an expert in the classics and Shakespeare."

"And where does he teach?"

Teach, thought John. So that's what Mathew must have told him.

"At Oxford most recently, sir"

The officer cast a glance at Mathew, then looked back at John. "What is the name of your mother?"

John's mind raced. Logically, Mathew would have said he was the boy's uncle. He even remembered Mathew joking about it when they first met. The only woman's name they both spoke of was Mathew's mother's name. Yes, that *had* to be it!

"Sarah, sir," said John calmly.

Hawthorne stood back from the boy and yelled to his men without taking his eyes off John.

"All hands return to the *Sentinel*"

As he turned to climb back aboard his ship, Hawthorne pivoted and looked back at the frightened boy run to the arms of the tall professor.

The marines had thoroughly searched the ship and had not found the man for whom they were looking. *He* was certainly not on this ship.

That evening, with the boarding by English marines a distant memory, Mathew was invited to dine with the *Sensato*'s captain in his quarters. Perhaps, Mathew thought, it was Torres' way of rewarding him for his intervention on behalf of the child.

He had spent a fair amount of time washing and tidying up his unruly locks in the early evening. He also wore a clean suit in respect for the invitation. At precisely seven-thirty, Mathew arrived at the captain's private quarters.

The cabin was not as large as a captain's cabin on a warship, but it was well appointed and comfortable nonetheless. Mathew was invited in by Captain Torres and entered silently, walking the four long paces to the table in the middle of the space. It was adorned with a fine linen cloth, a thick candle, two plates, and a bottle of Madeira wine. He heard Captain Torres close the door behind him, and walk toward the table.

"I expect you are wondering why I've invited you here tonight, Señor Dunn," the captain said.

"I believe it may have something to do with the events of earlier today."

"Indeed it does, señor."

Mathew stood at one end of the table, the captain at the other. With the room dimly lit by the lone candle on the table, the men could see each other, but the rest of the room was predominantly engulfed in darkness.

"Though it was not *my* idea to invite you here tonight," Torres clarified.

"It was mine!" said a strange voice from the darkness.

Mathew turned toward the voice. Approaching the table from the shadows was the monk Mathew had run into that morning on deck. Only he had replaced his worn brown tunic with a fine suit. Though short, rather plump and balding, the man had a certain undeniable presence and confidence.

"Thank you, Captain Torres," said the stranger. "I appreciate the use of your quarters this evening. We'll need absolute privacy for the next couple of hours."

Mathew couldn't decide on what was more awkward – the fact that this man wanted to speak with him for a few hours or that he was asking the captain to leave his own quarters, and the captain seemed only too willing to oblige.

"Si, señor. You have my quarters for as long as you need them."

"Muchas gracias, Capitan," responded the stranger, as he escorted the captain to the door, locking it after his departure.

He turned back to Mathew, approached the table, beckoned him to sit, and picked up a corkscrew to open the bottle.

"Mr. Dunn, is it?" asked the man as he uncorked the wine. "First of all, I wished to meet you face to face to offer my heartfelt gratitude for what you did for my son this morning."

"Your son?"

"Yes, Mr. Dunn. I believe you've forged quite a nice little friendship with young John. He is my son."

"I see. John is a wonderful child – you should be very proud of him. And congratulations on your remarkable recovery, Mr. Smith."

"Oh, a bit of misinformation, Mr. Dunn – a prevarication in order to elude my pursuers. I'm not sick, in fact, I feel in excellent health. And I am proud of my boy. I would be devastated beyond description if something had happened to John today. As you have no doubt surmised, I am the one that the British navy is so keen on intercepting. They must have been tipped off that I was traveling with my son."

Why would the British navy want to track down this well-to-do gentleman? Mathew wondered. He must be some sort of spy for the colonial war effort, but he did not seem the age or the type to be a spy. Perhaps that was precisely what made him a good spy. Though why would he involve his son?

The man seemed to sense Mathew's confusion, but rather than clarify further, he said, "Now, John tells me that you are a scholar from Oxford. How remarkable!"

"Yes, sir," Mathew replied, unsure if this information could harm him. He chose to answer the question directly rather than describe his schooling in greater detail.

"John says that you may wish to teach at a college in the colonies, is that so?"

"It is a consideration of mine, yes."

"Well then, I may be in a position to assist you in gaining employment at the most prestigious college in the colonies."

Mathew's eyebrow's raised, for the offer was as generous as it was surprising. While he had considered such an occupation during the Atlantic crossing, he had concluded that it was highly improbable. He was without any references or accreditations as Mathew *Dunn*. As Mathew Carrigan, he would be well received, but Mathew Carrigan was known to be dead. Could his action on John's behalf earlier in the day have opened a new door towards this pursuit?

"It is small compensation for what you did for me today, and according to young John, you are eminently qualified in the area of classic literature. I happen to be a somewhat influential graduate of Harvard and would be willing to lend a supportive hand on your behalf."

Mathew thanked the stranger for his generous offer of assistance, adding that Harvard was highly revered in England, and he would be a fool not to at least consider such a path. The man's next statement shocked Mathew.

"I mean, it's not like you're going to re-join the Royal Navy now, is it?"

"What?...Why would you assume I was in the Royal Navy?" Mathew asked, pleased at his rather quick recovery, unsure if his initial surprise was obvious.

"Oh, come now, Mr. Dunn. John tells me you can make all kinds of intricate knots rapidly, and I saw you use a sextant on deck one evening. And given your impeccable speech, I would say that somewhere underneath all that hair is an officer in the Royal Navy, and if not for your youth, 'Lieutenant' or perhaps 'Lieutenant Commander'. Am I correct?"

For some inexplicable reason, Mathew was beginning to trust his insightful and mysterious host, and he could sense that the man wanted to fully trust him. It was an awkward few moments, but Mathew decided to offer the first bold gesture of good faith.

"Captain, actually," he said, looking straight into the eyes of the strange and formal little passenger.

"Captain?! Really?! I am impressed, sir. I would have thought you for only about twenty-five years of age!"

"Twenty-three."

"Incredible! And did you really attend Oxford, too?"

"Yes. I enlisted in the Britannia Royal Navy College following commencement and advanced... faster than usual."

The man looked intently back at Mathew. "Mr. Dunn, are you still in the employ of His Majesty's Royal Navy?"

Now, it all made sense to Mathew. John's father was being hunted by the English. John says he met a nice Englishman on deck. John's father sees this Englishman use a sextant. John's father must have thought Mathew to be a naval spy and in some way a danger to him and his son. This explained John's reticent behavior in the middle of the voyage. But Mathew's behavior today must have surprised John's father. Mathew stared back at the man, enjoying having the upper hand, if only for a brief moment.

"No, sir. I am no longer an officer of the Royal Navy. And I mean neither you, nor your son, any harm."

The man stared quizzically at Mathew, seemingly satisfied with the answer, but clearly still curious as to the circumstances. "And how is it that a promising young officer of His Majesty's Royal Navy is allowed to resign his commission, grow his hair to such lengths and sail away as a private citizen toward North America, with whom it is currently at war?"

"A promising young naval officer would not," responded Mathew, "but a *dead* young naval officer..." he let the partial phrase hang.

The little man, still sizing up Mathew, was fully intrigued now. "Now I understand your using the Spanish name *Mariposa*...'butterfly', is it not? The metaphorical cocoon of England is cast aside for a new and better life of beauty and freedom? A rebirth, so to speak?"

"Something like that, yes."

The questions would have kept coming, but Mathew decided

he had shared enough already and that a change in tack was in order. As the man opened his mouth to begin another line of inquiry, he was abruptly interrupted by Mathew.

"Now, sir, with all due respect, I believe it is my turn to ask some questions of you!"

"Oh, very well, Mr. Dunn. You are indeed entitled. But let me start out by saying that this is a most fortuitous turn of events. It is as though the very fates have ordained our acquaintance. Please accept my apologies for not introducing myself earlier. *Smith*, by the way, is my wife's maiden name. My real name is *Adams*...John Adams."

✝

Chapter 13: Proposition

*M*athew sat in stunned silence. He knew the name John Adams very well. This was the Massachusetts barrister who, at great risk to himself and his family, had represented two of His Majesty's soldiers in a murder trial in Boston before the colonial rebellion. Against great odds and strong local sentiment, the soldiers had been acquitted.

John Adams was a name many in England held in high regard. But then a few years later, this same man who showed sincere courage and conviction in representing British soldiers who had fired upon a colonial mob was elected to what the colonists called their Continental Congress, a local governing body not recognized by the king. In time, this Congress directed a number of grievances to King George III. The most famous was entitled the *Declaration of Independence*, of which Adams was a chief proponent and architect. No one worked harder in rallying the colonial representatives in America to break free from British colonization.

No wonder the navy wanted to intercept him at sea.

"Mr. Adams," Mathew began slowly as he stood to shake the man's hand, "it is indeed an honor to make your acquaintance. I am an admirer of your courage and conviction. The colonies are fortunate to have you representing them."

"Thank you, Mr. Dunn. But there are many in America who would dispute that sentiment."

"Really? You defended those British soldiers in Boston. That must have been very difficult to place yourself on their behalf against such strong emotion in the local community. That took great courage. And the same conviction you gave to those men, you also give now to your cause of independence."

"Some would say that I was elected to represent the will of the people - that I should vote the popular opinion and keep my own traitorous sentiment to myself."

"'A representative owes the people not only his industry but his judgment, and he betrays them if he sacrifices it for their opinion'," Mathew quoted.

"Classic democracy, Mr. Dunn? ancient Greek, political theory? Let me guess...Pericles?"

"No, Mr. Adams. Actually, those are the words of a member of English Parliament - Edmund Burke."

Adams smiled as he reached for the bottle of wine. He poured a full glass for Mathew and one for himself. Mathew was still trying to grasp the fact that he was sitting down, alone, discussing democracy with the most outspoken leader of the colonial rebellion.

"Well, this has become a rather interesting journey," said Adams finally.

"That reminds me, Mr. Adams. What were you doing in Europe? And how is it that the British knew to look for you?"

"Two very good questions, Mr. Dunn," Adams began. "Since formally adopting the Declaration of Independence," Adams began, "each of the fifty-six signers are guilty of treason in the eyes of the Crown and can be hanged as traitors, if captured. There is no point remaining in Philadelphia and making it easy for the British army to find us."

Mathew nodded, understanding the man's reasons for taking flight. "But what were you doing in Europe?"

"We all have important duties to carry out. Just because I've signed my death warrant, doesn't mean my job is finished. Far from it. The Continental Army is depending on many of us to enlist the support of other people and nations in our quest for independence. This is a momentous opportunity, not just for our small country, but as a precedent for the world. We understand all too well that we have no hope of defeating the best army in the world alone."

"What kind of support?"

"Food, loans, guns, cannons, salt peter, supplies, troops, you name it. We are not in a position to be selective."

"And other countries are supportive?"

"My dear boy, please don't take this personally, but it is a rather easy request to make. Most countries in Europe would dearly love to slow or otherwise hold at bay Britain's growing military supremacy. My platitudes on fighting for independence and freedom typically fall on deaf ears, but the chance to knock England down a few pegs is highly enticing to say the least."

Mathew stared at Adams. Amazed at how much the man was confiding in him, though only a few moments ago they had been strangers.

"Now, it is your turn again, Mr. Dunn. I have exposed my identity and motivations to you. Do you trust me enough to do the same?"

Mathew had been sitting at the very front of his chair, taking in all Adams had to say. Now it was his turn to reveal his identity. He made a calculated decision that he would tell Adams everything.

"Well, Mr. Adams," he began as he sat back in the chair and lifted his wine glass to his lips, "it is a rather long story."

"Mr. Dunn, we are not due to arrive in America for four more days. I have both the time and the sincere interest. Please do continue."

"Very well," Mathew began. "*My* real name is Mathew Hatley, though I have not been known by that moniker since I was seventeen."

Mathew proceeded to tell Adams all about his father and mother, his education at Oxford, his love of the sea, his fencing skills developed under the tutelage of Santos, the wreck of the HMS *Pinnacle* and the popular backlash against his father's memory, his mother's hasty and forced return to Virginia, his enlistment in the Royal Navy, his meteoric progression to the rank of captain, and his discovery of the truth about the night his father died.

Adams listened intently. There was a respectful silence for nearly two minutes between the men after Mathew had finished his saga.

"Now I understand why you risked so much for my son," Adams finally said.

"How's that?"

"Your father was taken away from you by the British Navy, literally. I was nearly taken away today by the same methods, which would have left young John Quincy fatherless, as well."

Mathew tried to grasp the logic. If Adams was right, it was due to a deep instinctual reaction and not a reasoned course of thought.

"Mathew, you are a remarkable young man. Your father would be truly proud. And your feelings of hatred and revenge are natural. You have been betrayed most despicably by your navy and your country. But your inner conflict and decision to walk away and begin anew is the most impressive of your many attributes. I only hope that if young John Quincy were in your shoes, he would do the same. I admire your conviction, sir."

Mathew was quiet, still emotionally spent from retelling his tragedy. Though describing the events to a relative stranger was somehow cathartic, as though he had now reached a point where he could move on with his life.

"What are you going to do now?" asked Adams.

"I want to see my mother. She deserves to know the truth."

"Of course she does, Mathew. You're a faithful son. You should go to her. And then?"

"And then, I don't know. I imagined it would become clear to me in time. I only know that my future is *not* in the Royal Navy fighting America."

The more Adams learned of Mathew's life and special talents, the more his visible enthusiasm grew about their coincidental acquaintance.

"Mathew, I am not a man who believes in luck or

PRIVATEER

coincidence. I prefer to believe in divine providence. I am certain we were destined to meet – that fate has brought us together."

"How is that, Mr. Adams?" asked Mathew as he reached across the table for some bread.

"Because you seek clarity, a new life, a purpose you can believe in."

"And you can provide all this to me?" Mathew had an uneasy feeling about what Adams was about to say.

"Indeed I can, Mathew. You see, I have negotiated a rather intriguing form of support from Spain last month. I believe you would be well suited to assist with this particular operation."

Mathew was lost. He thought he heard the words *support* and *Spain* uttered in the same sentence by John Adams. Yet he had read in newspapers how King Charles' emissary had promised the English Court that Spain would remain neutral in the colonial rebellion.

It had only been fourteen years since the Spanish navy had surrendered to the British fleet, and Spain was not likely inclined to take up arms against England's supremacy again so soon.

"Mr. Adams, did you say Spain is providing support for your cause? I have read the very opposite in both British and Spanish newspapers."

"Have you indeed? Well, then that must be so," Adams said with a playful smile.

"I don't understand, sir."

"Not everything is as it seems, Mathew. Publicly, the colonial request for assistance was denied. However, *privately*, King Charles and his advisors had a rather unusual and intriguing proposition to make." Adams took a sip of wine.

"In a battle of this magnitude, alliances are our key to victory. As I said, we realize we cannot defeat England alone. We are waging a war on every front. Not just on the battlefields in Massachusetts and New York. Battle lines are being drawn across Europe, as well. Thomas Jefferson and Benjamin Franklin are in Paris at this very moment, making great progress in bringing France into the war. I have already secured military leadership and resources from both Poland and Prussia. Holland has agreed to large loans on our behalf. While not direct military aid, can you imagine the Dutch underwriting loans to our cause if it were truly hopeless?"

"Incredible," Mathew exclaimed. "You're succeeding in building an arsenal of European powers against England."

Mathew knew that no one in the Royal Court or the British military had likely contemplated the colonies actually gaining the aid of the fractured European powers. Only a decade and a half prior, the colonists and English fought side-by-side against encroaching French settlers in what the colonists called *The French and Indian War*. It was where a young English soldier would take part in his first military skirmishes. Now that same soldier, by the name of Washington, was leading the Continental Army against the very army that trained him.

"Oh, it wasn't easy, Mathew. Everyone abroad initially doubted our potential for success as much as England has. There was no reason to get involved in an obvious losing effort – and I didn't entirely blame them. I have made several trips to Europe for this purpose. Once one country made a pledge, we knew we had some momentum on which to build. I have no doubt that Jefferson and Franklin will continue my efforts and successfully enlist the French to fight with us in force."

"Mr. Adams, how on earth was this kept a secret?"

Adams pondered the question. After a sip of wine, he looked outward to the windows lining the back wall of the cabin.

"Our very success depended on an impenetrable veil of secrecy. The British knew we would need to enlist the aid of European countries. That was obvious. But they presumed they would either intercept us or that we would fail in our negotiations. Frankly, their presumptions were right. The odds were heavily stacked against us."

"Than why did you continue against such odds?"

"Because there are no alternatives. There will be no surrender. We are committed to the ideal of an independent state far, far more than we are concerned with the risk of death."

Mathew studied Adams, taken aback by the passion in his voice.

"On that point," Adams continued, "England has made its tragic mistake in underestimating colonial will. Not just of the diplomats like me, or the soldiers like Washington, but of the people of the land. It is precisely that desperate fighting spirit that European emissaries have seen in our soldiers that has swung the tide to our favor."

Mathew reclined in the wooden armchair. Was this all true? It seemed so fantastic and yet almost plausible. Why was Adams freely discussing the details behind the veil of secrecy with him?

"So you see, Mathew," Adams said, "what was once a fantastic dream is coming ever closer to reality. But we are not there yet. We need to take advantage of every possible resource that comes our way."

"Of course you do, sir."

"Mathew, I'm talking about you. I would like you to consider joining one of our ships."

"But, Mr. Adams, you don't have a colonial navy."

"You are well-informed, young man. We do not have a colonial navy yet. In fact, I have been given the responsibility of establishing our navy. But this is not a colonial naval vessel to which I'm referring."

Mathew sat silently, looking up at the American diplomat with a quizzical look on his hairy face.

"The ship is the *Sea Dragon*, and she's a frightening beauty. More narrow and deeper-keeled than British war ships. This ship was built for destruction and speed. She happens to be a generous gift from Spain's King Charles."

"What?!"

"I have brokered an unusual arrangement. The Spanish get to test a modernized design that may be the most deadly new form of battle ship in the age of fighting sail, all without the risk of joining the war – no one will attribute the ship to Spain. And we get much needed relief from the blasted British convoy of supply ships bringing an endless supply of soldiers and resources to our shore."

This was too fantastic for Mathew to accept without question. "Mr. Adams, if such a ship were to be built, the fact that a Spanish ship was attacking British ships would immediately pierce your precious veil of secrecy. It would be clear that Spain had entered the war on the side of the colonies. I'm surprised

King Charles would allow this."

"The ship is not under construction, Mathew. She is already built. I've seen her sail off the coast of Valencia, and she is the most formidable war ship I've ever seen. Her crew has been carefully identified and selected for our particular mission. And you are correct, King Charles would not take the chance that England would learn Spain was assisting the colonies. The terms of our arrangement strictly prohibit recognition as a Spanish ship."

"I see. So, she has an English name and doesn't fly the flag of Spain, but instead some colonial flag. You'll pardon me for saying so, Mr. Adams, but it will be a temporary disguise at best. The English will know there is no way the colonies could raise a navy so quickly without external assistance."

"You keep referring to her as a naval vessel! Why? Who said anything about a naval vessel? Spanish, colonial or otherwise. Not everything is as it seems," Adams repeated. "She will have no direction from, or report to, any country or government."

Mathew looked down at his wine glass, swirled the contents, and then abruptly stopped all movement. When he looked up to Adams, the statesman was nodding, as though he knew Mathew had fully grasped the identity under which the ship would sail. A smile broke out across Adams' face first, then on Mathew's.

"Of course! Pirates," Mathew said, nearly under his breath.

"I believe *privateer* is the most accurate description, Mathew. Why, you already have the look about you with your wild hair and beard. You would be an ideal addition to the crew, along with nearly five hundred of the most dangerous cut throats and marauders the high seas have ever seen!"

"Spanish mercenaries," corrected Mathew.

"The elite of the elite among fighting sailors; specialists from gunmen to swordsmen. Apparently, there's even a chemist who happens to be extraordinarily handy with creating explosive devices. The only thing missing from this crew is someone who knows British naval strategy and tactics, and preferably one who speaks Spanish. Do you happen to know of anyone who might fit that description?"

"I'm not your man, Mr. Adams," Mathew concluded

adamantly.

"Mathew..." Adams began.

"No, Mr. Adams," Mathew interrupted. "I appreciate your efforts and will keep everything you've revealed to me this evening in confidence, but I will not take up arms against the Royal Navy. In addition to the remarkably low probability of the mission's success, I refuse to attack my own country."

"Which country is that, Mathew? The country where high-ranking naval leadership plotted your father's death? The country that drove your mother, in her darkest hours, to retreat to a distant land currently at war – for her own safety? The country you run from now because you refuse to support the war?"

The two men remained in pensive silence for a few moments before Adams spoke again.

"In any event, I was not asking you to attack your old country; I was asking you to defend your new one."

"There's no difference."

"That is where you are wrong, Mathew. There is a very real difference. Whether a man is a hero or a traitor is merely a matter of perspective. In Boston, I am lauded as a patriot whereas in London, I am vilified and to be hung if captured. I don't look upon my efforts as destructive to England at all, but rather as *constructive* for Massachusetts and the other twelve American colonies."

"You're asking me to attack His Majesty's military and cargo ships. That is attacking England."

"Yes, but consider this mission from a different perspective. Think of this as defending your mother and her family."

Mathew silently pondered his mother while staring at the tabletop. The last time he had seen her, she had informed him of his father's death and had clung to him tightly. He closed his eyes and winced as a tear fell from his eye. He imagined a burned-out farmhouse and recoiled at the prospect of her being in danger. He was prepared to do anything to defend Sarah. He looked up at Adams and slowly nodded.

"You are in limbo, my friend; a man with no country. You're no longer English, and you're not yet American. You are to be temporarily forgiven your lack of direction, but the moment you land in America, you will no longer have the luxury of neutrality. The battle wages whether you like it or not, Mathew. You will soon find you'll need to pick a side. I think we both know what side that will be, and I think I know the best way for you to make a difference in this blasted conflict."

"You make your point persuasively, Mr. Adams," Mathew complimented.

"I should hope to never be accused of less, Mathew."

"I shall consider your request over the next few days."

"That is fair. We're three days out of South Carolina."

"It is a very intriguing idea, Mr. Adams. I will say that much. But I must tell you my reservation. It has been my experience that Spanish sailors would not likely take orders from an officer of the Royal Navy."

"*Former* officer of the Royal Navy."

"Either way," Mathew said, with a wave of his hand, "it would be presumptuous of you to place me on that ship before the men know anything about me."

"I can see your point, Mathew. But you leave that up to me. You are a unique asset to this endeavor. The men may be coarse, at first, but they will recognize the value you bring to the mission. For now, I offer you a purpose for which you are eminently well suited and, I dare say, appropriately motivated. You are to join a crew of elite Spanish sailors to intercept and disrupt the shipping interests of the British as much as possible, masquerading as pirates. The only flag you will fly will be the dreaded Jolly Roger."

"And what of prisoners?" asked Mathew sincerely.

"Prisoners?" Adams gave a loud laugh, but his gaze was as sharp and hard as the edge of a sword blade. "I don't believe I've ever heard of pirates taking prisoners!"

◆

The port of Charleston, in the southern colony of South Carolina, saw little activity that day, two ships from the European continent sailed in and one sailed out bound for England.

Very few people were there to greet the few passengers who

had completed the cross Atlantic journey, though there were several large, strong men who assisted in the loading and unloading of the cargo from the ships. As the *Sensato* docked, her passengers watched as some of the cargo was unloaded. They waited, impatient to depart and continue on to the Caribbean.

Two well-dressed colonists announced themselves as harbor officials and came aboard to inspect some of the cargo. In fact, they were Loyalists, colonial citizens loyal to the English Crown, and acted as spies against their own neighbors whenever it was convenient. They had strict orders to search every ship that came in for secret munitions and diplomats. They had specific orders over the last few months to be on the lookout for a short, heavy balding man and his ten-year-old son.

They would not find John Adams or his son John Quincy as they had transferred to two long boats a mile off shore during the dark of the prior night.

The American diplomat and his son, as well as the revolution's newly recruited secret weapon, were rowed to a sheer cliff with barely any shore, a mile or so to the north of the port. At the base of the cliff was a small cave. Mathew grinned silently in the night realizing that his first steps on the shore of America were into a damp dark cave at night. At the entrance to the cave, a gangly, weathered colonial named Ethan Parkinson met them with two flickering lanterns and an excited smile.

"Welcome to Smuggler's Cave, gentlemen," he announced. "This secret entry is usually reserved for smuggling shipments of rum and the like under the nose of the harbor inspector. Since George decided to tax our trade to service his own debts, we've been using it a lot more than usual, and for more than just rum."

Parkinson led the guest trio as they ascended an old wooden stairway adjacent to the cave wall.

"We thank you for your assistance, Mr. Parkinson," John Adams said, holding Parkinson's second lantern low in order to negotiate the steps.

"My pleasure. You gentlemen are a top priority according to the Sons of Liberty. Anything they ask, we gladly will do!"

"That is most reassuring, friend," Adams said then turned to face Mathew, although seemingly still talking to Parkinson. "This battle we wage has many fronts and it will take many acts of courage and effort to lead to independence one day."

"Besides, the stinking Loyalists are checking every ship that comes into port," added Parkinson.

After another minute, they reached the top of the steps, and a bent over Parkinson slammed a fist against the wooden barrier above them. The hinged barrier opened upwards and the men climbed into a candlelit parlor in a private home, where they waited comfortably for a half hour.

"Transportation is here, gentlemen, and right on schedule," Parkinson said, standing at the window, peering cautiously outside through the drapery.

A grateful John Adams reached out to offer a handshake to Mathew as young John Quincy looked on.

"Take care, Mathew. May God watch over you and the men of the *Sea Dragon*."

John Quincy looked up at Mathew. "Good-bye, Mathew. And thank you!"

Mathew saw the strange look in John Adams' eyes, as well as his odd body language, as if Adams was certain he'd never see Mathew again. While it was clear the mission ahead for Mathew would be exceptionally dangerous, he had expected the round little diplomat would have made a far better effort to and at least feign some display of confidence in its potential success.

Adams seemingly sensed Mathew was reading his thoughts, gently pulling his hand from the large man's grip and stammering somewhat.

"When all this is over, Mathew...call on me...in Boston. Maybe I can help you land that teaching position at Harvard after all."

Idle words thought Mathew. He already saw it in the man's face — there was no way Mathew would likely live to see the end of the war, let alone Boston. The odds of survival for more than a year on this mission would be astronomically high. He knew it, and Adams most assuredly knew it.

"I give you this list of friends to our cause in seven coastal towns of Virginia and the Carolinas. You'll soon find that what it lacks in length, it more than makes up for in spirit. Each one of these people is unwaveringly loyal to the cause and will assist you with munitions and supply exchanges as we discussed. Guard the list closely, Mathew. For it would be ruinous for many should it fall into the hands of the enemy."

Mathew accepted the list and quickly glanced at its contents. He saw a simple list of seven names written in Adams' scrawl, each name identified by the name of an inn, its town and colony. A code phrase and appropriate confirmation response was included at the bottom of the list.

In each coastal town, a network of spies would monitor British military presence. If the "coast was clear" of British soldiers, a large white sheet would hang from a specified cliff, well-hidden from sight on land by high trees or rugged coastline, but easily spotted from a great distance out at sea.

"How on earth can you expect them to help me, Mr. Adams?" Mathew asked. "I cannot approach them looking like this and sounding like I do. They'll kill me on the spot!"

"That is a good point. I would recommend you speak with a colonial accent from now on, young man. I know you have a talent for languages and I'm confident you must have picked something up from listening to your mother's voice for two decades. May I presume this will not be an issue?"

"You may presume so, sir. There will be no issue at all," Mathew said in a colonial accent, so realistic that Adams grinned widely. "But how can we expect them to trust a complete stranger?"

"Because you will not be a complete stranger. Leave that to me. When you make contact with each, they will know you as *Chameleon*. They will know nothing of the *Sea Dragon* or how you obtained the supplies, but they will trust you implicitly."

— Mathew offered a job gets Privateer

— Cargo ship gets to America

†

Chapter 14: Acquaintances

As the jolly boat pulled silently across the small bay toward the massive war ship, many of the crew leaned on the bulwark sizing up the newest member of their ranks. From his cabin below the poop deck, the captain withdrew the looking glass from his eye. He had never seen such an unruly and frighteningly unkempt sailor.

He whispered a prayer in Spanish pleading that this new sailor would be more than what was shown on the surface. He had a strong rugged look about him to be sure and he seemed large compared to Javier and Pedro, who were rowing the jolly boat. Yet there was something that bothered the seasoned captain.

This hairy man sat upright with excellent posture in the rowboat, which was bothersome. To the captain, he had the body language of a pompous Englishman who would probably feel entitled to lead the ship simply due to his English heritage and upbringing, whether or not merit warranted.

The captain reminded himself of his prayer and vowed not to judge too quickly and merely by appearance. *Trust Mr. Adams*, he told himself. But he couldn't help looking down at the cabin floorboards and shaking his head.

The captain knew that his crew would not look too kindly on the new sailor. All they knew was that he was a former English sailor who had come highly recommended by the man who managed and financially supported their strange seafaring charade. He would be despised the moment he stepped aboard the ship, if he was not already. His being English guaranteed that reaction from the Spanish crew. And betraying his own country would make him even less trustworthy in the eyes of the sailors awaiting his arrival.

How the stranger conducted himself would speak volumes to the captain, who didn't have the luxury of spending a lot of time getting to know him before putting to sea the next day. The captain decided to await the arrival in his cabin. He sat back in his chair, closed his eyes and listened intently, trying to hear the footsteps and voices on the deck.

The crew was eerily silent as Mathew climbed the rope ladder of the strange looking ship. They stood back a few paces as he threw his legs over the bulwark and stepped onto the deck. Normally, the men would have extended a hand at the top of the ladder to one so highly recommended. The lack of cordiality was not lost on Mathew.

As no one approached to formally greet him, he turned and stared at the men. "Buenas dias," Mathew offered, seeking to end the uncomfortable silence.

No one responded.

Then a voice in the crowd on deck called out in Spanish, "I see you wear a fancy sword, señor. Is that supposed to impress us? I doubt you know how to use it, English baboon!"

From behind the first wave of sailors encircling Mathew, a lone sailor approached. When he was within six yards, the sailor drew his sword and began an attacking move. Mathew instantly drew his own sword and sized up the situation.

The impending sword fight was not entirely unexpected, and Mathew was confident in his own ability. However, it would be impossible to win in any traditional sense. Mathew would not dare kill the man, for fear of being attacked by the entire crew immediately thereafter, though the attacker was clearly not constrained by the same circumstance.

Rather than wait for his assailant to reach him, Mathew approached his assailant, cutting down the distance between the two of them, and taking away what his aggressor would have felt was comfortable attacking distance. It worked. As Mathew advanced, he could see the expression in the eyes of the Spanish sailor change from confidence to concern.

Their blades connected in a flash of steel. A loud roar came from the rest of the crew on deck, who were pulling for their mate. Their cheers suggested the man's name was Barones.

The eruption of cheers on deck brought the captain instantly out of his chair and running to his cabin door to witness the commotion firsthand.

Mathew began the engagement fighting with his right hand. His counter-attack on the assailant immediately turned Barones into an unexpected defensive position. As Mathew parried and advanced, some of the cheers for Barnones turned to gasps.

Two additional sailors drew their swords and approached the fight. Mathew could sense their attack from his left side. With only one sword, he was at a decided disadvantage. Rather than face them and turn his back on Barones, Mathew leaned backward and completed two consecutive backward hand-less flips. The two attackers from the left thrust forward, though no one was standing there anymore. The rest of the men on deck were frozen in bewilderment. Mathew turned around and pulled the sword from the sheath of the stunned sailor in front of him, and returned to the fight.

He engaged the two attackers with his left hand, keeping them both at bay, while Barones rejoined the fight on his right side. He, too, could not get past the slashing blade. After thirty furious seconds of fighting the man, the swords stopped, and the men took three steps back.

One of the attackers on Mathew's left moved to his own left so that he faced Mathew straight on. Mathew's opposition was now essentially three points of a triangle around Mathew in the center. The next wave of the attack was set. Mathew saw in his peripheral vision that Barones was the first to attack. Mathew let him come.

Mathew looked toward the other two men. Their motionlessness meant Barones was nearly upon him. Mathew spun around just in time to meet Barnones' thrust to his mid-section and easily slap it away. But Barnones was moving at Mathew with such speed that once his sword was pushed harmlessly away from Mathew, his body was out of control and balance. Mathew pivoted around Barnones as a bullfighter spins as the bull passes by. His foot lifted underneath Barnones' stride and sent to man flying through the air towards the attacker on his left.

Barnones fell hard to the deck. Not only was he momentarily stunned, but his bulk impeded the attack of the man from Mathew's left. That left Mathew, with two swords moving swiftly to the attacker facing him.

The two steel blades in Mathew's hands moved like precision instruments, flailing about in the air but not touching each other. Only the swooshing sound of flying blades could be heard as Mathew reached the overmatched assailant who was slowly moving backward, as were the rest of the crew not far now behind him.

The retreating sailor tripped backward over a coil of rope on deck. Mathew spun around to subdue Barones and the other assailant.

Rather than join the fight, they had spread out cautiously, resizing their opponent for a more strategic attack. This allowed the tripped sailor behind Mathew to rejoin as well. In a moment, the triangular attack would be on again. Only this time, Mathew surmised, they would not attack one-by-one, but together.

Mathew's instincts were correct. In the next instant, each of the three attackers charged at him. There was nowhere on deck for him to move this time. Any direction would take him closer to one of his assailants. Even if he defended himself the other two would be on top of him instantly. The only course of action was risky, but truly his only remaining option.

Just as the three blades converged toward his body, Mathew crouched and jumped. His vertical leap into the air approached four full feet. His leap left the attackers thrusting toward each other.

Suddenly, Mathew's defense from the attackers turned offensive. At the apex of his jump, Mathew extended his legs in opposite directions with a horizontal kick. The soles of his boots connected with two of the attackers. The combination of their motion toward Mathew and Mathew's boots kicking them straight into their faces lifted the two men off their feet and sent them flying backward. Barones was one of the unfortunate attackers to receive an unexpected kick to the face. He landed hard on the deck, his nose streaming blood.

In that instant Mathew's feet landed back on the deck of the ship. He lowered his head and swords toward the deck. His head slowly rose to regard the third crewman. The lone remaining fighter looked back at him with disbelief. His hand was shaking and he dropped his weapon.

Just as Mathew raised his swords, he heard the unmistakable click of a pistol's hammer pulled backward into firing position. He didn't need to turn around to know the gun was aimed at his head from only a few feet behind him.

The crew ahead of Mathew parted quickly, as if to protect themselves, while staring just behind the large Englishman. Mathew lowered his swords. There was no defense - no acrobatic response - to a bullet fired from a pistol at close range.

"Bravo, señor!" said the captain. "Now, slowly put the swords down on the deck...and no sudden moves!"

Mathew did as he was told knowing the gun was still pointed at the back of his shaggy head.

"You fight like a tiger, señor. Where did you learn to fight like that?" asked the captain.

"Here and there," Mathew replied, lowering his swords to the deck.

"And these evasive moves...quite graceful and impressive. Who taught these to you?"

"My mother," Mathew replied, which brought a round of bellicose laughter from the crew.

"Your sword fighting technique is truly brilliant. It is a shame you cannot join this crew."

"Excuse me?" Mathew asked. "Why not?"

"Because I'm not sure my crew wishes to allow an Englishman to join their ranks, especially one who is a traitor. Why would you turn against your own country, señor?"

"I have good reasons," Mathew responded still facing away

from the captain with his hands out at his side.

"I should like to hear these reasons…and I believe my men are entitled, as well."

Mathew still hesitated.

"No matter how well you fight," the captain said, "you cannot be a part of this mission until you have the absolute trust of the crew and its captain."

"The Royal Navy killed my father and drove my mother away," Mathew said.

"That is most unfortunate, señor, but I do not think that…" the captain stopped speaking suddenly. "Your father…he was an officer…in the Royal Navy?"

"Yes…sir" Mathew stammered. "How…how did you know?"

"And your mother…she returned to…Virginia?"

"How could you possibly know that?" Mathew asked

"And this sword you carry? This was given to you by the man that taught you to sword fight."

Mathew slowly turned to face the man pointing the gun at him. The captain lowered the pistol and carefully replaced the hammer while the crew watched in silent suspense.

"Because I am the one who gave that sword to you, Mateo!"

Mathew's jaw lowered while his face registered disbelief. Slowly, he began to shake his head as if to confirm the man before him was merely an illusion.

"I am so very sorry, Mateo. Please forgive me!" Santos holstered the pistol, stepped forward, and embraced Mathew.

"Santos!" Mathew whispered his recognition while returning the hug. "I thought you were dead."

Captain Santos quickly stepped away from Mathew. "Your father, Thomas…what…what happened? Did you say the *Royal Navy* killed him?"

"Yes, sir. There was a mutiny on a secret naval mission. The entire ship was destroyed and all aboard her murdered by a handful of mutineers on the Mediterranean Sea. When they returned to England, they told a fantastic tale of the ship running aground due to my father's recklessness. They claimed the crash into the rocks triggered an explosion and all but a few hands were lost. The murderers were hailed as heroic survivors while my father's name was dragged through the mud. In England now, Thomas Hatley is regarded as a reckless failure, not a hero."

"Dios mio! This cannot be. Your father was the most honorable man I have ever met. And your mother...she returned to America because the British turned their back on her?"

"Yes, though her treatment was more pronounced than that. She was driven away by dangerous threats against her life and property. She had to flee for her own safety."

"Unbelievable! She was the kindest lady in all England! How cruel a tragedy is this?"

"I ran from England willingly, seeking to start over in the New World, Santos. I didn't seek a fight, merely a rebirth."

"And you believe fate brought you to this reunion today, to join in battle against your English brothers?"

"No, sir, fate had nothing to do with me taking up arms against England; Mr. Adams suggested it."

"Bah! That Adams is an obnoxious, selfish little man. He is interested in what suits him and his purpose. Do not be fooled by his fancy words and persuasive ways; he does not do this for *you*, he does this for *him*. This is not your battle, Mateo," Santos implored. "It is possible that the solution to your anguish is not to turn to violence."

"It wasn't what Mr. Adams said that persuaded me to join this mission."

"Then why?"

Mathew explained how the young officer that he had wounded long ago in a reckless fencing match had been the very one who murdered his father, and how Mathew had discovered his father's remains in the water on the island of Xirokos. When Mathew completed his description of the events, Santos looked downward to the deck of his ship and shook his head in disbelief and sadness.

"Mateo, I am so very sorry for your loss. Truly I am sorrowful this day. As wonderful as it is to see you again, my heart cannot rejoice because of the terrible tragedy your family has suffered. But revenge, this is a dangerous business, Mateo. I understand what is in your heart. I, too, have lost loved ones to the evil of men. But think of our lessons. You fight better when you can reason. Emotion must be entirely withdrawn from the battle. I fear your heart may overpower the reason that comes from your head, and that puts you at a decided disadvantage, my son."

"Santos, I appreciate your concern. But I have not acted rashly. I have thoughtfully calculated my future. I became an officer in the very navy that produced and then turned on my father. I had no idea that I would learn first-hand of the events of his murder."

"Mateo, the Royal Navy did not kill your father. Some very bad and dangerous men conspired to murder him, but not the Royal Navy, not all of England."

"I met him!"

"Excuse me?" Santos asked.

"Hours after I discovered the wreck of the *Pinnacle*, my captain introduced me to the very man who murdered my father."

"And he did not recognize you as the young swordsman that scarred his face?"

"No. He was smug and aloof. I could have killed him right then and there. But I did not. I reasoned that to kill him would not bring my father back, but provide only momentary satisfaction."

"You acted wisely, I am impressed and proud of your decision under such difficult circumstances."

"That's not all. I subsequently learned that the plot to kill my father and the crew was conceived within the Admiralty of the Royal Navy itself."

Santos stared at Mathew with raised brows.

"The final straw was when I made captain. After the ceremony, they informed me I would lead a fourth-rater against the colonial rebellion in America. I was to go to war against my mother's land – a land my father had always held in the highest regard. I faked my own death to rid myself of England and the Royal Navy and begin anew in America."

"And what now, Mateo? Now you are prepared to engage sailors in the Royal Navy and kill them?" Santos asked.

Mathew looked out toward the sea for a moment before speaking again. When he turned, he stared Santos in the eye with undeniable conviction.

"I was powerless in England to set things right. I was powerless in the Royal Navy to bring the guilty to justice, even when I discovered who the guilty were. Now England seeks to quell the colonial pursuit of independence. I cannot help my father, but I can support my mother. I am certain I can make a difference, and I will now gladly take up arms to defend my mother and her family."

"Mateo, your intentions are noble, but you must understand that we have a very dangerous mission ahead of us. If we are ever captured, we shall be hung on the spot as pirates. There will be no reasoning, no trial, no prison, only death."

"I understand, Santos. That means we fight to the end. There is no surrender and no quarter given. Accept me now into this crew, and you will enhance the strength of this mighty vessel."

Santos moved to Mathew and embraced him once more. He then stepped back and called out loudly in Spanish to the crew.

"Listen to me well, men. This man is like a son to me. It is true that I tutored him in fencing several years ago. I have lived many years and traveled to many lands and have never witnessed his equal with the sword. His heart is true. He fights for the American colonies and that is consistent with our purpose. Please accept him immediately into this crew."

With that the crew approached Mathew, circled him tightly and patted him on the back and shook hands with the newest member of the *Sea Dragon*. Some of the men began to chant a name that Mathew couldn't quite make out.

"It seems they readily accept you, my son," Santos said. "They have even given you a fitting name!"

"What are they saying?" asked Mathew.

"Azogue! Azogue! Azogue!" the chants grew louder as the crew looked at each other and nodded at the moniker's appropriateness.

"Azogue," Santos said. "With your two-handed sword fighting and lightning-like speed of the blades, it makes sense."

"But I don't understand, what does it mean in English?"

"*Quicksilver!*" answered the grinning Santos. "A fitting name for a pirate, no? Welcome to the Brotherhood of the *Dragon*."

—Mathew becomes Pirate

— Pirates accept Mathew)

— ~~the the~~ Mathews new p~~irate~~ name is "Azogue" (quick silver)

†

Chapter 15: Dragon's Breath

*M*athew spent his first few days on the *Sea Dragon* with the crew teaching them advanced technique with the sword. Most, including Barones, were eager to watch the step-by-step walk-through demonstrations on deck each afternoon. However, it was his physical fitness training that captivated the Spanish crew.

Inverted push-ups usually drew the most attention from the watching men. From a kneeling position, Mathew would lean forward and put his head on a cushion lying on the deck. With his hands spread out on each side of his head for balance, he would come off his knees and thrust his entire body into the air above the base of his head and hands. Knowing the crew on deck was staring at his inverted position, Mathew would then slowly push himself up away from the deck with the strength of his arms.

For three days, a number of sailors attempted to emulate the inverted push-up, but to no avail. Only four men could stand on their head, and none had the strength to push their inverted bodies upward more than an inch or so.

While watching Mathew's acrobatic fitness regimen, one sailor asked what many in the crew were likely thinking: were these mandatory Royal Navy exercises to build strength and flexibility? The unspoken concern was that many men in the

Royal Navy were capable of these feats of strength and fencing dexterity.

Mathew laughed and shook his head, explaining that he had learned these from his American mother as a child and had continued them just about every day to this point, though always in private. He then added, somewhat playing to the crowd, that many in the English navy were slovenly, rum-drinking baboons.

The fact that Mathew was an impressive additional weapon on their side seemed to make the crew comfortable with his presence, but it was his friendliness and openness that ultimately gained their trust. His willingness to share his private regimen and openly discuss fencing moves was well received. Mathew not only felt at home among the impressive crew, but he knew that trust was critical to his being fully accepted on this arduous mission. He could tell he was becoming a trusted member of the crew when the men felt comfortable enough to jeer his English upbringing.

"Where's Mateo?" asked one sailor loudly on deck one day.

"Probably taking tea on the aft deck!" answered another, drawing an eruption of bellicose laughter from the crew, as well as from Mathew.

Between fencing lessons and individually getting to know the crew, Mathew spent time walking the line of the ship. Mr. Adams' description of the *Sea Dragon* was indeed accurate. She was not only unusually narrow and with a deeper keel for improved speed and traction in the sea, but there were some odd mechanical additions bolted to the fore and aft decks.

"I see you are admiring the ingenious carpentry," offered Santos, laying a caressing hand on the intricate mechanical woodwork.

"Yes, but what is this?" Mathew queried.

"What does it look like?" Santos responded.

"It looks like a trebuchet or catapult."

"Precisely."

"I've never seen or heard of a trebuchet on a ship. What in the world would you launch from the deck of a ship?"

"Clay orbs, about the size of a cannon ball, but lighter," Santos added.

"That doesn't sound menacing," Mathew concluded.

"The orbs themselves may not be menacing, but what we fill them with is extremely lethal." Santos turned from the contraption to face Mathew. "Mateo, I seem to recall you had a head for naval history. Do you recall the Arab attempted siege of Constantinople in the late seventh century and again in the early eighth century?"

"Yes. The Byzantines successfully defended the city on both occasions, though they were far outnumbered."

"Very good! And how did they accomplish such an unlikely victory?"

"The legend is that they used a new form of weapon, devised by a Greek alchemist named Kallinikos, something called *Greek fire*. Supposedly, the complex formula he discovered created a fire that couldn't be put out by pouring water on the flames, in fact, water would actually spread the fire."

"That's right. Go on," Santos urged.

"It was used primarily at sea and was said to be responsible for many Byzantine victories over Arabs, Vikings, and even Venetians during the Fourth Crusade. It may have been the primary reason the Eastern Roman Empire survived into the fifteenth century, until the Ottomans burnt Constantinople to the ground and the closely guarded formula was lost."

"Was it?"

"Well, there have been no historical references to its use since then."

"True. People assume it was lost because Greek fire has not reappeared in battle. But there is actually more to this story, and you wouldn't find it in all of the history books and manuscripts at Oxford."

"What do you mean?"

"Legend has it that when Constantinople fell to the Ottomans, a monk responsible for a number of precious records, including the safe-keeping of the Greek fire formula, escaped the siege and ended up years later in a monastery in southern Europe. There, he kept the complex formula secret until, in his advancing years, he decided to pass it on to another. It was protected through the centuries by a small brotherhood that sought to prevent it from falling into the hands of those who would use it to dominate others." ⁄|

"Good God," Mathew said.

"There's more! The brotherhood called themselves *Prometheans*, after the Greek mythological hero Prometheus, who disobeyed the gods on Mt. Olympus and, with good intentions, provided fire to mankind."

"Prometheans? I've never heard any group calling themselves the Prometheans," Mathew countered.

"Of course you haven't. Through the centuries, the Prometheans kept their small brotherhood as secret as the recipe for the frightening weapon itself. It was not an especially difficult task since the formula was presumed lost forever – no one knew they had it."

"But why would they have kept the formula at all? I would think the original monk would have wanted it destroyed."

"On the contrary - the monk understood the awesome destructive power of Greek fire, but - like the mythical Prometheus - thought it could potentially have a positive use for man." |

Mathew frowned.

"Something puzzles you?"

"Pardon me, Santos. It's such an unbelievable story. Even if the formula somehow survived the siege of Constantinople, and was kept secret throughout the centuries by the clandestine Prometheans, how is it that you know so much about it?"

"A fair question that warrants a direct response." Santos slowly raised the cuff of his coat and shirt to reveal a copper bracelet at his left wrist with a raised insignia of a torch and flame. He took it off, and Mathew saw a highly detailed formula engraved on the inside of the bracelet. "I happen to be the sole remaining member of the Prometheans."

At the first glimmer of dawn, the anchor of the *Sea Dragon* was pulled up and the sails were raised. The wind was moderately soft from the northeast and the mighty ship began to move, slowly at first then effortlessly progressing to a pace of nine knots through the placid morning water.

As the ship emerged from Cowell's Cove at Blackbeard Island along the coast of Georgia, the crew moved across the deck almost silently, as though in a well-rehearsed dance.

Mathew knew the Royal Navy did not have a ship as sleek and lethal as the *Sea Dragon*, and he doubted any British naval crew was, from top to bottom, as finely trained and motivated.

Unlike in the English navy, each of the men on the *Sea Dragon* was an overqualified volunteer. No press gangs forced young inexperienced men to join on, for the crew was entirely made up of highly experienced naval soldiers, avidly pursuing an opportunity to confound and defeat the vaunted Royal Navy.

Mathew would soon experience his first engagement versus his former navy. To the northeast of the *Sea Dragon*, the HMS *York* bounded across the sea on the last leg of her long journey to the colonies from England.

By the time her distant sail was spotted on the grey horizon by the lookout, Santos was already spying the *York* through his telescope, knowing they were likely entering a natural shipping lane. Mathew stood near at hand, and noted his adrenalin increasing rapidly.

Santos barked a command to change course immediately to intercept the British cargo ship. Within one minute, the entire *Sea Dragon* was deftly turned and sails were adjusted to optimize her harvesting the gusting wind. Santos mentally plotted the course that would cross paths with his ship's prey in less than a half hour.

Just as the *York* was visible to the *Sea Dragon*, so too was the *Sea Dragon* visible to the *York*. It was entirely likely that the watch on the *York* had alerted their deck to the presence of a ship to the southwest. From such a distance however, it was unlikely that the watch would have been able to immediately gauge the *Sea Dragon*'s direction. It was perhaps a two-in-three probability that the *Sea Dragon*'s sudden change of course in order to descend upon the *York* was unnoticed.

While the gap between the ships narrowed as each headed west, the crew of the *Sea Dragon* prepared for battle and Santos kept a close vigil on the horizon beyond the *York*. Mathew, in turn, watched his mentor study the distance and not the prey, understanding his captain's concern.

"Escorts?" he inquired.

"None that I can see," responded Santos without pulling the telescope from his face, continuing to scan the horizon slowly. Mathew noticed Santos's hands suddenly tighten on the grip of the telescope. He twisted the front portion of the lens in order to focus on something in the distance.

"Damn!" Santos said. "I was hoping our first encounter together was going to be an easy one."

"What do you see?" asked a suddenly concerned Mathew.

"A war ship, third or fourth rater I think, 10 degrees to the right of the prey." Santos handed Mathew the telescope. "Royal Navy, Mateo. Are you truly ready for this?"

"Absolutely!"

"Bueno, because it is going to be quite a battle." With the telescope still raised to his eye, Santos cursed again.

"What now?"

"Another war ship, two degrees to the right of the first. Here take a look." Santos thrust the looking glass at Mathew.

As the *Sea Dragon* crossed the bow of the *York* within one hundred yards, no one on the English ship took any notice of the two clay orbs flying silently through the air toward them.

As the spheres reached the *York*, the ship bounded down in between great swells, catching the stealth bombs harmlessly in her sails like a soft cushion. Instead of exploding on impact, the clay balls rolled down the length of the sails toward the deck, but never reached it. Both orbs smashed into the horizontal beam above the heads of the sailors.

It was then that Mathew, looking through his telescope, understood the design of the orbs. The sphere was separated into two half-spheres by an inner clay wall. The chemical compounds on each side of the wall were harmless on their own, but once mixed together would ignite into an uncontainable fire.

In an instant the great broad beam was alight in Greek fire that rapidly climbed the sail itself, aided by the wind and the rising heat of the flames. In a matter of a minute the entire mainsail was gone and the mast was engulfed in a line of fire that reached well above the crow's nest where the lookout had already jumped away toward the rigging.

It was not the precisely intended target, but its destruction was actually better than what the crew of the *Sea Dragon* would have dared plan.

With her mainsail gone, the ship would progress toward the American coast at a snail's pace and her cargo would likely remain intact for the *Sea Dragon* to plunder once she defeated the war ships. *If* she defeated the war ships.

The *Sea Dragon* turned hard to the right to take on the oncoming HMS *Albemarle* bounding straight for the *York* along the building swells at over twelve knots. Interestingly, the *Albemarle* moved more in a line to assist the *York*, which had inexplicably burst into flames, than to strike against the *Sea Dragon*, which it briefly noted was flying the Royal Navy's Red Ensign. It was as though the *Sea Dragon* was invisible.

As the *Sea Dragon* and *Albemarle* passed each other within seventy-five yards, the privateering ship unleashed a formidable attack on the unsuspecting and distracted British third-rater. The entire set of forty-five cannons on her starboard side spat fire and red-hot cannon balls into the sides and decking of the *Albemarle*, whose deck shuddered under the surprise attack.

The bounding sea made the attack on the *Albemarle* even more lethal. Several of the shots, including the catapulted Greek fire bombs, tore through the canvas sails and hemp rigging. Two of the masts were badly damaged by direct hits from the iron cannon balls that had been pre-heated to a blazing temperature.

The crippled *Albemarle* would not have time or the resources to regroup quickly. Like a sitting duck, she could not catch enough wind to outmaneuver the pirate ship that was turning away from the wind. The captain of the *Albemarle* could see the *York* was immobile, but in better shape than his own ship. He implored his men to prepare for the second wave of attack, knowing that the HMS *Phoenix* was moments away from joining the battle.

As the *Sea Dragon* completed its wide turn and bounded directly toward the stern of the *Albemarle*, it was not clear on which side she intended to pass. Clever, thought the *Albemarle*'s captain, that she won't show her hand until the last moment. As such, he called down to have both sides of his ship prepare to fire their cannons. But with all the commotion of the damage and fires on deck, he knew that his men would only be able to muster firing half of the cannons once the attacking ship chose a side on which to pass.

Just as the *Sea Dragon* was within fifty yards of the *Albemarle*, she veered to her right and then suddenly turned hard to the left. The captain of the *Albemarle* turned white with fear as he understood what was soon in store.

Rather than pass the British war ship on either side, the aggressor turned to bring her cannon alongside the stern of the ship to strafe the *Albemarle* with no threat of being fired upon herself.

It all happened so fast. From the stern, the *Albemarle*'s captain witnessed an expert and flawlessly executed turn that would have torn the masts off a British ship in such strong winds. He was looking right down the barrel of forty-five cannons just as they exploded in near unison.

He dove to the deck, but realized that his movement was futile. In the next split second, the entire rear of his ship was cut up into splinters.

From the quarterdeck of the *Sea Dragon*, both Santos and Mathew confirmed that the giant rudder of the *Albemarle* was shattered and rendered entirely useless. Now they could focus on the oncoming *Phoenix*, though the element of surprise was no longer available.

The *Phoenix* fired one of her few forward facing cannons toward the *Sea Dragon* a half mile ahead of her. The shot fell harmlessly to the port side and the crew of the *Dragon* never flinched.

"Hard to starboard, men!" Santos yelled, as his crew scurried at blinding speed to adjust the sails and complete a rapid turn to the right, directing the *Sea Dragon* delicately around the burning *Albemarle*. The wounded British ship fired fifteen of her cannons at the odd looking ship that turned to pass on her left. The pitiful barrage was unsuccessful, as most of the shot never reached its target, and those few that did glanced harmlessly off her thick hull.

The *Phoenix* did not fire again for fear of hitting the badly damaged *Albemarle* that the *Dragon* had tactically used as a shield, but turned to her own right to head off the wide path of the privateer that was just striking her colors. The men on the advancing *Phoenix* felt a sudden rush of fear as the black flag snapped hard in the wind.

The *Phoenix* crew had witnessed the destruction of the *Albemarle* in what appeared to be only a few minutes. The *Dragon* ended its wide turn and bounded straight for the *Phoenix*, like the black knight angrily kicking his steed into attack during a joust.

Within one minute, the ships would be upon each other in accurate firing range. And that is when the crew of the *Phoenix* first heard the strange whistle seconds before the deck around them burst into flames. Several men moved to put out the flames with water, but their efforts only spread the fire further.

"Jesus!" stammered the *Phoenix*'s Captain Elliot, "The fire can't be quelled!"

"How is that possible!?" quipped his quartermaster.

There was no time to respond, for the ships pulled within firing range, and the *Sea Dragon* had the distinct advantage due to the mass confusion on the deck of her adversary. A deafening blast came from the starboard side of the *Dragon* as the *Phoenix* prepared to send their first volley.

Seconds after the blasts from the *Dragon*, the cannons of the *Phoenix* erupted to life, sending twenty-four pound shot across the fifty yard expanse to smash into the menacing pirate ship.

Once more, fate intervened as the moment the cannons fired, the *Phoenix* was at the apex of a large swell, while the *Dragon* was sliding down a trough. The privateering vessel took only minor damage, as most of the cannon balls from the *Phoenix* sailed harmlessly overhead, and missed the sails, masts and riggings.

Santos could not believe their good fortune. He was certain that it would not last.

The catapults on the deck of the *Dragon* had been reloaded

during the barrage from the *Phoenix*. More clay balls filled with Greek fire were flung toward the British war ship with great accuracy. Two shots landed on the deck, while two more smashed into the side of the third-rater. Although the deck of the *Phoenix* was itself a scene of confusion and hysteria, the real damage was below decks.

One of the earthenware orbs that rocketed toward the Royal Navy ship neither landed on deck nor smashed into her hull but actually pierced the hull by passing right through an open cannon portal.

While the sphere itself hurt no one, it exploded into hundreds of pieces against the base of the main mast. However, the resulting fire burst into life and young boys ran to the fire, thrusting buckets of water toward it to stop the fire's spread. It was only after the boys had thrown six buckets or so that they realized their unintended folly.

The increasing heat of the cannon area was unbearable. The men that labored in this part of the ship rarely left it, taking their meals and sleep in the same space in which they worked. On any ship, it was a foul smelling, congested compartment. The cannon crew was used to the cramped foul conditions, but not the intense heat of the fire and the thick, choking smoke filling their tight space.

Several of the cannon crew left their posts and pushed the young boys aside in order to get the flames under control. They performed the same water throwing operation as the boys with the same futile results. In a matter of three minutes, all the cannon crew on that particular deck abandoned their posts in order not to be burnt alive.

While the *Phoenix* tended to her escalating damage, the *Dragon* sent over volley number two. She had pulled even closer alongside the British ship, and the impact of her blasts was even more lethal. Sails, riggings, and sailors were ripped by the barrage of shot. The captain of the *Phoenix* watched helplessly. His ship was being destroyed, and flames lapped at the sky from nearly all parts of the deck. The acrid black smoke from beneath the decks was pouring out of the cannon portals and the parts of the main deck began to collapse. His ship could hold out no longer.

The captain turned to order one of the crew to raise the white flag of truce, but the words never left his mouth. He was cut in two by another blast of heated grapeshot from the *Sea Dragon*.

His demise preceded that of his ship only by seconds, for as the *Dragon* sped past the near motionless *Phoenix* into a pocket of the sea free of battle smoke, the *Phoenix* exploded in an inferno.

The battle that had started twenty-two minutes prior had ended with the *Sea Dragon* destroying two third-raters of the Royal Navy while taking hardly any damage herself. The crew of the cargo ship watched helplessly from the long boats they'd lowered into the water. Everything seemed to have happened too fast. There was no stopping the demon pirate ship. It was as though the heavily armed British fighting vessels never had a chance.

The remaining *York* crew prayed in their long boats that the *Sea Dragon* would leave as quickly as she had come. There were men in the water scrambling to reach long boats or floating debris.

The wind suddenly turned, pushing the thick black smoke to the west instead of the north. The harrowing pirate attack had ended, and the ship, which they could see was appropriately named the *Sea Dragon*, disappeared into a black curtain of smoke, ending a frightening nightmare.

†

Chapter 16: Odyssey

In the pre-dawn of her last day in England, Alison sat upright in bed and stared across the room to her east-facing window. The sky was still dark, but would slowly turn a delightful shade of charcoal grey. She could just make out silhouettes of the tall trees across the entry courtyard of the house. Soon, the most anxiously awaited day in her young life would begin. After eight years away from her beloved father, Alison Davis was finally going home. Sleep was, of course, entirely out of the question.

She found herself recalling the series of events that led to her living in London during her teens.

Her father, Benjamin Davis, had been a young and promising physician in London, but surprised his friends and family when he left his small practice in 1756 to start anew in the distant colony of Massachusetts with his loving wife and long-time best friend Rebecca. The challenge of building a thriving medical practice in the New World had always been a secret dream of the determined Benjamin. Rebecca had quickly warmed to the idea when Benjamin first discussed the concept, as the Atlantic Ocean seemed an appealing distance from his overbearing wealthy parents in London.

Over a short period of time, the Davises had become well

History

nd neither Benjamin nor
ning to England. In the
laughter and named her
the next several years,
en off far beyond what
London and the family
and happy lifestyle.

tunes, the general mood in
husetts and specifically in
There was a growing sense
ed toward King George III
and the British rami... minantly due to England's
decision to tax the colonies for revenue to be used back in
England. The newly announced Stamp Act tax was met in
Boston by angry mobs of citizens lining the streets. The first
Stamp Act Officer in Boston was threatened and so frightened
that he immediately resigned. Though the Stamp Act was
repealed the following year, it was replaced by the Townshend
Acts leading to additional taxes on numerous common items in
the colonies. A few years later, the Townshend Acts taxes were
also repealed with the notable exception of a continued tax on
tea.

In 1769, less than a month after Alison's ninth birthday,
Rebecca Davis died rather suddenly from pneumonia. It was a
very difficult year emotionally for both Benjamin and his young
daughter. At the same time, political tensions had grown to an
alarming level in Boston. Benjamin had seen firsthand – and
treated - the results of increasing public conflicts, from fisticuffs
to thrown objects and even knife wounds. The violence as well
as the absence of Rebecca led to Benjamin's concern for the
safety and proper guidance of young Alison. He began
mentioning that year that he was contemplating sending her away
from Boston until such time that the violence passed. Every time
the subject came up, Alison would end up in tears, fearing she'd
be sent away never to see her father again.

The last straw, coincidently, had come on Alison's tenth
birthday. On a nasty, bitterly cold March evening in 1770, a gang
of noisy young men began to badger the shivering British sentry

at the east end of the Old State House, not three blocks from the Davis home. What began as verbal taunts, escalated into snowballs, then stones and clubs. More British troops rushed to the scene from nearby guard posts. The mob, too, had grown as had the severity of the verbal exchanges. Within minutes, panic ensued and the soldiers opened fire on the mob, leaving five colonists dead on the frozen street and several others wounded.

Alison had heard the shots fired. Within minutes, the dining table that had previously been strewn with ribbons, cakes and toys had been replaced with two very bloody, near lifeless bodies. She watched in horror as the scene played out so quickly. She recalled not hearing the sounds of the commotion, as her eyes were fixated on the bloody humps on the dining table. The only sound that eventually pierced her silence was her father yelling at her to get upstairs and stay there.

She remembered instantly running up the stairs at full pace and shutting her door once in her room. She was crying so hard she could barely breathe. Her sobbing and gasps could not be heard downstairs over the multiple emotional exchanges over what had happened and whether the people on the table were going to live to see the next day.

It had not been her father's yelling that frightened her, nor was it the deadly and sorrowful situation that became known as *The Boston Massacre* that engulfed her otherwise festive evening. On her tenth birthday, she realized she would almost certainly be sent away from her father. The powder keg that was Boston, as Benjamin had described it to his daughter, had exploded and Alison's life would dramatically change.

She remembered the following day as an even more emotional one. Her father, fatigued from sleep deprivation and stress, reluctantly reasoned that the safest place for Alison to temporarily continue her development into a fine young woman was very far away, in the last place she wanted to go. It had been Benjamin, however, that shed the most tears during their discussion. Alison had few tears left over from the prior night. Her emotion had turned to pure hatred of England. It was the king and Parliament that vexed so many Bostonians, and it was English soldiers that were ultimately responsible for separating her from her father. She had pleaded with her father for over an hour, but ultimately resigned to his decision, as she knew his concern for her safety had been warranted.

He had written his parents who had responded that they would be pleased to take Alison in and see to her continued education and social development in London for as long as the hostilities in Massachusetts continued. They had confirmed that this was the only sensible strategy for her well being and appealed to him to return, as well. They were disappointed, though not surprised, by his polite refusal of their offer of sanctuary for himself.

From her first days away from home, she missed Boston terribly. She would often close her eyes and reminisce about walking hand-in-hand with her parents through the winding cobblestone streets near her home, the smell of freshly caught fish and the sounds of bustling crowds around the State House and Boston Common.

In 1775, she had been frightened to learn that a war in the colonies had actual begun in a battle at Lexington, not far from Boston. While she feared for her father's safety, she remained strong given the confidence exuded by her grandparents in their son's safety. They reminded her of the necessity for medical specialists in any war and that he would be well treated by both the colonists and the British. She was overjoyed to receive each letter attesting to his health. He ended each with the prayer that they would soon be reunited back home.

The second half of 1777 was perhaps the most pivotal period of the war. In the autumn, the colonial city of Philadelphia had fallen to troops under the guidance of British General Howe. At the same time, however - in Saratoga, New York – the Continental Army's General Gates had won an unlikely triumph over British General Burgoyne.

France was so impressed by the colonial spirit and impressive victory at Saratoga that it signed the Treaty of Alliance with the American colonies, officially entering the war in February, 1778.

By the spring, an immense fleet of French naval ships sailed for Boston harbor. For the first time, Benjamin Davis felt the Continental Army could possibly win the war. Interestingly, Boston – the city where the war had started - had become the safest city in the colonies, courtesy of the French navy.

Dr. Davis wrote to his parents in London, instructing them to finally send Alison home, through the English-controlled southern colonial port of Norfolk, Virginia.

Upon receipt of Benjamin's request, Mr. Davis arranged passage for his granddaughter on the *North Star*, a strong and sturdy merchant ship that would be escorted by two large British war ships delivering soldiers and supplies to the colonies. Sparing no expense and even calling in a few favors to secure special accommodations for Alison, Mr. Davis ensured her a comfortable and safe voyage home.

At dawn, four hours before their coach would depart, Alison was already downstairs nibbling on a piece of bread with a sweet marmalade spread. Her belongings, packed away in a trunk, had been brought downstairs the prior evening and placed near the entryway door.

Her grandparents had generously provided love, hospitality, and private schooling for the past eight years, as well as a much improved wardrobe of fashion as Alison's growth spurt rendered her colonial clothes useless. The two large sacks in which she had carried her belongings en route to England had since been replaced by expensive luggage.

Alison was still every bit the feisty colonial girl in her mind, but by all appearances she was a proper English lady. Local men were especially cognizant of Alison's graceful transition into maturity and beauty.

She had nearly every local male eye on her over the past four years. Though somewhat rough around the edges and perhaps a crude work-in-progress socially, there was no denying her allure and attractiveness. The deep blue eyes, radiant smile and sandy blonde hair had been there from the start. Over time, a fit and shapely body had taken the place of her thin, awkward trunk and gangly legs.

Her manner was different, too. It was clear Alison understood she had developed, as her mother had, into a beautiful young woman, but she was especially careful to show modesty to the world, while internally she could not extinguish a certain pride in her appearance.

Although never intentionally flirtatious, she had discovered that under certain circumstances, a particular glance or mere turn of her head could, for some inexplicable reason, set some young men into a whirling dervish of activity. She quickly learned she had a command over the affections of young men.

Though many competed for her attention, she was consumed with returning to Boston and did not wish to become close to any particular young suitor. Careful not to upset the delicate balance of her rising popularity, she became adept at politely declining the advances of young gentlemen without tarnishing their fragile egos.

Young gentlemen turned away by Alison Davis were numerous. Many gave up after their initial failure to win her heart, content that to remain friends was better than not knowing her at all. A few remained friends on the surface, though in secret their internal affections remained as did their hope that Alison might one day see them in a different light.

In the mid-morning, her grandfather descended the stairs quietly and slowly. He saw his granddaughter all dressed and ready to go, standing in the center of the drawing room turning a slow circle as if to memorize a 360-degree picture of the room. In her final few hours in England, Alison was suddenly nostalgic for her residence of the past several years.

She gave repeated hugs and kisses to her grandparents throughout the morning, thanking them profusely for their generosity, love and wisdom. It was perhaps a more emotional display than a properly raised young English lady should show, but it was nonetheless cherished by the grandparents.

By the late morning, young gentlemen had called upon Alison at three different intervals. They were each there in a futile attempt to reason with the young lady and convince her to stay at least a while longer in England. She was moved by their affection and sent each away with the assurance that she would not forget their kindness.

At noon, the coach arrived in front of the house and the footman proceeded to load the luggage from the entryway. Alison entered the coach, followed by her grandparents who would join her all the way to the wharf area in Dover. Unused to the emotion that was welling within them, the grandparents confided in Alison how they had originally feared the worst when she was en route from America, and how they were pleasantly surprised when she arrived.

Grandfather Davis explained that it would probably be wise to adopt an English accent on the voyage. The sailors of the naval escort would not be inclined to be so polite if they heard her colonial dialect, especially now that the result of the war was in question.

When they arrived at the Dover wharfs, Grandfather Davis made the final arrangements for Alison with the ship's captain, while Mrs. Davis and Alison shared a tearful good-bye. One last bear hug was reserved for her grandfather, who stoically resisted his tears until Alison was safely aboard the *North Star*.

Of the three vessels that sailed from Dover that day as a small convoy under the Royal Navy's Red Ensign, one was distinctly out of place. The HMS *Atlas* and the HMS *Gemini* were third-rater ships-of-the-line, measuring 180 feet from prow to stern, with three decks and 84 cannons each, while the *North Star* was built for the comfortable transport of cargo and passengers.

She was 140 feet in length, with two decks, a broader beam and no cannon ports. Her cabins were more spacious and comfortable than other ships of her class and a decided luxury compared to those of the accompanying war ships.

On this particular journey, the *North Star* had been chartered by the Royal Navy and was heavily laden with supplies for Britain's war effort in the colonies, including guns, gun powder, soldiers, and medicine.

The naval crew who sailed her was the envy of their peers. Most of the sailors had won their coveted place in a random, lottery-like drawing. Even though the men had to share cabins, it was still far better duty than to serve in traditional cramped, claustrophobic conditions on the *Atlas* or *Gemini*.

In addition to the crew, there were several civilians that had purchased passage on board the *North Star* to cross the Atlantic.

Normally, no civilians were allowed on a military vessel, yet this was a naval ship in name only. The proceeds raised from the civilian passengers' fare helped defray a sizeable portion of the trip itself, and with no established colonial navy, the only practical threat to their safety, albeit slight, was the weather.

With a trained naval crew and two large and lethal escorts accompanying her, the *North Star* provided as safe a passage as ever there was.

Beyond the stateliness and comfort of the *North Star*, there was still another reason that duty on board her was so highly coveted. One civilian in particular, a woman that would occupy a small cabin near the aft of the ship on the starboard side, was spotted coming aboard by a platoon of soldiers and sailors and caused quite a commotion.

She was uniformly described to those who had the misfortune to be below deck upon her arrival as the most physically stunning woman they had ever seen. Word spread rapidly among the crew, including the officers, that the gorgeous young lady was traveling alone.

While the crew admittedly could only dream of the pleasure of her company, some of the officers were more bold and proactive with their imagination. A series of bets were established, among many of the officers, as to who would win the heart of the fair maiden. The odds, according to the money being wagered, heavily favored one officer in particular.

Lieutenant Commander Roger Bartlett was a young officer who seemed especially mesmerized by the woman's presence. "Randy Roger," as he was known, was a handsome man with a solid physique, and he utilized – to full potential - the benefits of his attractive features. He was accustomed to taking women whenever and wherever he pleased, though his enlistment in the Royal Navy had materially set back his legendary pace of romantic conquests.

As such, enlistment had been the farthest thing on Roger's

mind - it had been the idea of his father, Lord Bartlett, famed and outspoken member of The House of Lords. His original intention had been to send young Roger off to get training in the navy for a few years, use every means of influence required to assure "safe" duty, keep him away from women, and learn if a non-distracted Roger shared any of the initiative and/or intelligence of his father.

Up until his *forced* enlistment, which he fought vociferously to no avail, his looks were seemingly his only asset. Roger had complacently resigned to never achieve or create anything on his own.

To Lord Bartlett, Roger had become something of an embarrassment over the past few years as well as a potential political liability. Recent rumors of Roger impregnating two different women caused his highly acclaimed and respected father to immediately put in place the naval enlistment concept that had originally been conceived as a last resort.

Aside from the forced enlistment, "Lord Reggie" - as Roger referred to his father - had seen to it that his son received special treatment at every turn. Roger's passage on the *North Star* was, in fact, not due to any stroke of good fortune, but rather to the far-reaching and substantial influence of his father.

Still, life at sea was no carnival for Roger. As powerful a man as Lord Bartlett was, he could not influence the weather or the sea, though he could influence events such that his son would not see any military action. Placing him on a naval frigate that continuously ran supplies to the colonies and back may not have been the most noble of duties, but since the colonies had no navy of their own, Roger was highly unlikely to come to any harm.

The only credible potential threat to Roger was the crew with whom he served. Sailors jealous of his good looks, wealthy upbringing, and family influence might consider taking out their envy of him physically. However, Roger had three things going for him that would render such threats extremely unlikely.

First, what Roger lacked in intelligence he made up for in personality. He was adept at getting most people to like him and to manipulating those who did not.

Second, he was protected by the aegis of his lineage. Even if he did not mention his famous father in order to improve his lot, which was rare, the officers had been previously apprised the crew of Roger's identity and sternly warned not to mistreat the young officer.

Finally, and perhaps most importantly, Roger had a taller and thicker-than-average build complemented by a fairly severe temper. When he didn't get his way, he was known to pitch a fit and physically strike out at things. Most of the time it was inanimate objects that incurred the wrath of his tantrums, but occasionally it was another man.

Britannia Royal Navy College had been something of a joke to Roger. He had never actually sat down in a personal interview, nor was he required to complete an entrance exam or provide references. His classmates regarded him as something of a pompous buffoon, and derided the intolerable favoritism afforded him by the Royal Navy.

His peers were comforted only by the hope that one day young Roger would end up in a situation where his famous father would not be in a position to prevent a well-deserved thrashing.

The first morning at sea found Alison Davis too timid to walk out on deck. She was aware of the distraction she'd caused upon boarding the ship the prior afternoon and was uncomfortable around the marines and sailing crew.

Captain Thadeus Harwick had introduced himself the prior evening at their supper in a private dining cabin reserved for the civilians. While pleasant, Alison's first impression was that he was perhaps too genteel and courteous to manage a crew of rugged sailors. She was careful not to judge on first impressions however, and reasoned that he was probably especially polite and accommodating with the civilians and that there was likely a different, more stern side to the captain.

At supper, Alison had politely inquired of the captain as to the best time for the civilians to take their air on deck. He responded that an officer would escort the civilians to the deck during the morning, midday, afternoon, and evening.

The hard knock on her cabin door startled Alison back to the present. One of the officers had indeed come down to the cluster of cabins occupied by the civilians on the first morning at sea and informed them he would be pleased to escort them to the deck, if they so desired.

Alison quickly and silently moved to the entrance and opened her cabin door just wide enough to steal a peek at the morning's deck escort. As a handful of civilians entered the narrow common passageway, the officer turned slightly and Alison could see he was rather tall and handsome.

She closed the door quietly in front of her and smiled to herself as the escort approached and knocked one more time on each cabin. Calling through her door that she'd be right out, she felt at ease all of the sudden. The door of the cabin opened and Alison stepped out to the common hallway. Her eyes rose slowly and met those of Lieutenant Commander Roger Bartlett.

"Good morning, Miss. You'll find it's a beautiful day on deck – a wonderful opportunity to see the ship and get some fresh air."

Though he was perfectly charming to her, Alison noticed his manner came at the expense of courtesy to the other civilians – a less than desirable characteristic, to her mind. He extended his right arm to Alison.

"Thank you, lieutenant commander, but I believe Mrs. Collins requires your arm more than I do."

Bartlett withdrew his arm, with a brief perplexed look on his face.

He led the civilians up the quarterdeck steps to the raised deck at the rear of the ship. Twelve civilians stood at the back railing and looked up to the giant clouds of sails and out to the sea. The sky was so bright that is was difficult to differentiate sky from the water's distant horizon.

Alison glanced down at the activity on deck and noticed many sets of eyes gazing back up at her. Were they staring at the entire group of passengers or just at her?

Lieutenant Commander Bartlett seemed to sense her discomfort immediately.

"All eyes fore!" yelled Bartlett. "Back to work!"

At his loud command, the movement and activity that had been momentarily interrupted begrudgingly began to build again. The reluctant crew went back to their tasks, and a sigh of relief could be felt, if not heard, from the civilians – especially Alison. The handsome escort turned back to the passengers and addressed them as one.

"I apologize for their rude stares, ladies and gentlemen. Please don't be startled or frightened. These sailors are not used to seeing civilians at sea."

It would have been more accurate to have substituted the word *ladies* for *civilians*, but the passengers appreciated his obvious delicacy.

Aside from the early glares of the crew, Alison admitted to herself that the trip up to deck had been worthwhile. The morning was beautiful and the cool air was a refreshing change from the stale, damp environment below decks.

When they returned to the civilian cabin enclave below, Lieutenant Commander Bartlett bid them a good morning and mentioned another officer would likely escort them up to deck again midday. Alison watched the escort leave and impulsively smiled. Turning around to enter her cabin, her eyes met those of Mrs. Ida Collins, who returned a broad smile back at Alison.

At midday, it was Lieutenant Chatholm that escorted the civilians to their defined area of the aft deck.

Ten minutes later, Lieutenant Commander Bartlett ambled on to the deck near the foresail, focusing his gaze over the bow for a few moments before glancing upward at the sails and riggings. It was a full five minutes before he allowed himself to nonchalantly glance backward to the aft deck.

His eyes quickly scanned the raised deck as his face registered disappointment. He blinked several times to confirm the gorgeous young blond woman was nowhere to be seen. She had consumed his every thought the past three hours. Her absence meant he would have to wait a few hours to potentially see her again, if even from a distance.

What was it about this girl that made him so emotional? She was beautiful indeed, but it was her shyness and proper manner that presented an irresistible challenge to him.

On the one hand, this could be a difficult conquest for him, and yet they were on a ship, so she was captive prey. They would sail together for approximately five weeks, and that would be ample time for him to work his charms. Relax, he told himself - *If not today, then tomorrow.*

Bartlett's momentary reflection on deck calmed his runaway pulse. He knew he needed to be more patient in order to make a good impression on the young woman. She would likely respond favorably if he pretended to be disinterested in her, though that would be difficult due to the spell she'd cast on him.

In the absence of seeing her in person, there was no harm in letting his imagination take over, as often it did. As he stood on deck, he closed his eyes and concentrated on her enticing lilac scent. He could almost see her pretty face and delicate figure. She was coming to him, arms outstretched. She reached up to pull his head closer to hers and gave him a soft kiss on his lips that quickly turned very passionate. As the kiss finished, she pulled back a half step and smiled eagerly at Roger and reached down to place his hands on her waist, as if guiding him to hold her and...

The mystical fantasy ended abruptly as two sailors scurried past to adjust the foresail rigging with the slight change in wind direction. The sailors looked back at him as he stood there with his eyes slowly opening and a deep smile on his face.

"God, I love the sea!" he exclaimed as he turned to return below deck.

The crewmen heard this and one of them shared a quip just loud enough for the other crewman to hear.

"Just wait until your first Atlantic storm, you pompous ass!"

✝

Chapter 17: Fury

Since the audacious attack on the HMS *York*, HMS *Albemarle*, and HMS *Phoenix* convoy, four other British vessels had been intercepted by the *Sea Dragon*. Unlike its initial battle, the other skirmishes were far less violent and a great horde of weapons and supplies were taken.

Word was spreading up the colonial coast of the thrashing the Royal Navy had taken several weeks prior, and it was more than lofty British pride that suffered. In addition to destroying the cargo ship *York* and her two battle-tested escorts, a winter's supply of medicine, food rations, munitions, and other basic military supplies bound for thousands of British soldiers was now resting at the bottom of the Atlantic.

Local British naval strategists made certain to warn fleets in other colonial ports as soon as possible. In the meantime, prudence dictated that cargo ships not sail without a military escort for as long as it took to hunt down and destroy the infamous *Sea Dragon*.

At dusk, six weeks following her first battle with the Royal Navy, the *Sea Dragon* sailed from a small cove in North Carolina used as a rendezvous to unload and transfer her stolen supplies to the Continental Army.

A nearly-full moon climbed slowly away from the calm sea

into the night sky. It had been Santos' wish to get out to sea in the night rather than remain in the secluded cove.

"There are no spies on the water!" he reminded his officers.

Setting a due easterly course, the *Sea Dragon* glided through the moonlit waves at a comfortable seven knots. It was one of the smoothest evenings at sea the men could recall.

Dawn saw no change in the placid sea and gentle weather. The *Sea Dragon* was fifty miles off the coast of North Carolina, and quite alone.

Two hours later, the look-out spotted a sail to the northeast. As the men on deck turned to see the ship, raising their hands to shield their eyes from the sun, Captain Santos burst out of his quarters and climbed up the raised aft deck with telescope in hand.

Mathew was already on deck studying the distant cloud-like shape through his own lens.

"What is she?" Santos asked as he located the ship and began to focus his instrument.

"Royal Navy, second rater, alone," Mathew responded in a level voice.

"How can you tell?"

"She's about 200 feet, three decks…maybe 90 cannons, and since we are in the path of the sunlight, we can presume she has seen us already, too."

"Bueno, Mateo!" Santos said, with his eye still squinting into his telescope lens.

"She's a big ship, Captain," Mathew reminded Santos.

"I can see this, Mateo. What do you suggest?"

"Stay the course and see if she turns toward us."

"And if she turns toward us?"

"We can outrun her."

"I believe we can, but why would we? As you can see, we fly a Spanish flag today. Spain is not at war with England. They will not fire upon us."

"And the name across our stern says *Sea Dragon*," Mathew pointed out. "You don't think that will get their attention? Surely, by now word about us has spread throughout the British naval controlled ports of the colonies."

"Si, but she is coming from the northeast, likely direct from England, and I do not believe word would have reached England in time for the king to send out reinforcements specifically to hunt us down. That time is at least three more weeks away.

"She's a great bloody ship!" Mathew repeated almost under his breath, which made Santos chuckle.

In the next instant, the huge Royal Navy ship suddenly turned to her left, veering toward an interception point with the *Sea Dragon*. Even at a distance of ten miles, Santos and Mathew could see it occur before the other sailors recognized it.

"British war ship, ninety-guns, just turned to intercept. Prepare to engage, but leave gun ports closed. Change the name on the stern...now!"

Santos' commands were met with an instant frenetic action among the crew. Four sailors raced to the back of the ship, pulled three large planks out from behind the pennant box and rappelled down ten feet from the stern. Placing the placards on adjustable pegs, the carved words *Sea Dragon* were covered up and replaced with the ship's new moniker, *Santa Croce*.

The HMS *Sentinel* carved through the water purposefully, with all sails raised. She shot a harmless blast well in front of the *Sea Dragon* as a universal warning to slow down, she intended to board. Mathew shot Santos a glance, which Santos did not return.

"Patience everyone, no need to panic," Santos called out. "Deck crew, prepare to invite them to board. Wear shoulder sheaths. Be hospitable. Defend yourselves if need be, but do not attack without my signal!"

Santos left the deck to quickly don his Spanish uniform, as did several of his officers.

Within a very tense twelve minutes, the huge *Sentinel* had pulled alongside the odd looking ship with a Spanish flag. Rather than politely request permission to come aboard, several British marines swung over and dropped to the deck, standing up with swords raised. None of the crew approached them, but merely stood back and raised their hands as if to suggest they would not move. After several more marines scattered across the deck, a voice called down from the English ship.

Mathew watched is disbelief as the man slowly swung across to the *Sea Dragon*. It was the same pompous captain that had nearly captured John Adams and his son John Quincy several months before. Out of the corner of his eye, Santos could see the reaction on Mathew's face.

"You know this man?" Santos whispered.

"I do, but not from the navy. He's the one that almost caught Adams at sea. He may recognize me, but only as an English professor en route to Harvard."

"You will have no trouble dispatching him?"

"None," Mathew confirmed.

The pretentious officer looked around slowly to study the Spanish crew. He looked upward and to the stern and viewed the Spanish flag.

"Habla Anglais?" he asked to a group of crewmen near the main mast, though they all shook their heads.

"Habla Anglais?" he repeated to a group of sailors on the other side of the deck, which brought the same predictable reaction.

"I speak English, Captain," Santos said, and the Royal Navy captain turned quickly to regard the man who spoke.

"Is that a fact? Well, that is indeed a relief as I'm afraid I've already used the extent of my Spanish vocabulary," he said mockingly to a few chuckles from the hard looking marines keeping their pistols and swords trained on the Spanish crew.

"The *Santa Croce* is a Spanish naval vessel, Captain. We are Spaniards. As you can see, my men did not rappel your boarding marines, though I must protest this act of aggression in the open sea."

"Silence, Spaniard!" bellowed the English captain. "You did not rappel my marines because we would have blasted your streamlined little racing sloop out of the bloody Atlantic!" he yelled at an increasing decibel with every word.

"We are not at war with England. Why do you board us?" Santos demanded.

"Of course you're not at war with England!" the captain said. "And why on earth would you be after the sheer dominance His Majesty's Royal Navy displayed in the Seven Years' War! I'm actually surprised Spain has been able to build seaworthy ships again so fast."

Santos stood firm and stared the captain down. It was a look that informed the British officer that he was neither impressed nor afraid of his English counterpart.

"As for boarding your ship, I am well within my rights as you are in British colonial waters presently!" the British captain concluded.

"We are fifty miles out to sea! What is this nonsense?!" Santos countered.

The volatile English captain looked down briefly at the deck to collect himself and seemingly prevent an eruption of temper. He raised his eyes slowly toward the Spanish captain and gestured for Santos to come forward.

Santos walked slowly toward the fuming captain. As he strode to the captain, his right hand was ready to pull his sword and thus send the signal to fight.

Mathew was ten paces behind the two captains who appeared to be discussing something privately. The English captain put his arm around Santos' shoulders in a strange friendly gesture.

Then the gun went off!

The shot from the pistol of the British captain tore through Santos's abdomen. Santos turned in disbelief to regard Mathew for a brief second before dropping to his knees and then toppling over on his side. Blood soaked rapidly through Santos' silk vest, while his eyes strained to stay open though his pain was unbearable.

Mathew lunged forward and he heard himself yell "No!", reaching Santos just as he fell to his side.

"I'm...so...sorry...my...son," Santos whispered to Mathew in Spanish. "You ... must ... des ... destroy ... ship ... do not let them ... ta ... take...fire!" Santos took the copper bracelet from his wrist and place it on Mathew's. "Pro ... pro ... tect ... the ... secret. God ... be ... with ... you."

His final words were barely audible gurgles, but the message was clear to Mathew, who knelt, stunned, on the bloody deck.

A sea of anger welled within him. Through his rage, his mind instantly concentrated on the situation. English naval officers had killed both of the men he loved as father figures.

"Do I know you?" barked the English captain standing above the kneeling Mathew and the dead Santos. He leaned over to get a better look at Mathew. "Show me your face!"

"I will," Mathew spoke slowly and in well-bred English, "so you will look on the man that is going to end your miserable life!"

"You!" the British captain gasped.

In that moment, Mathew gained the upper hand, for as the captain's eye's met his, he did not see Mathew pull Santos's dagger from its sheath.

Mathew sprang upwards like a tiger and cut through the English officer's belly before anyone on deck could fathom what had just happened.

In that instant the Spanish crew who were still holding their hands up high, reached behind their heads to the guns holstered across their shoulder blades, pulled them down and fired at point blank range. Fifteen British marines lay dead on the deck, and seven more were seriously wounded.

From the crow's nest, several clay balls were tossed onto the deck of the HMS *Sentinel*, sending its crew scurrying to put out the fire.

In the time it took for the remaining marines to react, Mathew had drawn his own two swords and cut down three more men.

Two more marines stood in front to challenge him but were quickly back-peddling for their lives. The two swords Mathew wielded were flying with such an amazing speed that neither man could concentrate on his thrusts. The morning sun glinted off of the blades. It looked as though they were on fire.

Another marine raised his rifle and took careful aim at Mathew.

"Click" was the only sound from the misfiring gun.

Mathew jumped forward and stabbed the two sailors foolish enough to challenge him. With his swords still in their bodies he released the hilts and spun a three-quarter turn, pulling a throwing knife in his right hand and letting it fly, burying it deep into the stomach of the disbelieving rifleman.

Officers on the deck of the *Sentinel* yelled to push away from the ship. Mathew knew that they would open their gun ports if they got a safe distance away from the *Sea Dragon*. The pirate ship would have no answer for the barrage that the *Sentinel* would lay.

"Tie up the ships!" he yelled to his crew in Spanish. "Don't let them pull away or we'll die. Jump to their deck and take the fight to them!"

Eerie yells arose from the Spanish crew as they swung over to the *Sentinel*. The British defense was not adequate enough to rappel the Spaniards as the Englishmen were confused and busy fighting the fire that was consuming nearly half their deck and reaching up their masts to their sails.

Mathew was in front of the charge. Still wielding his two swords, he thrust at any man that would stand near him. He cut down four sailors before shots rang out above his head and one of his own men, Barones, pulled him down to safety.

The sound of steel cutlasses clashing filled the air, and Mathew was nowhere near quelling his raw anger. He spied two sailors racing toward the battle on deck with pistols at the ready. Timing his lunge perfectly he jumped up and grabbed the closer man's forearm turning it toward the other man and firing. The other man in turn saw him pop up and turned to shoot but ended up shooting his colleague, who had just shot him.

Meanwhile, the fire was eating through the top of the mainmast and there was only a minute or two before she would topple over, possibly onto the deck of the *Sea Dragon*. Six *Dragon* crewmen fought their way to the hatch openings of the gun docks below, emptying an entire sack full of small clay hand bombs into the crowded gun ports. The fire soon spread around the gun ports on the second level of the big ship. The gun ports opened to allow the smoke to escape the cramped space where oxygen was nearly gone.

As the port doors opened, a shower of rifle shots from the already opened gun ports of the *Sea Dragon* rained out across the space of no more than ten feet.

The mainmast gave a loud crack that signaled it was nearly burnt through. Had there been any strong wind to speak of that morning, it would have already snapped.

Mathew barked the order for everyone to get back to their ship. Even as the last Spanish crewmen sailed over to the *Sea Dragon*, shots were still being fired from rifles across the decks. As the crew cut the ropes that bound the two ships loosely, the *Sea Dragon* had already raised its sail and was away from the *Sentinel* free and clear.

The mainmast of the *Sentinel* broke in two, sending a rain of flames and wood down onto the burning deck littered with dead bodies. The mighty HMS *Sentinel*, that had served so gallantly in two previous wars was rendered immobile and would likely sink within a half hour.

Mathew looked around and saw that the vast majority of the crew was intact. He also noticed that the gunners manning the catapults were lining up for the killing shot. They turned at the last second to look at him, believing he might wave them off as the *Sentinel* was defenseless.

"Fuego!" barked Mathew, with a sword in his right hand held high. "Por Santos!"

The *Sea Dragon* unleashed what would soon become known around Atlantic maritime circles as *dragon's breath.* As she sunk, the once proud *Sentinel* continued burning. A tremendous concussion erupted from the water as the fire reached the explosives stores just as the ship dropped below the waterline.

Mathew fell to his knees on the deck where Santos lay dead. Exhausted, he reached his arms upward and looked to the smoke filled sky, crying out in English, "Why?!"

By nightfall, the *Sea Dragon* was within ten miles of the American coast again. Mathew was busy penning a letter to the British Admiralty, denouncing the aggressive posturing in international waters of a foreign ship that they had witnessed. So profound was the dereliction of appropriate diplomatic custom, that the *Sea Dragon* proudly intervened and destroyed the HMS *Sentinel*, leaving no survivors.

A knock at the doorway of the opened captain's door brought Mathew back to the present. Barones walked in and sat down.

"I am very sorry for the loss of Santos, Quicksilver. He was a great, great man. But we still have a mission to complete. He would say this if he were here."

"He was like a father to me, Barones. I knew this mission was dangerous, but I never thought he would die."

"He clearly loved you very much, Quicksilver. I think he would agree with what I was sent to tell you."

Mathew looked quizzically at Barones as the hard faced Spaniard began to speak again.

"The crew has elected a new captain. I am pleased to say that it was unanimous," Barones said as he stood to salute Mathew. "We chose you to lead us, Quicksilver!"

Mathew pushed himself to his feet. "Are you all crazy?! I acted stupidly out there. It was pure rage that consumed me. You want that quality in a captain?"

"You saved us all, and defeated a mighty war ship. You were smart enough to command us to pull closer rather than break apart during the battle. That alone saved all our lives most likely."

"You don't know what you're doing, putting me in charge," Mathew pleaded.

"I think we do. You are the best fighter, and you understand the enemy inside and out. I used to not think that was important. Santos told me it was. Now I believe it."

"Then I will accept the captaincy on one condition."

"What is that, Quicksilver?"

"That you all vote again in two days. Let the emotions of today die down and vote with a clear conscience. If I'm chosen then, I will serve as you wish."

"Ahh, you see? That is what the men said you might say. We will do as you ask, for it is wise."

†

Chapter 18: Ungrateful Attention

It was three full days before Lieutenant Commander Roger Bartlett got another glimpse of the young Alison Davis. The duration between sightings was so long it was nearly unbearable to the infuriated sailor. Had he a natural method of running into her each day, he might have been sated by the brevity of her few appearances, but now nothing short of his fantasy seemed to suffice. He was literally haunted by the woman, and he despised not being in a position of control.

At the end of the first week at sea, she partook of an escorted deck sojourn with eight other civilians. Roger was with two other officers guiding the raising of the foresail when the civilians appeared on deck far behind them. It was evident that the civilians had emerged because the crewmen raising the sail, as one, momentarily turned and scanned the back of the boat. Roger did not turn around, tired at being disappointed. But the smiles that crossed the faces of the crewmen told Roger that Alison had made one of her rare deck appearances, for they would never react that way to the matronly Mrs. Ida Collins, no matter how long at sea.

Roger again elected not to turn. Surely she was there and surely she would notice the lone person not gawking at her. If there was one thing of which Roger Bartlett was confident, it was his ability to stand out in a crowd.

Once the foresail was adjusted, it was all Roger could do not to turn and look at Alison. What was the probability that she would look at him the moment he stole a peek at her? All too high, Roger recalled from his past exploits utilizing the rare *disinterested* strategy. It was a delicate game he played, for he didn't want his avoidance of her to be obvious. His natural path was back to the aft deck after the foresail was adjusted, but he took his time and closely examined the rigging along the port side of the ship as he made his way to the stern.

Alison was enjoying the midday air, having ventured to deck only once in the past several days. The glare of the overhead sun was a welcome distraction. She raised a hand to shield her vision and stared out across the ocean, wondering when they would see land again. With her hand still raised to her eyes, she allowed herself to look out at the sea of activity on the deck. She saw some sailors looking back at her, but for the most part, they were busy adjusting sails or cleaning the deck.

One of the officers was directing them to do something to the sail. His arms pointed to various parts of the rigging as he talked them through their exercise. Though he never turned around, Alison recognized it was Roger Bartlett, who had escorted the civilians to deck the first full day at sea. She realized she had not seen him since that time but didn't dwell on the thought.

Her thoughts followed her gaze upward to the sails themselves, to the man in the crow's nest, and eventually to the clouds and sky above. She dropped her hand from shielding her vision, closed her eyes, and enjoyed the warmth of the midday sunshine on her face. With her eyes closed, her other senses were heightened. The salty smell of the sea air filled her nose, and she felt the sturdy push of the cool wind from the starboard side of the vessel sweeping across the deck of the ship.

After a few moments, she joined a conversation with two of the older civilians who were standing near the very stern of the ship, Henry Foster and Ida Collins. They were discussing their recollection of the town of Boston, and were impressed at how much the young Alison Davis knew of the colonial city. After somewhat aghast stares from her elders, she confided that she'd actually been in Boston before. Both Mr. Foster and Mrs. Collins still couldn't believe that one visit could have such an indelible impact on a young English girl.

It was an awkward moment for Alison who suddenly became conscious of perhaps sharing too much information with the other civilians. She recalled how her grandfather had admonished her not to speak with her normal American dialect and not to tell anyone she was from Boston.

Just then, two of the young officers climbed the stairs of the raised aft deck. One was Lieutenant Commander Bartlett. Alison was saved by the distraction. She wanted to leave the conversation immediately and saw her opportunity.

"Good day, Lieutenant Commander Bartlett," she blurted out, hoping to draw the other civilians into a new conversation. "Are we still on course and on schedule?"

"I beg your pardon, Miss," responded Bartlett as he turned toward the direction of the voice, apparently not hearing the question.

"I asked if we're still on course and on schedule," she repeated, now looking directly into his eyes from ten feet away.

"Yes to both, Miss. But there is still a lot of ocean ahead of us," he replied. "Is everyone comfortable on the voyage so far?" he asked to the other civilians. They all nodded appreciatively.

"Mrs. Collins, you look beautiful today. Sea travel obviously agrees with you!" Bartlett harmlessly flirted.

"And Mr. Foster, you just let me know when you're ready for that shift in the crow's nest," he joked, as the other civilians, including Mr. Foster himself, began to chuckle heartily.

Alison was glad to have had the conversation on Boston interrupted so seamlessly by the young officer. She returned her gratitude with a smile.

With Alison's innocent gesture imprinted in his mind and confident that he'd improved his chances with the young woman, Roger Bartlett begged the forgiveness of the collective civilians and returned to his responsibilities on deck. Years of experience had taught him that it was better to leave the conversation early - and on good standing - rather than risk boring or losing his audience. It was a most difficult task, but he didn't dare risk the good will he'd just built up with Alison.

In her smile, he felt what he assumed to be her undeniable attraction to him. Soon he would be able to make a more direct and romantic advance.

The supper that evening was rather uneventful in every detail but one. Roger Bartlett walked in as the civilians were finishing their meal, asking everyone if the food and accommodations were still acceptable.

As he worked his way around the table, he was careful to make eye contact with each and every diner. He patted some of the males on the shoulders gregariously. To some of the women, he bowed graciously before moving on to speak to the next person.

He finally got to Alison and, with all eyes in the room on him, and all conversations quieted, he made his romantic move.

"Good evening, Miss Davis."

"Oh...Good evening, Lieutenant Commander Bartlett."

"How was your dinner this evening?" he asked nonchalantly.

"Very agreeable, thank you."

"Good. I wonder if you would care to join me on deck for an evening stroll."

"No, thank you, Lieutenant Commander," Alison responded. "I am quite tired and wish to retire to my cabin directly."

The conversations hastily began again. Alison turned to Ida Collins and bade her a restful evening before standing.

"Then I shall escort you, Miss Davis," Bartlett said. Alison turned to face him.

"That won't be necessary, Lieutenant Commander. It is but a few strides away from this salon."

"It is no trouble, ma'am," he called out as he pursued her to the doorway.

Alison left the salon with Bartlett in tow. The civilians looked at one another and smiled. It was clear to them that Roger

Bartlett was attracted to the beautiful young lady. They also presumed that Alison was probably infatuated with the handsome young officer, but was so shy as to turn away from the attention he gave her. They began their traditional round of port wine before retiring to sleep.

Alison strode across the short stretch of wooden planks that separated the salon from her cabin. Confident that they were away from earshot, Bartlett sped past her and attempted to cut off her path.

"Miss Davis, I apologize for my forwardness in the salon, but I just wanted a word with you."

"I'm really rather tired, Lieutenant Commander," she replied matter-of-factly. "Please, excuse me." She sidestepped him, but he jumped in front of her.

"Miss Davis, the voyage is coming to a close soon and I wanted to formally offer my assistance to you at its conclusion."

"No, thank you, Lieutenant Commander," she responded somewhat curtly. "I'm sure one of the crew can ably carry my luggage to the dock."

"You misunderstand, Miss Davis. I offer my services as a guide and guardian. America can be a barbaric land and most colonists are essentially animals and not to be trusted. It would do well for such a beautiful young lady to have an experienced escort at her side."

As he spoke, Bartlett moved closer to Alison and placed his hands on her waist.

Alison stood rigid, then quickly removed Bartlett's hands from her body.

"What did you just say…about America?" she asked.

"Well, ma'am, I fought in Boston earlier in the war," Bartlett lied in order to sound experienced about Americans. "Trust me, colonial rebels have no respect for women and might treat a young English lady very badly. I'm not certain you fully comprehend what type of environment you are about to enter in America."

His ploy to offer himself as her guardian would either be welcomed by the girl if she was suitably frightened by his coloring of Boston, or refused politely. Either way, he was sure that this protective tact would produce at least gratitude and, possibly, bring them together in a tender moment for a kiss.

"And you really fought in Boston?" Alison responded as if accepting his word as the truth.

"Absolutely, the rebels were relentless, but we put them down all right!"

"Were you part of any of the battles near the St. George River or the Old South Church?"

"Miss Davis," he replied while slowly shaking his head from side to side, "I killed seven men in a fierce battle along the St. George, and I was nearly killed myself near the Old South Church."

Alison Davis stared at him for several seconds. When she finally spoke, it was with clarity and conviction.

"Lieutenant Commander Bartlett, first of all, it is clear to me that you have never actually been to Boston. The river is called the *Charles* River and the church is The Old *North* Church. Furthermore, if I were to walk with you anywhere in America, I would be *more* of a target of derision, not less so. You and your brutal red-coat colleagues are not welcome in America, which you wouldn't know because you've never been there before. Trust me! *You* would be the target, not me! And finally, Lieutenant Commander, and more directly to the point - I am not remotely interested in you. Now, leave me alone!"

Bartlett did not move. His face flushed red at being caught in the lie. More than her rebuke, it was her tone that rattled him. In her anger, she had unknowingly let down her guard and, in so doing, her English accent.

"Very well, Miss Davis. I apologize and bid you a pleasant night," he said, his voice under his command, though he was still seething inside.

His discovery of her colonial identity would certainly change everything in his interaction with the girl. It was bad enough to be so coldly refused by a refined British lady, and quite another by a pretentious colonial harlot. He moved aside to let her pass and stood at attention.

She opened the cabin door and entered without returning a courteous "good evening". Without turning to face him again, she slammed the door.

Alison turned the lock and collapsed on the bed. She stared at the door envisioning Bartlett still standing outside. The mere sight of the man would, from now on, make her blood boil.

Alison presumed that he had usually had his way with just about any female he set out to conquer. Unfortunately, her own general coldness and outright dismissals had only seemed to encourage him to redouble his efforts. It had reached the point where Alison was becoming fearful of the man. He was conniving, treacherous and persistent.

Before falling asleep that evening, she was resolute to report her concerns to Captain Harwick immediately the next morning.

- Alison meets Bartlett
- Bartlett lies about being to America
- Alison ends their relationship

✝

Chapter 19: Confrontations

Alison's complaint about Bartlett directly to Captain Harwick was delivered lucidly, but with enough emotion that the captain of the ship fully appreciated the severity of the matter.

Harwick was aware of Bartlett's legendary reputation for womanizing and actually found it refreshing that the pompous cad had finally suffered ignominious defeat. However, he internally cursed his bad luck to have been stuck with Lord Bartlett's son on the voyage, and the young officer's stupidity that led to this awkward predicament. The formal complaint lodged by the civilian woman warranted the captain's delicate involvement.

The captain courteously acknowledged Alison's assertions, apologized on behalf of the Royal Navy, and promised to see that Bartlett would be kept away from her. This solution sent the agitated young lady back to her cabin openly skeptical, but reluctantly satisfied.

Alison's grandfather had made it clear that she was to be afforded privacy and protection on the trans-Atlantic voyage. Harwick had personally accepted a sizeable purse to ensure her safe and comfortable passage. Thus, the ship's highest officer felt responsible for the young girl. On the other hand, Bartlett would certainly not take well to any admonishment, the consequences of which - Harwick feared - would involve the influential Lord Bartlett altering his own, suddenly cloudy, future at sea.

A hard knock at the door jolted the captain out of his quiet reflection. The attending sailor ushered Bartlett into the sizeable cabin, turned and left, closing the door behind him.

"Lieutenant Commander Bartlett, good morning. Do you know why I've summoned you here today?"

"No, Captain. But I'm most anxious to discover why?" Bartlett gave a world-weary sigh. Harwick could not be certain, but he accepted the statement as blunt and highly inappropriate sarcasm. There were two distinct ways to address the issue, he thought, and Roger Bartlett was in essence requesting the rougher version.

"You're here this morning because I've listened to a formal passenger complaint lodged against you."

"May I remind the captain that this is a military vessel, chartered by the Royal Navy and under British naval control. As far as I'm concerned, the civilians are not even here."

"Lieutenant Commander Bartlett, Miss Alison Davis has lodged a formal complaint about your general conduct and unwanted advances."

"Ridiculous! I've made no advances whatsoever toward the woman."

"There was no mistaking her tone today, Lieutenant Commander! And since I wasn't there to witness the interaction between you two I've elected to relieve you from civilian escort duty for the duration of this voyage."

Bartlett didn't respond at first, though the captain could see the flare of temper in his eyes. The young officer didn't dare complain about the captain's arrangement. For if he complained, Bartlett knew it would appear that he was emotionally charged and that the woman's accusations were well founded. Even Roger Bartlett grasped his precarious position and maintained a moderate tone in front of his superior.

"It is most unfortunate," he began, "that Ms. Davis makes such an ugly accusation. I cannot understand where she has misread my intentions. However, I am only too willing to abide by your order and will happily stay clear of the woman, as well as the other civilians. Annoying post anyway, if you ask me…playing nurse maid to a group of non-military personnel."

Harwick was surprised and somewhat relieved to hear Bartlett handle the matter so maturely. This would be the end of it, he thought, and he could continue his unremarkable career in the Royal Navy without fear of reprisal from Roger Bartlett's influential father. He was confident that if Lord Bartlett himself were present, he would have approved of the private and non-punitive handling taken by the captain.

Roger Bartlett left the captain's quarters calmly, but he seethed in the short hallway outside that led to the main deck. His boundless temper was close to eruption.

It took the utmost restraint for Roger Bartlett to return to his berth on the *North Star* and not make an argumentative stop at Alison Davis' cabin. Anger had taken the place of his raw lust for the attractive young lady. Reassigned to regular naval duties, his temper was barely controlled whenever the thought of Alison crossed his mind.

A full week later, in hindsight, the captain's private reassignment enabled Bartlett to maintain his dignity among the crew, for he comfortably lied that he was no longer interested in the woman. Most had inferred from his tone that this could only mean that he'd already had the woman. It was very much in Roger's character to completely lose interest in a female, no matter how beautiful, once the conquest was complete.

That evening, Bartlett and two other officers oversaw the navigation and sailing. The howling winds had the *North Star* bounding mightily over the rolling Atlantic swells. It was difficult for the crew to maintain a steady course under such conditions, and required Bartlett's undivided attention. Engaged in commanding the sailing crew that evening, Bartlett glanced backward only once, to see how the sailor was holding up guiding the huge vessel through the turbulent sea.

It was in that unfortunate instant that he saw Alison Davis on the raised aft deck behind the struggling helmsman. Lieutenant Mullins stood next to her closely and she was wearing his coat as protection against the cold sea winds.

Mullins had just placed the coat on her shoulders and, for only that brief moment, clasped a hand on each of her shoulders. It was an innocent motion that served to convey that it was draped about her frame appropriately and would not fall off. He meant it no other way – and she did not think otherwise.

He immediately stood back away from Alison, but this was not seen by Bartlett, who had turned instantly toward the foredeck upon seeing the man's hands on Alison. His expression was one of disbelief, and the image of Mullins' grasp of the beautiful girl was indelibly imprinted on his frantic mind.

Alison Davis lay in her bed later than evening, content that her grievance lodged with the captain had kept the annoying Bartlett at bay, though she wondered how long it would last. Whatever had been said to the persistent Lieutenant Commander, the effect was powerful.

She realized that he had seen Lieutenant Mullins place the coat on her shoulders that evening and yet there was neither a glaring stare nor awkward recognition. Since she had gone to the captain, Alison felt her complaint might actually have made things worse. Content enough that she was safe from provocative stares and advances in her locked room, she allowed herself to drift into a joyful dream of Boston.

Now a little more than a week outside of Norfolk, Virginia, she concentrated and could recall the smell of her home town, and the faces of the people that she happily remembered. She was forced to keep up with news of New England from decidedly slanted British journalism, for her father dared not risk including very much mention of the war in his correspondence with his daughter overseas.

Alison wondered sadly not *if*, but *how many* of the people she knew had perished at the hands of the overpowering British military, fearing it would be a depressingly high number. As she felt herself drifting off to sleep, Alison felt she could hear the thunder of shells exploding all around her neighborhood. The pounding sounds increased even though she tried to block them out.

Boom, boom, boom!

She startled herself awake breathing heavily – what an eerie dream to have made her jump!

Boom, boom, boom!

Then she realized it was no dream that produced the noise. Someone was pounding on her cabin door.

Still drowsy, she stumbled to the door and opened the lock. For a split second, her faculties sharpened, and she regretted unlocking the door, but before her hand could correct her mistake it was already too late.

The door burst open and slammed into her hard, sending her flying backward to the cabin floor.

In strode an enraged and somewhat drunk Roger Bartlett, who casually closed the door and locked it behind him before Alison recovered enough to understand what was going on. He reached down with his powerful arms and picked her up as though she was a small batch of straw. Though still dazed, she could feel the vice-like strength of his grip on her upper arms.

"How dare you go to Harwick and have me admonished like a little school boy!" he hissed through clenched teeth.

"Leave me alone!" Alison pushed against him.

"Oh, I'll leave you alone alright…just as soon as I've taught you a lesson! And you'd better keep your damn trap shut about this or I'll see to it that you vanish over the bulwark, tramp!"

Alison was fully alert now and completely frightened.

She screamed as loud as she possibly could, but the closed doors of the cabins muffled the sound that barely registered over the shrill of the piercing wind surrounding the ship.

As the breath required for her scream purged the last bit of air from her lungs, the back of Roger Bartlett's right hand connected squarely with the right side of her face. She flew backward again, this time landing on the bed just a few feet behind her.

Before her mind could register, Roger Bartlett was on top of her, straddling her waist and holding her arms down to the bed.

He kissed her sloppily. The repulsed Alison spit bloody saliva in his face. Enraged, he released his grip on her arms and ripped open her nightgown. Alison screamed, but again to no avail.

Roger stared down at her with hot eyes. "I've always wondered what a colonial girl tastes like!"

Just as he was set to pounce, the locked door behind him burst open, sending splinters of wood in all directions.

Before he was able to turn his large frame, a thick rope was thrown around his neck and yanked aggressively.

It was Roger Bartlett that flew backward this time, landing awkwardly and painfully on his head and shoulders. Instantly collecting his wits and rising to his feet to fend off the intruder, he pulled at the tightened rope around his neck and stood erect. He was facing two soldiers with their rifles trained on his upper torso from barely four feet away.

A voice behind them shouted, "Shoot to kill if he makes even one move!"

The look on the faces of the soldiers was unmistakable – seemingly willing the loathsome officer to make a desperate movement. Even in his inebriated state, Roger Bartlett seemed to know that nothing would please these soldiers more than to kill him on the spot.

◆

When word reached Rear Admiral Christopher Fairchild, the Royal Navy admiral with direct responsibility for the southern colonial region, of the destruction of his nephew's naval vessel and theft of valuable war supplies that were desperately needed by British forces, he responded with a thundering barrage of expletives that shook the walls of his Charleston, South Carolina office.

"Let me understand this clearly," he bellowed toward the commanding fleet officer that delivered the news. "We lost another of His Majesty's prize ships-of-the-line to a band of pirates? And without firing a single damned shot? Please do explain to me how the hell something like that is possible!"

"According to reports, admiral, his ship spotted a rather

strange looking ship flying Venetian colors. Captain Charleton and thirty of his best soldiers boarded the ship without incident, but were ambushed silently by Quicksilver and his crew."

"Quicksilver!? Again?"

"I'm afraid so, Admiral. He's intercepted and destroyed dozens of vessels around the southern and mid-colonial coasts, including nine ships-of-the-line, counting the *Courageous*."

"Commander, I was under the impression that we were outfitting our war ships these days with cannons!" Fairchild barked.

"The pirate attack was by stealth and occurred within seconds, according to the few survivors," the commander explained, disregarding the belligerent tone of the admiral.

"Where's Henry now?"

"I'm very sorry, Admiral...Henry is dead, apparently killed by Quicksilver himself."

The admiral began to slowly shake his head in disgust and confusion. "It just doesn't make sense! How could a pirate crew overpower an elite troop of Royal Marines without a sound?"

"High tension cross-bows, Admiral. They killed the boarding party and the ship's lookout without a sound."

"Very well." The admiral nodded his head as though the approach to catching and eliminating Quicksilver were suddenly clear to him, "I shall pull some of our best war ships to track and run this Quicksilver bastard to ground. We'll catch him, Commander! By God, we'll catch him! And I will not rest until I see his limp body swing from the yardarm over this port."

◆

After transferring the huge and valuable cargo of supplies from the HMS *Courageous* through one of the pre-established secret revolutionary channels, the crew of the *Sea Dragon* had earned a night off on board the ship as well as a delicious dinner courtesy of the Argonaut Inn's proprietor.

Across the small, hidden cove and up on the land, Mathew and five of the crew sat finishing their dinner in the moderate dining room of the inn. It was a quiet evening and they were the only patrons in the inn.

Four of the sailors gradually pushed themselves from the table and stood, informing Mathew they would return back to the ship. With a quick nod from the big Englishman, they turned and left while Mathew and Barones stayed behind to settle their charges for the evening's meal as well as the replenished food supplies for the ship.

Mathew walked to the back of the room and politely summoned the proprietor.

The Argonaut's proprietor was absent at the moment, but his wife responded to Mathew's call. She was every bit as loyal to the cause as her husband and offered the evening's meal as gratitude for their dangerous service.

Ever the gentleman, Mathew thanked her for her family's gesture but politely refused and placed a small velvet pouch of coins in her hand.

"God bless you, sir," she said before turning to leave the dining room.

Just then, the entrance to the inn burst opened, as though kicked hard from the outside.

The frightened proprietor's wife looked up at Mathew and slowly sank behind the oak beamed bar. Mathew didn't turn around. He knew by the woman's reaction that there were British soldiers standing in the entrance's door frame. The only question was how many.

He glanced down at the woman crouching behind the bar and calmly whispered the question. As the men stormed into the dining room, she quickly peeked around Mathew's bulk and sank back into her position of relative safety on the floor. She held up three fingers.

Barones was the lone patron the soldiers could see. They approached him assuming Barones to be the wait staff. By their loud and rude manner, Mathew could tell they were standing together in the middle of the room.

"Fetch us ale, boy!" yelled one of the soldiers.

"C'mon, boy, move your ass! We're thirsty," said another.

Barones nervously glanced toward Mathew at the bar. His command of English was rather poor, and although he understood the command for "ale" and that they had mistaken him for the proprietor, he was frozen with anxiety.

"Ale, now!" commanded the first soldier, with a thundering voice that seemed to shake the very beams of the small tavern.

"Si, ale!" Barones answered in a rather poor attempt to remain calm. The soldiers stared at Barones as his verbal response betrayed his Spanish heritage.

"Well, what have we got here?" said the thunder-voiced soldier, now frighteningly calm in his speech. "We've found ourselves a little Spaniard! A bit far north of Spanish territory aren't you?"

The soldier eyed Barones from head to toe and back again. "And what a portly little fellow. All of a sudden I believe I'm hungry for some Spanish pig! What shall we do with him boys? Slice him up here or take him back to the regiment?"

Scouts thought Mathew, and there was no telling how far ahead of their regiment these soldiers were.

The goading laughter from the other two soldiers told Mathew there was no chance of avoiding trouble. He silently cursed the situation and the lack of warning from his carefully established spy network. He had to do something fast.

Barones could not understand the words, but their tone and intentions were translated instantly. He very slowly reached for the sword sheathed at his side. The collective eyes of the soldiers picked up the almost imperceptible movement of his hand and noticed the hilt of his sword. They instantly drew their swords.

"None of that, Spaniard! Touch that sword and we'll slice you up right here!"

Mathew could wait no longer. He burst into what sounded like drunken laughter, though still facing away from the soldiers, calling attention to himself from across the room.

Only one of the soldiers took his eyes off Barones and regarded the hairy slumped man at the bar. By the awkward position of his legs, the soldier could see the man would have fallen over and passed out if not for the bar itself propping him up.

"Slishe...Shlishe him up...hee hee hee...we're go...going to have a pig roast! Hee hee!" bellowed Mathew.

"Shut up, drunkard! Leave this establishment at once!"

"But I...I haven't fin...finished my ale..." Mathew stammered slowly, buying time as he secretly pulled a throwing knife from the inside of his coat.

"Leave at once I say! I am a lieutenant in His Majesty's Army and I order you to leave!" This time the command closely approached the thundering voice Mathew had heard before.

"But I...I haven't...finished my..." Mathew purposely knocked over a half-empty ale tankard that clattered to the floor.

The tense situation turned comical for a brief moment as Mathew's gasp feigned tragic loss at his precious spilled drink. The soldiers laughed.

"You've finished your drink now. So go, drunkard!"

"But I...don't want to go...I want...I want to watch you roasht...roasht...the pig!"

"Last chance to leave, drunkard! Either out that door this instant or in a coffin! I really don't care which!"

Mathew heard the other two soldiers quickly beseech their comrade not to continue his present course of action - from the sound of the hammer being pulled back on a pistol Mathew deduced he was about to be shot in the back.

In the next split second, Mathew pivoted to face the soldier and in the same motion let fly the throwing knife which struck instantly and deeply into the soldier's upper chest. The movement was so quick and precise that the man had barely enough time to register surprise before the knife had plunged into his body, killing him instantly.

His eyes were wide open in shock as he stiffly fell backwards, while the reflexes in his fingers fired the pistol harmlessly into the oak ceiling beams of the dining room just before his body hit the floor.

Before the other two soldiers could react, Barones had drawn his sword as had Mathew. The soldiers registered both confusion and fear when they saw the large size and dexterity of the man presumed to be drunk only a few seconds prior.

Mathew approached slowly with a sword in his left hand. His right hand was raised with another throwing knife ready to fly.

"Not a sound, gentlemen," Mathew commanded in a quiet,

level tone. The soldiers froze.

"Sheath your swords, lay your pistols and dispatch bag on the table and leave. If I wanted to kill you, you would already be dead."

The soldiers briefly glanced at the corpse that had been their colleague a moment prior. They shook their heads and backed away toward the door ever so gradually.

"Don't try to leave, gentlemen. Your friend's gunshot will have brought more of my men to the tavern. If you open that door with swords in your hand, you will be killed. I will spare your lives if you lay down your weapons quietly right now."

The soldiers continued moving backwards toward the door, with increasing fear in their eyes.

"Touch that door and I will kill you!" warned Mathew. "Don't be stupid! You don't have to die."

The soldier closest to the door grabbed the handle behind him and threw open the large door. Mathew's hand came down in a blur and the man at the door dropped to his knees like a dead weight, clutching the hilt of the throwing knife now lodged into his neck.

The third soldier dropped his sword and ran outside. Mathew and Barones immediately gave chase, but the soldier was already striding his horse and leading his comrades' horses when the two pirates exploded out of the inn's doorway.

In a moment, the soldier would be gone. By the morning, the town would likely be razed in search of those responsible for the death of two British military scouts.

Mathew stood motionless outside the inn. There were no other horses around and the man was nearly out of sight.

They would have to act quickly now, as the hunters became the hunted. A whirlwind of thought crossed Mathew's mind as he watched the horse gallop away in the dusk. Get rid of the bodies. Weigh anchor and sail away as fast as possible. He had no idea how many soldiers were following behind this scouting detail. It could be only a few and a very long ways off, or hundreds on the edge of town. He realized then the flaw in his spy network – it was rendered useless at night due to darkness.

Just then shots rang out from rifles about twenty feet or so behind them. The unexpected blasts made Mathew and Barones jump. Neither was hit, though Mathew was certain he heard the whiz of bullets as they flew past his head.

Both turned slowly to face the riflemen, hands extended high in the air, reluctantly accepting that the next shots would not miss.

~Mathew fights
off British
soldier

~Alison is
attacked

†

Chapter 20: Three Kings

"*Got* him in the shoulder!" claimed the first rifleman.

"Lower middle back" bragged another.

"The neck," said the third in a smug tone that suggested he'd won some sort of competition.

The three men concluded congratulating each other and approached a very confused Mathew. They spoke in a colonial dialect and carried extended-length hunting rifles.

"Evening. Saw you were in a bit of trouble with that red-coat so we took care of it for you. Hope we didn't startle you," said one of the riflemen.

"I beg your pardon," asked Mathew, careful to change his accent to colonial. "You just said you took care of it for us?"

"Yeah. Shot the bastard dead!" said another of the riflemen with a wide grin.

Mathew turned to look at Barones, then looked out into the distance of the evening. He could see nothing.

"He's about 150 yards ahead; fell off his horse to the right. He's dead," confirmed the third man looking out into the same darkness as Mathew.

Mathew instructed Barones in rapid Spanish to run down the road and confirm the riflemen's bold claim. He then turned to the three men and noticed a similarity in each of their faces.

Probably brothers he presumed.

"If he's 150 yards away, how could you have possibly hit him?" asked Mathew.

The three men smiled and gently patted the rifles in their hands without saying a word.

At this point, several of the crew of the *Sea Dragon* came bursting out of the nearby bushes, brandishing pistols and swords. The three riflemen stood very still, their bravado instantly washed from their faces, and replaced with an ashen color.

Mathew quickly ordered the crew in Spanish to lower their weapons and explained that the men were not a threat, and may have greatly assisted a moment ago. As the crew lowered their weapons, the riflemen gave Mathew an appreciative nod.

Mathew asked the men who they were.

"We're Joseph, Jeremy and James King. We are part of a detachment of Pennsylvania rifleman serving in the Continental Army up north. We've been sent down here on special assignment."

Just then, Barones sprinted back to the crowd outside the inn and excitedly verified that the English soldier was indeed dead and that the shots hit him in the shoulder, back and neck.

Mathew turned back to the riflemen with a quizzical look on his face.

"We're not very good soldiers, but we are the best long-range shots in the Continental Army," James said. "We've killed over a hundred red-coats from distances that would make your head spin. Apparently, we rubbed some feathers the wrong way with some of the continental officers and got reassigned to duty down here."

"Gentlemen, I am impressed," Mathew said, "and I thank you for your assistance a few moments ago. But why would you be assigned here so far from the war?"

"Can't say," Jeremy said.

"Well, I understand the need for secrecy of course, but since we're clearly on the same side, I thought I might help you find your next assignment."

"No. You don't understand, mister," Jeremy added. "We

can't say because *we* don't know."

"You were told to travel this far south and report to no one?" asked Mathew.

"No. We were told to report to someone all right, but all we have is the name of this inn and a code name," answered Joseph.

Sensing that Adams might possibly have sent the sharpshooters to serve on the *Sea Dragon*, Mathew extended his hand to the closest King brother.

"In that case, gentlemen, allow me to introduce myself, for I believe that it is I whom you seek. I am *Chameleon*."

The King brothers let out an exasperated sigh and congratulated one another for finally finding their contact. Jeremy King reached into an inner panel of his worn coat for a wax-sealed note and handed it to Mathew.

"Mister, you don't know how glad we are to finally find you," Joseph said.

The note was explanation enough for Mathew and was signed by a code name that Adams knew Mathew alone would recognize: *Father John*.

♦

Far out to sea that same evening, Lieutenant Commander Roger Bartlett, bound in manacles, slumped silently in the cabin of Captain Harwick. Two soldiers stood behind him as Bartlett looked up to face his distraught captain across the broad oak desk.

"What am I going to do with you, Bartlett? You've committed a felonious crime after having ignored a direct order from your captain."

Bartlett sat quietly with a disturbing grin on his face.

"Out of respect for your father," Harwick added, "I merely pulled you from civilian escort duty, but this…this is a reprehensible act."

"She's colonial!" blurted Bartlett, as though his surprise discovery somehow warranted his foul behavior.

"Her lineage is of no consequence to the matter. She is a lady and you have disgraced England, the Royal Navy and your family."

The grin on Bartlett's face turned slowly into a fatigued yawn, as if to goad Harwick into anger.

"The standard punishment regulated by the Articles of War for your senseless act tonight is clear," Harwick slowly began as he took his eyes off of Bartlett and down to the papers on his desk.

Two can play at that game, reasoned the captain, and he had a decidedly advantageous position. *Let's see how you like what I'm about to say*, he thought.

"A dozen lashes, followed by salt water on the wounds, tomorrow at 11:00," Harwick mentioned matter-of-factly. "Nasty punishment - still, you have it coming, by God."

The captain looked up and met the gaze of the hardened soldiers behind Bartlett. Their usual stoic faces registered a pleasing agreement with the stated punishment as they glanced downward at the loathsome offender. The look on Roger Bartlett's face had immediately changed to one of sincere concern.

"That can't happen, Captain," said Bartlett with a panicked look that conveyed his hope that a negotiation might be in order. "There is a special circumstance that should be taken into account here, and I request a private council with you before any formal sentence is passed."

"You are an officer of the Royal Navy. I will listen to your confession and any circumstances you feel are relevant to the crime," Harwick began as he noticed the grins on the faces of the sentries were replaced with looks of disbelief. "But make no mistake, Bartlett, you will be punished harshly for this violent and indefensible act!"

The grins reappeared on the faces of the sentries. Harwick motioned for them to leave as he addressed them.

"Please remain outside the door, and no one disturbs me for the next ten minutes – I don't care if the bloody ship is sinking!"

The sentinels nodded their understanding and left the cabin, shutting the door firmly behind them. As the door closed, Roger Bartlett looked deep into the Harwick's eyes and smiled.

♦

"Intriguing," Mathew said as he finished reading the note handed to him by Jeremy King.

Though rather cryptic in its delivery, the content was clear. The King brothers were the best long-range shooters in the Continental Army, but were nevertheless a headache for the military's attempts at unity, drilling, and teamwork. Their heralded exploits notwithstanding, the army thought it more productive to have them fight in a small, tactical operation than to serve alongside hundreds of colonial troops where their undisciplined behavior was counter-productive. In personal correspondence with General Washington, Adams had learned about the King brothers and persuaded Washington to transfer the snipers to the underground movement led by his cousin, Samuel Adams. *The Sons of Liberty*, as the movement was known, used the King brothers' special skills on a few assignments before John convinced Samuel to usher them to the south to join Chameleon.

"Says here you men are great long-range snipers. I have already seen this to be true," Mathew began. "But it also says you lack modesty, discipline, and a sense of team."

"Yep!" Joseph King agreed emphatically as his brothers burst out laughing.

"That's too bad then," Mathew said as he folded the note and put it in his overcoat's inner chest pocket. "You came all this way for nothing. Off with you, now. I have no use for peasant farmers on this mission."

"Excuse me!?" said one of the Kings incredulously. "You're sending us back to the Continental Army? You can't do that!"

"Gentlemen, let me make something perfectly clear to you. I have the authority from your provincial government to do anything I see fit. *Anything!*" Mathew enunciated the last word very loudly and slowly to make his point. "And no matter how fantastic your skills are with those rifles, your behavior or lack thereof will not work on this particular assignment. I can promise that if the enemy didn't kill you soon, one of my men probably would do the job neatly, that is, if they beat *me* to it."

The three brothers looked at each other and then to the sea of malicious faces surrounding them as Mathew continued.

"We are the most destructive fighting force in America. We act as a well-honed team. We treat each other like family. Every one of these men would die for the other, and I include myself in that commitment. Based on this note and your arrogant display of attitude, I can only surmise that you would not fit into our particular fighting unit nor get the chance to use your talents."

"But we're damned good fighters, mister!" countered James.

"Really?" Mathew said with a lift of his brows. "Gentlemen, ours is a very tightly run and dangerous operation. We do not shoot at the enemy and hide behind a tree or a rock! There is no guerrilla warfare in our theatre of battle. We meet the enemy head-on and to the death."

"What the hell kind of soldiers are you then?"

"Exceptional!" one of the Spaniards said in very clear English.

The King brothers conferred briefly and turned to face Mathew again.

"Sir, we don't know what kind of unit you're talking about, and we'll abide by your decision to send us back. But before you do, know this. Not one of your men could have made the shot that felled that Brit. Each of us did it, and in twilight yet! As for our attitude, please don't let that stand in the way of using us; we'd desperately like to use our talents to a more productive use, even if that means we're in greater danger ourselves. If you'll consider using us on your team, we'll quit the attitude and take orders as well as any of your men here."

"And I am supposed to believe that?" Mathew asked.

"Sir, we've already lost a brother, our father and mother and our farm to the British. We're not afraid of death. In fact, battles allow us to exact our personal measure of revenge. Please don't take that away from us. If you fight the British, take us with you and you won't be sorry. Put us at the lowest rank, we don't care, but put us in harm's way and we promise to serve you well until we die."

Mathew was moved by their plight and spirited words, and the idea of using such remarkable sharpshooters did present an intriguing new tool for battle. In truth, Mathew did not wish to turn them away, but to modify their behavior instantly, and his tactic appeared successful.

"Very well, gentlemen. I seem to have developed a soft heart for anyone who wishes ill on His Majesty's forces," Mathew said. "But please understand that I swear I will kill you myself if your attitude *ever* presents an issue. You will not see it coming. You will not have a chance to explain. And I promise you will have to work harder than you can possibly conceive, and you'll have to take orders from Europeans. Is that clear?"

"Yes, sir!" the brothers snapped to attention.

"In that case, gentlemen, I have one additional question before we accept you into our fold."

The brothers visibly gulped awaiting the question that might make or break their enlistment in the elite team, as smiles registered across the faces in the Spanish men surrounding them.

"Have any of you ever been out to sea?"

◆

Captain Harwick sat alone in his cabin, deep in thought contemplating the rich prize awaiting him back in England; the spoils of a trade made with Bartlett in exchange for leniency in punishment.

Bartlett had conveyed that through his influential father, Harwick would be promoted one full grade, as well as receiving a sum of five hundred pounds. Though he initially had no intention of allowing Bartlett to bribe him, Harwick eventually succumbed to a private arrangement as the amount of barter steadily increased.

They agreed to communicate that Bartlett would be lashed once ashore and processed through a military court. In reality, both men knew that Bartlett would not be punished at all.

Harwick reasoned to himself that no amount of punishment would undo the terrible act of aggression against Miss Davis, and Bartlett would be confined to his quarters for the remaining week of their voyage, with the exception of midnight duty in the crow's nest atop the mainsail.

The captain was confident that even Roger Bartlett would not step out of line in that week's time, for the punishment for any indiscretion would be immediate death. Once ashore, Roger's secret release could be handled behind closed doors, and no one would know differently.

Less than an hour after Captain Harwick dismissed Bartlett from his cabin, there came a knock at his door.

"Enter," Harwick called, somewhat dismayed at being tugged back into reality from his daydream of the monetary bonus and promotion awaiting him.

Lieutenant Mullins stepped into the captain's quarters, careful to close the door behind him securely and walk closer to the captain before speaking.

"Captain, I understand from the sentries posted outside his berth that Bartlett is to be turned over to a military tribunal in Norfolk for punishment."

"That is correct, Lieutenant."

"Well...Captain...why?"

"Why what, Lieutenant Mullins," the captain stalled as he knew what the officer was driving at.

"Why not punish him here on the ship...tomorrow?"

"I see. Tell me, Lieutenant Mullins, are you aware of the punishment for his level of crime?"

"Yes, Captain. Public flogging, twelve lashes at 11:00 am."

"And are you so anxious for a pound of flesh, Lieutenant Mullins?"

"I am anxious to see just punishment for the crime, Captain."

"Lieutenant Mullins, do not suppose for one moment that you have a better grasp of the issues than me," shot back Harwick, visibly disturbed at the impeachment of his judgment. "This has been a most unusual voyage in that civilians were along," the captain continued. "In light of this circumstance, I believe it would be detrimental to flog anyone in public right now. You have probably not witnessed a flogging before, but I have. It is a most cruel and disturbing form of punishment. Does Bartlett deserve it? Hell yes he does, but NOT...ON...THIS...SHIP!" Harwick finished his comments with a roar so as to eliminate any thought of Mullins continuing the discussion.

"Yes, Captain," Lieutenant Mullins responded meekly as he turned to exit the captain's quarters.

On the way back to his own berth, Mullins thought about what the captain had said. Something didn't seem right. He was, of course, correct to be concerned with the civilian presence, but the flogging could be done when the civilians were below decks. Public flogging on a ship was meant not only as a punishment for the perpetrator of heinous crimes as sea, but also as a deterrent to others who may have similar designs of impropriety.

At dawn the next morning, Roger Bartlett was relieved of his duty in the crow's nest. He climbed down the riggings to the deck below where two armed guards were waiting to escort him back to his cabin. He was too tired to argue with what he deemed to be the unnecessary effect of an armed escort. It was probably the captain's idea, reasoned the fatigued sailor, to play up to the crew in terms of how seriously he was taking things.

While turning uncomfortably in his hammock a few hours later, Bartlett arose and opened the door to his berth. All the young officers who shared this cabin with him were gone. He was alone. In fact, there was no sentry at the door, which confirmed his suspicion of Harwick sending the escort in the morning merely to placate any observers.

Roger returned to his hammock and wandered into a sleepy daydream. He was imagining how he would have concluded his time with young Ms. Davis had he not been interrupted.

As Bartlett was falling asleep, Alison walked briskly towards the captain's quarters.

After pressing a visibly distraught Lieutenant Mullins a few minutes prior, she had discovered that Bartlett's punishment would take place on shore, once in Virginia. Just one day after her attack, Alison's emotions were running high, fueled by rumors that Bartlett might be punished lightly.

Against the earnest recommendation otherwise by Lieutenant Mullins, Alison was determined to let the captain know her feelings first hand. Mullins had tried to appease her, telling

Alison how he himself had argued the point the prior evening only to be angrily dismissed.

After rapping heavily on the door to his private quarters, Alison stood with steely determination ready for a verbal confrontation with the captain. As he opened the door, she saw his eyes widen in shock at her facial injuries.

"Captain Harwick, I demand a private word with you!"

Harwick knew from her fire and loud knock that this was not a social visit. He presumed word had potentially spread over the ship of Bartlett's sentence postponement.

"Come in, Miss Davis. Come in. And please do sit down," Harwick said, in order to take some of the bite out of her impending bark. "Let me first state how very sorry I am that this unfortunate circumstance has occurred."

He walked her over to a soft sedan chair, his mind rapidly plotting how to explain to the beaten young woman why he was seemingly going soft.

"Captain Harwick, it has come to my attention that Lieutenant Commander Bartlett will not be punished for his crime. Is that so?"

"No. That is not so, Miss Davis!" Harwick gladly fielded her initial grievance. "Lieutenant Commander Bartlett is being punished in a number of ways. In fact, he has spent the entire night in the crow's nest on lookout as his first form of punishment."

"I would gladly serve night duty in the crow's nest every night rather than go through what he did to me last night!" retorted Alison careful to not sound too emotional.

"Yes, well…" the captain stammered, "that is just the first of multiple punishments, Miss Davis."

When he made his private deal with Bartlett, he had not anticipated ever facing the young lady. Now, she stood before him with her swollen and split lips, closed black eye, and badly bruised jaw, unable to grasp how such a fiendish act would not receive swift punishment.

A feeling of self-disgust began to well in the pit of the captain's stomach. How could he possibly have bargained with the crazed and desperate Bartlett? It would be just like Bartlett to forget or even purposely rescind their arrangement. Harwick had no wife or daughter, but suddenly imagined how he would feel in front of this beaten woman if she were his child.

Then Alison Davis did the one thing that turned the captain inside out. The defiant strength in the battered young lady that had driven her across the deck to his quarters and demanded a private discussion, broke down. Alison slumped in the sedan chair and began to cry. At first, it was a quivering lip, then it escalated to a shaking body. When she cried openly, it was as though the floodgates had opened a torrent of tears and emotion came all at once.

Harwick knelt down next to Alison and took her hand and patted it. He was trying to comfort her, but to no avail. Her great sobs and tears were beginning to tug at Harwick's own heart. He felt awful that his selfishness led to his benefiting at the woman's expense.

"Please, Miss Davis. I'm so very sorry."

His pangs of sorrow for the woman and anger at himself turned instantly to a renewed sense of hatred for Bartlett. He had been duped by the wild exaggerations and likely hollow promises from the desperate sailor.

He silently calculated the effects of a retraction of his arrangement with Bartlett. Of course, he thought, I could still flog the bastard on deck this very day. No one would mind. He would, in fact, be carrying out the explicit sentence for the crime.

But what of the arrangement itself? What if Bartlett announced that he had struck a deal with the captain and that the captain reneged? Would anyone believe him? Of course not. Harwick was alone when the deal was made. He would simply deny the allegations, and it would be the word of the captain versus the ranting of a loathsome thug that no one liked.

Bartlett would then certainly threaten reporting Harwick and the flogging to his father, Lord Bartlett. But how would Bartlett explain things to his father? Harwick had witnesses and the girl victim who would certainly back him up.

Bartlett had no way of conjuring up a scenario that would paint Harwick in an unfavorable light to his father. In fact, he almost hoped it would reach such a state. It would be the ruination of both Bartlett and, potentially, his father if it ever got to that stage.

"Miss Davis," Harwick resolutely vowed, still on bent knee at her side, "I am greatly sorry for your treatment and for the rumors of leniency circulating among the crew."

Alison continued crying, but turned her head toward the captain who looked pleadingly into her one half-opened eye.

"My dear," he continued, "I don't know what rumors abound on this ship, but I can personally commit to you that Bartlett will suffer deeply for the way he's treated you. He is to be flogged on deck this very morning. I know punishing him, no matter how harshly, will not undo his senseless act of violence and rage against you, but he must be made to pay nevertheless."

Alison continued looking at the captain, her crying seemingly slowing.

"I can only imagine," the captain continued, "that the rumor was a product of my conviction not to flog him *in front of the civilians.*"

The lie seemed to appease Alison somewhat.

"Please do not think me soft, Miss Davis. I shall be only too happy to carry out the sentence myself if necessary, but I highly doubt that will be an issue. There is not a sailor on this ship that would not like to crack the cat-o-nine-tails down hard on Roger Bartlett. Why, I've a good mind to ask the sailors to bid and pay for each lashing. The sum would likely pay for our return voyage to England!"

His feeble attempt at humor was lost on Alison, but she was grateful for the clarification nonetheless.

"Captain," she tried to calm her crying in order to make one last lucid request, "I understand your policy of privacy from civilians, but is there any way you could possibly change your policy for me?"

He stared back into her one, partially-opened, pleading eye and couldn't control his own words, "I think so, dear, if it is that important to you. But I must inform you that it will be very brutal and you should not be seen by others on deck. You can remain in my cabin and view from the slightly opened door if you promise to stay out of sight and quiet."

Alison nodded her understanding. "Then may I remain here now until the sentence is carried out?"

"Of course, Miss Davis. Make yourself at home. The flogging will take place in less than an hour. Afterwards, we shall wait and I will personally escort you back to your cabin in the afternoon."

Alison again nodded her appreciation and understanding.

"After the flogging, Alison, he will be locked below decks, you have my word upon it. You have nothing more to fear. I will have the ship's doctor check on you daily and you should get as much rest as possible."

The captain stood and moved slowly away from the woman trying so hard to compose herself after her uncontrolled display of grief. Harwick reached the door and turned to say something else, but was interrupted by a loud yell from several sailors on his deck.

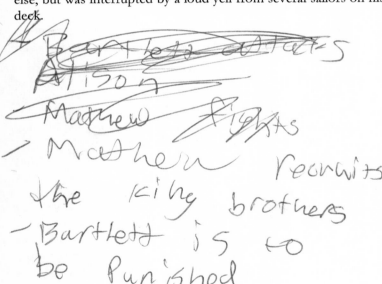

✝

Chapter 21: Pirates Closing!

"All hands on deck! All hands on deck! Pirates closing fast from the southwest!"

Captain Harwick leapt out of the cabin, instantly forgetting about Alison and focused on the horizon as he reached the aft deck above. One of the officers handed him a telescope and gestured to the southwest where a distant cloud-like sail was coming into view. In the air, the thundering sound of all the soldiers and sailors running about the deck, taking positions and arming the deck cannons.

Harwick viewed the approaching pirate ship and felt intrigue rather than fear, for he looked on each side of his own ship and saw two of His Majesty's finest warships as his escorts. It was an impossibly low probability that this approaching vessel could defeat one Royal Navy warship, let alone two. The HMS *Atlas* and HMS *Gemini* were fully prepared for the battle that would begin in a matter of minutes.

It was a very foolish pirate, thought Harwick, to show such an aggressive tactic as to attack warships. Even from a great distance, the size and build of the warships would be easy to discern, not to mention the Red Ensign flying on all three ships. Attacking supply ships was understandable, but cutting off a British military convoy was sheer suicide.

"What the hell does he think he's going to do?" said one nearby junior officer aloud. Harwick was puzzled with the same thought.

"He'll be crushed in minutes!" said another junior officer, brimming with confidence.

Harwick suddenly felt uneasy. Inexplicably, he had developed a very bad feeling deep down that would not allow him to share the confidence of his fellow officers. He looked at the seemingly invincible force presented by the two naval escorts and back to the advancing pirate ship.

There must be some reason why they run toward us, thought Harwick, though he could not fathom what possible strategic ploy dictated such an outrageously overconfident maneuver. He once again raised the telescope to his left eye.

He had expected to see some form of generic pirate flag long ago dubbed *Jolly Roger*, a ubiquitous term coined by the French long before, as the earliest pirate flags were usually bright red. The French referred to these flags as *jolie rouge* or "pretty red" flags. Black had long since taken the place of their red field, but the message was the same as the century before - surrender or die! The flags were meant to frighten the crew of ships into submission without a battle taking place.

Gaining an automatic surrender was important to all pirates, for it meant not only would they not have to risk their own lives, but a battle-less victory provided intact plunder, including the ships themselves.

Often their identifying flags contained figures suggesting a violent death to those that dared oppose them, such as skeleton's, skulls, bones, swords, dripping blood, and even hourglasses, suggesting that time was running out on the lives of those who looked upon the fearful pennant.

The advancing pirates were now running their colors up their main mast. As the flag unfurled and snapped crisply in the open sea wind, Harwick's heart sank. Of all the flags in the Atlantic, this was the one no Royal Navy ship ever wanted to see.

There was a large black field with a grotesque fire-breathing dragon coiled into a circle, and a saber protruding from the bottom of the circle forming a large letter "Q". There was no doubt that the vessel was the *Sea Dragon*, captained by the dreaded pirate Quicksilver.

The legend of Quicksilver had grown rapidly, and was known to many sailors in the Royal Navy. A vicious, brutal pirate who usually fought with a large saber in each hand, and so blindingly fast that no one could best him. It was said that he could cut down twenty able swordsmen in only a minute of battle. One legend even suggested he could not be killed, and that immortality was due to his being the son of the Devil himself.

Quicksilver's ship was also said to possess devilish properties, including a fearsome weapon called *dragon's breath*. Harwick could not imagine what dragon's breath was or what victims thought they saw, and he didn't want to find out. Though as with many stories born on the sea, there was likely a large degree of exaggeration wrapped around a shred of truth.

The crew of the *Sea Dragon* was nearly as feared as their captain. In preparation for battle, apparently they often smeared white face paint on themselves which gave them a frightening look, like fighting skeletons. Fortunate survivors of battles with the *Dragon*, as the ship came to be known, agreed that its crew fought with impeccable precision and tactics, as strong as any British navy crew.

Harwick looked on at the impending sea battle with nervousness, as the ships were within five hundred yards or so of using their cannons against one another. He silently prayed for victory, for he was in a defenseless position on a merchant ship after all, the few deck cannons notwithstanding.

Suddenly a silent explosion created a raging inferno on the deck of the *Gemini*. Though no cannons were fired, half their deck was ablaze. Sailors raced about the deck trying to put out the flames, but their attempts were feeble. As they threw water on the deck to quell the fires, two more silent explosions erupted sending flames all the way up the mainsail. The entire deck seemed engulfed in fire now, and several of the *Gemini*'s sailors were diving into the ocean, seemingly choosing to drown rather than burn. *Dragon's breath*, thought Harwick.

Before the *Atlas* could come about and pour a thundering blast of its cannons toward the *Dragon*, she too was alight in flames. This was indeed the hand of the Devil, thought the panicked Harwick, now understanding why the infamous pirate ship had attacked so confidently and aggressively. How could she cause the British warships to burst into flames without firing so much as one cannon?

Then, as if they heard his thoughts, the *Dragon* was in position to let loose a cannon barrage that instantly crippled the *Atlas*. Meanwhile, the flames that had engulfed the *Gemini* had spread below decks, perhaps due to falling debris or just the caving in of the weakened deck structure. Harwick turned to see another handful of sailors dive into the sea just as the fire above decks met with the stores of gunpowder below decks. The concussion of the enormous blast nearly threw the disbelieving sailors on board the *North Star* off their feet. The deafening explosion echoed as shards of the *Gemini* were projected into every direction.

At that same moment, the mainsail of the *Atlas* was collapsing. It would be only another minute or so before she suffered the same fate as the *Gemini*. With her mast weakened from grapeshot and cannon blasts, and her sails torn and burning, she could not move to gain position to fire upon the pirate ship.

The unscathed *Dragon* disappeared behind the burning, listless *Atlas*.

Harwick and those on the *North Star* deck, could not see it, but they heard the unmistakable thunder of the *Dragon*'s cannons explode towards the *Atlas*. Again, several sailors – some of whom were on fire themselves - jumped off the ship attempting to swim toward the as yet untouched *North Star*. The second round of cannon blasts blew the *Atlas* out of the water. Her explosion, like that of the *Gemini* was as horrific as it was loud.

Harwick stood on the raised aft deck of the *North Star* petrified. Only minutes ago, two mighty British naval ships sat proudly on the water, ready to take on the approaching threat. Now there were no warships at all - just burning debris spread across an enormous expanse of the sea in front of the merchant ship.

Even the ocean itself gave the strange illusion of being on fire where the ships once were. Then all was quiet. Among the burning debris and dead seamen, cries of sailors still clinging to life lifted into the smoke filled sea air.

The officers surrounding Harwick were as agitated as their captain, with the only difference being that they visibly showed their fear. Harwick gathered himself quickly and yelled his command.

"Send up the white flag immediately!"

For the first time in minutes, he surveyed his deck. The sailors were either looking back up at him or at the cloud of black smoke that took the place of the *Atlas*. They were dejected and frightened, but seemed visibly relieved that they would not be asked to fight. The *Dragon* was mysteriously nowhere in sight, hidden by the thick smoke on the water, but they knew that would not last long.

The white flag was raised high on the main mast, and all heads turned to the acrid black cloud on the water. In dramatic fashion that could not have been more effective had it been planned, the *Sea Dragon* broke through the black smoky veil as if it were spat out of Hell itself coming directly at the defenseless *North Star*.

"Stand down, men!" commanded Harwick loudly. "Drop your weapons and extend your arms. Let no man put up a fight if you want to preserve your life!"

The dumbfounded sailors gladly complied with their captain's order.

As the *Dragon* approached and came about, the frightening grin of the devilish serpent on its flag served its intended purpose. The highly trained and experienced fighting sailors on the merchant ship had never seen a battle like the lopsided one just fought, and were frozen in abject fear.

The crew of the pirate ship, now visible, had their faces painted as skulls, which seemed to verify all other rumors about the *Sea Dragon* and its dreaded captain. Hooks and ropes were tossed to pull the ships bulwarks together.

The King brothers had moved up into strategic positions, one in the crows nest, one near the stern and one near the bow sprit of the *Dragon*, ready to provide covering fire in case the soldiers on the deck of the merchant ship decided to attempt to repel boarders.

Within three minutes the entire naval crew was silently gathered on the foredeck – their swords and guns taken by the pirates. One pirate whistled back towards the pirate ship. Captain Harwick remained on the aft deck, nervously awaiting the imminent arrival of the one called Quicksilver.

At last, a large menacing figure emerged from the smoky air swinging over on a rigging line. The man had very long, thick curly black hair and a black beard nearly as long as his locks. Three long braids complemented his full beard, one from each cheek and one hanging directly downward from his chin. He was as large as the rumors suggested. There was no doubt in the mind of Harwick and the others on board the *North Star* that the man was very strong and likely as dangerous without a sword as he was with one.

Quicksilver walked deliberately slowly from the mid-deck to the steps leading up to the poop deck, giving Harwick a long and menacing glare before speaking. Harwick didn't dare speak first.

"What be yer name, Captain?"

"Harwick, Captain Thadeus Harwick," the captain blurted out belying his fear.

"I see. And do you know who I be?" asked the big pirate captain in the broken English speech commonly found in the Caribbean region.

Harwick nodded slowly, "You're Quicksilver."

"Yer intuition serves you true, Captain Harwick"

Quicksilver slowly glanced across the deck to the gathered British sailors and back again to Harwick.

"What be yer cargo, Captain?"

"Munitions, food, medicine, and various supplies for the British war effort," he stammered.

"First of all, try to relax. I have no intention of killing ye or yer men. If I had, ye'd be dead by now. You respected the black pennant of Quicksilver and ye shall be spared!"

Harwick couldn't restrain a gulp.

"But lie to me just once, and I'll cut yer throat open before you see the blade coming! Do ye comprehend me, Captain?"

Harwick silently nodded.

"Good man. Now, what else are ye carrying?"

"I...I...don't understand. Just munitions and other war supplies...oh, and a handful of civilians," remembered Harwick.

"Civilians?!? On a ship chartered by the Royal Navy, and whose bright idea be that...fat George?"

As the pirate captain approached and stood next to the captain of the *North Star*, Harwick explained that, while rare, civilian transport was a way to assuage the cost of the voyage of shipping war supplies.

Quicksilver turned and stood at the railing, overseeing the deck of the *North Star* with his back to Harwick who didn't dare move. After a moment of reflection, the fearsome pirate captain turned back to Harwick again.

"Here be what we'll do. Have yer men bring the stores of goods to the bulwark. We'll be taking your entire cargo, less enough supplies to see you and any survivors in the water comfortably back to England. Be that clear to ye?"

"But, we're less than a week from Norfolk?" Harwick said, then immediately was sorry for his instinctive reply.

Quicksilver winced as though in some brief pain or discomfort. He spoke surprisingly gently after a few seconds of silence enabled him to swallow his anger.

"I would appreciate it, Captain, if ye would be so kind as to simply agree with me. If there is a disagreement, I'm liable to get angry. And if I loose my head, ye be losing yours. Understand?"

"Yes, Quicksilver. I'm sorry. England it shall be."

"Now, if ye don't mind, some of my men are going to inspect yer ship. Ye've got nothing to worry 'bout so long as ye be telling me the entire truth."

Quicksilver made a series of quick hand gestures to his men who, in turn, sprang into activity. The onlooking Harwick was impressed with the silent hand language of the pirates. Other than the handful pointing blunderbusses at the British sailors on deck, the rest of the men scurried through the ship like starved rats for cheese.

The silence was an eerie departure from the recent thunder of the exploding ships. The British crew had witnessed the raw power of the *Sea Dragon*, and now – with ears still ringing - were watching the tactical skill and economy of movement of the experienced crew. This was indeed a disciplined operation, thought Harwick.

The civilians were soon escorted to deck.

"A head count of the civilians, if ye don't mind, Captain," requested Quicksilver.

"Nine, ten, eleven…" Harwick finished his counting out loud while pointing to the collected group at the bow of the ship. But there were twelve civilians. One was missing! Then it hit him. For a brief moment, he weighed the idea of not disclosing that Alison was in his cabin, probably hiding by now.

No, he thought. As much as he wanted to protect the girl, he wanted to appear as conciliatory as possible with Quicksilver to save the entire crew. Besides, one of the pirates would probably find her anyway. It wasn't worth risking anyone's neck over, particularly his.

"And there is one more. A young lady who has been injured, she is in my quarters presently."

Quicksilver stared into the eyes of the British captain with a look that seemed as sharp as his blade.

"Company for the captain during the long voyage, eh?"

"Certainly not," Harwick protested. "Nothing like that! She was injured the night prior and I was having a discussion with her when the nest alerted the ship to pirates on the horizon. I swear it."

A quick whistle burst from Quicksilver's teeth. Two men standing below him on the main deck looked up in his direction. He gestured again. Although Harwick knew this time what the communication was likely about, the hand signals were so rapid that he could not follow their meaning. Immediately, one of the two men broke off and entered the captain's quarters.

A moment later, the pirate crewman emerged gently escorting a young woman by the arm. Quicksilver stood on the deck above the captain's quarters. He could not see the woman's face, but he heard the gasps and watched the reactions across the deck of the British crew and civilians turn empathetic as though they'd seen something rather gruesome. His curiosity piqued, Quicksilver made his way to the steps down to the quarterdeck and called out a single word command: "Wait!"

Alison did not look up. She stared straight out across the deck above the faces of the British sailors and civilians gathered at the bow. The only sound was that of large boots coming down the stairs and walking slowly across the deck toward her. She already knew whom it was coming toward her, and yet was too sad to be frightened. As she had witnessed the destruction of the escort ships from the captain's cabin moments prior, she realized that a more terrible fate than Roger Bartlett loomed near.

As the large pirate captain walked into her line of vision, she stood erect with her shoulders back, defiant though her lips quivered and tears ran down her lone open eye. She did not look Quicksilver in his eyes, and he did not force the issue.

Visibly seething, the frightening pirate leader turned his glance upward to the raised aft deck where Harwick still stood looking back down at him.

"It was not me that did this, Quicksilver!" Harwick offered, anticipating the pirate's thoughts.

"Then who be responsible?" the pirate captain responded in a slow, deliberate drawl.

"One of the officers tried to molest her last evening. He was caught in the act and sentenced to be flogged on deck this morning."

Quicksilver looked back down at Alison who still stared her one open eye toward some point way off beyond the ship's bow.

"Be this true?" he asked in a surprisingly gentle voice.

Alison nodded, but the admission of the molestation made her lips tremble even more until she broke down and openly cried. Quicksilver pulled out a clean linen handkerchief and handed it to her. Then he brought his face in closer to hers so that only she could hear.

"Shhh, darling. Please don't cry. I am not going to hurt ye, I swear it."

Still crying, Alison allowed herself to look into the eyes of the infamous pirate captain. Though his size, clothes and long beard and locks made him menacing looking, there was something incredibly sincere in the two eyes that had to be the deepest blue she had ever seen. And up close, it was immediately apparent that his complexion was not like sun-baked parchment as she would have presumed, but clean and youthful. Up close, the face did not precisely fit the voice and reputation of the feared pirate commander.

"What be yer name, my dear?"

"Alison," she offered, though barely above a whisper, still too frightened and weeping to speak up.

"Alison, I want ye to listen carefully. Can ye point out the officer that did this to ye?"

Alison nodded slowly and managed a softly whispered question, "What do you intend to do?"

"Well, Alison, that's up to you, but with yer permission, I'd very much like to settle the score with the one that did this to ye."

Between sniffling, Alison spoke purposefully, "As much as I would like to see him dead, please don't. Death is *too good* for him!"

"Indeed," responded a moved Quicksilver. "All right then, how 'bout if I inflict wounds similar to yer own? An eye-for-an-eye, so to speak."

The arrangement was highly satisfactory to Alison. If she was to die or be kidnapped today, at least she'd have the pleasure of watching Roger Bartlett receive the beating of his life. She nearly laughed out the sarcastic words, when she responded to the seemingly sympathetic pirate, "Can I hit him first?"

"By thunder, yer American!" whispered the pirate.

For the second time on the voyage, Alison had inadvertently let down her guard and responded out of pure emotion. "Yes, but please don't hurt me?"

"Hurt ye? I don't hurt civilians of any country. Besides," he added even more quietly, "ye and I are on the same side, as you might say. Now listen closely, I'm going to send this ship back to England, but I offer to take ye to the colonies."

"Really?"

"Truly," he promised. "Where is home?"

"Boston," Alison murmured cautiously.

"Upon my word, I will see that ye arrive safely in Boston this month, though I can take ye only so far as southern Virginia m'self. However, I can arrange a coach to take ye the rest of the way up to Boston."

Alison sized up the offer. It was better than going back to England to her mind. However, willingly going with fearsome pirates was inconceivable. And yet there was something in the eyes of their leader that made her feel calm. There was one way to test his trustworthiness.

"Will you be offended if I remain on this ship?" she asked cautiously.

"No, Alison. I believe I understand yer dilemma. I can't make ye trust me, but I meant what I said. The offer stands, the choice is yours."

"I just want to go home, sir."

"Done. But there is one little problem - ye can't be seen to be going with us willingly. I hope ye understand, and I do apologize, but I'm going to ask two of my men to physically take ye to our ship. They will be firm but gentle. Ye, in turn, need to put up something of a fight for appearances sake. I will announce that we're taking ye, but please don't be frightened by the words I may say. Is that acceptable?"

Alison feared the scene about to be created, but still somehow trusted the pirate captain fully. She nodded slowly to him.

"Are ye sure, dear?" Quicksilver said, offering her one last out.

"I am now!"

"One last item, Alison - as they escort ye out, beg them to stop so ye can say farewell to one of the crew. Find the one that did this to ye and slap him hard - I'll do the rest. Can ye do that, dear?"

Again, she nodded, and Quicksilver immediately turned his attention up to the trembling captain of the *North Star.*

"Captain Harwick, may I rely on yer honor to see that the man responsible for this young lady's injuries is severely punished by flogging?" Quicksilver called up to the aft deck, but loud enough for all on deck to hear.

"You have my word, the sentence will be carried out."

"In that case," yelled Quicksilver, "we will leave ye now." After a few seconds pause, he added, "And we're taking the girl!"

"Noooo!" screamed Alison, who struggled on cue most convincingly.

"Quicksilver, take the stores, take what valuables you've found, but the grace of God, please leave the civilians," pleaded Captain Harwick.

The menacing pirate turned back to face the British captain. He crossed his arms so that each hand firmly grasped the sword hilt on the opposite hip. He stared back at the captain, seemingly daring him to say just one more word so he could draw his swords.

The gesture served its intended purpose well, for the captain stood in stunned silence. Harwick was not about to risk his own life, or that of the entire crew based on what he'd witnessed a few minutes prior. Quicksilver let go of the swords and let his arms uncross, but he continued his menacing stare at the captain a few seconds more.

"I leave yer ship intact, Captain. I have hurt none of yer men, and I leave ye with plenty of stores for yer safe return voyage to England, including the men you'll soon pluck from the sea. Do not make the mistake of presuming my generosity goes further!"

Meanwhile, Alison was being escorted by two terrifying pirate crewmen. Her wild struggles to tear herself free from their grasp seemed hopeless.

The entire line of English sailors watched in shameful despair, save one. While the crew's collective faces reflected sympathy for the young woman, the corners of Roger Bartlett's mouth turned upward in an uncontrollable grin.

Alison's lone open eye found Bartlett, who not only smiled smugly back at her, but winked.

Just as she and her captors passed a number of officers, she pleaded to them to let her say one last good-bye. The captors turned to Quicksilver who nodded from afar. They relaxed their grip momentarily, and Alison composed herself, walked closer to the line of sailors, stopping in front of Roger Bartlett.

"Lieutenant Commander Bartlett, I want to give you something to remember me by," she said as she walked to within inches of him. Her knee jerked up so quickly that the confused sailor never had a chance to ward off her blow. The thrust of her leg into his groin sent a shockwave through Bartlett, who instantly fell to his knees, doubled over in agonizing pain, and clutching his crotch.

The two pirate crewmen swooped in and grabbed her to take her bodily over the transom of the ship, and she resumed her kicking and screaming.

Roger Bartlett stumbled to his feet and lurched forward to grab the back of Alison's flowing hair. Alison jerked away from him as a large hand grabbed Bartlett by the shoulder. The grip was so ferociously strong that his whole body was thrust into an awkward turn.

Before he could react to the force that had impeded his movement and spun him around, a gloved hand connected solidly with his jaw, shattering it instantly. Bartlett fell to the deck like a large sack of flour. Incoherent, he spat blood over himself as the gloved hands lifted him up by the lapels of his coat.

"No, no…we're not finished quite yet," said Quicksilver slowly.

Before Bartlett had a chance to raise his hands and cover himself, the second blow was delivered, connecting with the bridge of his nose, smashing the cartilage into fragments and bloodying his entire face. The only reason Roger Bartlett remained on his feet was the powerful grip of Quicksilver that held him upright for one final blow.

"Was this how ye treated that girl?"

The pirate captain released his grip on Bartlett's lapels and watched the beaten officer crumple to a bloody heap on the deck.

Quicksilver looked upward toward Captain Harwick, "I spare this wretched man, Captain, because I have yer word of honor that he'll receive his due flogging in full. Is my presumption accurate, Captain?"

Harwick regarded the beaten, bloodied Bartlett. His lips

quivered as he began to form his response.

"I see." Quicksilver drew one of his sabers and raised it in the air to finish the man.

"Wait!" pleaded Harwick. "Yes, of course, you have my word that the man will still be flogged...today."

Quicksilver rapidly spun his sword around his hand and replaced it in its sheath without taking his eyes off Harwick.

"He had better be, Captain," Quicksilver replied as he turned to walk away to the bulwark and return to the *Sea Dragon*.

In the ten strides that it took Quicksilver to reach the side of the *North Star*, Bartlett foolishly pushed himself up onto his knees and pulled a knife from his boot.

As he pulled back his right arm above his head to throw the blade into the back of Quicksilver, three different long-bore rifles fired as one deafening blast. Each of the three bullets tore through - at different angles - the right hand of Roger Bartlett, causing him to drop the knife that harmlessly stuck, blade down, into the deck by his side. His hand still raised in the air, Bartlett turned his head upwards disbelieving the site of his bloody, mangled hand.

Quicksilver was standing on the bulwark of the *North Star* and addressed the silent crowd on the deck.

"Consider yerselves fortunate! That feeble and cowardly attempt nearly cost ye all yer lives! Or do you think this here ship can tame the dragon's breath that swallowed yer escort ships?"

With his wrath building, Quicksilver took in a deep breath and roared his last command: "Now back to England with ye and the Devil's own curse on any who venture across the Atlantic again!"

— Mathew Meets
Alison
Takes out 2 British
Ships

✝

Chapter 22: Aboard the Dragon

From the captain's quarters on board the *Sea Dragon*, Alison heard the loud final command from Quicksilver before he rejoined his ship. His booming voice was terrifying and her intuition was suddenly telling her that she perhaps had made a colossal mistake in trusting the infamous pirate captain. As she weighed her internal concerns, the door opened to Quicksilver in the passageway.

"Brava, Alison!" Quicksilver declared, "I congratulate ye on a magnificent performance. Why I thought ye were truly frightened m'self!"

"That's because I *am* frightened," she confessed. "I am also confused, and I'm beginning to think I may have made a tragic choice."

"I see. Well, I can't blame ye for being scared, but I can assure ye that you'll be perfectly safe on board this ship. Besides, you'll be in Virginia within the week. Now, until we reach America, ye have free reign of the ship - go anywhere ye like. Ye will be fed and treated well. The only time I would ask ye to stay below is if we're going into battle. Is that reasonable to ye?"

Alison looked up at the pirate, weighing his words.

"*You* are skeptical," he concluded.

"*You* are a pirate," she shot back without thinking.

"A fair point, dear," agreed the pirate captain. "However, don't judge things too hastily; things aren't always what they appear to be."

Quicksilver studied her, his gaze unreadable.

"Why are you helping me?" Alison broke the short, awkward silence feeling the weight of his stare.

"Yer cuts and bruises are fresh, probably no more than a day or two old. Yer an attractive young lady. It's not difficult to deduce what probably happened to ye." Quicksilver paused. "Let us just say that I take great offense to those who force their strength and will upon others."

"Well, thank you. I appreciate your exacting revenge on Lieutenant Commander Bartlett."

"Be that his name? Th' man's not fit enough to sail on a Royal Navy ship, much less wear an officer's uniform. I'm very sorry ye had to endure the likes of him."

"That's just it. He's never accomplished anything on merit. He wouldn't be an officer if his father had not set everything up for him."

Quicksilver's eyes widened in surprise. Then his brows drew together.

"He is the son of Lord Bartlett. How paradoxical that he wears an English naval officer's uniform and acts as a savage, whereas you seem so kind and yet you have the reputation of a vicious, cold-blooded pirate," Alison said, then bit her lip, worried she had insulted Quicksilver. "Oh, I'm so sorry, I didn't mean..."

"That's quite alright, dear. No offense taken personally. In fact, I'm rather glad to hear it."

"You are? But why?"

"Well, as I said before, things aren't always what they appear to be. In any case, it's important to have something of a vicious reputation in my line of work."

"I suppose so."

"In fact, it's probably my most important weapon in battle. I would rather see a crew surrender as soon as they recognize the dreaded flag of Quicksilver. We're trained fighters, to be sure, but it's preferable to take a ship without a fight."

"Why did you spare the men of the *North Star*?"

"Dead men tell no tales!" pronounced Quicksilver slowly and ominously.

"What do you mean?" Alison asked, suppressing a shiver.

"It means I spare men so that they can tell wild tales about me that will enhance my infamous reputation."

While Alison mulled this over, Quicksilver stood up as though he had pressing business elsewhere on the ship.

"Alison, I meant what I said - you are entirely safe on this ship. Feel free to make yourself at home in my cabin. I will bunk elsewhere."

"Thank you, Captain Quicksilver."

"Alison, that brings up another little matter. I need to ask a favor of ye."

"You need something...from me?" Alison asked hesitantly.

Just then the cabin door opened and two rough looking sailors entered unannounced, approaching the table near the rear of the cabin where Alison sat. The noise and their approach startled Alison.

"Oh, don't be frightened, Alison," Quicksilver began as he noticed her jump. "I asked them to join us."

One sailor was carrying a plate of food, including bread, soup, and salted meat along with large cup of fresh water. The other was carrying an odd looking bag.

"These men are here to make you more comfortable. This is Ramirez, the ship's cook. And this is Pietro, our ship's doctor."

Ramirez placed the food on the table in front of the young woman and placed a linen cloth across her lap.

"It is a pleasure to serve one so beautiful, miss," he said in a thick Spanish accent as he bowed.

"Thank you very much, Ramirez," Alison replied, as he turned and strode out the door. Meanwhile, the doctor opened his small leather bag and removed a few items.

"Let me see your face," he asked in an even more pronounced Spanish accent, as he felt around her face delicately without waiting for her reply. As much as Ramirez was considerate and warm, the doctor was clinical and cold.

"Please don't move," added the doctor. "Ah, your cheek

bones have not been broken, and your nose is fine."

He then examined her swollen black eye closely. He gently pulled back the eyelid to see into the eye. "I'm sorry if this is uncomfortable, miss, but I need to examine the eye itself. It won't take long."

He turned to Quicksilver and asked him to hold up a candle nearby for additional light. He then closed her eye and opened his medical bag. "You will have blurry vision out of this eye once it opens, probably for a couple of days," Pietro pronounced. "But there seems to be no permanent damage. The bruises and split lip will likely heal by the time you reach your home."

The doctor reached into his bag, removed a small jar and handed it to the girl. "Here, rub this salve on the damaged portions of your face and lips each night before sleeping, understand?"

"I will, thank you. But what is it?" asked Alison.

"You don't want to know," the doctor answered. "If I told you, you probably wouldn't put it on your face. But it is one of the most powerful substances for healing broken skin and preventing scarring and infection. In any event, I don't know the English words for this."

Alison listened as Quicksilver spoke to the doctor in rapid Spanish. It wasn't what the doctor replied back to Quicksilver in rapid Spanish that made Alison wince, but the grimace on the pirate captain's face when he was informed of the ingredients in the salve.

"Ye don't want to know!" Quicksilver confirmed in English to Alison with a wry smile.

"Also, you would do well to stay out of the sun," added the doctor with no emotion as he began collecting equipment into his bag and stood to leave. "Sunlight would be moderately uncomfortable for your wounds and will lengthen the healing process."

Quicksilver stood as well and shook the hand of the doctor while speaking in Spanish again. After walking him to the door, Quicksilver turned to Alison.

"Forgive the interruption, Alison, but I thought it best to feed ye and look after yer wounds as soon as possible. Now, where were we…oh yes, I need to ask a favor of ye," began the large pirate. "When ye do get to Virginia, there will be a lot of questions to answer. They'll want to know how ye got there ahead of the *North Star* for starters. Then you'll have to explain how ye escaped the *Sea Dragon*. They'll also want to know what we…did…to ye," trailed off Quicksilver uncomfortably.

"I need ye to tell them that we locked ye in a cell below for the entire trip and that ye were allowed air on deck once or twice a day under close supervision. Ye escaped when a drunken pirate escorted ye up for night air one evening. No one was watching and ye slipped over th' side and swam ashore."

"I just don't know…" the girl began.

"Of course, we could accommodate the story by literally locking ye up…for authenticity sake," the big pirate grinned.

"Oh, no, that won't be necessary," Alison countered quickly, "I have no problem protecting your generosity to me with a lie."

"Good. Now if you'll forgive me, I need to speak with the crew on a number of issues. Eat your food and make yerself comfortable. If ye need anything, I'll be back in a half-hour or so, and I will knock first."

Alison watched the previously terrifying pirate leave the cabin and gently close the door behind him. She wasn't sure, but she thought he smiled back at her as he shut the door, but with her one-eye vision and his thick beard, she couldn't be certain.

As she turned again to her food on the table, she looked up through the aft windows and watched the *North Star* disappear into the horizon. For the first time in a long while, Alison Davis felt a peculiar sensation of safety.

A gentle knock at the door, nearly imperceptible, brought Alison back from a deep and restful sleep.

"Come in," she called out as she propped herself up on one elbow.

Judging by her own state of drowsiness and the shadowy hue within the cabin, Alison figured she'd been asleep for several hours. Indeed, as the door opened, the sun that had been high in the sky when she was carried over to the *Sea Dragon* was now low in the western sky and lit up the room once the door was opened. The unmistakable silhouette of Quicksilver appeared in the doorway and slowly entered.

"I'm sorry to wake ye, Alison. You've been asleep for quite some time, and I need to take a look at some charts."

"I'm so sorry. You should have knocked louder," Alison offered.

"Oh, no. Ye need yer sleep more than I need the charts. We're making very good time. Anyway, how do ye feel?"

"Confused. So much has happened and all so fast that I don't know what's real and what's not."

"Well, let me try to clarify things for ye," said the pirate as he sat on the edge of the bed. "You've been kidnapped by the ruthless pirate Quicksilver and been made a slave of the *Sea Dragon*."

"Very funny," she bemoaned, her confidence in him growing rapidly. "By the way, will you be dining with me tonight?"

"If ye like," Quicksilver offered.

"I would like. I would especially like to know what such a hardened soul is doing on the high seas with a complete set of the works of William Shakespeare on his bookshelves," she added as she held up a copy of *Hamlet*. "You are a most peculiar pirate."

"Those? I'm afraid the truth is not so interesting, dear. We stole those off a ship about six months ago, and I thought they'd give the cabin a nice cultured touch."

"They're filled with hand-written notes and passages that are underlined," Alison said.

Quicksilver gently pulled the book from her hand and looked at the pages to which it opened as though he'd never perused one of the books yet. "Well, apparently we stole them from someone who really enjoyed reading this kind of stuff."

"Stuff?!" Alison shot back. "Did you say 'stuff'? Do you know who Shakespeare was? He is one of the most wonderful and influential writers of all time, and second to none in the English language. You should do yourself a favor and read these sometime. They're beautiful!"

"I'll consider it, dear, when I have more time," Quicksilver replied in a disinterested tone that didn't quite ring true. "For now, I need to plot a course for our cove in southern Virginia."

Quicksilver stood up from the edge of the bed and began to walk to the table that contained several nautical charts in a compartment under the lid.

"Mathew Carrigan!" Alison said slowly.

Quicksilver stopped in mid stride to his table and turned back around to face Alison, unable to physically hide his shock.

"Excuse me?!" asked the pirate.

"I said 'Mathew Carrigan'," Alison repeated, "See, his name is written inside the cover of each of these books, and underneath it says Warwick College, Oxford. I'll bet that this Carrigan fellow was either a student or quite possibly - given the amount of scribbling inside the margins - a don at Oxford."

"Interesting theory, Alison," Quicksilver responded in what seemed as relieved tone as he turned again to approach his desk. "But I need to plot that course now."

He walked back over to his table, opened the table top and rummaged through some nautical charts of the American coast. As he pulled the one he was looking for, Alison stood up herself and wandered over to where he was leaning over the large table examining a map closely.

"Quicksilver?"

"Yes, Alison," he answered without interrupting his plotting a course with a long straightedge.

"At the risk of annoying you, may I ask you another question?"

"Do I really have a choice?" he asked with a smile, again without looking up.

"No," Alison echoed his smile. "Why did you become a pirate?"

Quicksilver momentarily pulled his attention from the map and straightened up. He looked down at Alison and gave her a knowing smile. "Well, I always wanted to travel the world, and as for piracy, it was not something that I necessarily set out to do, but it turns out I'm rather good at it."

Alison smiled back at the man. There was something she just couldn't put her finger on, but he was an undeniably intriguing person. He was as far from the mold of a frightening pirate as one could be, yet she recalled how earlier that day he had crushed the British naval escorts and struck a terrifying chord in Captain Harwick and the British sailors. His polite evasiveness to her questions was almost rather charming.

"I'm going back on deck for a few moments to direct the crew. The sun is low enough that it shouldn't be a problem for ye. Yer free to join me," Quicksilver offered.

"Oh, yes. I'd like that, thank you."

As they emerged from the captain's quarters, Quicksilver escorted Alison to the center of the deck. He called attention to the men on the deck in Spanish with a booming voice. His pronouncement was met with much laughter by the crew and a quizzical look from Alison. One man yelled something back which really made the crew explode with laughter.

"What did you just say?" she inquired.

"I said that ye were very pleased at the way you've been treated and that ye were thinking of joining th' crew," explained Quicksilver. "And Javier added that yer too beautiful to be a pirate, but that ye might look good on the front of the ship as our figurehead."

Three gangly men walked up and introduced themselves in English, "Good evening, miss. On behalf of the English speaking contingent of the crew, welcome aboard the *Sea Dragon*."

"Oh, you're American!" Alison exclaimed. From her first moments aboard the *Sea Dragon*, she had quickly developed a high comfort level with her host and had happily dropped her false English accent.

"Yes, ma'am, militia from Pennsylvania."

"Militia?!?" said a shocked Alison, "what ever are you doing on a pirate ship in the middle of the war?"

"*Deserted* militia," corrected Quicksilver quickly as he gave them a glare from behind Alison, "came to claim their fortune on the high seas with us. A better prospect than marching against red coats in Pennsylvania, New York and New Jersey, eh men?"

"Yeah, that's right," laughed the three American men uneasily.

"Well, Alison, yer free to roam the ship. We've got a good strong wind and a following sea. Dinner won't be served for another couple of hours. Welcome to the crew of the *Sea Dragon.*"

With that, Quicksilver bolted across the quarterdeck and pointed to the compass in front of the helm while giving instructions to the crewman steering the mighty vessel. The sailor nodded his understanding and turned the ship slightly. With hands set on his hips, Quicksilver barked out some additional orders to the crew in Spanish, which generated a flurry of commotion among the men, sending them to multiple positions about the deck and into the rigging to adjust the sails.

The adjustment in the course and in the sails made a noticeable difference in their speed. For the next few hours, the ship raced across the water at a healthy clip, far faster than the *North Star* ever traveled thought Alison.

She began to think about getting home soon. Only two days prior she feared for her very life on board a British merchant ship, and now she felt an ebullient rush through her body as she felt the great pirate ship slice through the ocean swells. After standing at the bow and staring out across the sea for several minutes, she turned to look back at the aft deck and Captain Quicksilver.

Questions upon questions filled her head, and she categorized them in her mind as they would have to wait until supper to be asked. She took in a deep breath of sea air and looked out westward across the sea again, squinting her one open eye and teasing herself into imagining that she could see the first, faint lines of America on the horizon. The radiant sunset of pink and orange in front of them was the most beautiful she had ever seen.

In high spirits, she turned back once again to view Quicksilver, imagining what he might look like without the thick beard and long, wild hair. As though he could read her mind, he looked down at that moment and their eyes met. He waved out toward her and she snapped back a mock salute. Even with only one good eye, she was sure that this time she saw him smile.

Though she was not especially hungry, dinner could not come soon enough for Alison. The two hours watching all the deck activity and feeling the nautical miles roll beneath her made her tired. She looked forward to a quiet evening below deck and especially to continuing her earlier discussion with Quicksilver.

She waved once more to the pirate captain as she passed beneath the aft deck and re-entered the captain's quarters.

There, in the middle of the room was a wonderful surprise waiting for her. Stacked next to the bed was her luggage that had been taken from the *North Star* by some of the crew. She had not thought to ask for it, and was saddened earlier in contemplating the loss of her lovely possessions, but suddenly all was right with the world.

She opened the wardrobe box containing her clothes and contemplated the appropriate outfit for her first night on board the *Sea Dragon*. While she presumed she looked hideous due to her unsightly wounds, at least she would *feel* pretty in one of her favorite dresses.

Just then, Ramirez walked in with two plates of what looked like a kind of stew and a loaf of bread. Under his arm, he carried a bottle of red wine. He laid everything on the captain's table that had been temporarily transformed into a fancy dining table, complete with linen tablecloth and candles in silver candlesticks. He lit the candles and turned suddenly as Alison cleared her throat.

"I'm sorry, miss. You startled me. I hope you like the food tonight. It is a little spicy, so I bring the wine, too."

The young woman walked straight up to the portly, unshaven cook, threw her arms around him and kissed him on the cheek.

As Ramirez turned bright red, an amused Quicksilver appeared in the doorway and chuckled.

"Oh, don't encourage him, Alison. He'll just keep bringing ye special meals and wines all day, and your family won't recognize the fat woman that gets off the coach in Boston!"

Alison shot Quicksilver a mock angered stare, "Well, I think it's sweet how Ramirez has gone out of his way to make me feel comfortable." She turned to address the cook directly, "*Muchas gracias, Ramirez, y buenas noches!*"

Though her Spanish was limited to only a few words and her accent severely lacking, Ramirez's eyebrows jumped up and he grinned widely.

"*Buenas noches, señorita!*"

"Oh, good Lord, now you've done it!" laughed Quicksilver, "I can't wait to see what's for dessert!"

Ramirez smiled back at Quicksilver, who thanked him in Spanish for the food and for making her first night on board especially comfortable. Ramirez responded that it was nice to have a woman in their lives again, if even for a little while, to remember what life is like outside of the violence of war.

Before parting, he added that the girl showed a rare strength of spirit and, the bruises and cuts notwithstanding, was truly beautiful on the inside. Quicksilver agreed, but admonished the cook not to get too comfortable with the situation, for it would only last a few days.

"Quite a remarkable collection of sailors, Quicksilver," Alison said after Ramirez left, "and they respect you tremendously - anyone can see that."

"They are indeed an exceptional crew," the captain agreed as he grabbed the wine bottle and studied the label pensively.

Alison sat and spread a linen napkin across her lap. "I didn't think I was hungry, but this smells so good. What is it?"

"It's a kind of stew that Ramirez discovered after we held out in the Caribbean for a time. It's quite spicy, but very good."

"Where are you from?" Alison asked, feeling suddenly awkward now they were alone at the formal table.

"Alison, I don't mean to be rude, but there are many things about me which ye cannot know, and try to understand it's for yer own good."

"But I swear I won't tell anyone about you."

"I'm inclined to believe ye, Alison, but ye can't ask me to divulge secrets that would put the crew or myself in danger just to satisfy yer curiosity."

"Well, can you at least tell me your first name?"

Quicksilver shook his head from side to side as he began to stir the stew in front of him. Alison tasted her portion and proclaimed it to be delicious.

"Really? Ye like it?" said a surprised Quicksilver. "I'd have thought it might be too spicy for yer taste."

"Oh, no. It's very flavorful. May I have some wine?"

"Forgive me, where are my manners?!" said Quicksilver as he uncorked the bottle and began to pour the deep red liquid into Alison's glass. "It's a lovely wine from Madeira, actually."

The dinner discussion focused primarily on Alison and her past, as Quicksilver expertly guided the conversation toward her and away from questions about his own past.

After the dinner, Alison requested some night air on deck before retiring. Quicksilver escorted her through the cabin door to the main deck, where the near full moon lit up their way almost magically. The sea was relatively calm and the breeze was half what it was in the day. As the pirate captain turned and checked in with the helmsman, Alison continued her stroll toward the ship's bow.

"What a wonderful night," Alison announced to herself after several strides. The combination of the cool night air and Madeira wine made her feel relaxed, and the reflection of the moon on the water was dazzling. She felt as though she were in a dream, wishing so much she could open her other eye and take in the perfect moment in full perspective.

There were a number of sailors on deck, and each politely bid her a good evening as she passed. She stood near the bow and looked directly up. Though the moon was bright, she could see hundreds of brilliant stars scattered across the sky and the horizon.

"A beautiful evening, t' be sure," said Quicksilver, who by now had caught up with her on deck.

"Magical!" exclaimed Alison. "Is it true one can set a course by the stars?"

"It is indeed. That's what I was confirming with Vasquez at the helm."

"I'm sorry I've been asking so many questions."

"No need to apologize, Alison. It's understandable. I just hope ye understand why I cannot share too much about myself or the men."

"I think I do," she replied.

They stood together in silence for a few moments, staring out at the blackness where the sea met the night sky. Both recognized the serene and romantic moment and yet neither would risk spoiling it by saying a word. Individually, they each drank in the moment wishing it would extend longer. After minutes of comfortable silence, Alison felt a chill in the air and crossed her arms to ward off the cold.

"It's getting late, Alison," Quicksilver said. "It's a beautiful night, but you've had quite a remarkable day. Ye should get some rest."

With that, he walked her back to his quarters, where he left her to sleep.

Just before crawling into the bed, Alison remembered to put the salve on her facial wounds. As she opened the small jar and put her nose to the lid, she nearly fainted from the pungent smell. She put a very light layer on her cuts and bruises and lay down, pleading silently for sleep to save her from the foul odor.

- Alison boards
Pirate Ship
- Alison likes
Mathew and get
comfortable

✝

Chapter 23: An Intriguing Journey

*A*ison opened her eyes slowly as the bounding ship stirred her from a pleasant slumber. She arose from the bed and put on her robe, as Quicksilver knocked at the door and announced himself.

"Come in," she called out.

The pirate captain entered and asked how she was doing as he approached her. Just then he stopped in mid stride, a strange grimace on his face.

"What's the matter?" Alison asked.

"Oh, it's nothing, Alison…nothing at all."

Suddenly Alison remembered the pungent smell from the ointment on her face, an odor to which she had somehow grown accustomed overnight.

"It's the salve, isn't it?"

"Well, it *is* a bit strong…but I've smelled worse," the pirate captain offered, in a noticeably poor attempt to not embarrass the young lady. "Actually, that's not quite true - that is the foulest thing I've ever smelled in my life!"

Alison looked up at the pirate who had a big grin on his face. She couldn't help but laugh herself.

"It is awful, isn't it," she confirmed, to which Quicksilver nodded. "Too bad I didn't have some of this on the *North Star* -

250

it might have kept Roger Bartlett away!"

After they both had a good laugh, Quicksilver added, "You're very brave to make light of that experience so soon, Alison."

"Thank you," said the young lady, "but something doesn't make sense to me. Why am I so lucky?"

"Lucky? What do ye mean? Ye were beaten pretty badly," reminded Quicksilver.

"True," agreed Alison, "But I was taken off that ship by a chivalrous pirate who is escorting me home. How did that happen?"

"I'm not sure I understand yer question," admitted Quicksilver honestly.

"Well, what kind of pirate attacks a Royal Navy convoy? I mean, it's got to be far more dangerous than taking on an unescorted merchant ship, and it's not likely you'll gain much wealth off of warships."

"It is true that we'd prefer to take on merchant ships, but the Royal Navy is not so dangerous as ye may think. I know their tactics, their strengths, and their weaknesses. And as far as wealth on warships, well...ye would be surprised. The munitions and supplies I take from the British I sell to the Continental Army. It's admittedly not as direct a profit as taking gold from another ship, but the one extra step in the process pays for itself handsomely."

"I see," Alison said in a quiet voice, somehow disappointed.

"Alison, I know yer American and you think it wrong for me to profit from this. But look at it this way – without me, there is no way the Continental Army could make or otherwise obtain the guns and supplies they need in the war. I am taking a risk, as ye said, and aiding the colonies. It is a mutually agreeable situation that had been negotiated fairly by their army."

Though the explanation was unsolicited, it did make Alison feel a little better about the rogue and his dealings.

After an informal breakfast of bread and fruit on deck with Quicksilver and several of the crew, Alison affixed a garish wide-brimmed hat to her head and stayed on deck most of the morning reading *Twelfth Night*, borrowed from Quicksilver's cabin. One of the Shakespeare's most beloved comedies the story of an individual who successfully carries on, falls in love and wins true love, all within a false identity.

She napped in the middle of the day and then avidly watched swordsmen spar on deck during a lesson led by Quicksilver himself in the afternoon. Late in the afternoon, she returned to reading *Twelfth Night* which lifted her spirits even more. As uncomfortable as she had been on the *North Star*, she was enjoying her brief stay on the *Sea Dragon* with its disciplined, but wonderfully pleasant crew.

Once again, Ramirez assembled a splendid evening meal from a variety of odd ingredients that Alison had never seen before. But it was the nighttime that particularly delighted her.

The calm sea and moderate breeze made for smooth and relatively slow sailing that night. Sailors gathered at mid deck to listen to five gifted musicians among the crew. One played violin as well as Alison had ever heard it before. In fact, he started the evening's revelry by playing a sad, melodic piece. After two songs that he explained to Alison were from his home in southern Spain, he was joined by another sailor who played the accordion, one who played a flute, and two more with percussion instruments. The songs they played were merry and lively, enticing the men, including the staid doctor Pietro to loudly stomp their feet and clap their hands along with the melody.

Before the next song started, one of the crew came over to Alison and extended his hand for a dance. She accepted the offer by placing her hand in his and allowing him to pull her to her feet. His English was no better than her Spanish, but he gestured for her to extend her right hand, as though for a dance. She smiled as far as her split lip would allow and the dance was on.

At first he moved slowly, so she could recognize the pattern of his steps. It was a rather simple dance, but the challenge came when the music sped up significantly. Aside from the racing music, Alison could hear the cheers of encouragement and whopping and hollering as she and her partner quickly danced around their area of the deck.

The song built to a fevered crescendo and ended in a flurry of quick moves. The moment the music stopped, a deafening cheer exploded from the rest of the surrounding crew. Alison gratefully curtseyed to her partner.

After another spirited song from the band, in which ␣ was whirled around again, this time by another crew m␣ Quicksilver stepped in and reminded everyone in Spanish she should rest and not be asked to dance every song. ␣ audible disappointment from the crew was all the translatio␣ Alison required to know exactly what Quicksilver had announced.

"It's alright, Quicksilver. I am tired, but I can dance one more song," she proudly proclaimed.

"Fine. Yer the captain tonight. Choose a partner and dance once more, but that's it for tonight. Ye need yer rest more than ye realize."

Alison looked around at the crowd of enthusiastic sailors as though carefully considering whom her partner would be for her last dance of the evening. Each extended their hands to ensure she noticed them.

In fact, Alison walked through the circle of crewmen spread around the dance area and grabbed the hand of the tallest pirate of them all, and the only one seemingly uninterested in dancing. She looked up into his eyes and smiled.

"Does the fearsome Quicksilver dance the bolero?" she asked, to which the captain of the crew merely shouted something quickly in Spanish to the musicians without taking his eyes off those of the young lady.

"Careful, Alison. You'll make a gentleman of me yet!" he joked.

The music began and the two dancers glided around the deck so fluidly that the entire crew was captivated. It surprised Alison that Quicksilver was so graceful, but not the men on deck. His own methods of teaching swordsmanship were based on many balanced and fluid dancing moves. When the dance was over, the entire crew cheered as though they had witnessed a professional ballet.

The musicians played several more songs, and instead of dancing, several of the crewmen sang along in a series of lovely ballads from their homeland. Alison sat quietly, listening to the romantic songs and watching the brilliant stars above. She

d up near the main sail and was carried
· one of the crew. Quicksilver threw a
the door to his cabin quietly behind
'h below deck.

₁ himself, sleep was slow to come. He
₋₋ₘking of Alison, her passion for Shakespeare,
₋₋al streak, and the bolero dance they shared that
₋₋ng. For the first time in his life, he had a strange and
powerful feeling for a woman. She was not like others he had
known in England; she was entirely unforgettable.

He also realized the cruel irony that he had, at long last,
discovered a woman he found both intriguing and delightful,
though he was bound not to let her into his chaotic life.

The *Sea Dragon* made good time on its westward course and
was within a day of the American shore. Alison's wounds were
healing quickly, thanks to the special ointment Pietro had
provided and her own discipline to stay out of the sun.

Considering all the wickedness she had endured on the *North
Star*, her engaging spirit could not have been brighter, and it
seemed the closer they moved toward America the happier she
became. The crew considered her as a wonderful young woman
and a terrific distraction from the rigors of their wartime
responsibilities.

Alison spent most of the middle of each day out of the
sunshine reading *Twelfth Night*.

After a casual meal on the deck with the crew that evening,
she made her way up to the raised aft deck, where Quicksilver
himself was at the helm of the *Sea Dragon*.

"We're close to America, aren't we," Alison asked as she
walked up to the captain's side.

Quicksilver nodded, "I expect we'll see it on the horizon
tomorrow mid-morning and we'll arrive tomorrow afternoon."

"I see," she said.

"Aren't ye pleased, Alison?" Quicksilver asked.

"Yes, of course I am. I'm thrilled!" Alison began. "It's just
that I will be leaving all of you and that makes me sad."

"Alison, remember your promise to me," Quicksilver admonished. "Ye must tell anyone who asks that we kept ye in the hold and that we treated ye civilly, but coldly. And that goes for yer family and any other trusted friends. Ye cannot betray our confidence because ye will be potentially hurting the very men ye would seek to describe on favorable terms."

"I remember, Quicksilver. I will describe my last week precisely as you request. I would never want anything bad to happen to anyone on this ship!"

"Good girl," Quicksilver added with a sigh of relief, as he kept a focused eye on the horizon and a firm grip on the helm wheel.

"But in truth, this has been a wonderful week," she continued. "Everything was as you said it would be, and I am ashamed I ever doubted you."

"That's because ye know us all now," added the pirate, "but in yer earlier situation, ye could not have been certain. And given what ye went through the night prior, I'm actually surprised – though gratefully so – that ye trusted me. No shame or apology is necessary."

After a long moment of quiet, Alison added, "It was your eyes!"

"I beg yer pardon?"

"Your eyes. They are the deepest blue and most sincere I've ever seen."

Quicksilver blushed slightly, and even though he had a thick beard and the evening was growing dark, Alison seemed to notice.

"Also, you gave me a choice," she added.

"I did?" he tried to recall as his eyes remained locked on the sea in front of them.

"Yes, you said you'd take me to America or I could stay on the *North Star*. Do you remember?"

"Now I do."

"That told me that you were sincere. A treacherous man would never have left it up to me. He would have just...taken me...like Bartlett, I suppose."

"He's long out of yer life, dear. Don't give him another

thought."

"I know. And thank you again for exacting revenge. I'm especially glad I got to witness the punishment you gave him!"

"That was entirely my pleasure," Quicksilver said. Then he gave a smile that was almost sinister. "I can assure you."

They stood there together in comfortable silence as the ship cut through the dark water tightly.

All of the sudden, an impulse seized Quicksilver and he reached out and grabbed Alison's hand. But rather than hold it in his, he pulled her toward the large wheel and placed her hands on the helm. Frightened at first by the thought of steering the large vessel alone, she eased into it slowly as her apprehensive face started to reflect confidence and, finally, exhilaration. She smiled widely.

It was at that moment, with the moon high on the western horizon, that Mathew noticed Alison's wounds were nearly fully healed. Her right eye was open and barely bruised. Her right cheek had returned to its normal rosy color as the bruise had finally faded away, and her lips were no longer cut and swollen.

The evening sea breeze fluttered through her sand colored hair. For the first time, his assumptions were confirmed visually – Alison was indeed a very attractive young woman. The outer beauty that was once hidden seemed to radiate from her as she smiled. Her thrill of guiding the big war ship in the open sea was contagious. She turned to Quicksilver and smiled.

In that instant, his heart was completely lost.

On the final evening, with the coast of False Cape, Virginia, its southern most point clearly in sight three miles away, Alison spent her last hour on board the *Sea Dragon* graciously thanking the crew for delivering her safely.

Though her expressions of gratitude in Spanish were broken at best, her sincerity was clear and her tearing eyes touched many of the rugged crew of warriors. All of them would miss her bright spirit and expressive confidence, but none more so than Quicksilver himself.

In one of the longboats cruising swiftly to the shore at dusk,

Quicksilver addressed Alison directly about her travels ahead.

"Alison, we're going to leave ye with some very trustworthy people. They are going to take ye by coach to Norfolk and wait until you've located yer family. It is a one-day ride comfortably from here. I'm confident you'll beat the bad news of yer...capture."

"I understand, Quicksilver. And thank you!"

"Ye will spend the evening at an inn ashore. Ye can get some food and stay the night, and start yer journey home in the morning."

The remaining few minutes moving toward the shore, Alison silently fiddled with the thoughts she wanted to convey to her hero that had literally saved her life and delivered her home. Was she feeling affection for the menacing pirate captain simply because he had been kind to her? Or did she see something else deep down in the man that led her to believe he might be something more than the fearsome bandit he appeared to be?

When they reached the shore and ascended the moonlit path up the cliff wall, Alison continued to fumble in her mind with her eventual good-bye to Quicksilver.

The first party from the *Sea Dragon* reached the inn and entered. Immediately the smell of a boiling beef stew welcomed the transient seafarers. Quicksilver spied the proprietor and approached with caution.

"Welcome! The setting sun brings weary travelers to my inn!" announced the thin, fifty-ish innkeeper.

"But the sun will never set on our cause!" responded Quicksilver.

The innkeeper grinned, and Alison realized Quicksilver had completed some sort of secret code.

"Andrews," the innkeeper said, extending his hand to Quicksilver. "It's indeed a great honor, sir!"

"Chameleon," greeted Quicksilver accepting the man's handshake. "We appreciate yer help!"

Alison watched from a table across the smoke filled dining room as Quicksilver privately sat with the innkeeper and detailed the valuable list of goods they had taken from the *North Star*.

At one point, he motioned over towards Alison, presumably

arranging her safe passage to Norfolk the following morning. The man seemed to nod his understanding, which made the fatigued Alison feel a sense of relief, knowing that she would reach her father quite likely within two or three days. When the two men at the table across the dining room stood, they shook hands and the innkeeper approached Alison.

"I will serve you some dinner, dear, as much as you like. Then you can take the room upstairs and to the right whenever you like. It's clean and vacant. Get a good night's sleep, and I will arrange tonight for a private coach to take you to Norfolk first thing tomorrow."

"You're very kind, sir," Alison replied.

"You're entirely welcome, ma'am. The gentleman made it very clear that you are to be afforded every possible courtesy."

"Well, that's lovely, sir. I just want to go home."

"In the morning, dear, I promise. Now have something to eat and get some rest."

Alison realized that she was as hungry as she was tired, and reached for her fork to taste from the steaming bowl in front of her. As the stew warmed her mouth and her taste-buds became reacquainted with grilled meat and fresh vegetables, she reached for the loaf of fresh bread placed on her table and glanced up towards Quicksilver who was leaving the inn.

As though the slamming doors woke her up from a daze, Alison stood impulsively from her table and ran through the entrance herself.

"Quicksilver!" she called to the man pacing away from her. He stopped and turned around.

"Yes, Alison?"

"I'm sorry, and I know you have to go, but I have to ask you something."

"Yes?" he replied as she walked up to him slowly.

"It occurs to me that if we had perhaps...met...under...well, very different circumstances, of course...that we might...we might...possibly be...friends," Alison inwardly cursed herself for handling her fond farewell moment so clumsily.

Mathew stared at the beautiful girl, touched by her obvious and awkward affection for him, and reached out his strong hands to hold each of her shoulders. "Alison, listen very carefully to me. Ye think I'm a wonderful person, but it only seems that way because Bartlett was a horrible man. Compared to that cad, I suppose I am quite a gentleman. But ye are a wonderful young woman and ye deserve a truly wonderful man. Promise me, Alison, that ye won't settle for anything less."

"I promise," she meekly responded in a quiet voice. "I won't forget you, Quicksilver. Please don't forget me," she added.

"I hardly think that would be possible, Alison."

"Will you do me one more favor, Quicksilver?"

"And what is that, dear?"

"Please read your Shakespeare. Specifically *The Tempest*, Act Three, Scene One, Line fifty-five," she said hurriedly and turned to hide her rapidly blushing cheeks.

"Good-bye," she whispered as she turned and ran back inside the inn.

Unbeknownst to Alison, Mathew knew instantly the passage to which she referred, where the beautiful Miranda professes her love for the handsome Ferdinand.

"I would not wish any companion in the world but you, nor can imagination form a shape besides yourself to like of."

He watched her disappear into the inn as he whispered the passage for no one to hear. A small tear formed in his eyes as he saw the young woman he had fallen in love with leave his life for good.

Inside the inn, Alison failed to conceal her feelings as the proprietor approached with a glass of wine.

"I suppose that the large cargo should fetch him a small fortune," mused the saddened Alison.

"There's no gold changing hands here, dear," the proprietor corrected her. "The supplies he brings us go directly to the revolution! Why, that man is one of the main reasons the tide of the war is turning for American independence!"

Alison sipped her wine gently as her tired mind slowly began to assemble the puzzle pieces that were Quicksilver.

- *See a Drayon Approches*
America
- *A lisar dances with Mathew*

†

Chapter 24: Trojan Horse

In the Spring of 1780, King George summoned a strategic session of his top naval commanders available in London to devise a plan to track and destroy Quicksilver. The initial thought was to commit a greater number of naval war ships and crush the lone pirate ship by sheer force.

"In my opinion, we would be committing thousands of men and several more British war ships to defeat," said Captain Harwick.

"Ridiculous!" was the shout from several other captains who had not dealt with Quicksilver first hand.

"Yes, it is," Captain Harwick agreed, "and yet it is true all the same. I saw him destroy the *Atlas* and the *Gemini* with my own eyes. He blew them out of the water before they could get a shot off. It must have been the dragon's breath, but he sunk those ships like they were paper boats in a pond!"

The disbelieving commanders looked at each other with renewed seriousness.

"If we cannot defeat the man in a sea battle, then let us try to defeat him hand-to-hand," reasoned Admiral Watts, who had sat quietly up to that point at one corner of the long table.

"I only wish it were possible. But I can tell you from personal experience that I've never seen a man faster with the sword," interjected another captain that had witnessed deck fighting in which Quicksilver had cut down several talented swordsmen as though they were ribbons.

"The point is moot because he would never try to board a British war ship; he would destroy it first," added Harwick.

"I see your point," one admiral agreed, as several others nodded.

"Then how is it that you live to tell the tale?" Watts asked.

All eyes turned from Watts and focused on Thadeus Harwick.

"Well, I suppose it was because I captained a merchant ship filled with supplies. We were not a threat as a war ship. We surrendered immediately and Quicksilver wanted to take our stores intact."

"Precisely!" said Admiral Watts.

"What is your point, Admiral Watts?" another admiral inquired rather indignantly.

"Gentlemen, suppose we send a merchant ship again, only this time with no escort. Instead of civilians, we send rugged naval fighters, the best swordsmen and fighters we have, only in civilian clothes."

The grim faces around the table began to see the advantage in Watts' concept and small grins started to form.

"We could practically invite them to board the merchant ship," joked another commander.

"And when they board, we'd be ready – extra men, extra guns. The element of surprise! We'll fight them to the end, including Quicksilver!" offered another.

The mood in the room brightened considerably.

"Admiral Watts," called out First Lord of the Admiralty Simon Hughes from the opposite end of the long oak table. The talking in the room quickly stopped. It was the first time he had spoken up. "Your strategy is reminiscent of the Trojan horse. The element of surprise may indeed be the advantage that enables victory."

"Thank you, My Lord," Watts replied, already preparing in his mind the obvious next question.

"Do you have a man in mind that would take on this dangerous assignment?"

"I believe I do, My Lord. Captain Artemis Shaw," offered Watts as the suggestions was generally met with nodding and verbal agreement.

"I must respectfully disagree," Admiral Malcolm Young said. "Shaw has sailed with me on two voyages as a lieutenant, and one as a commander. I have found him to be aggressive and impetuous, borderline ruthless. I'm still not comfortable with his being named a captain in His Majesty's navy, to tell the truth."

"I agree with every one of your insightful observations, Admiral Young," Watts concurred to the confusion of the rest of the leadership around the table. "Captain Shaw is everything you say, perhaps worse, and yet these are the very reasons I would send him."

Watts then turned from facing Admiral Young to face the entire table.

"Gentlemen, this is not a conventional naval enemy. We may need to consider sending someone *unconventional* to deal with this unconventional threat."

"Send a pirate to catch a pirate!" offered one unseen commander as a few laughs broke out amid general nodding around the table.

"That is essentially my suggestion," Watts concluded.

There was a long pause before the First Lord of the Admiralty spoke once more.

"Admiral Watts, your plan is intriguing and your logic reasonable. I will personally present His Majesty the plan this morning. You will arrange for Captain Shaw's immediate transfer and brief him on his new assignment."

◆

At ten minutes past four o'clock on the afternoon of June 23rd, the watch in the crow's nest of the *Nottingham* called out that another ship approached from the southwest. The sun was particularly bright that day and the ocean surface uncharacteristically calm. Between the bright sun and the reflecting glare sparkling on the water, the distant ship approached the *Nottingham* from an angle that made it difficult to see clearly.

On the *Sea Dragon*, the watch called out the British merchant ship in the distance. Mathew thought the approach perfect. The brilliant sun was in the eyes of the enemy, whereas he could clearly see his own adversary on the horizon.

When the *Nottingham* was within telescope range, Mathew elected to raise their pirate flag and thus frighten the British merchant ship crew, perhaps into an early surrender. Indeed, almost as soon as Quicksilver's terrifying pennant was raised, so too was a white flag of surrender from the *Nottingham*.

Interesting, Mathew thought, *and too easy*. That had to be the fastest surrender on record. It was almost as though they had the white flag already out and ready to be raised. He scanned the entire distant horizon in every direction, concerned that the seemingly unescorted cargo ship was bait for a trap.

As Mathew refocused on the cargo ship, another strange feeling came over him. There were some rather large and homely women standing on the deck facing the *Sea Dragon* - the heaviest and ugliest women Mathew had ever seen. But more than their appearance, it was the strange way they stood still on the deck that tugged at Mathew's intuition. The few times Mathew had intercepted British merchant ships, the civilians – especially women – had always run below deck. Why on earth would these large, homely women stand staring out at the approaching menace?

As the gap between the ships was reduced to just over five hundred yards, Mathew figured out the ingenious trap. These were no women! Indeed, these were not likely civilians. This was most likely a clever rouse to spare the ship from the dragon's breath and coax a hand-to-hand battle on deck. If that were so, then there was most certainly an entire company of soldiers below deck waiting for the call to come out and overpower the boarding pirates.

On the *Nottingham*, Captain Shaw crouched behind the bulwark near the aft of the ship, a fiendish grin frozen on his face, already enjoying what he perceived to be a pending slaughter.

"Drop yer sails!" came a loud and craggy voice from the one that must be Quicksilver. "We intend to board ye!"

"Drop the sails!" repeated the small man on the aft deck of the *Nottingham*, pretending to be the captain. A handful of sailors jumped into action to accommodate the order.

As they approached the cargo ship, Mathew saw that the bright afternoon sun would be in the eyes of the adversary.

"Prepare to board!" Quicksilver yelled to his crew loud enough for the entire deck of the *Nottingham* to hear him, before addressing the *Nottingham* directly. "Avast English ship, lay to. We're coming aboard!"

"We surrender! Please don't harm us," yelled back their captain. "We are defenseless!"

Thirty seconds later, the *Sea Dragon* pulled up alongside the *Nottingham*, and grappling ropes were thrown to draw the two ships closer.

Quicksilver smiled as he waited what seemed an intolerably long period of quietness before he gave the fateful order.

"Board her!" he yelled, and with his command, his men yelled and stomped on the deck like savages before crouching to a low position on deck. The terrifying sound of movement and screaming from the deck of the *Sea Dragon* was the cue for the men of the *Nottingham* to spring into action.

As one, the British sailors jumped up and stared into the blinding sunlight on the horizon, firing their pistols and rifles wildly and well above the *Sea Dragon* crew crouching behind their own bulwark.

In the next six seconds, while the crew of the *Nottingham* was straining their eyes to see, the King brothers let loose three quick rounds each that dropped nine men. With each shot, they put down the rifle and it was immediately reloading with their special filament packets by another member of the crew. In another twenty seconds or so, nine more British sailors would be seriously wounded or killed by the talented snipers.

The man in the *Sea Dragon*'s crow's nest, Marco Villareal, waited patiently for the right shot. His one objective was to shoot his counterpart in the *Nottingham*'s crow's nest. As he raised his rifle and aimed at the other crow's nest, he saw no one.

As he waited patiently, a few seconds after the battle began, a man peered over the edge of the nest and prepared to fire down at the *Sea Dragon*'s aft deck toward Quicksilver. Villareal squeezed the trigger of his rifle gently, as the King brothers had trained him, and watched the man across from him fly back over the side of the nest and fall over fifty feet to the deck, though likely he was dead before his horrifying impact.

The biggest surprise however was waiting for the reserve soldiers that were about to come up on deck. At the initial burst of gunfire from the soldiers on deck, the captain's cabin door flew open and the first of a stream of thirty more men came filing out into the sunlit deck, squinting.

On cue, several of the pirate crew fired crossbows, killing the first few men who came out on deck. After their fallen bodies created a small barrier for the others to pass, small ceramic hand bombs were thrown into the area behind the doorway. Their explosions sent flames back far into the cabin, setting the rest of the men trapped in the cabin, as well as the cabin itself, on fire.

At the same time, another twenty-five British sailors began pouring through a deck hatch near the bow of the *Nottingham*. Prepared for this tactic, several of the *Sea Dragon* crew fired crossbows, silently killing the first two men out of the portal before lobbing small vials of Greek fire into the open hatch. The fire spread quickly, essentially sealing the others sailors below deck.

Within thirty seconds of his first boarding command, Quicksilver gave the second command. The chaos of the fire and destruction on deck was an advantage for the *Sea Dragon* crew. Artemis Shaw squatted in his original position, dumbfounded at how his plan could possibly have failed. More angered at his failure than fearful, he rose up and prepared to cut down the first boarding pirate he could find.

He saw the first wave of the boarding, as fifteen agile men jumped aboard as one and fired blunderbusses into the disorganized British crew and lay flat on the deck. The next wave was only a second or two behind, another fifteen agile men leaped over the transom with blunderbusses firing into the rapidly waning British crew and then they lay on the deck. By the time the second wave of pirates had discharged their weapons, the first wave stood and whipped out their hand pistols and fired again into the remaining crew on deck. Then the second wave of the crew dropped their blunderbusses, reached for their pistols and fired as their colleagues crouched.

The confounded British crew had finally returned gunfire, striking down four of the pirates, two of them dead. However, the surprise barrage and subsequent fire had limited the fighting crew on deck, and the first and second wave of boarders had killed or wounded all but twelve British sailors on deck.

With sabers now rattling, Shaw crawled up the aft deck stairs and crouched low. He watched as his men were quickly losing ground to the more numerous and skilled pirate crew.

He, too, would be cut down for fighting through a formal surrender, and so he valiantly decided he'd kill as many pirates as he could before being caught. If only he could find and kill the one called Quicksilver, he would know that his mission had not been the total failure he was witnessing on deck.

As flames lapped upwards through the middle of the aft deck, Shaw raised his head and shouted loudly and slowly, "Quicksilver!"

By the time, he had finished calling out his adversary's name there was a loud thump of boots on the deck behind him. Shaw turned swiftly and saw the menacing pirate who ruled the colonial seaboard through fear.

The crazed man was at least six foot three inches tall and thick. He had long ratty hair and a long black beard to match. His blue eyes were so strangely deep and piercing that Shaw could see how the rumors of his being supernatural may have surfaced.

Quicksilver thrust both hands toward opposite hips and drew two shining sabers. Shaw could see right away that he'd have no chance to beat the pirate with the sword. He instinctively dropped his own cutlass and pulled both pistols from the leather holster-sash about his chest. Quicksilver approached the man with swords drawn high ready to pounce.

"Fool! Ye can't kill me!" a defiant Quicksilver yelled as he continued to approach Shaw.

The next five seconds appeared to every man on deck, British and pirate alike, in slow motion. The two pistols in Shaw's hands discharged at close range sending bullets into the torso of Quicksilver, who was lifted off his feet from the blast and thrown down hard to the smoldering deck.

The stunned pirate crew had never contemplated the death of Quicksilver, and looked up toward Artemis Shaw with a mixture of disbelief and raw anger.

"There, you see," Shaw yelled as he pivoted to face the motionless deck fighters. "He's no Devil! He is a man the same as you and me. And he is dead now!"

Several of the *Sea Dragon* crew were about to break off their deck battle and rush Shaw.

"Stay back!" Shaw ordered, "or I'll cut off his head and throw it into the sea!" The desperate threat surprisingly seemed to work, for the advancing pirates slowly moved back.

On the deck of the *Sea Dragon*, the King brothers all lined up shots to the head of Artemis Shaw. Their fingers slowly squeezed the firing pin in their long-bore rifles. But each pulled back at the very last instant, as something peculiar caught their attention.

Amid the emotional confusion on the deck of the *Nottingham*, the pirates looking upwards towards the aft deck began to gasp in horror.

"By the Devil!" exclaimed one of the British sailors, "Captain, look!" and he pointed to the area behind Shaw.

Shaw turned slowly and nearly jumped out of his own skin.

There, standing no more than ten feet away from him was a very alive Quicksilver. There were two bullet holes in the mid-section of his shirt, but no blood, and some of the Greek fire that had lapped on deck was on his thick coat burning and smoldering harmlessly, giving a most frightening effect as though he had just returned from Hell itself. The pirate captain's face was contorted in the most gruesome display of anger Shaw had ever seen on any man.

At that point, Shaw was prepared to believe that Quicksilver was the Devil himself.

The pirate captain still held a large saber in each hand and approached the English captain who was too stunned to move.

"Any last words, Captain?" Quicksilver spoke between tightly clenched teeth.

"Go to hell!" Shaw spat defiantly.

"You first!" responded Quicksilver, as he stabbed Shaw through the torso with both swords. As the pirate quickly extracted his swords, Shaw stood for a few seconds – his face still registering disbelief - before toppling to deck dead.

The British crew looked up to the aft deck in disbelief and dropped their swords immediately.

As the pirate crew raised their own swords for one final, emotional attack, Quicksilver yelled out to them: "Lay to!"

Even in his wounded state, Quicksilver was clever enough to realize that survivors of this particular battle would be eminently more useful to spread the wild legend that would reach even the king himself. With the *Nottingham* now burning in two large areas, it was only a matter of minutes before she felt apart and sank. Quicksilver called for his men to speedily transfer the surviving British sailors to the *Sea Dragon*.

◆

"Are you quite certain?" one of the admirals asked while all others were thinking the same impossible thought.

"No mistake, Admiral," the sheepish naval officer replied. "Shaw fired two shots directly into his body. I watched him clutch his belly and fall backward hard to the deck!"

"And he didn't even appear wounded?" asked another admiral from the sea of startled faces around the room.

"No, Admiral. It just seemed to…make him…angry."

Admiral Watts sat stunned as the other admirals all around stared at him. He had no explanation for the disastrous failed attack on the *Sea Dragon* that had been described in harrowing detail by its second in command.

"Admiral Watts," began First Lord of the Admiralty Simon Hughes, "your thoughts?"

Watts sat with his gaze riveted on the table in front of him. "Well, sending one ship against this pirate was, in retrospect, a mistake. Therefore, I suggest we try again but with greater resources."

A din of arguing naval commanders rose instantly, debating with one another the reasonableness of Watts' suggestion. "And from what theatre shall we pull these resources, Admiral?" one of loudest senior officers bellowed. "Surely, you can't suggest pulling ships from the Caribbean. We've too much at stake there as France - and Spain as of a month ago - have joined the war and desperately covet those islands."

"Not from the Northern theatre!" yelled another from the crowd of admirals. "New York is exposed to the French navy now that they've signed the Treaty of Alliance with the colonies. We cannot afford to dilute our naval efforts from the northern colonial ports!"

"Neither, gentlemen. I propose we send three warships from here. The *Imperial* and the *Atlantis* are due to be completed any day and are not yet committed to other duties. After dealing directly with the *Sea Dragon*, they can add to the support of either the northern colonial or Caribbean theatres. They have to make their way out there in any event."

The arguing instantly began again as seemingly each admiral had a differing strong opinion he wished to make loudly, in unison with the others. After a few seconds, First Lord of the Admiralty Hughes stood up and raised his hands. The roar of the other admirals and commanders quieted immediately.

"Gentlemen, the war in the colonies is not going well at all. Now that the French have joined the Americans, the Royal Navy will play an expanded military role. As such, we can spare neither our ships nor our focus at this time. And yet we cannot allow Quicksilver to continue to terrorize the colonial seaboard. Therefore, we will send three ships of the line, as Admiral Watts suggested, to track down and finally destroy the *Sea Dragon* before joining the war effort in the colonies."

In early 1781, the newly complete ships HMS *Imperial* and HMS *Atlantis* began their inaugural mission. Joined by the HMS *Avenger*, the three ships-of-the-line convoy left England with the sole purpose to hunt down the *Sea Dragon* and destroy it. The three captains had strategically agreed not to separate by more than a few miles. If Quicksilver were to be found, he would have to defeat all three war ships at once. The crew's confidence was boosted by the fact that the three ships would sail closely together. Like a pack of wolves that hunt for and attack prey in groups, the war ships would track their prey together.

The convoy rushed at full sail all the way to the American colonies to an area considered by the Admiralty as the middle of all the reported *Sea Dragon* attacks on British ships.

Once they reached the point where America could barely be seen on the distant horizon, they turned to the South and patrolled the waters off the Carolinian coast no more than a mile apart.

For three days they headed southward without coming across the *Sea Dragon*. When they did see a slight wisp of a cloud that could be a ship, they raced towards it with the reckless abandon of a pack of wolves that had not eaten for days.

Just off the southern coast of the colony of Georgia, the wolf pack turned to retrace their tracks heading north. With the stakes of their mission high and their patience running thin, each of the captains felt as though their odds of running down the pirate ship would be materially improved by spreading out further from each other. Communicating through small nautical flags, they agreed to spread out just to, but not beyond, the limit of their vision.

There had been a captain's pledge before they left England to never move out of sight from at least one ship. Though the three war ships cut a wider swath in the sea spread apart, none of the captain's dared move too far ahead or away from the other ships. Victory, and more importantly the reward, would be shared equally among the three ships, admonished First Lord of the Admiralty Hughes. Any motivation to be the first ship to engage the *Sea Dragon* or to individually defeat it was removed right from the start.

This pledge had been of paramount importance to gaining the confidence of the three ships' crews, giving them a sense of relative comfort that no ship would fight alone. If one ship spotted the *Sea Dragon*, a signal would be sent immediately to enable the other ships to join the battle.

— Sea Dragon
takes out
another
war ship
sent out
+1 destroy
them
- Mathew gets
shot twice
but survives

†

Chapter 25: The Wolf Pack

In the early November afternoon of 1781, three British war ships sailed northward in parallel lines, the closest just over a mile off the South Carolina coast well south of Charleston. The sea was relatively calm, though a veil of fog had developed on shore and sat stubbornly over the first mile of sea.

The HMS *Imperial* was the middle ship in the wolf pack, as they referred to themselves, nearly five miles due east of the HMS *Avenger*, visible on the distant horizon, and the HMS *Atlantis*, nine miles to the east of the *Imperial*.

Each ship had an officer staring through a telescope at the ship to its side. The *Imperial*, by virtue of her being the middle ship, had an officer of each side of her deck staring continuously at the ships on her flanks.

Unbeknownst to the crew of the *Avenger*, the rare fog off the Carolina coast rendered their ship nearly invisible to the distant *Imperial*.

"I'm losing the *Avenger*!" the lookout on the port side deck of the *Imperial* yelled, without taking the telescope from his eye. "She's blending with the damned fog!"

"Signal to her to move closer to us!" barked Captain Yarborough loudly from atop the ship's quarterdeck as he raised his own telescope to find the giant white sails of the ship veiled against the fog to the west. At his command, several crewman positioned small flags on a line that would form the signal "thick fog - come east."

As the line was quickly raised up the mainmast, the lookout on the *Avenger* read the message in his head, twice to be sure, and turned to yell out to his own captain, but the words never made it from his mouth. A roar from the crew on the opposite side of the deck received the full attention of the captain.

"War ship off the port bow!" four of the men yelled in near unison.

Everyone on the deck of the *Avenger* turned to face toward the coast, trying to spot the ship shrouded in the now thickening fog.

As the men peered through the mist, the oncoming ship turned at the very last moment to avoid collision and pulled alongside the *Avenger* to within fifty feet.

The narrowly avoided collision was a momentary distraction for the crew of the *Avenger*, though the same could not be said for the other ship. With her cannon doors open and guns primed with short fuses for a fast barrage, the *Sea Dragon* unleashed a ferocious volley at extremely close range. The crew of the *Avenger* was thrown to the deck literally before they knew what had hit them. Several rifle shots erupted from the deck of the pirate ship and nearly a dozen British sailors lay wounded or dead on deck.

The *Avenger*'s captain loudly commanded his crew to prepare to return fire, but by the time they could prep the cannons, the *Sea Dragon* had passed by the wounded British war ship and was comfortably out of the firing line. The attack was over in seconds and the mystery ship had presumably turned quickly to the west to disappear into the thicker fog toward the coast.

The *Avenger*'s captain considered making a run for it by turning directly east and heading out to sea and the safety of his colleague ships. In a few moments, he believed he would shed the fog and could signal to the *Imperial* who, in turn, would presumably signal the *Atlantis* to join the battle. He quickly reasoned that this was the only course of action, as he looked upwards and noticed the sails and rigging were intact. The initial blast from the *Sea Dragon* had been so close that the barrage had been principally contained to the port side hull.

"Prepare to come about and head east!" the *Avenger*'s captain yelled.

Within a split-second, the orders were repeated down across the deck and a flurry of sailors collectively coaxed the large war ship to turn to the east. Without being told, the crew understood that the strategy would be to draw the unsuspecting aggressor out toward the other Royal Navy war ships that would soon be speeding their way, if they were not already.

The shifting fog was dense around the *Avenger*, but the crew knew they would get to a position of visibility within a few short minutes.

After the initial attack on the HMS *Avenger*, the *Sea Dragon* had continued on a path away from the rear of the British ship, but had turned to the east, contrary to what was presumed by the officers of the *Avenger*.

As the *Avenger* achieved its new easterly course, the *Sea Dragon* surprisingly reappeared out of the thin fog to the east coming right for her. Once again, the crew was caught off guard, but this time they were not entirely unprepared. The captain commanded the gun positions on the starboard side of the war ship to set short fuses and prepare to fire. There was precious little time, however, as the *Sea Dragon* had harnessed the northeasterly wind more efficiently and was coming in fast.

The *Sea Dragon* let loose another volley of cannon fire from close range, this time to the starboard side of the British war ship. Again, its close proximity limited the damage to the side of the newly completed English vessel.

The *Avenger*'s gunners took advantage of the passing ship and returned a volley of cannon fire, and the amount of damage sustained by the *Sea Dragon* was unusually more than that sustained by the *Avenger*. The *Avenger* had shot fewer cannon balls and more shrapnel aimed upward toward the sails and rigging of the pirate ship rather than her bulwark.

The *Avenger*'s captain audibly rejoiced seeing the damage sustained by the pirate ship, and raised his arms high in the air.

Prudence dictated that he outrun the now visibly wounded pirate vessel out to sea and allow the other ships of the wolf pack to join in and finish the fight. But the surprisingly effective blow delivered by his ship swelled the pride within the captain such that overconfidence and emotion dominated any remaining sense of reason.

So confident was the captain of the *Avenger* that the *Imperial* and *Atlantis* would soon arrive, that he decided to move in for the kill rather than continuing eastward. He commanded the ship to turn north and circle back to take on the ailing *Sea Dragon*. While the three captains would share equally in the financial reward, he visualized his name going down in British naval history for ages to come as the hero who defeated Quicksilver.

In the invisibility provided by the fog, the weakened pirate vessel made one more surprising move. Instead of proceeding toward the shore, she turned to the north to circle back toward the *Avenger*, coming about on the unsuspecting Royal Navy ship's port side.

Let's take the battle to them, thought Quicksilver. If he could surprise the *Avenger* one more time, he might take the ship by boarding her, which meant a better chance of survival than remaining on the badly damaged *Sea Dragon* and trying to outrun the British warship.

Quicksilver called out for Diego Rincon, and within a few seconds a short, brutal-looking sailor sprinted up the ladder to the raised aft deck and approached his captain. Quicksilver spoke for a moment, after which Diego smiled a ruthless grin and nodded his understanding of responsibilities, turning to jump down to the main deck. He quickly called out for two other sailors to assist him in his assigned task, and disappeared below deck.

Quicksilver verbally willed his damaged ship to gain on the *Avenger* that was, for some inexplicable reason beginning to turn, shortening the distance between the ships and presenting the opportunity to catch up.

The *Sea Dragon* limped alongside the *Avenger*, and the pirate crew let fly the grappling hooks to bring the ships closer together. Following a series of several gun shots from the King brothers that took out the first wave of defense on the British ship, the crew of the *Sea Dragon* charged over to the *Avenger* deck with blunderbuss guns pointing ahead, ready to blast away. Guns fired from both sets of crews as the pirates landed on the *Avenger* deck and rolled. The initial volley took a heavy toll on the *Avenger* crew, and nearly no toll on that of the *Sea Dragon*.

The roar of blasting guns was replaced by the sound of long steel blades connecting. While the British seamen were well taught, few had actual experience, as this was a predominantly novice crew.

The *Sea Dragon* sailors were winning their various sword battles on deck by a measure of nearly five to one.

The *Avenger* captain looked on in shock as the pirate crew quickly gained the advantage in hand-to-hand combat. He regretted his foolish decision to finish the ailing pirate ship alone instead of leading it out to sea for support from the other ships of the wolf pack.

Additional shots rang out from various locations on the pirate ship, adding to the death toll and chaos among his crew. He looked up to the crow's nest to see if his sailor atop the mainsail could confirm the *Imperial* was heading their way. He could see no man in the nest. Fearing the worst, his eyes followed the length of the mainsail downward. There lay the lookout that had been shot from his perch and plummeted to the deck, his impact contorting his body into a mangled pile.

The fog was beginning to recede, and the *Avenger*'s captain looked out to sea to note for himself if the other British war ships were closing in on the action.

As he stood at the front of the aft deck, squinting through the lifting fog and hoping the immense outline of the *Imperial* would magically appear, a loud thud came from the deck just a few yards behind him. Pulling his sword quickly from its sheath, he wheeled around to face the oncoming threat. The size, the two swords, the beard; there could be no mistaking his adversary's identity. The *Avenger*'s captain gulped with fear as he recognized the pirate captain Quicksilver.

As Quicksilver strode toward the *Avenger*'s senior officer, he crossed his arms as each hand grabbed the hilt of the sword on the opposite hip. He tore the swords out from their sheaths and primed them in the air. Within a few strides of the *Avenger* captain however, he stopped abruptly and stood looking at the man. Momentarily stunned, he had never expected to draw swords against this particular Royal Navy captain, a man he recognized immediately.

Over the past few years, he realized that his efforts might bring him face to face with one of his former captains or officer training classmates. He had often wondered how he'd react if he were to battle someone whom he respected in his former capacity as a British naval officer.

While he recognized the captain immediately, the frightened face he stared into now was certainly not one he had ever respected in his past. The hideous scar under the right eye and the brutish way he held his saber made Quicksilver grin widely.

Silently thanking God for the ironic twist of fate that brought him together with Captain Jack Wilson one last time, the big pirate slowly approached his father's murderer. Unlike other situations, where he willingly spared the lives of captain and crew to spread the tale of the *Sea Dragon*, there would be no mercy given.

Jack Wilson nervously awaited the charge by Quicksilver, who grinned fiendishly as he moved forward very slowly, eagerly anticipating a battle that he believed he might purposely prolong in order to savor the moment. The voice of Santos reverberated in his head, urging him not to take foolish risks or fight emotionally. *There was no way to fight this man without emotion,* reasoned Quicksilver to himself.

But in a flash, Jack Wilson ruined the dreams of the pirate captain. The one move Quicksilver could not have predicted, Wilson made with blinding speed. The Royal Navy captain dropped his sword to the deck and surrendered.

Rage spewed forth from the large pirate, "PICK IT UP!"

"No, I will not," Wilson answered, his shoulders shaking. "I know you have spared the lives of many British captains over the years. I will not duel with you. I surrender."

"The charity of which ye speak ends today, pig! Pick up yer sword!" Quicksilver commanded even louder than before.

"No," Wilson replied. "If I pick it up, you will surely kill me. If I do not, there is a chance I will survive this day."

"You've got it all wrong, filthy dog! If ye don't pick up that sword I will run ye through. Yer only opportunity for survival is to defend yerself."

Wilson stood his ground, shaking his head slowly, afraid that one more audible rejection would end his life.

"And this is the legendary bravery of the Royal Navy?!" asked Quicksilver rhetorically while cocking his head, attempting to goad his adversary into a duel. "Yer miserable little island has long ago seen its best days. I shouldn't be surprised if wee Ireland comes down and takes over yer pathetic little rock!"

The tactic didn't work. Wilson stood there, with pride noticeably wounded, but not one flinch to suggest that the insults had motivated him to even consider taking up his sword.

Quicksilver considered killing Wilson on the spot, but something else deep inside warned that the immediate gratification would still not be worthwhile. He recalled how a badly-beaten Alison Davis had requested he not kill the despicable Roger Bartlett and how much more the man suffered in humiliation, flogging scars, and a disfigured right hand. Death would have been too good for him. Quicksilver knew the quick death of Wilson would similarly not be enough to sate the pirate's lust for revenge.

Just then, a loud yell of alert came from the crow's nest of the *Sea Dragon*. "British war ship approaching from the east, four miles and closing fast!"

Both Quicksilver and Wilson turned to view the oncoming *Imperial* through the patchwork mist, perhaps less than twenty minutes from joining the fight. Wilson turned to Quicksilver and grinned confidently back at the pirate.

"Found yer courage, have ye?" Quicksilver asked, hoping Wilson would pick up his sword.

"I'll go down in history as the one who destroyed the *Sea Dragon* - the captain who defeated Quicksilver!" Wilson announced, shoulders straightening.

Quicksilver had heard enough. It would be just like Wilson to turn the events at hand to suit his heroic stature. Even if he were to die, he would get credit for the destruction of the *Sea Dragon* and his memory would be enhanced in the annals of British naval lore.

The big pirate plunged with drawn swords at the loathsome British officer. Wilson cowered knowing his life was to end in that instant. At the very last moment, Quicksilver pulled up from his assault and merely decked the face of the captain with his right elbow. Wilson dropped backward to the deck hard, spitting blood from a mouth that had three fewer teeth than when the day had started.

"Don't kill me! Don't kill me!" Wilson pleaded.

"Get up, pig!" barked Quicksilver. "I'm not going to kill ye...not yet, anyway."

Quicksilver sheathed his swords, kicked Wilson's cutlass aside and grabbed the lapels of the fallen officer to lift him quickly. The pirate captain called down to two of his men who promptly rushed up to his side. After a quick order in Spanish, they turned to the bloody-faced British captain, grabbed him and ushered him to cross over to the *Sea Dragon* with them.

Quicksilver called out to his men who were finishing off the last few men of the British deck defense. Many in the pirate crew turned and stared at Quicksilver, urging him to repeat what seemed an incomprehensibly strange command. He repeated it, twice as loud and so angrily that none dared ask why.

As the men quickly fulfilled his odd command, Quicksilver dropped down to the main deck and grabbed a rope to swing back to the crippled *Sea Dragon*.

Once he'd landed on his own ship's deck, Diego Rincon approached him and let him know his prior command had been completed. Quicksilver disappeared below the deck.

Within twenty strides, Quicksilver approached the broad circumference of the base of the main sail's mast below decks to which was tightly tied Captain Jack Wilson.

"I demand to know what's going on?" Wilson said.

"Oh, we've suddenly developed a backbone, have we? A bit late, Captain! Ye had a better bargaining position on deck with the sword in yer hand."

"You can't outrun the *Imperial* and the *Atlantis*? What do you think you're going to do?"

The menacing pirate merely grinned as he walked up to the face of the British captain, "Ye and I are going to have a little talk," Quicksilver said as he drew one of his swords and held it up horizontally and close to his own eyes to examine its sharpness. While he focused his vision on the middle part of the blade, the end of the saber was purposely less than an inch from Wilson's face.

"Lie to me and loose parts of yer body. I believe I'll start with yer ears," Quicksilver said as Wilson nodded slowly.

"There are many legends about me. Why some even say I'm in league with the Devil," Quicksilver continued, while Wilson laughed nervously.

"Actually, that one happens to be true, Captain, and I promise you that I will know when yer lying. I'm going to ask you a few questions. Don't be foolish and test me or I will hurt ye badly. Tell the truth and I'll neither hurt nor kill you. I'll leave ye alone. Understand?"

Again, Wilson nodded.

"Very well, let's start with an easy one," Quicksilver seemed to ponder what would be an easy test of the officer's sincerity. "Where did ye get that scar on yer face?"

"From a battle with pirates in the Mediterranean," Wilson said with a lift of his chin.

Quicksilver was not entirely surprised that, even in perilous circumstances, Wilson's vanity was stronger than his common sense.

"LIE!" Quicksilver took a step away from studying Wilson and hacked quickly with his blade. The bottom lobe of Wilson's left ear dropped to the dirty wood flooring. Wilson screamed out in anguish, but the pirate reached a gloved hand over the Englishman's bloody mouth to silence him.

"Shhhh. If yer too stupid to take sound advice, you won't last more than two minutes. I promise ye this – if I am to kill ye, it will be so painfully slow that ye cannot imagine such a fate. Now stop the blubbering; I only took off the lobe. The other one comes off with the next lie. Understand?"

Wilson nodded quickly, his tearing eyes squinting against the pain.

"Where did ye get that scar on yer face?" Quicksilver repeated.

"From a duel with a young Spanish boy in London about thirteen years ago."

"Ridiculous..." the pirate toyed with his nervous prisoner, "...and yet ye speak the truth," he pronounced as Wilson let loose a sigh of relief. "Let us continue. At which island did the HMS *Pinnacle* sink?"

Wilson's face went blank.

"Ye are Captain Jack Wilson, are ye not?" Quicksilver asked, to which Wilson nodded.

"Well, then I will repeat the question, only once. Silence or any utterance other than the truth will cost you dearly."

Before Quicksilver repeated the question, Wilson blurted his response out, "Malta, the island of Falfla!"

"LIE!" Quicksilver stepped backward and instantly cut off the lobe from Wilson's right ear. Wilson shrieked out with pain, but again his cry was muffled by the glove of his pirate captor.

"The captains of the British navy are truly as stupid as they are cowardly!" Quicksilver said. "Ye don't have to suffer, idiot! Ye literally bring this suffering upon yerself."

"The Greek island of Xirokos!" Wilson cried out after wresting his mouth away from the gloved palm of the pirate. "I swear it!"

For dramatic effect, Quicksilver took a few extra seconds and pretended to study Wilson's face from the side. "How very interesting...ye speak the truth."

Quicksilver stepped back and scratched his head in mock pensiveness. "Then why did the *Pinnacle* sink?"

This time, Wilson told the gory truth about the mutiny and destruction of the vessel including leaving the captain to drown.

"Ye speak vile, cowardly words, Wilson," Quicksilver began, "but ye speak the truth."

Suddenly Diego Rincon appeared in the doorway and called out to Quicksilver in Spanish, announcing that the approaching war ship was within five minutes of firing position on the *Sea Dragon*. Quicksilver thanked him for the reminder and told him to get immediately to the deck of the *Avenger* and cast free from the *Sea Dragon.*

Diego reminded his captain that their time was limited and that he should come right away. Quicksilver turned and blasted a verbal tirade at the Spaniard in Spanish so angrily that spit flew from his mouth like a rabid dog, and Diego disappeared before the harangue was completed.

Quicksilver drew several deep breaths and again faced the bloodied Wilson. "What was the cargo of the *Pinnacle* on that fateful voyage?"

"Gold! Crates and crates of gold coins. I swear."

"Ye speak the truth," Quicksilver said, to the evident relief of Wilson who was near fainting. There was so much pain on both sides of the British captain's face, as well as his mouth.

"Who betrayed the mission? Who was it that orchestrated the murderous plot?"

"Admiral Josiah Watts," Wilson responded. It was clear to Quicksilver that Wilson had finally learned the value of telling the truth.

"Ye speak the truth!" proclaimed the pirate. "Who else knew of this plot? Did the king know?"

"Of course not," Wilson shot back. "No one else knew. Watts engaged me to carry it out with a handful of trusted men. That was it. Not even the cargo ship that picked us up knew what was in the crates. I swear it."

"Last question, Jack! Where's the gold now?"

Wilson impulsively skewed his eyes toward the big pirate and considered remaining silent, lying again or pretending to faint.

"Faint on me now and I swear you'll never wake up!" warned Quicksilver, anticipating Wilson's thoughts. He withdrew his sword and placed its razor-sharp blade against Wilson's sweating neck.

Wilson explained that the gold was stored at the estate Watts had purchased in Hastings. As for the handful of crew in on the plan, they had entrusted Watts with their share in exchange for a discounted, though nonetheless large, value in cash.

"Ye speak the truth. Our conversation is concluded." Quicksilver turned to leave.

"Wait!" Wilson called out. "You said you'd let me go!"

"Wrong!" Quicksilver shouted as he stood in the doorway of the room that was now taking on nearly a foot of water. "I said '*tell the truth and I won't harm or kill ye*' and I am not going to kill ye...the water will. Ye will drown in a matter of minutes, Jack. Time to make peace with yer God...if He'll have ye."

"Wait!" Wilson pleaded, looking down helplessly at the water rising up to his knee. "Don't leave me here to die. You can't do this to me!"

In perfect English diction, the brawny pirate replied, "I'm giving you the same chance you gave my father, you filthy bastard! And I shall enjoy watching you share his terrible fate."

Quicksilver watched Jack Wilson's face go entirely blank. It was all too confusing for the panicked thief to even contemplate.

Moving quickly to the cannon area, Quicksilver lit the core fuse expertly set by Diego Rincon. The cannons were primed to fire in less than two minutes from both sides of the ship.

On the port side, cannon shot was used, while on the starboard, nothing but gunpowder. As the big pirate moved to the next chamber, he found the remaining components of the Greek fire, previously safely separated in storage compartments on opposite sides of the ship, now bundled dangerously together. Quicksilver removed the top of two of the barrels. If they tipped over, broke or their contents were otherwise mixed, the back middle of the ship would become an inferno even as the ship was sinking.

Above him the grappling hooks had all been removed, and the *Avenger* was slowly pulling away from the *Sea Dragon*. Quicksilver ran the length of the main deck, gesturing wildly to the *Imperial* in the distance, and sprinted back toward the captain's quarters. Before bursting through his own cabin doors, he noticed his odd instructions had been followed to the letter. As many as twenty British sailors from the *Avenger* stood, tied to the riggings in various threatening but statuary positions, in pirate clothing with mouths gagged and faces painted white.

Quicksilver flew across the captain's quarters and immediately lunged for the rope hanging in the open window. It was unraveling as the *Avenger* pulled away. He could see there was only ten feet of rope left before he was halfway across the cabin. He had no chance to catch the line before it disappeared out the window. And yet he willed his body to pick up speed and dove headlong through the open portal just as the last foot of the line reached the window, clutching it tightly on his arc downward to the sea, preparing for a harsh impact.

His body hit the ocean with a terrific jolt. His head speared into the water with his hands extended, still clutching the line from the *Avenger*. With surprising strength he pulled himself forward several feet and ran the line around his leather belt. He had successfully created a harness to better hold himself through the water.

In the next moment, he was pulled by a massive force, as several sailors on the *Avenger* hauled him through the water and up on to the British war ship.

Less than a minute later, he was lying on the deck drenched and physically spent from being towed through the ocean.

"You have a flair for the dramatic, Captain! We were not sure you were going to make it," Diego Rincon said.

Before Mathew could answer, a thundering burst of cannons sounded from the *Sea Dragon*, riding low in the water, sending cannon balls at the *Imperial* now approaching her port side, and nothing but explosive sound toward the *Avenger* which was in the process of circling for another attack on the pirate ship. The *Imperial* let loose its own barrage from forty cannons, as did the *Avenger* on the other side of the badly damaged infamous pirate vessel. The seemingly coordinated barrage from both Royal Navy ships destroyed much of the remaining top deck of the *Sea Dragon*.

The heavily damaged hull was breached and the ship began listing. The sea would swallow the legendary pirate ship and her crew within another five minutes. Crews from both British war ships cheered as flames rose up high in the wounded vessel, all the way up the main mast. Eerily, the ship was sinking fast and yet was still on fire below decks where water had clearly breached the hold.

On the *Avenger*, amid his crew dressed in English uniforms and garb, Quicksilver pulled himself up and glanced back at the mighty Spanish vessel for its last moment above the surface of the sea. She went down in a violent explosion of wood, flames and water. The concussion of the blast threw many on both Royal Navy ships toward the deck.

Gone was the *Sea Dragon*, gone was the Greek fire, and gone was the treacherous Captain Jack Wilson. All in all, it was a more than fair trade off, thought Quicksilver.

But the danger was far from over. Quicksilver barked orders in rapid Spanish and men scurried about the deck in order to comply. "We're not out of trouble yet, men. Raise these flags in this precise order right away," he ordered as he pulled a number of colored pennants from the locker on deck.

As the men assembled the small flags and raised the signal to the *Imperial*, Quicksilver stepped back and peered through the fog at the spot where the *Sea Dragon* had just sunk. The water gurgled and let forth intermittent gasps of air, and an odd layer of smoke hung low on the surface, as though the ship were burning underwater.

A grin crossed Quicksilver's face as he verified the death of the man who had killed his father. He pulled a large knife from his right boot and sliced off of his wrist the leather strap that had once bound his father.

"For my father!" he said aloud as he tossed the leather strap off the deck and into the ocean toward the spot where he last viewed the *Sea Dragon*.

His vengeance, however, was not complete. In the annals of British naval lore, the name Captain Jack Wilson was still revered and his celebrity would be enhanced with his part in the sinking of the dreaded *Sea Dragon*. Somehow, Mathew would have to communicate the truth back in England, and Admiral Josiah Watts would have to pay dearly for his duplicitous crime.

- Mathew kills
  Wilson
- Mathew takes
  out newar fleet
  but boards another
  ship because the Sea
  dragon was destroyed.

†

Chapter 26: Loose Ends

From the deck of the *Imperial*, which had burst into a triumphant roar celebrating the defeat of the *Sea Dragon*, one junior officer peered through his telescope into the mist shrouding the HMS *Avenger*. While his colleague celebrated, the officer kept an attentive vigil on the *Avenger*'s deck. When he was certain what he thought he had seen, he turned to yell to his commander.

"'Victory. Minor damage to ship. Meet in Charleston'," called the officer loudly to the HMS *Imperial*'s Captain Yarborough.

"Bloody foolish of Wilson to take on the *Dragon* directly," Yarborough yelled back to the junior officer over the hysteria on deck. "He's damned lucky it was only minor damage. Very well...send a confirmation message back to the *Avenger*."

Yarborough turned and called out to his helmsman, "Midshipman Roth, prepare to come about. Make to the east in search of the *Atlantis*. We need to get out of this blasted fog and signal her to meet in Charleston."

It took nearly twenty minutes for the *Imperial* to finally pierce the veil of coastal fog, and Captain Yarborough was astounded to see that the *Atlantis* was literally nowhere in sight.

"Forty-five degrees, Midshipman Roth," Yarborough

bellowed. "We need to head northeast as the crew of the *Atlantis* seems to have their collective head up their arse." The *Imperial* crew broke out in laughter at the expense of their colleagues on the missing *Atlantis*.

"If we can track the bloody *Sea Dragon*, I should think we stand a reasonable chance at finding the damned *Atlantis*!" he added, as he attempted in vain to suppress a wide grin. The crew moved about on deck with renewed vigor knowing they would be considered heroes when they returned to England, and were due a material financial reward, as well.

"Dios mio! It worked!" cried one of the crew aboard the *Avenger*, as there was an audible sigh of relief from his shipmates. They peered through the mist at the now barely visible *Imperial* that had just signaled back its confirmation to go find the other ship and meet back in Charleston Harbor. The crew on the deck of the *Avenger* quietly rejoiced for a few seconds before scurrying about to turn the ship to the west, heading away from the British warships as fast as possible.

The damage sustained by the HMS *Avenger* in its clash with the *Sea Dragon* was by all accounts remarkable given the broad, direct attack in close quarters from the legendary pirate vessel. While "minor" - as had been communicated through nautical flags to the *Imperial* - was a decided understatement of the damage, the ship would indeed make it to their intended destination.

The commandeered British warship *Avenger* sped toward the cove of Port Royal, South Carolina, over fifty miles to the south of Charleston.

As they entered the Port Royal Sound, with St. Helena Island on their starboard, Mathew peered in the distance through a telescope. They were perhaps three nautical miles out of Port Royal and he could clearly make out the white flag dangling from the cliff. He grinned, with the telescope still held up to his eye, as he stared at the signal he had concocted with John Adams to communicate from a great distance that the "coast was clear" of British military presence.

Two-and-a-half hours later, the HMS *Avenger* crashed violently into the jagged coastline of South Carolina.

The ship, sailing at full sail, careened off the first few rocks it hit and tilted on its right side at a 45-degree angle, finally coming to an abrupt stop upon a set of rocks that ripped open a length of nearly fifty feet of the ship's starboard hull. The foresail, already damaged from the original attack by the *Sea Dragon*, snapped in two like a dried twig from a long dead tree.

The instant the ship settled awkwardly on its rocky perch, the few crewmen aboard went to work. They ventured below decks to recover the bodies of the thirteen Royal Navy seamen that had died in hand-to-hand combat with the *Sea Dragon* crew earlier in the day. Left in their uniforms and placed on scattered rocks near the ship, the bodies would substantiate that the *Avenger*'s crash was accidental.

Mathew slumped in his chair in a back corner of the Pelican Inn, savoring the first few sips of cool ale that raced down his dry, salty throat. His exhausted body was devoid of adrenaline and achingly demanded rest. He sat back and recalled with pleasure his final exchange with the despicable Captain Jack Wilson.

It was late and the Pelican Inn was occupied exclusively that night by the crew of the *Sea Dragon*. One by one, sailors approached Mathew and patted his sunken, weary shoulders, congratulating him on their collective fortuitous fate that day. In between well wishes, Mathew tried to make sense of the information he had interrogated from Wilson.

The young proprietor of the inn, a staunch advocate of the revolution, slowly made his way to Mathew's table.

"Beg your pardon, sir. Are you…?"

"Chameleon? Yes, I am," Mathew responded.

"In that case, sir, The Pelican Inn is yours for as long as you like."

"Thank you,…"

"Graham, sir. Michael Graham."

"A pleasure, Michael Graham. Thank you for
We'll need to make arrangements to transport the
as possible."

"Don't worry about that, sir. My cousin is the cou
goods you deliver. I'll go talk to him tonight."

"Fine," Mathew said. "And while you're out, do you
favor and remove the giant white sheet from the cliff."

"Of course, sir," Graham agreed. "Though you're welcome
long as wish, how long do you think you'll need use of the inn?"

"You're very kind, but we'll likely stay only for the night, Mr.
Graham."

"Very well, sir. Let me know if you need anything at all," the
owner stood, shook hands with the exhausted mariner, and
turned to leave.

"Oh, I nearly forgot," he added as he turned back to Mathew.
"I've been carrying it around for a couple of weeks now in case
you ever showed."

Graham reached into a pocket of his waistcoat and withdrew
an envelope that he placed on the table in front of Mathew
before leaving him alone.

Mathew stared at the envelope that read simply Chameleon
on the front. While bringing his ale mug to his lips with his left
hand, he extended his fatigued right arm and flipped the letter
over, noticing it had been sealed with red wax for secrecy.

The letter had to be from John Adams, and was likely one of
seven identical notes sent to the seven drop points agreed to in
advance of Mathew's privateering exploits.

Mustering his waning energy, Mathew leaned over the oak
table, pulled the flickering candle closer, opened the letter and
began to read.

Boston, November 12, 1781

*Heartiest congratulations, Chameleon! Thanks in large part to your
brave and improbable success over the years, the fate of the war has turned.
No longer is the concept of an independent America an unlikely dream, but
a tangible reality.*

victory in Saratoga, New York in
he entire war, the battle impressed
re! France joined the war in 1778,

s defeated a British fleet at
and reinforcements headed for
General Washington himself
in which Cornwallis surrendered to a
force just a few days ago.

rave men that serve you have rendered our new nation an
debt of service. However, I have appealed to those with authority
grant each man thirty acres of land in the colony of his choosing, a
commission in the newly formed American Navy if desired, and the
equivalent of £1,000 to be paid over the next five years. For you, the
position of your choice in the new American Navy awaits your acceptance.

Please respond to this letter as soon as you are able - if I do not hear
from you by spring, I shall regrettably presume the worst has occurred.

I pray that this letter finds you in good health. God be with you always!

Father John

Mathew read the letter again to ensure he wasn't
hallucinating. He chuckled lightly as he got to the bottom where
John Adams had used the pseudonym that only Mathew would
understand, as it dated back to his disguise as a monk on the
Atlantic crossing where they originally met.

The news was incredible. Aware that his efforts had materially
aided the American Revolution, Mathew had carefully
conditioned himself over the years not to become too optimistic.
The revolutionary cause, though noble, pitted an undermanned
and unfit group of volunteers versus the strongest ground
military and naval arsenal in the world. But it had been Mr.
Adams' vision that with guile, ingenuity, and a massive and
timely supply of luck, they might be able to motivate European
skeptics to join their war and defeat a common enemy.

Mathew summoned the energy to stand and address his men
in Spanish. As he stood on his chair, the boisterous gathering
quickly quieted.

"Gentlemen, this is indeed a proud day. I congratulate you all on a superb mission that started fast and ended up with the peculiar destruction of one British war ship and the Royal Navy believing we are all dead!"

Cheers and laughter rose from the men until Mathew raised his arms to quiet the crew in order to address them further.

"It is also a most fortuitous day, my friends, for I have received word that the British have surrendered to the American General Washington up in Virginia a few weeks ago."

The word *surrender* was followed by an explosion of cheers that shook the walls of the Pelican Inn, drowning out the details of where and to whom the military concession took place.

"We have no ship, but it doesn't appear we need one anymore!" Mathew added to hearty laughter that took several seconds to subside.

"Additionally," he continued, waving Adams' correspondence over his head, "we have been offered handsome compensation from our sponsor."

The men began to cheer, but quickly became silent to learn the details of the Adams' generous rewards, which Mathew read slowly. More cheering followed audible gasps of disbelief and genuine surprise.

"Gentlemen, there is one last item," he added as the crew calmed down to hear Mathew's solemn voice.

"You shall have the everlasting gratitude of the senior leadership of this new country, a country that can never formally recognize your names or your efforts, but will owe its very existence to your brave and selfless deeds. I advise you all to concoct your own version of the last several years, for we can never discuss the truth with anyone outside the *Brotherhood of the Dragon*. Is that clear?"

A disciplined affirmative response, loud and in unison, roared from the men, as though they were following an order aboard the *Sea Dragon*.

"Finally, gentlemen, I propose a toast to Captain Santos and the fallen colleagues of our brotherhood. While their brave sacrifices cannot be honored publicly, we will celebrate them in our hearts for all our years to come. May God bless them!"

Several minutes later, as the crew headed for the rooms of the inn, Mathew made his way to the King brothers to communicate - in English - the good news of the war and their share of the generous compensation. The exhausted captain was about to stand and retire to a bed for the night, leaving the Kings to ponder their future.

"What about you, Cap? Any thought to where you're headed next?" James King asked Mathew.

"No set plans as yet, though I need to return to England first," Mathew said, as the King brothers flashed a collective stare of disappointment. "There are a few loose ends in my life that need to be tied up, gentlemen," he added, which seemed to appease the patriotic brothers from Pennsylvania.

"But you're not exactly welcome back in England now, are you?"

"True," Mathew concurred, "but remember I am the chameleon, gentlemen. If there's one thing for which I've developed a talent, it is for adapting to new environs," Mathew added in perfect English diction, reflecting his advanced education at Oxford.

"Be careful, Cap!" said one of the brothers.

"It would sure be nice to see you again, sir," said another.

As the brothers stood to retire for the evening, Mathew stood with them and snapped a formal salute. Taken somewhat by surprise, the brothers, who had little formal training in military etiquette, uncontrollably snapped back a smart return salute.

"How do you like that?" Jeremy King mused. "The first time we salute an officer in the entire war and it's to an Englishman!"

"American!" corrected his brother Joseph, who extended his hand in a firm handshake to Mathew, as did the other two in turn, "Welcome *home*, sir!"

◆

It took two days for the wreckage of the HMS *Avenger* to be spotted by a British scout ship. Though the flames from its explosion had long died down, the ship was still smoldering, providing an eerie beacon for search ships.

Upon closer inspection, a number of bodies were found drifting in shallow water amongst the debris and strewn on the rocks. Four of the dead were positively identified by sailors from the ship that had discovered them. A search in and around the vessel wreckage yielded no sign of Captain Wilson or any other sailors. Those that were missing were presumed dead and lost to the sea, and the tragic discovery concluded one of the strangest sea battles of the American Revolutionary War.

A careful examination of the remainder of the ship suggested that she had been accidentally driven up on the rocks while traveling under full sail. It was thus presumed that the fog had shielded her vision of the coast, and her speed, as well as the jagged rocks of the coastline, combined to rip a gaping hole in the belly of the great war ship. Likely the listing vessel would have suffered spilled powder, and one broken lantern would have been enough to set off the gigantic explosion that destroyed the ship and killed the men.

News of the *Sea Dragon*'s defeat began spreading rapidly throughout the southern colonies as soon as the HMS *Imperial* and HMS *Atlantis* landed in Charleston. As word reached British and Continental troops alike, as well as the general citizenry, it was met with a variety of responses.

British troops remaining temporarily in America heralded the news of finally cutting down the marauders that had interrupted naval transport and supplies for years. With the war lost, they were eager to hang their winnowing pride on any notable victory.

Continental soldiers hearing the news were disinterested, though the civilian population of the colonies generally took the news hard. Over the years, Quicksilver had become something of a dashing hero, fighting a common enemy with a legendary success rate.

Within a month, the news of the *Avenger*'s victory and subsequent tragic destruction reached England. The Admiralty of the Royal Navy was guardedly pleased to have finally rid the Atlantic of Quicksilver, though it was a small consolation for losing the war.

For those British sailors and officers that had actually

encountered Quicksilver in person, the reports of his death were received with understandable suspicion. Skeptics questioned whether the pirate captain could be killed at all.

However, several of the *Imperial* crew claimed they could positively identify the pirate captain from the white-skull-face-painted *Sea Dragon* crew wriggling with freakish movements on the deck of the ship as she went down. Multiple accounts confirmed the large, bearded pirate captain raised his fist in a threatening gesture toward the *Imperial* just as she crossed the *Sea Dragon*'s bow. Consistent independent testimony further described Quicksilver turning and running across the deck towards his cabin at the ship's stern. In any case, he was confirmed to be on the *Sea Dragon* by multiple witnesses immediately before it sank.

Even the skeptical gradually grew more confident of the infamous pirate's demise as time passed with no new reported sightings or attacks.

Captain Wilson's memory was posthumously raised to the level of one of the greatest naval heroes in British history. Given his courageous heroics in the HMS *Pinnacle* disaster near Malta earlier in his career, his notable victory against the infamous Quicksilver, and the sorrowful death in the line-of-duty in a distant foreign land, Wilson's name would be heralded for decades, if not centuries, to come.

- News spreads about the Sea Dragon Sinking - everybody thinks Mathew is dead
- Mathew Recieves a letter from John Adams about the generous reward Crews defending America too

†

Chapter 27: Collaboration

In the quiet of a cool April evening, Andrew Dunn decided to relax on his terrace for a post-dinner pipe and cognac. He looked forward to reclining in his comfortable chair while watching stars light up the sky. After retrieving a blanket to ward off the chilly spring air, he wandered into his study to pour his drink and select his favorite pipe and Virginia tobacco. As he entered the large room, something out of the ordinary caught his eye.

Upon his oak desk lay a long, narrow box with a thick ribbon securing the contents and an envelope slipped under the ribbon. He pulled the small envelope and read the card:

To my dear friend,

Your sincere kindness and immeasurable support over the years have helped me on many occasions. I shall forever be grateful for all you have done.

As a small token of my esteem, please accept these unique gifts that I know you, especially, will appreciate. Perhaps they can be added to your private collection of precious nautical artifacts.

The gesture seemed genuine, yet the fact that there was no

signature was intriguing. Dunn pulled at the bow and unwrapped the heavy paper to reveal a leather tube-like valise. Untying the leather straps securing the top, he peered in a pulled out a long steel object that turned out to be a badly tarnished sword.

Judging by shape of the hilt it was that of a naval officer, but it was in poorly corroded condition. He examined the area where the blade connected to the hilt and noticed there was an engraving that had somehow survived the elements that had otherwise worn down the blade's once sparkling luster.

Dunn struggled to read the engraving and did not believe what he thought he was seeing. He bent down and moved closer to the bright lamp on the large desk and picked up a magnifying glass to get a better look. His eyes registered the name, but his mind didn't initially accept it. How could it be true? In his hands was the broad sword of his long time best friend, Captain Thomas Hatley.

He gently placed the sword on the desk and slowly shook his head, unintentionally beginning to softly speak out loud.

"I...cannot accept this!"

"Of course you can. He would have wanted you to have it," answered a familiar voice from behind the study curtain, which made Dunn nearly jump out of his skin.

Dunn recovered his composure, turned, and smiled. "Come out here, boy, so I can get a good look at you!"

Mathew stepped from behind the drapery and walked toward Dunn with a beaming grin and extended arms. Dunn was so pleased to once again see the son of his best friend, but as the young gentleman got closer to the light from the desk, he could see a dramatic change in the lad's physical appearance.

"I dare say I would hardly recognize you!" Dunn added as he threw his arms around Mathew.

"That is the intent, Uncle Andy. It wouldn't do if someone in London were to recognize me."

Mathew wore a resplendent suit of colorful silks. His curly hair had been trimmed to a stylish mid-length cut, and his once thick and wavy beard had been reduced to a neatly trimmed moustache and goatee. He wore an interesting pair of glasses that, though the lenses were clear, made him look older and effectively diluted the deep blue in his eyes.

"It's grand to see you, my boy, just grand!" Dunn held the tall man by the sides of his muscular shoulders. "You must stay for a while. Tell me where you've been, what you've done. I want to hear all about it."

Then the gentleman wearing a blanket around his shoulders let go of his unannounced guest and dropped his head as his tone became sorrowful. He paused briefly before his next statement. "Oh, Mathew, there is much to discuss. I don't know whether or not you're aware...Wilson is dead."

"I am aware," Mathew responded slowly as though he had finally come to accept the fact. "I cannot stay more than a few days, but you're right about having much to discuss." Mathew nodded toward the leather valise on the desk, "Aren't you going to look and see what else is inside."

Dunn recovered and raised his face again, pleased that Mathew had already known of Wilson's death, and for the fact that the young man seemed accepting of the passing of his long term target of revenge.

"Of course, my boy. Forgive me," Dunn moved toward the leather satchel. "But we'll discuss your father's sword in a moment. In any event, Wilson got what was coming to him after all. I must say I'm somewhat relieved that there's no need for you to put yourself in harm's way any longer to settle a blood score."

As he peered into the leather tube and reached in to pull out the second object, Dunn could have sworn he heard a faint smirk from Mathew.

It was another sword, but very much unlike the first one. This sword was more like a fighting saber with a shining blade and intricately decorated silver and gold hilt. Dunn held it in his two outstretched hands and examined the steel. It was thick and razor sharp. The heavy sword was as uniquely impressive as it was frightening. The mere sight of this cutlass would immediately frighten an opponent in any battle.

Dunn immediately prized the rare blade and looked down toward the intricate hilt. Among the fancily engraved design work was a hideous serpent coiled into a circle, with a saber laid across its body, forming the letter "Q". Dunn shuddered as he flipped over the blade and read the engraving.

"Quicksilver!" exploded Dunn out of complete shock. "Is this authentic? How in the world did you ever come by this, Mathew? They said that monster's dead and at the bottom of the sea!"

"He is," Mathew confirmed immediately, then slowly added somewhat under his breath, "...in a manner of speaking."

"But how did you...did you receive this from him directly?" Dunn rephrased his question.

"Yes, Uncle Andy. I received this sword directly from Quicksilver."

"Without a fight?"

"Without a fight!" Mathew confirmed.

"But...I don't understand...a pirate like Quicksilver doesn't just give up his sword!"

"That's certainly true."

"Then how..."

"Uncle Andy, I am...Quicksilver."

Dunn drew a breath of surprise. Of course - it made perfect sense as he considered the revelation. The legend was born and grew during the years Mathew was away. The expert skill with the sword should have pointed to Quicksilver possibly being Mathew before, but the heinous legends describing his anger and viciousness, not to mention, demonic references and immortality prevented Dunn from considering it in the past.

"Quicksilver is not real, Uncle Andy. He was a legend built up to torment and confuse the Royal Navy. He was nothing more than the captain of a naval vessel for a country with no established navy. The circumstances and resources at the time required the American Navy to be built essentially from privateers, and Quicksilver was more legend than truth."

Dunn sank down in his high-back leather chair.

"We killed as few sailors as possible, Uncle Andy. We targeted only British war ships and destroyed them in a way that preserved the vast majority of the crews. It was a method of taking British munitions and using them for the colonial revolutionary cause."

"But they say he...you...couldn't be defeated...you single-handedly destroyed multiple ships of the line...but how?"

"I'm afraid I cannot tell you, Uncle Andy. Sufficed to say, the skills, tactics, weaponry, and crew that enabled our heralded victories have since been disbanded."

"And Wilson?"

Mathew grinned. "I killed him. It was fate that brought us once more together...and I could not let him go again."

Dunn nodded as he stood and looked at Mathew solemnly. Slowly he smiled and stepped toward his large guest and hugged him again.

"I will keep this secret, lad...just as I have your others. It is a shame I can't show anyone this beauty," referring with his eyes to the sword on the desk. Then he strode out of the room momentarily and returned with a prized bottle of French wine.

"I have saved this particular bottle for an extra special occasion. I cannot imagine one that would top this. You and I have much to discuss tonight."

◆

When word of General Cornwallis' surrender to Franco-American troops at Yorktown, Virginia reached King George, his mood seemed to permanently turn sour. It was only in the past year that the possibility of losing the American colonies to independence went from "impossible" to "highly unlikely", and then from "improbable" to "probable", which weighed heavily on the English monarch.

Failure had never been contemplated. Even as news of lost battles reached the Royal Court over the years, the reasoning was that the ragged Continental Army had been lucky or that poor weather conditions or uneven terrain had assisted. These were freak events out of the control of the English army and would not likely have a great impact on the war.

As improbable colonial military successes began to mount, the king could see that an originally disinterested Europe became increasingly intrigued. As several countries eventually joined in to assist the colonies, it seemed that England was fighting the rest of Europe and on many fronts, including the Mediterranean as well as the Caribbean.

The king realized that his pride was greatly at fault, leading him to spurn peaceful solutions proposed early on by colonial statesmen and then to have grossly underestimated the military resolve of the colonies. And it was his pride that was now taking a beating as America became the first colony in history ever to break from its parent country. To add insult to injury, even the general to whom Cornwallis had surrendered was a former British military officer, George Washington.

As word of Cornwallis' surrender in Virginia spread throughout England, many who had vociferously pleaded to allow the colonies improved treatment and some form of legislative representation felt vindicated. Their final pleas before George III had tacitly declared war was that it would end badly. Even they did not believe the colonies would win the war, but that a military response would long scar the tender relations with this important area of the New World and England's most valuable set of colonies.

The British surrender was discussed in Parliament in April of that year, ultimately prompting Prime Minister Lord North to resign his position and the British House of Commons to vote to officially end the war in America.

By the end of April 1782, to characterize King George's mood as permanently ill-tempered would have been a vast understatement. His closest counselors altered their number and form of direct communications with the king thereafter. There were even rumors that the monarch was beginning to go mad. A number of the staff at the palace had apparently witnessed tantrums and other childish behavior out of the blue on a number of occasions. Some palace staff had mentioned that they heard him talking to himself at times, and ran in terror when his talking grew to an angry tirade with himself.

In these confusing and solemn days, to deliver any kind of potentially disturbing news to the monarch was to invite an eruption of anger on par with the legendary blast of Mount Vesuvius that buried Pompei.

In light of the king's delicate temper, Lord Roberts had the distinct displeasure of delivering the most unexpected and disturbing piece of news he had ever seen, including Cornwallis' surrender at Yorktown. So remarkable was this particular letter that Lord Roberts went to great lengths to verify its authenticity, having brought in an expert to examine the signature. The content was so shocking and disturbing that Lord Roberts personally covered the text of the letter as he watched the expert cautiously examine, under a magnification glass, the signature at the bottom. He slowly compared it to another document that bore the signature of the same man from a few years prior. Hoping to save his monarch certain heartache and anger, Lord Roberts silently hoped the analysis would cast a reasonable shadow of doubt as to the authenticity of the signature and document. However, the independent verification suggested the signature was genuine.

Having exhausted all hope of the correspondence being a forgery that morning, Lord Roberts reluctantly approached the king in the afternoon. It happened to be a day when the king was relatively calm and in a fairly pleasant mood. In front of an immense array of windows providing abundant natural light, the king was reviewing some papers at his grand desk. He paused momentarily at the sound of the large oak doors opening and took off his reading glasses.

"Greetings, Lord Roberts. I understand you wished to speak with me about a private matter. What is this about?"

"Thank you, Your Majesty, for seeing me. I received a communication by courier this morning intended for you. It is rather disturbing in both its origin and its revelation, so I took the liberty of independently verifying its authenticity, though careful to conceal its content. I am sorry to inform Your Majesty that the letter appears to be a valid confession."

"Let me see the letter, Lord Roberts," the king ordered without emotion.

"Yes, Your Majesty," the counselor responded as he approached the king and placed the piece of parchment on his desk.

The king remained seated, but leaned forward to collect the correspondence. After replacing his reading spectacles, he settled in to his cushioned silk chair and began to read. Lord Roberts remained silent, dreading the imminent eruption. After a few moments, the lack of any emotional outburst from the king began to confuse Lord Roberts.

"Who else has seen this?" the king asked.

"No one other than myself, Your Majesty," Roberts responded.

"And do you believe this to be authentic?"

"Unfortunately...I do, Your Majesty. I had hoped that the gentleman analyzing the signature would confirm otherwise."

"Still, it could be a very clever forgery."

Lord Roberts simply raised his eyebrows as if to suggest that that chance was highly unlikely.

"Oh, I almost forgot...," continued the royal counselor, "...there was something else inside the sealed envelope."

Lord Roberts removed a gold coin from his pocket, stared at the markings one last time, and placed it on the desk in front of the king.

By the king's shocked reaction, the appearance of the gold coin had abruptly pulled him back into reality. Without taking his eyes off the coin on the desk, the king spoke again in a defeated tone. "I'm sorry to say, Lord Roberts, that the addition of that coin means the letter is indeed authentic."

◆

The Spyglass Inn, located in the southern coastal town of Hastings, was an appropriately named establishment as it was nestled on a bluff jutting out southwards towards the Atlantic, and catered to travelers that usually requested a room viewing the sea. In most circumstances, such requests were met as all of the bed chambers, save one, had some view of the rugged coastline, either directly or to the east or west.

It was quite rare for a guest of the inn to request a room with no view of the sea. In fact, its proprietor could not recall when last such a request came. Nonetheless, that morning a hunched-over, caustic, grey-haired gentleman with a cane insisted he wanted the room that faced away from the sea. The proprietor had pleasantly suggested that there were rooms available with dramatic ocean views, to which the guest scowled beneath his worn eye-patch and mumbled something unintelligible about being sick of the sea and much preferring to gaze upon *terra firma.*

The unusual request was granted, along with an agreement not to disturb the man under any condition, while the coachman who had delivered the man assisted in transporting the luggage, in two trips, up the stairs for the frail man to his room on the third level.

The proprietor caught the eye of the coachman on his second trip down the stairs, offering a slight smile and shake of his head to convey the absurdity of the old man's request. The coachman grinned back and shrugged his shoulders, disinterested in why the crotchety guest had requested the worst room at the inn.

Once the door was shut and locked from the inside, the old man approached the window and opened the thick wooden shutters. As was confirmed by the proprietor, there was no view of the sea. The view was back toward the town of Hastings as well as some grand estates nestled in the hills just beyond the town. The man smiled.

Carefully, he set down his cane across the table at the end of the bed, and began to open his luggage bags.

From the various pieces of luggage he pulled a number of delicate instruments and laid them out on the bed. Within minutes, he had expertly assembled a powerful telescope for gazing at the stars. However, this telescope was not pointing toward the heavens, but directly over the town to a particular estate in the distance.

Peering through the completed apparatus, the man grinned wider when he saw clearly the front oak doors of the estate, as though he could reach out and touch them himself.

Downstairs, the proprietor had his hands full with two guests drinking heavily and yelling loudly in the dining area of the inn. It was not uncommon to have seafarers as guests and for them to request rum or tankards of ale in the mid-morning.

Every so often, the noise required a stern warning by the proprietor that he would cut off their supply if they persisted in being bothersome to him and other guests. In most instances, the threat of losing one's ale privileges was enough to motivate even the most boisterous guests toward immediately improved behavior. Thankfully, this was another such occasion.

A moment after the downstairs fracas had ended, there was a gentle knock on the door of the grumpy old man. The knock was not the usual two or three bumps with closed fist but a kind of code with two knocks, followed by a pause, one knock, another pause, then three knocks.

The guest walked upright and quickly to the door, detached the lock and pulled open the door slightly. In the hallway stood the coachman who, upon the door's slight opening, gently pushed the door open and slipped past the older man who closed and locked the door quietly behind him.

"It's all set", Dunn exclaimed to Mathew. "No one saw you come up here?"

"No. There was a timely little distraction from two guests in the dining room. I shuffled in without being seen or heard." Mathew walked the length of the room toward the telescope.

"Haven't seen him yet," Dunn said. "It's your turn to watch."

"Are you sure he's there?"

"I was able to check with a reliable source that confirmed he isn't currently at sea. They haven't seen him in London for weeks. Where else would he be?" Dunn lay on the bed next to the window and telescope.

"By the way, you make a convincing old grouch." Mathew sat down and stared through the eyepiece of the great telescope.

"Thank you, my boy," Dunn remarked as he lay down on the bed. "You know, the only part that was difficult was remaining stooped over for so long. That really began to hurt my back."

Mathew pulled his head away from the device and shot a stare of mock anger at the man. "I am so very sorry to hear that. Bringing all this heavy equipment up to the third floor was a real pleasure," he said as he turned his head back to focus his gaze through the eyepiece.

"I still can't get over it. You...Quicksilver!" whispered Dunn after a lengthy silence, as his head lay on interlocked fingers and he stared at the ceiling. "There was a rather prevalent rumor that Captain Shaw shot you with two pistols right in your abdomen at point blank range."

"Not a rumor, that actually happened." Mathew continued to look through the telescope lens. "Knocked the bloody wind out of me, but didn't penetrate."

"You're joking! How is it that you live to tell the tale?"

"Mail," Mathew confided, now smiling, though his gaze was still on the far away mansion.

"I beg your pardon?"

"Chain mail, Uncle Andy…hundreds of connected iron ringlets under a thick leather vest, a form of defense borrowed from the knights of the Middle Ages, you might say."

"Too bloody brilliant! Well, this Quicksilver bloke was a clever, resourceful character!"

"Handsome, too," Mathew added, and both men shared a hearty chuckle.

"I also heard what happened to that twit Roger Bartlett. I bet that felt good knocking the smirk off that bastard's sallow face!"

"He's lucky to be alive at all. I was so consumed with rage I would have killed him. Beat the tar out of a lovely young girl, all because she refused his advances. She's the one that asked me to spare his life, and merely hurt him badly."

"Remarkable!"

"Yes, she certainly was," Mathew agreed as he pulled away from the lens to relieve his neck muscles by rolling his head in a circular motion.

"I meant the restraint you showed," Dunn clarified.

"Oh,yes…well," Mathew stammered.

Dunn turned on his side to regard Mathew and smiled, though Mathew, with eyes back at the telescope lens, never saw it.

The next several minutes were silent.

"There he is!" announced Mathew triumphantly. Dunn bounded off the bed and replaced Mathew at the eyepiece of the apparatus.

"There's the blighter!" Dunn responded as he spied the distant man on his horse at the back of the estate. "Out for a morning ride, eh? Enjoy it, you damned bastard, it's going to be your last in this lifetime!"

An hour later, the man reappeared in their sight having returned from his ride. There was no sign of any servants assisting him with his horse or any activity in the large house while he was gone. The only man that could be seen through any of the windows was the owner himself.

The man had acquired the twenty-five acre parcel very privately, through an intermediary, in early 1775. For a tidy sum, paperwork had been created to appear as though the land and luxurious home had come to him through a distant family connection.

Dunn and Mathew switched off on one-hour shifts. The monotony of spying on the distant estate was tiring, but the purpose made their task well worthwhile and the potential spoils would be incalculable.

"Tell me about the girl," Dunn said while looking through the eyepiece.

"From Boston, parents emigrated from England just before she was born. Mother died of fever when the girl was about ten." Mathew stared at the ceiling from his prone position on the bed. "Father's a doctor and raised her; never remarried. Bright, well-educated girl. Beautiful. Engaging. Rather lovely really."

"What happened to her?"

"Took her off the *North Star* that was part of a military convoy. Saved her from that fiend Bartlett. She traveled with the *Sea Dragon* to America, got her safely to a secret cove and arranged for her safe passage to her father who would have been waiting for the *North Star* in Norfolk."

"And that was it?"

"Well, I didn't think a marriage proposal was appropriate at the time...her being an American and my being a wanted pirate!"

Dunn waited a few minutes before continuing the conversation delicately. "Have you thought much about her since, Mathew?"

"Every single day," Mathew confirmed. "She was as wonderful as she was beautiful. She even loves Shakespeare."

"Never! Well, that clinches it, my boy. You've got to track

this young lady down now that the war is over."

"Believe me, I've considered that. But I can't."

"Why?"

"For one thing, she's probably already married. Even if she isn't, she would never take up with someone like me."

"Nonsense, Mathew! Why you're precisely the kind of man that…"

Dunn broke off and quickly adjusted the telescope. His movement startled Mathew, who climbed off the bed and stood next to his seated partner.

"He's got visitors!" Dunn announced. "King's Guards! Oh, and they're not fooling around either. Jesus, there are four of them!"

"Let me see!" Mathew gently nudged Dunn away from the telescope lens. He could see two guards on horseback at the lead of the coach, one guard on the coach and another walking up the steps of the entryway.

The guard at the door pulled back the knocker and slammed it hard three times. It was eerie to Mathew how clearly he could see these men through the intense magnification of the telescope, and yet there was no sound from the knockers due to the distance.

The door of the estate was opened by a footman, who was visibly shocked to see King's Guards at the door. He recovered and motioned them in. One of the guards must have spoken because the footman nodded his head and gestured toward the upstairs. The guards entered the house as the footman disappeared from Mathew's sight, and the large oak door remained open.

Within ten minutes, Admiral Watts had changed into his uniform and left his estate, as his footman watched from the doorway. The guard ushered the admiral down the entryway steps to the awaiting royal coach, showing no sign of force or coercion. In fact, it looked to Mathew as if Watts went willingly. Clever, thought Mathew. The king obviously did not want to alert his prey to the coming confrontation.

"Looks like the king bought the Wilson confession letter!" Dunn said, wringing his hands as though what was unfolding was going precisely according to their strategy.

"As clever a forgery as that signature was, it was Diana's coin that did it!" Mathew said. "The king would have no choice but to believe its authenticity."

"It sure took them a while to send for Watts," Dunn added.

"I expect that the counselor that read it must have analyzed the signature very closely before bringing it to the king," Mathew said as he stood away from the telescope.

"There they go, and fast as lightning," Dunn said, peering once more through the telescope. "You had better get going. No telling how long it will take you to find the gold. And that's if it's in there and if you can get yourself in, and if you can avoid the footman. I figure you have less than four and-a-half hours. Good luck, my boy."

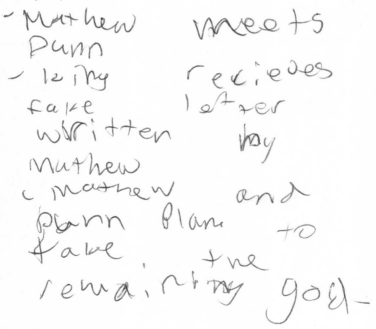

- Mathew meets
Dunn
- king recieves
fake letter
written by
Mathew
- mathew and
Dunn plan to
fake, the
remaining gold-

✝

Chapter 28: Retribution

*R*iding in the coach from his estate in the southern coastal city of Hastings to St. James Palace in London, Admiral Watts considered the details of his requested presence at the palace, blind to the landscape outside the carriage that passed in a blur. While it was not unusual for the king to call a special meeting of admirals, one with so little notice was rather rare. Only nine days into a long-overdue month's hiatus, he longed for the day when he would finally control his own schedule.

Watts eagerly deduced that the important meeting might have something to do with ending the war with the American colonies. He had nearly retired several months prior, with the news that his Wolf Pack mission had successfully rooted out and destroyed the dreaded pirate Quicksilver and his demonic *Sea Dragon* crew.

The perfect way to go out - he had thought – *now that he was back in good favor with the Admiralty and the king.* In any event, Watts concluded, he could retire soon enough.

The prevailing conventional wisdom was that the war with the colonies had been lost, though Watts didn't personally care about the disastrous outcome. He had served in the line of danger for many years and had secretly obtained a phenomenal level of wealth. Losing the American colonies wouldn't affect him in the slightest. He would still live out his days in ridiculous luxury, womanizing, and leisure.

Within two hours, the carriage reached St. James Palace and a larger-than-life sentry opened the coach door, moving quickly aside to allow the admiral to step out. Upon entering the palace, Watts was met by Lord Roberts who cheerfully greeted him.

As they walked the long entrance hall, Watts inquired as to the purpose of his unscheduled summons.

"An important naval matter, I'm told," the royal counselor responded.

Lord Roberts had walked past the strategy room where it was customary to meet with the king in planning battles or otherwise discussing British naval operations around the world. The immense maps adorning the walls of the strategy room were apparently of no use in today's discussion. An odd feeling of curiosity gnawed at Watts.

He was then led up a stairway and down another hall to a part of the palace where Watts had never been before. Several strides later, Lord Roberts ushered the visibly confused admiral into the comfortable waiting room outside the king's own office.

"Please wait here," requested the counselor before leaving the room through a thick door in the far wall.

Watts' began to daydream of how he would soon spend his lavish days of retirement when the door in the far wall opened again. Through it stepped Lord Roberts.

"Admiral Watts, His Majesty will see you now," pronounced the royal counselor.

The curious admiral entered the large office and approached the great oak desk of the king who was seated, looking down intently at some papers. The afternoon sun was rather bright outside and the light pouring in through the wall of windows behind him gave the king an appearance of a shadowy silhouette. From his perch behind the desk, King George addressed Watts.

"Admiral Watts, so good of you to come on such short notice. I appreciate your indulgence."

"It is my pleasure, Your Majesty," the admiral said, becoming instantly more relaxed at the friendly opening of their conversation.

"Do you know why I have summoned you?" the king inquired.

"I was not told a thing, Your Majesty; only that you required my presence immediately. I can only presume an important naval matter."

"Indeed it is an important naval matter, Admiral Watts, and I shall be the one to enlighten you." The king stood up and walked behind the cushioned silk high-back chair.

Upon this physical cue, Lord Roberts barked at the guards who instantly drew their swords and placed their razor-sharp points at the admiral's chest. Lord Roberts quickly wheeled in front of the stunned Watts and removed the admiral's sword from its sheath.

"What is the meaning of this!" demanded an outraged Watts.

"Do you know the penalty for treason, Admiral Watts?" the king asked in an eerily calm tone. Watts was frightened more at that moment than at any time in his dangerous, event filled life, and he had no idea what was coming next.

"Yes, Your Majesty...death" Watts responded, "but surely you don't believe I would commit treason."

"I have received a disturbing bit of correspondence from the grave, as it were," offered the king. "It seems the intolerable weight of Captain Jack Wilson's shame was ultimately greater than his loyalty to you. He explains it all rather clearly in this confession letter that was to be delivered to me upon word of his death," he added as he held up the piece of parchment on the desk.

Watts was stunned. His mind raced to grasp any plausible deniability, but without reading the letter himself, he did not know how much detail it contained. Through it all, Watts could not fathom that Wilson would have done this to him.

On second thought, it might have been a clever method for Wilson to protect himself from any unfortunate *accident*, the likes of which abruptly ended the other conspirators' lives. After all, Wilson knew that Watts had seen to poisoning each of the surviving crewmen when he exchanged their portion of the gold for cash.

But it still didn't make sense. The protection would only be useful if Wilson had informed Watts of this clever insurance policy – which he hadn't. And it was far too unbelievable that the brutal and loathsome Wilson would have suddenly developed a spiritual conscience that would explain this desperate act of contrition after his passing.

"Your Majesty, I don't know what treasonous claims are made in that letter," Watts said, "but I do know that Captain Jack Wilson was a good man and would not implicate me in any outlandish claim of impropriety. The letter must be a forgery by someone out to harm me."

"Bravo, Admiral Watts," congratulated the king. "A spirited rebuttal. I have valued your loyalty to the Crown and to England for many years and I came to the same conclusion directly, isn't that correct, Lord Roberts?"

"Yes, Your Majesty," confirmed the counselor.

"And yet an independent expert verified the signature as authentic," the king said. "Still, the allegations made are so repulsive that I held out hope that they were untrue."

"I assure you, Your Majesty. I have committed no act of treason."

"Several years ago, Professor Hutchins from Oxford comes to me with a miraculous discovery in the Mediterranean. I brought together some of my top admirals in London at the time to secretly bring back this immense treasure to England. It was simple. I was even going to handsomely compensate all involved. But an unlikely tragedy occurred instead."

"I remember, Your Majesty, but surely that letter doesn't suggest that I had anything to do with running the *Pinnacle* aground!" Watts exclaimed.

"No. But it was you who handpicked then-Lieutenant Wilson for the mission. And according to Wilson's confession, it was you who came up with the scheme to kill the crew and remove the cargo, and you who arranged for its secret transport back to England by the coincidental charter of the *Avalon*."

"Your Majesty, forgive me, but that is absurd. The *Pinnacle* disaster occurred in 1774…fully eight years ago. If I were to have orchestrated such a despicable act, why would I still be in the Royal Navy? I would have left for a warmer climate and safer occupation. Don't you think a thief would want to leave the scene of his crime?"

"That's true," the king agreed. "That would be sensible."

"There, you see. I do not live in extravagant wealth, Your Majesty. I serve you and England in the Royal Navy."

"And Wilson," the king reasoned out loud, as if thinking through the absurdity of the charge, "he could not possibly back up this claim of stealing the cargo and transporting it back to you because he didn't even know what the cargo was. Only Captain Hatley and Professor Hutchins knew!"

"Precisely!" Watts agreed.

"Lord Roberts, show the admiral what was delivered with the letter," the king said.

Without a sound, Lord Roberts moved from behind Watts to in front of him and placed a shining ancient Greek gold coin on the desk. Watts looked at the coin and turned red. He immediately tried to work up a plausible scenario to explain how Wilson had obtained the coin without Watts knowing about it.

"Do you recognize the coin, Admiral Watts?" the king asked.

"I do, Your Majesty," Watts said, as a brilliant idea came to his cunning mind. "But this proves only that he possessed some of the cargo. He may have taken a few coins before or even after the crash. Yes, I am the one that nominated him for that position in the crew, but I did not inform him of the contents of the cargo, nor did I plot an elaborate scheme of mutiny, theft, and transport."

The king stared at Watts from his stance behind his chair. "Very well, Admiral Watts. I shall make you a proposition. I shall not repeat myself, so please listen carefully."

Watts stood very still, thinking he had successfully created enough doubt in the mind of his king that he would escape punishment.

"In spite of your claims of innocence, I find myself believing the letter more. As such, I hereby find you guilty of treason against the crown and country. Your punishment shall be a lengthy set of tortures tonight, to be followed by a public flogging and beheading tomorrow at the Tower of London. If, however, you wish to avoid this fate, I give you one last chance.

Leave at once, with my guards of course, collect your share of the gold from the *Pinnacle* and bring it to me. For your admission of guilt and restoration of the gold, I shall - against my better judgment and propriety - grant you a full pardon. You will resign your commission in the Royal Navy, but otherwise avoid public scandal as well as torture. You shall die of old age rather than the blade of an axe," the king finished.

Watts showed no emotion, but calculated his options over and over in his head. He saw no way out. If he continued to contest his guilt and the king didn't change his mind – which appeared to have a high probability – he would be tortured mercilessly and die. If, however, he confessed to the truth, he would spare himself certain torture and imminent death.

"Do you understand the terms of this proposition as I have described them?" the king inquired as Lord Roberts smiled and Watts slowly began to nod. "What will it be?" inquired the king unemotionally.

"I am deeply sorry, Your Majesty." Watts broke down instantly in a torrent of shame and tears. "I *did* orchestrate the crime of which you speak. I do have the majority of the gold at my estate in Hastings. I will use it now to buy my life."

"Very well," the king answered showing little outward emotion, "but if the gold amounts to more than a few ounces, you've grossly overpaid."

◆

Within twenty minutes of leaving the third floor room, Mathew reached the gates of Watts' estate. From the distant room in the Spyglass Inn, Dunn nervously watched his colleague approach the grand oak door and take out a small tool from his waistcoat pocket that allowed him to pick locks.

"Quickly, quickly," Dunn implored as though Mathew could hear him.

Dunn's eye caught some movement in a large bank of windows two rooms to the right of the front door. It was the footman arranging and replacing some books in the library. It appeared Mathew's fiddling with the front door lock had not been heard inside the large house.

Suddenly, Mathew stood, pushed the front door of the estate open, and waved at Dunn watching from afar.

"Stop fooling around, boy," Dunn admonished in a whisper. "You'll need all the time you have!"

As though he sensed Dunn's instruction, Mathew disappeared behind the door and shut it gently.

Dunn turned his gaze back to the library, but the footman was nowhere in sight. His heart started racing. There was no way he could see through the house into the hall. Where was Mathew? Where was the footman?

While it was Sunday and most of the staff of the house would be gone for the next several hours, there was always the chance of a stray chambermaid remaining inside or a guest. There were also two stable hands that Mathew had seen earlier, but they would not enter the main house.

Dunn studied the library carefully and let out a large sigh of relief when the footman returned into view carrying a tea tray. He placed it on a table near the bank of windows and then walked across the large room to select a book from the vertical stacks. Walking back towards the bank of windows, the footman stared outside towards the distant sea, unaware that he was being watched.

The footman sat down at the front edge of a leather reading chair facing away from the windows and poured some tea. He lifted the book off the table and reclined in the chair.

From across the town, Andrew Dunn let out an audible gasp at the temerity of a servant relaxing in the master's part of the house. "Can't imagine there's anyone else there if the footman is reclining with a book and tea," he reasoned out loud.

Dunn then realized that his heart was beating at a more normal pace. He removed his eye from the telescope just long enough to peak at his pocket watch. Less than four hours to go.

Just as he returned to the telescope, Dunn noticed the footman jump up rather startled. Good and bad. A noise from elsewhere in the house would only make a man jump if he thought he were alone. No one other than Mathew and the servant was in the house. However, Mathew must have made a sound that brought the footman out of his chair. He moved out of Dunn's vision, no doubt to investigate.

Dunn noticed movement in the room again, but this time it wasn't the footman.

Mathew strode purposely towards the table at the windows, waved his hand over the man's teacup and quickly moved behind the curtains to the side of the windows, still visible to Dunn watching from afar, but hidden from the footman who would return at any moment.

As the servant returned into view, Dunn's felt his heart race again. The footman stared out the windows. Was he watching for movement on the property? Was he admiring the beautiful distant view and the sunlight pouring into the library? Dunn held his own breath as he saw that Mathew, no more than five feet away from the footman, now clutched a large knife.

Apparently satisfied that the noise was nothing to worry about, the footman returned to his reading chair, reached for his tea and sipped from the cup. He picked up the book and reclined in a position of comfort. Dunn could now only see the top of the man's head. Three times over the next few minutes, he reached over to the table with his left hand for the teacup.

There was no change in movement for the next ten minutes, which seemed an eternity to Dunn. Slowly, Mathew made his way around the curtains and approached the footman's chair. Dunn could see only Mathew now, and his left hand holding the knife raised to his side. It appeared Mathew would slash the footman's throat in a blinding flash, but the next movement was not what Dunn expected.

Quickly Mathew sheathed his blade back into his boot and turned to face out the windows toward Dunn. He gestured with his palms together, fingers aligned, and head tilted to a rest on the back of his hands with his eyes closed. The footman was asleep!

The first room Mathew elected to inspect was the study, eyeing closely the paneling of the dark wooden walls. It took him less than ten minutes, but he finally found a door ingeniously hidden in the wooden panels.

Almost imperceptible to the eye, one would have to be

looking very closely to possibly find it. A slight push on the door released the spring that forced the door to open toward him an inch or so. Mathew pulled the door open further and peered inside.

Much to his surprise and dismay, it was nothing more than a closet. In it hung three coats, a greatcoat, two hats, and some old shoes and riding boots upon the floor as well as a couple of blankets on a shelf. Dejectedly, Mathew brought his lantern closer to the doorway and lit it. The closet lit up brightly, as did Mathew's hopes, for there in the floor of the closet was a very thin line that appeared to be the faintest crease where another door, this time in the floor, could barely be seen.

Certain he was getting closer to the treasure of the HMS *Pinnacle*, Mathew put down the lantern, cleared the floor of the shoes and boots and pulled the door open with his fingers. Nearly the entire floor of the closet opened upward.

There were steps leading down into darkness, which Mathew descended slowly after retrieving his lantern. He wished Dunn could be there with him, but it was too much of a risk for the wealthy and notable shipping owner to be caught in the house. Besides, if a hasty retreat were necessary, Mathew would be better able to evade detection if he were on his own.

As he reached the bottom of the stairs, Mathew marveled at how large the basement area was. He could see up to twenty feet ahead of him and at least that much to either side.

There was not much furniture in the cellar - just a large carpenter's table with an iron vice grip at one end and a few odd tools near the middle.

The wall to his left was built entirely of large stones, with the exception of one very solid oak door. The door had what looked to be an intricate lock below the handle. Mathew sensed he was on the right path, as though he could almost smell gold. He put down the lantern and pulled out his lock-picking tools. This lock was far more difficult than the one on the door of the house itself, but nevertheless, he had it open in just under five minutes.

The thick oak door opened slowly and Mathew lifted the lantern to light up what was inside.

In that first moment witnessing the contents of the locked

storage area, Mathew felt a giant wave of shock nearly bowl him over. If each of the crates before him was each filled with gold, he might be witnessing a treasure that would surpass the wealth of the king himself.

He reached in and grabbed one of the crates. It didn't budge until he placed a hand on each side and lifted with his strength. Sure enough, the case was extremely heavy.

He pried open the lid with one of the tools from the table outside the vault door, and as the light from the lantern illuminated the contents, the entire room seemed to glow in a deep golden hue. In the crate, which measured approximately eight inches by twelve inches by six inches, there were several neatly stacked rows of gold coins. Mathew reached in and pulled up one of the coins to his face.

They were not the ancient Greek coins that Hutchins' daughter had revealed to him, but English guineas. The face on the coin was that of King George, with the Latin words *Georgivs III Dei Gratia* – George III by the Grace of God. On the reverse, a crowned shield with the arms of England, Scotland, France, Ireland, and Hanover.

On top of a few crates to the right of the vault door there was another hundred or so coins in neat stacks. These, however, had the original ancient Greek markings. Watts had somehow come up with a way to erase the origin of the coins and convert them into standard English currency, which made them far easier to pass on as payment to anyone.

Just past the stack of coins that had yet to be altered, Mathew recognized at once the tool that enabled Watts to change the look of the coins.

It was a thick piece of black iron with numerous components. In conjunction with the iron vice grip on the table outside the vault, Mathew could imagine using the strength of the vice to push together two coin molds that would take a gold coin and literally imprint a different relief picture on it.

Very clever, thought Mathew. In 1774, nearly twenty million worn gold guineas featuring previous monarchs were melted down and recast as George III guineas. Watts was able to recast the Greek coins at a time when suspicion would not be raised.

Mathew recalled that gold was an easily malleable metal, and that with the exponential strength of the vice grip, a man could probably re-imprint up to fifteen coins in the span of an hour. If his calculations were right, it must have taken Watts over three-and-half years to alter the coins, one-by-one.

Instinctively pulling out his pocket watch, Mathew saw that he had less than three hours before the King's Guards might reappear. Now that he had found the gold, he was presented with a new problem: transporting the heavy crates up to the house and, eventually, out of the house.

One by one, he began to carry the crates up the stairs of the cellar and outside to an area just behind the rear of the house.

From across Hastings, Dunn momentarily withdrew from the eyepiece of his telescope for a few seconds of welcomed stretching. The footman in the library hadn't moved for hours.

As Dunn glanced to the north, something far off in the distance caught his eye. The panicked Dunn nearly bolted from his seat. Interrupting his vigil of Watts' estate, he retrained his telescope on the distant road leading toward the seaside town. The cloud of dust rising was no mirage, but a team of coaches traveling at top speed. As they drew closer, he could clearly see they were royal carriages, and that Mathew's time was up.

Nine King's Guards occupied the three royal carriages racing to Watts' estate. The admiral slumped forward in one of the bounding royal coaches a defeated man, perplexed at the confession letter from Wilson. He still could not fathom what possible motive his accomplice had to pen a note of contrition.

The return journey took slightly less than two hours. It went all too fast for the condemned former admiral, for he tried to breath in all the passing trees and countryside. As the carriage slowed down in front of his expansive grounds, Watts looked out the window with nostalgic eyes, knowing it was likely to be the last time he would look upon his beautiful estate.

The coach had seemingly just come to a stop when the door

swung open abruptly in the hand of a large, intense looking guard who seemed to have been personally offended by Watts' crime. The guard reached into the coach and extracted Watts in one quick thrust that brought the bound prisoner to his hands and knees onto the circular drive in front of the estate.

"Get up!" he ordered Watts.

As the admiral pushed himself awkwardly to his feet, one guard knelt down to unlock the manacles around the prisoner's ankles, while another moved in to free his wrists.

"No!" the lead guard commanded to his colleagues. "He stays bound."

Then the ranking guard stepped in front of Watts vision. "Show us the gold now! And don't try any tricks," the giant man announced as he pulled a large knife from a sheath on his belt, "I would be following orders to kill you if you try to escape, and it won't be a bullet for you. Trust me, nothing would give me greater pleasure than to slice you open very slowly and painfully, filthy maggot."

Watts nodded his understanding, trusting the man was entirely sincere.

The lead guard then ordered three of his colleagues to remain with the coaches, instructing them to shoot and kill Watts if he came out of the house unaccompanied.

Watts led the six guards up the marble steps that led to his front veranda. As they reached the landing, the large oak door was opened by the visibly nervous footman.

Inside the great house, Watts led the guards to his study. He focused on the paneling in the wall, found the seam and pushed to release the secret door. When the paneling revealed only a closet, the soldiers appeared confused and disappointed, but when he removed the boots and shoes and pulled up the floor to a latch on the wall, revealing steps down to a cellar, several pairs of eyebrows raised.

"We'll need a lantern," Watts mentioned to no one in particular and, within fifteen seconds, one was thrust in front of him.

"Wait!" the large, lead guard shouted. "Jones, go first! The admiral and I shall remain up here until you get down safely and light up the cellar." The imposing guard pulled Watts up from a squatting position at the floor opening, and thrust the large knife against his neck.

Jones reached the bottom of the stairway without issue and lit the candles along the wall, before calling up to the others. Within two minutes, the six guards and the admiral were standing in front of the massive vault door.

Watts made his way to the vault shoulders slumped as he reached for his key. Feeling the click of the lock opening, he reached over to pull down the lever and turned toward the soldiers as he pulled opened the thick door, watching their expressions change when they saw the enormous cache of gold.

Only there was no change of expression. All eyes viewed the vault and turned back toward him. Watts didn't understand. Perhaps the soldiers presumed it would be a room full of gold coins and not neatly stacked wooden crates. He felt the giant hand of the lead guard grab his shoulder painfully and angrily shove him backward into the vault. Bracing himself for painful impact with the crates, Watts stumbled to the cleared floor with surprise.

Two guards entered the vault behind him with lanterns illuminating the chamber in a flickering glow. Watts was dumbstruck. It was unimaginable to contemplate, but there were no crates. No gold! Impossible!

"What the hell is this?!" the lead guard barked. "Where is the gold?"

"I...I...I swear I don't know. This is...this is where...I kept the gold...but it...but it's...gone!"

"We can see it's not here, maggot!" the guard snapped, "I asked you where it is!"

"I don't know...I don't know...someone's stolen it...I've been robbed, but...but...no one knew I stored gold here, and no one could get to it even if they thought it might be here!" Watts reasoned out loud in front of the impatient guards.

"Major, I found something!" one of the guards announced to his superior. The one named Jones knelt to pick up something shiny that was laid on top of a piece of paper in the middle of the vault floor. He stood and turned around, placing the items in the large outstretched gloved palm of his superior, whose face seemed to register increasing anger by the second. In the light of the lantern, the commanding guard could see that the shiny object was a coin of pure gold.

"Beautiful, though not nearly enough to buy your miserable life, I'm afraid," the lead guard said in mock concern for Watts. Then he unfolded the note that had been left under the coin.

Even in the flickering shadows of the cellar vault, Watts could see the pulsating veins in the neck of the lead guard nearly pop through his taught skin. His serious face contorted into an expression of building rage.

"What kind of stupid bloody joke is this?!" he said, thrusting the note into Watts' face. The note contained three words only - three words that increased the likelihood that Watts would not live to see the outside of his own vault.

For my king!

Watts nearly fainted. He was in a terrible dream, unable to make sense of or control any of the absurd events around him. As he wobbled in place and nearly fell, he felt his collars being clutched by the commander of the guards. The guard's voice sounded like thunder to the dazed Watts, whose mind was still racing trying to grasp the theft of his gold.

"Listen to me, you filthy shit. I have been given authority directly from His Majesty to exact your punishment on the spot if you tried to escape or if it should turn out that you refused to take us to the gold. I will ask you only once more and the wrong answer will end your life right here." The giant guard lifted Watts by his lapels nearly off the ground. He looked directly into the eyes of the defeated former naval officer.

"Where...is...the...gold?"

Watts felt as though he was already dead. In all the shock of his fortune disappearing and the note and the stress of imminent death, he was resigned to his punishment. There was nothing else he could think to say.

"I...I...don't know," he whispered so softly that it was barely perceptible to the guard holding him up. The guard nodded slowly for a few seconds and tossed Watts to the ground.

"In that case," the guard began, "on behalf of His Majesty, George III, I have been granted authority to carry out your sentence for the act of treason committed willingly against your king and country, for plotting the murder of the brave men of the HMS *Pinnacle*, and for theft of the property of the Crown. The penalty for these crimes is death by beheading," the giant pronounced in an emotionless, formal tone.

Fine, just get it over with, thought Watts, ready to end his frightening nightmare.

Then the large guard came closer to Watts and kneeled down so that his voice would be heard by the defeated admiral only.

"I swear I will carry out the king's command, but first I have something of a private score to settle with you."

Watts could muster only enough energy to crane his neck to regard the man appearing as a frightening silhouette against the soft glow of the lantern from the ceiling above.

"You see, my brother and uncle were sailors on the *Pinnacle*," the guard said, "and you committed them to a violent and senseless death, you avaricious old shit! What I am about to do to you is for them, as well as the rest of the crew. You will leave this earth in immeasurable agony, and then you'll rot in Hell for eternity!"

The guard stood up again, slowly withdrawing his large knife, and turned his head slightly to the other guards standing in the cellar outside the vault door.

"Clear out, men," he ordered, "Wait for me upstairs."

He turned back to look at the feeble, defeated man on the vault floor and called out once more.

"Sergeant Jones, go to the coach and retrieve the sack!"

◆

From the Seaview Inn all the way across Hastings, a nervous Dunn sat glued to his telescope, praying silently that the King's Guards had not discovered Mathew within the admiral's home.

Then he saw the large commanding guard emerge from the front door of the estate with a sack, tied at the end with chord.

He threw the sack to one of the other guards closer to the coaches, who placed it into a box, strapping the container down at the rear of the carriage.

Another guard approached his commander at the top of the veranda and threw him what appeared to be a large cloth. The guard rubbed it all over his red vest and coat, and the color seemed to run onto the cloth.

There could be no doubt what was inside the box, and judging by the contented look on the guard's face, Dunn was just as certain that Watts had suffered tremendously before his execution had been carried out.

— Mathew Dunn and break into estate steal the and the gold
— Admiral Watts gets killed

✝

Chapter 29: Epilogue

In the weeks following the execution of Admiral Watts, a royal proclamation was circulated that clarified the events of the HMS *Pinnacle* destruction. Though there was no mention of the vast stores of treasure, the mutiny and murder were detailed and the names Watts and Wilson became immediately synonymous with treason and treachery.

The news of the crime was followed by an announcement that the fallen crew of the *Pinnacle* would be honored in a special ceremony and monument near the harbor area of the Thames.

Captain Thomas Hatley, who had been wrongly accused all these years of breach of judgment, reckless endangerment of his crew, and dereliction of duty was exonerated in full.

A separate announcement came a few days later that several present and former Royal Naval officers had commissioned a bronze statue commemorating the decorated career of one of England's most heroic naval officers. The inspiring collective sum was doubled by a generous anonymous donation shortly thereafter.

Andrew Dunn arrived home and showed his guest the newspaper that detailed the upcoming ceremony to finally pay official tribute to Captain Thomas Hatley. There was even mention that one of the prominent members of The House of

Lords had paid touching respect to the legendary sea captain, as well to Hatley's charming wife who had been run out of England many years ago back to her home in the American colony of Virginia. He volunteered to pen a formal apology that, on behalf of a grossly deceived England, the entire House of Lords should sign. There was not one objection.

"I'm going to my father's ceremony!" Mathew announced.

"You're not serious, Mathew!" Dunn protested, "With all that's been accomplished, I'd say we're damned lucky to have righted the ship, so to speak. Let's not get greedy, my boy! There will be hundreds of naval personnel there. Someone's bound to recognize you!"

"I'm going to my father's ceremony!" Mathew repeated.

"Be reasonable, Mathew. Don't muck up the situation. Do you know what would happen to both of us if just one person recognized you? And what of your father's memory?"

Mathew looked down at the table and stewed knowing Dunn was absolutely correct. While he would gladly give the entire massive fortune he now possessed to attend the ceremony, it was not worth the risk of his being recognized and ultimately executed as a traitor, tarnishing his family's name on the day it was to be celebrated.

Upon further reflection, Mathew found solace in the fact that his revenge against Wilson and Watts was complete, their horrible crime was made public, and his own father's name had finally been cleared.

◆

On a late spring morning in 1782, the London ceremony commemorating Captain Thomas Hatley's long service to Great Britain quietly began. The sheet covering the twice-life-size bronze statue of the legendary seafarer waved in the breeze. The long war to put down the upstart colonial rebellion had been embarrassingly unsuccessful and England was starved for an occasion to celebrate something positive. Long overdue public restoration of the character of one of her previously most cherished and respected captains brought out a crowd of no less than four thousand.

First Lord of the Admiralty Simon Hughes gave a stirring eulogy that touched many in the crowd as the overcast skies of the morning gave way to blue skies with wisps of distant clouds. It was a day that turned out to be beautiful, and those in the crowd would remember it as the day that a certain amount of pride was restored to England.

Far off to one side of the densely packed crowd, a ragged servant pushed an old man in a wheel chair. They slowly made their way toward the platform where the highest-ranking officer of the Royal Navy addressed the massive gathering. The grey-haired invalid had a thick blanket across his useless legs and was hunched over awkwardly in his seated position. Under a wool sea cap, his ratty grey moustache and beard could not adequately hide the habitual motion of rubbing his toothless gums together. His weathered, wrinkled face suggested a long, hard life at sea.

At the conclusion of the ceremony, the large bronze statue was finally unveiled and a deafening roar rose from the crowd for the memory of the great Royal Navy officer.

While most continued their cheers loudly for nearly a minute, the old man stooped in the wheel chair began to openly weep. His tears were not tears of sorrow so much as an emotional overflow of long repressed pride for how his father would be remembered ever more. For most of his life, he had purposely distanced himself from his father's lauded name in order to ensure his own successes were based on merit, and now he happily joined the crowd in proudly celebrating the great captain.

The feeble figure in the chair then began to gently clap along with the crowd and motioned his caretaker to wheel him closer to the statue. Unnoticed by anyone around him but his caretaker, the man slowly reached a gloved hand to his pursed lips and placed a kiss at the statue's marble base.

◆

The Thompson's independence party was to be Boston's social event of the summer, making up for the lack of social engagements over the previous years in one long night of revelry.

The large and elegant Thompson home was decorated with red, white, and blue throughout, and there wasn't one invitee who declined. By the time Alison and her father arrived, it was already a loud and exciting affair.

Alison was soon separated from her father by three of her closest friends. Though lovely young women in their own right, together they were a loud and giddy bunch. The four girls congregated by the punch bowl, laughing loudly and pointing out to each other certain eligible young gentlemen in attendance. The music would commence soon and after several minuets, the up-tempo fiddler, drum, and flute combo would touch off a wild dancing celebration that would consume the entire ballroom.

In preparation for the dancing festivities, some of the more confident young gentlemen were making eye contact with the small group of pretty girls and approached from across the room. Even in her celebratory mood, Alison didn't feel like dancing very much, but she was careful not to be seen as aloof or dismissive.

For goodness sakes, don't worry so much, it's just a dance, she told herself. *It's all right to have some fun, sharing a dance is not a marriage proposal!* One by one, her friends were pried from her by young men.

Ironically, as the music began, it was Alison who was ultimately left alone. Most of the men in Boston it seemed, like their counterparts in England, were intimidated by Alison and felt they would be refused outright if they asked for a dance. Or perhaps they had presumed her dances were probably already pledged. However, there were several in the room who – upon seeing her alone as the music began - would not make the same mistake for the next minuet.

Alison felt awkward standing there alone and scanned the room for her father. Though sensing her gaze as he was talking with the hosts of the party, he glanced across the large room and noticed his daughter. He excused himself from the conversation politely and walked towards Alison.

"Is everything all right, dear?" he asked.

"No takers." Alison shrugged with a half-smile.

"In that case, may I have the privilege of this dance, young lady?" her father requested as he bowed to her.

"Why, yes, sir. I would be delighted," she answered, bowing her own head and curtseying.

As they stepped into the movement of the dance, she squeezed her father's hand. "Thank you, father," she spoke softly.

He returned her gratitude with a smile. On the arm of a capable and comfortable dancing partner, she let her mind drift until she was lost in the music and truly relaxed for the first time in recent memory. She thought about her lone, magical dance shared with Quicksilver on the deck of the *Sea Dragon* on a moonlit night off the southern coast of the colonies.

As the music concluded, they found themselves near the outer fringe of the dance floor, where many people stood watching the dancers. One young man in particular nodded and smiled to Mr. Davis, alerting him that he was about to introduce himself.

Mr. Davis quickly took his cue to leave his daughter and bowed while he thanked her for the dance. Alison again curtseyed with her head bent in a half bow. Her father then silently departed, revealing in his place the young stranger who began to speak.

"Good-evening, Alison. You look beautiful tonight."

Alison looked up slowly to the voice, somewhat startled, and regarded the handsome stranger cautiously.

"Thank you. I...I...apologize. I've been away for a few years and don't remember...have we met?"

The young man lifted his eyes to the ceiling as if in pensive thought. "Well, we've never been *formally* introduced, but...yes...we have met."

Alison smiled back while trying desperately to place the stranger. His voice was only vaguely familiar, and he was so handsome she was sure that she would have remembered him had they met recently. It had to be someone from well in her past.

She looked around to see if her girl friends could provide a silent clue. Instead of knowing looks, they were gawking at the man themselves. It was clear that they didn't remember him either but were equally moved by his attractive features and confident presence. She noticed a number of other young women around the ballroom now staring at the striking young man that, for the moment, she had to herself.

"I do apologize, sir, but I seem to require a…hint."

"No apology necessary, Alison. I really wouldn't expect you to remember me; I have changed quite a bit, after all," the stranger admitted.

"Then, where and when have we met?" she asked as she studied his face, enjoying the challenge of deducing his identity. She couldn't place the chin, or the smile or the nose.

Then the stranger reached out, took her hand and spoke in a hushed tone with an English accent:

"I would not wish any companion in the world but you, nor can imagine form a shape besides yourself to like of. Hear my soul speak. The very instant that I saw you did my heart fly to your service."

For a second or two, Alison's mind didn't quite register what her ears thought they had heard. Her face reflected confusion.

"What…did you just say?"

In that moment, her ears and mind finally connected. It was the same passage from Shakespeare's *Tempest* that she had instructed Quicksilver to read when she left him standing outside the southern Virginia inn.

Then her eyes focused on his eyes; eyes that she could never forget.

She pulled back her hand from his suddenly, and her mouth opened wide in shock as if to announce she'd seen a ghost. In the next instant, she gave a cautious smile while her eyes searched his in hopeful anticipation.

The stranger nodded his silent confirmation as he returned her smile.

Out of reflex, Alison brought both her hands to her mouth, as if to suppress her surprise.

"I…I…don't understand. I thought…I *heard* you were…dead."

"Let us just say that…Quicksilver is dead," he selected the

words carefully as he leaned close to nearly whisper, "as his services in support of the American Revolution are no longer required."

Alison's friends noticed from across the ball room her brightest smile they'd seen since her return, and were shocked when she uncharacteristically threw her arms around the tall and handsome stranger after only a few words of apparent introduction. The stranger wrapped his strong arms around Alison, as well.

As the females in attendance looked on longingly, the males in the ball room saw their own spirits dashed as it seemed every dance with Alison would now be taken by the stranger. No one could figure out who he was or from where he came.

"I'm so pleased you're alive!" Alison said as she pulled away from their embrace. "But what are you doing here?"

"Do you remember our discussion when I dropped you off near Norfolk? You wondered aloud if, under entirely different circumstances, we might have become friends and enjoyed each other's company?"

"I do," she said looking back in his deep blue eyes.

"Well, with your permission," Mathew began as he glanced around seeing most people in the room still staring at Alison and him, "I'd very much like to test your hypothesis."

Alison beamed. There was something wonderfully intriguing about his bashful demeanor around her. It was a decided departure from the commanding presence he displayed on the deck of the infamous *Sea Dragon*.

"I'd very much like that, too," she agreed as she took his arm. "Are you planning to stay in Boston long?" she added, attempting to hide her blush.

"That all depends," Mathew began. "I'm also in town to see a rather influential old friend about a teaching position at the college."

— Mathew meets
Alison again
at her party
— Mathew attends
feathers Unieval

331

About the Author

Privateer is the first novel written by Michael Scandalios. Since early childhood, he has been an avid student of the American Revolutionary War and of the founding fathers of the American political system. Michael majored in political science with an emphasis in international relations at UCLA, where he also played on the baseball team. After earning a master's degree in finance and accounting from the University of Chicago Booth School of Business, he has enjoyed a 20+year career in the fields of investment management, investment banking and investment consulting. In his free time, Michael enjoys surfing, playing guitar, reading, writing, traveling and spending time with his family at their home in Northern California. — Hillsborough!